REALM
OF THE
CONSPIRATORS

Pete Lans

REALM OF THE CONSPIRATORS
PETE LANS

Copyright © PETE LANS 2018

Author: Lans, Pete
Title: Realm of the Conspirators
Edition: 1st ed.
ISBN: 978-0-6483227-1-9

All Rights Reserved

Cover design Rebecca Timmis 2018

To the Future

More Books by Pete Lans

About the Author

Pete Lans is in his sixties now and has at last decided on a career: being a writer. After a lifetime of optimistic inventing and building, all without a hint of commercial gain, his two daughters have advised him to stick to what he's good at: telling stories.

He lives in Brisbane, Australia, but is considering joining the endless migration of nomads traversing the country in search of free camping and friendship.

Or, if the opportunity presents itself, he would like to develop the Roadworks Learning concept mentioned in his novel, *Realm of the Conspirators*, and do his bit to transform the lives of children and to help them escape the programmed future for which they are presently destined.

PART ONE

Chapter One

The moon had gone down behind the ridge. Twenty-six-year-old Owen Lucas knew that dawn was still a chilly hour or so away. He'd been woken by an incredible noise. The echoes still rang in his mind.

He let the corrugated tin door of the hut close behind him and trod on bare feet down the steps to the cold sand. Barra, his black and grey kelpie, whined softly somewhere ahead. Using his peripheral vision in the dim starlight, Owen made his way to the small holding yard. His horse, Stella, rose to her feet and shook herself inside her canvas rug. She came towards him and he waited at the rail until he could stroke her forehead.

... no point in saddling up at this hour—it's too dark...

Owen shivered with cold. Stella jerked back her head.

... whatever that noise was, it'll have to wait until it gets a bit lighter before I can investigate...

It wasn't thunder, of that he was certain; the sky was a glittering vault of stars. But so loud! For a few moments after he'd surfaced from a deep sleep, he had no idea where he was. His heart had raced as he listened to the echoes coming off the ridges—confused rumbles that lingered long enough for him to know that it wasn't a rifle shot.

... what, then?...

He'd flown the chopper over most of the area earlier in the week and hadn't seen any vehicles or camps. The following day, he'd saddled up and headed to the waterhole at Yappar river. It was only forty kilometres, but the land was rocky and rugged and he didn't get to the hut until sundown on the second day. He'd had a swim in the deep pool at the base of the escarpment, made a meal on a fire in front of the steps to the elevated hut, sat for a while sipping at his cocoa and catching the occasional falling star, and wondered about where he was going to go in his life. Then, he'd opened the tin door and let Barra push his way inside. After rolling out his swag and checking for wildlife, he'd fallen asleep in an instant.

Owen pulled Stella's rug up on her neck and tip-toed carefully back to the steps, hoping that he wouldn't tread on the thorns of a bullhead. He climbed the steps and brushed the sand off his feet. Now he was cold. He straightened out the swag that he'd folded to keep in the warmth, wrapped himself tightly in the canvas and pulled his beanie down to his neck.

A curlew's mournful call resounded in the night. It suddenly came to him that, on this flawless night, somebody had died. His last wakeful thought was of a plane crash— his subconscious had registered the sound of a plane flying over just before the noise that had woken him.

The kookaburra's first calls lifted Owen from his slumber. He'd become attuned to their strident laugh. The curlews and nightjars could whoop and hoot all night long without disturbing his sleep, but the first hollow call from a kookaburra would wake him.

There was just enough light for him to saddle Stella, and by the time he had lashed on a canteen and filled the pocket of his long jacket with a few nut bars, he could see enough to pick his way through the gidgee and spinifex alongside the dry river bed.

Stella poked along lazily with the occasional clack as her hooves collided. Owen smiled and shook his head.

It was no wonder that the Blackfellas never adopted the horse in the way that the American Indians had; horses were high maintenance, slow and vulnerable. He was only able to do this trip at this time of the year because he had made a food drop in the chopper a few days earlier—and most of it was for Stella.

Two days of long walking to the hut had just about used up her reserves. Owen had filled a drum with chaff, and she had hardly drawn breath as she hungrily munched and snorted. It continually amazed him that the early explorers and pioneers had made such astonishing treks. Of course, they took their time and worked in with the seasons as best they could, but the likes of Stuart and Leichhardt traversed country that was not well suited to horses and the welfare of their mounts must have been a continual concern. Not that there weren't enough brumbies infesting the country nowadays, but they merely survived—they didn't work.

Owen took a cattle track that led up to a rise. When he reached the flat, rocky clearing at the top, he could see what he had been expecting— smoke. But this wasn't bush smoke—this was jet black, and it spiralled thinly upward and dissipated into the yellowing morning sky. With his head cocked to one side and with a thoughtful purse to his lips, Owen estimated that the smoke was about two kilometres away—but he had no idea what was causing it. He feared the worst.

Most times when he went out on horseback he would take the satellite phone. His father had been insistent.

'There's nothin' out there that you can't handle, Owie... you're more likely to be killed by your bloody horse.'

Another reason why horses were a liability—they'd get spooked, they'd get tripped, and sometimes they just did unpredictable things that could leave the rider hanging in a tree or flat on their back in the spinifex.

Owen leaned forward and ruffled Stella's ears. He recalled his smart-aleck reply to his dad when he was only sixteen. 'But the phone is in the saddlebag, Dad... how am I going to use it if me horse takes off?'

Two weeks later, the mail plane brought a parcel.

'That one's for you, Owie,' his father had said. It was an Epirb— small enough to fit in his pocket, and powerful enough to send a distress signal to a satellite. From then on, he always took it with him whenever he went out alone, and later, when he started flying the chopper, he clipped it to the dash.

It was only a year ago that he'd casually looked at the label on the

Epirb and realised that the ten-year expiry date had just elapsed. So, he went back to taking along the sat-phone—if he remembered to. This time he'd forgotten.

It was the smell that jolted him out of his reverie—the pungent odour of burnt technology. Looking down, he saw amongst the spinifex a piece of interior lining panel that he knew was from a plane. There were other bits of wreckage all around. Owen realised that he was inside the debris zone of a plane crash.

The smoke was still a little way ahead. He urged Stella onward over ground littered with plastic, metal and glass.

Then, close to a big, white gum tree, he came to the smouldering remains of a plane— just the after-section with the two engines still attached. It was a business jet of some sort—he'd seen enough of them over the years. Many of the stations in the area were owned by foreign interests, and none of those executive types had any interest in traversing hundreds of kilometres over outback roads. When it came time for an inspection, they flew—usually, turbo-props. Jets were rare.

… now would be a good time to have the sat-phone—although it's not going to be of help to anyone on board this flight…

Owen felt a sudden flutter of anxiety. There were bound to be bodies nearby. He fixed his gaze on a shiny, metallic object some distance away. He didn't want to see any bodies. He wasn't going to be of help here anyway—no one would have survived this crash—the pieces were just that small.

He felt slightly nauseous at the realisation that this patch of scrub was the scene of awful deaths. He was unprepared for this; he had intruded into a site where one of the most profound achievements of humans and their technology had come to a blackened end.

He nudged Stella onward. He would ride straight out of the crash site. There was nothing for him to do but to get back to the station as quickly as possible.

As he neared the shiny object, he saw that it was a metal briefcase reflecting the just-risen sun.

Reining in, Owen examined the case from the saddle. It was still closed. It looked expensive.

A gust of wind wafted a curl of acrid smoke his way. Stella fidgeted.

Not taking his eyes from the case, Owen dismounted. He didn't want to touch anything from this area—not because it was an accident scene—but because he sensed that there was something evil about the circumstances. And yet, he knew in an instant that he would never be satisfied with his actions if he didn't take the case, because, attached to the handle was a set of handcuffs, with the loose cuff closed tightly around thin air.

Owen curled his fingers around the handle and consciously refrained from looking at anything nearby. He remounted one-handed and urged Stella onward, looking at nothing but his horse's mane.

It wasn't cowardice—Owen instinctively knew that there was nothing to be gained by his witnessing a disfigured body. The memory would stay with him forever. There was no need for that.

Stella plodded through the scrub until there were no more pieces of debris. He let her take her own path and felt considerable relief that she hadn't shied at anything. Maybe the smell of the smoke overpowered any other smells—human smells.

Barra flitted in and out of sight. He seemed unusually subdued when the trio, having skirted around the crash site, doubled back to the rocky rise.

Owen dismounted, put the case down beside him, and gave Barra a comforting rub. The dog panted and looked askance at the distant plume of smoke. Something had clearly distressed him too.

On examination, the case seemed very light for its size—almost as though it was empty.

... documents, then? But why handcuffs? A circuit board—micro-chip...

Barra sniffed at the case, his nose following the dangling handcuffs. He lingered on the ring of hardened steel. Against the rim, there was a scrape of skin. Owen grimaced and searched around for a twig to remove the flesh.

The briefcase latches required a key. Owen raised an eyebrow. Here was a challenge.

... the angle grinder with a super thin cutting disc—or, if it's titanium, the hinges can be ground to the pin, with argon to keep it cool...

All possible once he got back to the station. But that wasn't going to happen.

He could see himself handing it over to Derick Overton when the police troopy arrived.

'Yeah, picked this up because somebody thought it was important enough not to be separated from it. Bit of a coincidence but—plane crashes with highly confidential material aboard. What d'ya reckon?'

Owen always reverted to a simpler, more accessible persona whenever he had to deal with Sergeant Overton—whose family graves in Julia Creek went back to the 1880's, and who took advantage of any opportunity to assert himself.

Part of fitting in necessitated concealing certain aspects of one's background. So, he would ask the rhetorical question, 'I suppose you're just gonna hand it in to the authorities, hey?' knowing full well that the reply would be, 'I am the authority, Owen... you've done the right thing.'

Owen grabbed the case and remounted. He wouldn't be back at the hut for another two hours. Then, he'd think about whether he still wanted breakfast.

For over an hour, the trio picked their way through the scrub. The sun dazzled in Owen's eyes.

Of course, if he did open up the case and discovered stuff that definitely should be handed over to the experts, then that would be a bit awkward.

... actually, it could get awkward pretty quickly if the plane's transponder was working as it should have...

At a bend in the river, where there was a stony shelf that accentuated Stella's hoof falls, Owen dismounted. He flicked the reins through a small gum growing in a crevice. Then, with the case under his arm, he scuttled up the rocks to a small outcrop and secreted it under an eroded, rocky overhang. He returned to his horse and continued the last couple of kilometres to the hut, deep in thought.

He heard the rhythmic 'whumph' of a helicopter—and this was a big helicopter, not a mustering chopper— when he had the hut in sight. It passed by to the East and was obviously headed towards the crash site.

Owen spurred Stella and covered the last half a kilometre at a canter, with Barra loping easily behind. He leapt off just before the slip rail and quickly tied Stella to the gate.

It was time to get his story right.

Whoever poked through the crash site would eventually see Stella's hoof prints. They didn't need to be a tracker. Any urban desperado with a dire need to find a valuable briefcase would have the presence of mind to follow his tracks—because this was the scenario that was rapidly becoming all too apparent to Owen. He was beginning to wish that he'd left the case alone.

Taking his lighter from his pocket, he walked over to a large clump of spinifex and knelt down. In a few seconds, he had a nice little flame glowing at the dry base that soon licked up into the tall clumps. The resinous smoke was black at first but turned a heavy grey as it billowed higher.

... there—that should be enough smoke to attract attention...

Owen checked his watch—*ten minutes past nine.*

A big chopper like that would have come from Mount Isa, Cairns or Townsville—all equidistant.

... probably Townsville. At 200kph—that would be about three hours. Dawn—pretty early start for an emergency response... but plausible...

But, out here, they'd be flying way beyond their range limit and would have to organize a refuel to get back—at a station—or on the road.

Whoever was on board had much more on their mind than a straight forward search and rescue.

... and, they must have been getting a signal to home in close enough to see the smoke...

The spinifex fire had burnt out, but high up there was a nice ball of grey smoke that was slowly being dissipated by the morning breeze.

Owen wondered whether the suitcase had a transponder in it. He'd find out soon enough.

... probably not—the owner had not been anticipating it to leave his person...

He knew it was a 'he'—the skin on the cuff had black hairs mashed into it.

A pair of Brahminy Kites wheeled at treetop height. He sat on the lower yard rail and listened to their keening. He was about to set fire to another clump of spinifex when the sound of rotors suddenly filled the air. The helicopter loomed into sight over the ridge top of the escarpment. It was above him in an instant.

... smart—they used the ridge to hide their sound...

The almost sub-sonic waves from the rotors wouldn't bend readily enough to reach into the valley. Any mustering pilot knew that. But why would the pilot do that now?

Martin Connelly looked down at the lone figure by the hut. 'Looks like there's just one... only one horse. Got his dog with him.'

In front, occupying the co-pilot's seat, Melvin Brecks checked his Glock 43. Specially designed for concealment, the weapon fitted unobtrusively in a holster against his massive rib-cage. 'Best be prepared,' he grunted, as he slipped the pistol under his shirt.

The two men could converse very easily. Inside the helicopter it was surprisingly hushed. That is what made twenty-five million so worth it—a machine that transcended common 'state of the art' by a couple of decades. This craft, an Augusta Westland 139, was rebirthed from a production business model in a secret facility where the cleverest technicians were encouraged to be innovative and discouraged from talking about it.

Next to Connelly, in the main cabin, Gina Wu scanned her laptop. 'Property owned by the Lucas family, apparently... two generations at least. Donald Lucas currently.' She craned her neck to look out the window. 'How old do you suppose he is?'

Connelly lowered the binoculars from his eyes and shrugged his shoulders. 'Doesn't look that old... hat getting in the way.'

'Could be the son, then—Owen Lucas.'

'Or any random roustabout,' Brecks volunteered from the front seat. 'Bit odd though, for an ordinary worker to be this far out on his own.'

Wu folded the screen of the laptop. 'He was definitely at the site... the hoof prints, and the dog. If need be, we can shock him.' She pointed at a blue cooler bag on the opposite seat. 'But go easy at first.'

Owen waved his hat and watched as the helicopter hovered over the river bed and settled slowly down on the embedded river stones.

... no dust that way...

The front and rear doors opened simultaneously. The two men, both in jeans and dark glasses, stepped to the ground and stooped as they trotted out of range of the rotors.

Owen walked towards them and gave a businesslike wave of his hand. He was suddenly a cattle-man who took a dim view of planes crashing onto his property, no matter how tragic the circumstances.

Connelly waved back. 'Good morning!'

Owen nodded and waited for them to reach him. He held out his hand. 'Owen Lucas,' he announced soberly.

'Hi there, Owen. Nice to meet you,' said Connelly.

With a squint against the sun, Owen glanced at the newcomer. About forty, tall and strongly built, he looked like one of those all-round sporty types that never make it to the elite level of any particular code and become thwarted and dangerous. Owen disliked him already.

Brecks came forward and deliberately crunched Owen's knuckles with his handshake but said nothing.

Connelly pointed in the direction of the burnt spinifex. 'Was that for our benefit?'

...okay, so you prefer not to introduce yourselves. 'Yeah... but, I guess you already found the crash.'

Connelly gave a slow, grave nod. 'Sure did... we've been there already... nothing we can do... it's terrible...'

Owen looked to the horizon—*just offer what they already know.* 'I heard a huge bang, crash, sort of thing, so I went out this morning to have a decko, and... yeah... it's not pretty...'

Connelly shamelessly scrutinized Owen with a slight smirk of disbelief. He lifted his glasses. 'Okay... good on you. Did you see anything?'

Owen did his best to wipe the effects of a university education from his face. 'Shit, yeah!... the place is a mess... total devastation... I took one look and headed back here. I was just about to head back to the station when you guys arrived.'

Connelly nodded thoughtfully. 'Sure, you were... yeah.' He gave an exaggerated frown and looked out towards the crash site. 'Now... did you find anything unusual... anything unexpected?'

'Apart from two smoking jet engines?' Owen was treading a fine line between jocularity and solemnity.

The eyes that bored back weren't amused.

Owen looked at the ground. 'Well, to tell you the truth... I didn't stay very long... there was no point... it was creepy,' he conjured a look of disarming candour, 'I got out of there quick smart. I was back here at just after nine.'

Brecks hauled himself well inside Owen's personal space—which in the outback is measured in yards, not feet. He jutted his chin. 'Are you sure... that you didn't find anything?'

Owen's eyes flitted innocently between the two men. 'I'm not sure what you mean... but if there's something you'd like me to keep an eye out for, just let me know.'

Brecks sneered. He turned and walked back to the helicopter.

Through the open rear door of the helicopter, Owen could see the silhouette of a woman with a laptop on her knees.

Connelly deftly plucked his phone from his pocket and commenced scrolling.

Owen gave a derisive snort. 'Not a chance... not out here.'

His answer was the hint of a smile from Connelly who continued scrolling.

Brecks was still at the door of the helicopter. The woman passed him a bag.

Connelly cleared his throat and bestowed a superior smirk on Owen. 'So... *Uther*! I bet that's a well-kept secret. In fact, your middle name doesn't even appear on your driver's licence.' He looked at Owen and laughed with noiseless spasms. 'Who was responsible for that?... it'd have to be your dad. Bit of a romantic, is he?'

Owen took an involuntary step backwards—*how the hell!*...

Languidly scrolling some more, Connelly nodded and pouted, '... honours in mechanical engineering. Well, well... aren't you a smarty. And, to think I wouldn't have been at all surprised if you'd had a gob full of chew-baccy and were yodelling about them-thar-durned-critters or some such thing.'

Brecks, with the blue cooler-bag in his grip, re-joined them and planted himself directly in front of Owen.

Connelly canted his head and gave an exaggerated frown. 'You almost fooled me, feller. Hey, I want you to have a look at something.'

Without taking his eyes off Owen, Brecks delved into the bag and pulled out a mangled human hand.

At the sight of the blood and draggled tendons, Owen felt faint. His vision tunnelled and a pulsing roar filled his head.

Brecks smirked.

Connelly stepped forward and took Owen by the shoulders. 'Whoa... you okay there, buddy? Here, why don't you sit down.'

Owen bent forward with his hands on his knees. He had that familiar nausea in his stomach—each time he'd had a bad knock—football—low blood pressure—it didn't take much. He could hear the two men laughing, but it sounded a long way off.

He came to, looking up at the blue sky. He felt so much better already. If he could just lie here in the beautiful dirt for an hour or so, it would be great.

Barra licked at his face.

Connelly looked down at him. 'Hey there, sleeping beauty... I was just about to get Melvin here to give you a kiss... we were getting worried.'

...Melvin!... he doesn't look like a Melvin.

Connelly knelt down. 'You're as white as a sheet. Look, I won't keep you, Owen... you've got ranges to, um... range, and we've got important work to do. But, look... I believe you. You didn't see what we're looking for... but I'd like you to get in contact with me if you find something unusual... anything at all.' He pressed a card into Owen's top pocket and stood up. 'Take care, mate.'

He left Owen's field of vision for a moment, then suddenly reappeared.

'Oh, Uther... your secret is safe with me,' he grinned.

Owen didn't want to get up. He didn't want to face the awkwardness of standing around while the two men boarded the helicopter. Anyway, lying low, literally, would bolster his case—that of an innocent stockman with no stomach for prying a severed limb from attaché case.

How close had the body been to the case? It could have been tangled in the scrub mere metres away. Come to think of it, there had been that big gum nearby.

...did the body fly through the air—briefcase snag suddenly in the fork of the tree—hand ripped off by the manacle—body falling some distance away—hand falls to the ground near tree.

Owen sensed a queasiness returning. He felt the gusts as the helicopter left the river bed.

...who knew that my tendency for the occasional faint would one day save me!

The Augusta Westland 139, already a hundred metres in the air, flew directly overhead.

Taking some deep breaths, Owen listened to the diminishing reverberations until the air was still again.

Barra came and sat by him.

Stirrups clanged against the steel gate as Stella shook herself.

Martin Connelly looked out of the cabin side-window at the spreadeagled body on the ground below. 'He really had no idea. Still, we'll give him till sunset—see what his story is then.'

Melvin Brecks cracked his knuckles. 'Why don't we just lean on him a bit—then we'll know exactly where we stand?'

'Not yet. We leave as few ripples as possible. It's just a damn nuisance that Lucas happened to be in the area... otherwise this crash would have remained a mystery for years.'

Connelly turned to the pilot. 'Head back to the site—we'll give it another once over. If we don't find it, we'll drop in on Lucas again—I think he's on 980.' He looked back for confirmation from Brecks.

Brecks nodded.

The pilot punched in the numbers on the plotter. Shortly, a blue dot appeared below the centre of the screen.

Brecks gave a derisive chuckle. 'Very obliging of him to faint for us. His horse is a bit skittish though.'

Connelly grinned.

Ahead, a slow curl of black smoke marked the crash site.

'We need to be back in the air with enough daylight left in case we have to deal with Lucas. After that, our rendezvous with the tanker isn't till midnight.'

Connelly unfastened his seatbelt as the helicopter settled in a cloud of dust. He turned to the woman sitting next to him.

Gina Wu raised an indolent brow and crossed her slim legs. She snapped shut the laptop in her hands.

Connelly breathed just a little bit deeper than usual and looked her directly in the eye. 'Okay?' he queried.

'I hope so, Martin,' she replied in a reproving tone. 'The thing is,' she continued with an assertive thrust of her chin, '... we know that the case is here somewhere. The hand proves that—it wasn't severed by the crash—that would be unlikely. If we don't find it, it will be because that cowboy took it—that is the logical deduction. My thinking is that he found it without coming into contact with any body parts—he's obviously not used to, or at least incapable of witnessing gore without feeling faint—hard as it may be to believe from a man of the land. He hid it when he heard us coming so soon after the crash. He obviously suspected something. When we interview him, I'll scan him.' She turned to Brecks. 'And there was nothing in that shack?'

'No... nothing. It's just bare tin. Nothing underneath either.'

'He's hidden it. But before you set to him, Melvin, we need to be absolutely sure that it's not out here amongst the wreckage.'

Connelly gave a decisive snort and reached for the door lever. 'Good—let's go.'

Owen turned in the saddle and scanned the horizon behind him. Just above the tree line, he could see distant clouds—bulky cumulonimbus prematurely blocking out the setting sun.

...haven't heard a weather report for three days—maybe a cyclone in the gulf?

Even though the going was slow, the day had passed quickly; there

15

was plenty to think about.

He looked ahead at the slight, bare rise that was Pepper Knoll. Barra trotted up the gentle slope. They were headed home. It seemed that all three of them couldn't get there quickly enough.

...not a lot of distinctive landmarks in this part of the world.

That was one of the things that attracted Owen to this part of the gulf country—the fact that only he and a handful of others could navigate their way through the featureless landscape. But, his train of thought was continually disturbed by his encounter with the crew from the helicopter.

...got to get out of here before either one of those storms catches me.

There was a good campsite on the other side of the plateau, where a dry tributary led into the dry Yappar River. He smiled and shook his head and wondered why anyone would take it into their head to live here.

A sound like distant thunder came to his ears. He turned—and froze rigid in the saddle. Against the mottled clouds, there was a black object which he immediately knew was a helicopter.

Exposed, on the middle of the plateau, there was nowhere to hide. But the light had faded so much already that he doubted he would be seen. Reining in Stella, he whistled at Barra and remained absolutely still. Barra dropped to his belly.

The helicopter came straight at him. In hardly any time at all, it was hovering just above the scoured stone of the plateau. Through the windscreen, Owen could see the faces of the occupants turned to him.

...how on earth?

He swung to the ground. With quick fingers, Owen unstrapped the pouches of the saddle bags. Inside one of them he felt something flat and cold. He pulled it out just as Connelly and Brecks came striding up to him.

Hefting the object in the palm of his hand, he turned to face the approaching men. 'This'll be yours then, I expect...' and lobbed the cool slab at Connelly who snatched it without even looking at it.

'Thank you, Owen... we like to recycle as much as possible in this day and age.'

Brecks smiled and glowered all at once.

16

Behind the two men, Wu climbed out of the helicopter and sauntered towards them, intently examining something she was holding in her hand.

Connelly eyed Owen with an inquisitive crank to his head. 'I'm glad we managed to find you.'

Brecks gave a menacing nod.

'... because we still need to ask you a few questions.' He turned to Wu who lifted the device to her eye and signalled she was ready.

'Righty, then... let's begin.' He folded his arms on his chest and spread his stance. 'Just answer yes or no, as much as possible—no need for complicated answers.' He gave a tight smile. 'So... this property belongs to your family?'

Owen gave a sullen stare but answered curtly, 'Yes.'

'... and you are fairly familiar with the territory out here?'

'Yes.'

'... and you have a degree in mechanical engineering?'

'Yes.'

'Are you going to make your career on the land?'

Owen shrugged. 'Don't know.'

'I see. Do you have a girlfriend?'

'What's that got to do with your line of enquiry?'

Connelly grinned. 'Do you fly a mustering helicopter?'

Owen took a big breath. 'Yes.'

'Were you born in this area?'

'In Cairns.'

'Do you like being out on your own?'

Owen flicked the reins over Stella's head. 'Look, I haven't got time for this...'

'Answer the question, Owen!' Connelly barked.

Brecks moved forward, massaging his fist with his palm.

Owen stilled with his hand on the saddle. 'Yes... I enjoy being out here by myself.'

'Thank you. What alerted you to the plane crash?'

'The noise... it woke me up... about four o'clock I think it was.'

'Did you ride out to the crash site?'

'Yes.'

'Were you surprised to see our helicopter?'

'Yes... I was surprised... and the type of chopper, too,' he nodded at the helicopter.

'Do you know a bit about planes?'

'... a bit. We have a Bell Sioux that I fly.'

'Were you surprised to find that briefcase?' Connelly's voice remained bland.

Owen stalled. Images of the briefcase came involuntarily to his mind. 'I didn't see a briefcase.'

'Did you look for it?'

'What? No, I didn't see a briefcase...' Owen looked over the heads of the trio in front of him. His heart was beating faster. He needed to calm himself. Something small moved above the tree line. At first, he thought it was a nearby insect, but he quickly realised that it was further away and considerably bigger. He furrowed his brow and tried to focus on the object, partly out of curiosity and partly to divert his mind from Connelly's probing questions.

'... would be likely to find it?' Connelly's question came into his consciousness.

'What? Sorry...' Owen resumed eye contact with Connelly.

'I said, do you know where we would be likely to find it?'

The object moved sideways then dropped below the horizon amongst the trees. Owen's eyes darted towards it but had difficulty locating it in the fading light. 'No...' he answered distantly.

...there! Just over that ghost gum...

'Owen, you seem to be losing concentration, my boy. No matter, I think we have enough to go on.' Connelly looked around at Wu, who responded with a tiny nod.

The four of them stood for a moment in silence—Owen trying to maintain a visual on the object, while the other three furtively eyed each other for some sort of verdict.

Eventually, Wu broke the silence. 'What *are* you looking at, Mr Lucas?'

...what is that accent?... British—establishment—recently acquired...

Owen summoned a look of mild anxiety. 'Just those clouds... could be a cyclone... not unheard of for this time of the year.'

The other three turned.

Owen resumed his search for the object but had no hope of finding it in the rapidly gathering darkness.

Connelly and co remained looking at the horizon.

...oh, I get it... if it does rain, it'll wash away any tracks—they're re-evaluating their next move.

The woman turned around. 'Thank you, Mr Lucas. You've been very helpful. You will never see us again—we had to perform something of vital significance to national security and I'm sorry that we intimidated you. We can't afford to be blasé about this issue, and that means that we have had to treat you rather discourteously... I do apologise.'

Owen raised his chin in reluctant acknowledgement.

...yeah, bullshit!

The trio turned and headed back to the helicopter, but not before Brecks managed a malevolent squint at Owen.

'Hope you'll be okay in the dark,' he said softly.

The redness of the setting sun filled the interior of the helicopter with a golden hue as it rose above the plateau.

Connelly looked across at the woman beside him. 'How did he score?'

Wu answered without looking up from her laptop. 'As expected—he's lying to us.' She turned the screen around so that Connelly and Brecks could see the image of Owen's face—an infra-red exposure that highlighted the hot-spots on his face that occurred whenever he flushed under stress.

Brecks flexed his fingers and cracked his knuckles, 'The little shit. Why don't we just beat the truth out of him?'

Connelly looked down onto the black landscape outside. 'Bit awkward now—now that we don't have a transponder on him anymore.' He turned to Wu. 'Why *did* we let him go? You knew he was lying as you were scanning him.'

Wu folded the screen. 'Our job is to find that case—with as little fuss as possible. The possibility of rain changes things a bit, I know, but if we brutalize him and, for some unexpected reason—medical condition—whatever, he dies, then we've lost any hope of recovering it. We can't take that chance. We're not set up for prolonged interrogation. Our best bet is to leave him alone, let him feel confident that we have exited his life, and then wait for him to come back for the case—because I'm certain he will. Or, failing that, we can pay him a visit when we're in a better position to threaten him—although,' Wu gave an amused pout, '... we won't be able to use his girlfriend as leverage, because according to the scanner, he doesn't have one.'

'Don't tell me he's...' Brecks blurted, before Wu silenced him with hostile eyes.

'Does he look that way to you, Brecks? I don't think so. However, speaking of fruity types, I want you to get hold of Dorian, or whatever he calls himself nowadays, and see what he can put together regarding monitoring the Lucas household. We want to stay informed of their intentions. My guess is that they'll take their helicopter out to look at the site, so tell him to make sure *that* gets bugged... and the kitchen table.'

For a long time, Owen sat motionless in the saddle, even after the last murmurs of the helicopter had faded. He felt too unsettled to make a camp. Kindling a fire and boiling the billy was something that was dear and comforting to him. After what had just transpired, he wouldn't enjoy laying in a sandy gully in his swag.

The moon had not yet risen. Dismounting, he reached inside one of the saddle bags and extracted his head torch. They would walk by torchlight for a few hours until the moonlight strengthened. There was plenty to think about and plodding onward was a good way to pass the time.

He'd be home before lunch.

Chapter Two

Don Lucas chatted to Theo, the tanker driver, as they supervised the filling of the overhead tanks with avgas. The pump droned steadily. Already, the morning was very warm and the men leaned in closer to the shade of the trailer.

A helicopter, a small Robinson R22, flew in from the south east and hovered above the cow paddock.

Theo inclined his head in its direction as it descended onto the grass.

'That's not one that I've seen before—you?'

'No, can't say I have. I wonder what they want. Probably lost and running low on fuel.'

'Won't have been the first time,' said Theo with a chuckle.

The two men stayed in the shade and watched as a man and a woman alighted and began walking towards the homestead.

Theo snorted scornfully. 'Whoa! Are you *sure* they're not friends of yours?'

The man was wearing a broad brimmed black hat with a streaming, coloured bandana. He wore a black 'duster', leather pants with stovepipe legs and red knee-length boots. The woman had on a leather flying helmet which she pried loose to allow her blonde hair to cascade over her shoulders.

'Jeez,' said Don, 'I suppose I'd better go over and see what they're after.'

Theo pulled on his gloves. 'Right pair of spangled drongos, if you ask me. Okay, I'll finish up here.'

Lucas walked across the dusty driveway to the new arrivals and gave a friendly wave. 'G'day,' he called, '... are you lost?'

The man pitched forward, thrust out his hand and gave Don's hand a delicate jiggle. 'Hi,' he drawled, 'I'm Dorian, and this is my associate, Jane.'

Don introduced himself.

Dorian gushed and waved his arms. 'Oh, my!... isn't this just quintessentially *outback*! Jane, what do you think?'

Jane cast her eye over the featureless landscape and nodded. 'Yes, it's perfect.'

Dorian put his hands on his hips, breathed in deeply and gave a long, thoughtful sigh. 'We work for Film Australia, and we're doing a site inventory—we're location scouts.'

Don gave an exaggerated nod of his head. 'Oh, right...'

'Look,' said Dorian, stepping forward and holding the station owner by the arm, 'I won't waste your time—you've got plenty to do, but we heard about this property from our network of spies,' he chortled conspiratorially, '... and, if you're interested, we would like to recommend your farm— oops, excuse me—your station, as the location for a film that's in the pipeline to be shot soon—a thriller... got Russell Crowe and Cate Blanchett in it. It's going to be big—isn't it, Jane!'

Jane scanned the outbuildings and replied with a desultory, 'Sure is.'

Dorian rolled his eyes and swatted at Don's shoulder. 'Believe me, it is.' He took a few steps nearer the homestead, held out his arms and made a rectangular frame with his fingers. 'This is so divine,' he said, peering through the aperture. 'Of course, it can get a tad busy, what with all the trailers and gear, but,' he squinted with concentration as he panned from the homestead across the horizon, '... the remuneration more than compensates for that... and, chatting with the stars!' he added with a precious grin.

'Fair dinkum?'

'Oh, yes! A place like this, for the duration of the scene, would be worth twenty or thirty thousand dollars—more, if we use your vehicles and do interior shoots of say, your house—I mean, homestead.'

Don pursed his lips. 'Wow, that's a lot of money.'

Dorian pawed Don's shoulder. 'No, it's not!... they throw around shit loads of cash when production starts... oops, excuse my language. Would you mind very much if we had a quick peek at the homestead— just the verandas and perhaps the kitchen?'

'We can do better than that, mate.' Don placed a gnarled hand on Dorian's shoulder. 'Why don't you have some smoko with me and my daughter, Jenna.'

Dorian gave a little clap and turned to Jane. 'Come along, Jane. We've been invited to morning tea—have you got your iPad? Oh good.'

Morning tea around the big dining table was a prime opportunity for Dorian to regale the Lucas' with exploits from his lifetime in the film industry—all of it a spontaneous stream of deceit, supported now and again with appropriate noises from Jane.

Jenna sat spellbound.

Half way through one of Dorian's anecdotes, the screen door creaked opened. Owen walked into the kitchen.

Jenna rushed off her chair and flung her arms around her brother. Don stood up with a big smile, Dorian moved back his chair in anticipation of introductions, and Jane took the opportunity to press the surveillance device in position underneath the table top.

Owen had spied the R22 in the paddock as he approached the homestead. He'd reined in underneath a river gum and contemplated his options.

It wasn't a helicopter that he'd ever seen before—*news crew perhaps?*

He was becoming a bit sensitive to coincidences, after what had played out in the last twenty-four hours. But there was no recourse other than to find out who was paying Yappar Station a visit.

Stella needed no urging to go onward. Owen rode her to the vegetable garden at the back of the house. He dismounted and let her inside, tying her to the gate post so that she had some grazing radius. Stella nibbled happily while he strode to the back door, pried off his boots and stepped silently inside.

In the hallway, he listened for about five minutes to Dorian's yarns until he thought he had a pretty good idea of what was going on.

Then he tip-toed back to the door, slipped on his boots and traversed the verandas to the screen door of the kitchen.

After the introductions had been made, Dorian promptly commandeered the conversation and suggested that he and Jane best be off— perhaps after they'd had a quick look at one of the outbuildings. '... maybe the hanger... to convey the extreme isolation of the station... the need to contend with floods and that sort of thing...' he gushed.

The party duly trooped down to the hanger where Dorian spoke ebulliently about sacrifice and hardship, mateship and self-reliance, and how the film would evoke all of these virtues in the most sincere and authentic manner.

Meanwhile, Jane tapped furiously at her iPad and took meaningful shots of dust and rusted corrugated iron, all set against the azure sky. She remained standing by the mustering helicopter, wholly engaged with her pad, as Dorian, fast running out of material, rabbited on about the Australian ideal, a magnificent rural utopia, and the vital role of the Country Women's Association in these changing times.

The group sauntered back to the R22.

It took only ten seconds for Jane to stick the bug underneath the cabin air cowling of the Bell Sioux. She caught up with the others just as Dorian was pawing his adieu to the Lucas's, trilling about how fabulous it was all going to be.

Enveloped in a cloud of dust, Jane pulled up gently on the collective pitch lever and kicked in some rudder. The helicopter spun and soared and was over the cattle ramp of the driveway in seconds.

Dorian threw back his head and closed his eyes. He suddenly opened the door and flung out his hat. The colourful bandana streamed to earth. 'Holy hell,' he exhaled, '... the things I do for a quid.'

Jane looked across at him and reached for the headphones hanging from the canopy. She dropped them into Dorian's lap.

He dutifully put them on.

Jane checked the GPS and set a course for Atherton. 'You were saying?' Even with noise cancelling headphones, having a conversation was going to be a trial.

Dorian called out, 'I was just lamenting the extremes I have to go to in order to make a living.'

Jane smiled to herself. 'I imagine that today's little charade probably netted you enough to live for a year in luxury.'

Dorian gave a sardonic grunt. 'I might say the same for you.'

Jane nodded slowly and kept her eyes on the horizon. 'I can't imagine that would be a regular gig for you, though… is it?'

'You should know the rules, sweetheart… however, this isn't the first time that I've been a location scout—or a screaming fairy. It gets me into a lot of places that normally are out of bounds. People are fascinated by the movie industry.'

'And its eccentric, ah…personalities.'

Dorian laughed. 'Especially out here. I'm odd and above suspicion. How about you—Jane… if that's your real name?'

'It's not. I usually fly for marine biologists—scientists, that sort of thing. Not regular enough, though. I won't deny that I look forward to the call to do one of these types of jobs. Happens surprisingly often, of late.'

'Good money, huh?'

'Ooh, yeah.'

Dorian smiled and nodded. 'So, did I provide you with enough of a diversion for you to complete your mission?'

Jane gave a curt salute. 'Mission accomplished.'

The two looked at each other with wry smiles and said nothing more.

The Lucas's moved back towards the homestead, but instead of going to the front veranda, Owen diverted them to the back of the house to where Stella was finishing off the last of the carrots within reach.

Jenna walked over and unsaddled her.

Owen took his dad by the arm and moved into the shade of a mango tree. 'I've got to tell you about something strange that happened out at the waterhole, Dad. But first, I need to know how legit those two were,' and he cranked his head towards the diminishing sounds of the helicopter.

Don shrugged. 'Said he was a location scout—going to shoot some thriller—with Cate Blanchett. She's a bit of alright, hey, Owie?'

Owen grinned and shook his head. 'Seriously though, something very weird happened to me out at the waterhole, and I'm wondering whether those two aren't involved in some way.'

Don looked his son in the eye. 'Okay, mate...'

Owen recounted the strange events of his trek to Yappar River— being woken by the sound of the crash, locating the wreckage site, finding the case, hiding it, the visit by the strange helicopter, the severed hand, the subsequent visit and his interrogation.

Don listened with deeply furrowed brows. 'And you think those location scouts are mixed up in this?'

'Dunno. The thing is, that crowd in the executive chopper had a massive amount of technology at their disposal, and it wouldn't surprise me if they'd decided to plant some of it here—know what I'm saying?'

'Son,' Don said with a distant look in his eyes, '... you'd better hand over that case. It's got nothing to do with us, and if, as you say, they can marshal the sort of resources that they appear to have, then they could make our lives very difficult.'

Owen nodded. 'I agree. I only took the case because, at the time, with the handcuffs on it and everything, I thought that it looked important enough to, you know, secure it for the authorities. Then, I hid it on instinct, because when I saw that flash helicopter so early in the morning, I had a feeling that something wasn't right.'

Don nodded with concern and walked back to the veranda. 'How do we get in touch with them?'

Owen suddenly remembered the card. He retrieved it from his top pocket. It was a normal business card size, white with rounded corners, but a bit thicker and stiffer than usual. It was completely blank on both sides. He looked at it from different angles, held it to the sunlight, breathed on it, clamped it between his palms, but nothing brought about a change.

Jenna approached, leading Stella. 'What's that?' she asked.

Owen sat on the edge of the veranda with the card between his fingers, thinking about ultra violet, microwaves and chemicals. 'Not sure,' he muttered.

Barra came up to Owen's knees and sniffed at the card. He gave a disconsolate whine. The card began to colour. In a few seconds there were vibrant hues in a mosaic-like pattern. The three of them lent closer. The card flashed brilliantly in the sunlight. It seemed to have a holographic quality to it. Deep inside the hologram there appeared to be numbers. Before the trio could get a good look at it, the card began to fade and within a few seconds it was completely white again.

All three of them looked at Barra.

'Here, Barra,' Owen said, '... do your magic.'

Predictably, the sudden attention spooked the dog, and he remained just out of reach, panting and trying to look inconspicuous.

'Where did you get that,' Jenna said. 'Do you think Barra's whine made it do that? Can I have a go?' She took the card from her brother's fingers and held it near her mouth. She did her best to simulate Barra's whine. The card gained colour straight away but faded within seconds.

'Bloody hell,' Don said. 'Give me a go.' He held out his hand.

Owen's father hadn't inherited any musical genes, but even his sonorous warble instantly brought about a result—this time with completely different colours.

The three of them looked intently at the numbers deep inside the tessellated hologram. The pattern lasted for quite a while before it faded.

'Did you get that, Owie?' Don said expectantly.

'Think so, Dad. It looked like a phone number.'

Jenna looked up with a quizzical brow. 'Did you notice anything peculiar? Apart from the fact that this is weird...'

Father and son shrugged.

'Well, I'm positive that the last phone number ended in seven, four. This one ended in five, nine.'

The three of them stood in quiet reflection for a moment.

Then Don said, 'Give it another go, son.'

Owen frowned. 'We don't want to waste its battery... if it has one.'

'It probably recharges on sunlight, for all we know,' Don said garrulously. 'Go on, sing to it and see what happens.'

Owen dutifully hummed at the card. Sure enough, a delicate blend of hues spread across the surface. Heads closed together as they studied the number within.

'Okay,' Jenna breathed, '... that was a different number again.'

The three of them sat in a row on the veranda and stared ahead, watching Stella, tail swishing, as she nibbled at the sparse lawn.

'Where did you get that?' Jenna queried. 'It's really cool.'

'Owen was given it by some guys in a mysterious helicopter out at Yappar waterhole, Jenna. It's something that is way beyond our ken. I'll tell you what we know in a minute.' Don turned to his son. 'So, you reckon those two in the R22 might have bugged the house?'

Owen shrugged. 'I'm starting to think that this card might even be a bug.'

They looked at the card, white and innocuous, in Owen's fingers.

'Doubt it,' said Don. 'Let's go and check the kitchen—that's the only room they went in.'

The three of them walked around to the kitchen door and went inside. Owen and Jenna chatted about what it would be like to have a film crew staying at the homestead, while Don checked the door frame, the benchtops and finally the kitchen table. He got down on hands and knees and looked underneath. Then he turned to his son and daughter and gave a thumbs-up.

Jenna took the initiative. 'Owie, have you taken care of Stella yet? She needs a rub down and a good feed.' She nodded meaningfully.

'Yeah, I was going to—it's just, with the visitors and everything...'

'I'll give you a hand, mate,' said Don.

'I'll come too,' said Jenna, 'I haven't said hello to her yet.'

They went outside and walked to the back lawn where Stella was munching the tall grass against the fence.

'Well,' Don began, '... the table has a bug on it—a little black rectangle up in the corner with about half a metre of thin wire coming out of it that's stuck to the underside.'

In silence, they retrieved Stella, who didn't look at all as though she needed a feed any more and walked her to the stable.

Father and daughter spoke quietly together as Owen washed his horse with the hose.

'... so,' said Don at length, '... whilst it sounds very mysterious and possibly a bit exciting, I don't want anything to do with this. We return the case—end of story.'

They watched as Stella rolled around in the dust after her hose down.

'I guess the bug makes it easier for us to contact them,' said Jenna, '... without being too obvious, of course.'

'Yeah,' said Owen, '... we can make it look like we're trying to use the phone number on the card—however *that's* going to work.'

Don looked serious. 'We have to have a discussion about the plane crash too, Owie—just as though we would even if we weren't doing it for the benefit of our listeners. This whole episode is...' Don struggled for a suitable word '... sinister, and I don't like it at all. We're caught up in something far beyond our control, and I'd like to leave it behind us as soon as possible.'

The three of them spent some time establishing how they were going to conduct their performance. Then, with nods all round, they walked back to the homestead and opened the squealing flyscreen door to the kitchen.

'I don't know, Owie,' said Don, '... this whole plane crash scenario sounds mightily suspicious to me—I haven't had any word from Darren or any other copper about a crash, and you'd reckon that by now the word would be out. Seems to me that whoever owns that briefcase has got enough clout to control the usual channels of investigation, and frankly, that worries me a lot.'

Jenna put the kettle on the slow combustion stove. 'The trouble is, Dad, we still don't know how to make contact with, well, anyone to do with that crash.'

Don cut in. 'Are you sure that they didn't give you instructions of some sort—just after you recovered from your faint. Maybe you don't remember...'

Owen let out a yell. 'Yes!... I remember now,' and he delved into his pocket and pulled out the card. He held it close to his face and spoke loudly at it. 'They gave me this—I'd completely forgotten. The guy said that if I found anything, I could contact him.'

Crockery tinkled as Jenna prepared the tea. 'A business card? That's a bit unusual. Does it have a contact number?'

Owen squinted. 'That's *all* that it has. Hang on, it's disappearing.'

The family went through the whole routine of 'discovering' how to bring up the graphic. After ten minutes of crooning and exclamations of amazement, plus discovering that the card never repeated numbers, they made the decision to call the next number that came up using the satellite phone.

With the phone on the kitchen table, Owen called out, 'Open Sesame' to the card and read out the number as Don dialled it.

They waited in anxious silence as the ring-tone burred.

The other end picked up. 'Horton's Earthmoving... Brian speaking...'

Don looked perplexed. 'Ah, hello... I'd like to speak to a Melvin, if he is available...'

'No Melvin here, mate—you must have the wrong number.'

Don quickly cut in. 'Oh, I do apologise, but just out of interest, which town am I ringing?'

'Wyndham, mate—and I know everyone in town and there definitely aren't any Melvins.'

'Okay,' said Don. 'Sorry about that.' He clicked off the handset.

The family looked at each other with brows of bewilderment.

'Shall we try again?' said Owen.

Don gathered the hand set.

'Okay, let's do this thing!' Owen said loudly onto the card.

A new pattern emerged, and Owen peered into the holograph and read out the number.

Again, the phone burred. It was answered by a woman's frail voice. 'Hello...'

Don replied gently. 'Hello... my name is Don Lucas, and I was wondering whether I could speak to Melvin, if he's available...'

'... oh...' came the tentative reply, '... I don't think so, Mr Lucas. Melvin didn't come back from the war. We waited for a very long time—we got a telegram. It was very sad...'

There was a sudden interruption on the other end and another woman's voice said abruptly, 'Hello, *who's* this?'

'Hello, I'm sorry to bother you—I think I've dialled...'

'You should be ashamed of yourself!' interrupted the woman angrily. 'Cold calling on hapless old people... they don't have any money and they don't need whatever it is you're selling!'

Don answered apologetically. 'Look, I am truly sorry. I'm not selling anything... I've accidently dialled the wrong number. But, would you mind telling me which town or city I'm ringing... please...'

There was a moment's silence on the other end before he got a grudging reply.

'You've rung the Trafalgar Aged Care facility in Bunbury.'

'Oh... Bunbury, in Western Australia?'

'Yes, of course!' came the terse reply.

'Thank you, thank you very much,' Don said, looking at the mouth piece.

The woman on the other end obviously didn't hang up the phone properly because the Lucas family could hear the conversation continuing on the other end.

'... I've told you hundreds of times before, Daphne... you're not to pick up the phone.'

'... but he was asking about Melvin... is he coming back?'

'Who is Melvin?'

'... my brother... Melvin... he went to the war...'

'Well, in that case, he's not coming back... now, it's time for lunch.'

Don clicked off the phone.

'How sad...' said Jenna.

They sat in silence.

The sat-phone suddenly burbled.

Don clicked on the receiver. 'Hello?'

'Hello, Don!' came a breezy male voice, '... I hear you've been hitting on little old ladies.'

Don's face darkened. 'Who is this?'

'I'm a friend of Owen... we met out at Yappar River yesterday—but you already know all that. Any chance of me speaking to him?'

Don wordlessly passed the bulky hand-piece to his son.

'I'm here...' Owen said tonelessly.

'Good man,' came the reply, '... listen, there's a little matter that we

31

have to sort out—you know what it is—and I'd like to do it on... let me see... bit late today. Let's make it tomorrow. You and your dad can fly out to the hut, say ten o'clock—wait for us there—don't bring any friends—you can show us where to go—we do the pick-up, and you'll be free to go. How's that sound?'

'Yeah, that's okay.'

'Excellent. Okay, we'll see you then. Oh, and Owen... let's keep this simple, huh?'

'No problem.'

'Good. We want to keep this *very* simple. Alright then, see you tomorrow.'

The phone went dead.

Once again, the three of them sat in silence around the table.

Jenna sighed deeply. '*Is* it in fact going to be that simple? What's stopping them from...' She couldn't finish her sentence.

Don pointed meaningfully at the table to remind his son and daughter that they were being monitored.

'Once they have the case, they won't care about what we say or do. We can report the crash—which we probably should, and the relevant authorities will do the relevant things—and we could make a big deal about a stolen briefcase... but, who's going to pay any attention? No one. They seem to be able to call the shots every time. Their plan, which no doubt included the downing of the jet, would have worked out fine if it hadn't been for the fact that Owen just happened to be in the area.'

'So, you reckon they won't try any funny business,' said Owen.

'I'm sure of it. They just want the case. Two missing stockmen would just complicate matters.'

Jenna put her hand on her father's hand. 'Don't you think it might be wise to have the police chopper drop a few men off at the waterhole this afternoon—they could position themselves somewhere handy... just in case...'

'Absolutely not!' Don exclaimed, 'You can count on the fact that they'll do a flyover, and that they'll be able to detect any warm bodies lying in ambush. No, that would be fatal—we go in alone, just as arranged.'

'Anyway, Jenna,' Owen added, '... the case isn't near the hut, so there'd be no point in trying to arrange protection.'

For the first time, Jenna looked deeply worried.

Don looked at his son. 'C'mon... let's get the chopper ready.'

Chapter Three

The next morning, Don and Owen were flying low over the undulating terrain towards Yappar waterhole. On the distant horizon, the towering cumulonimbus gleamed like clusters of pearls.

The two men had seen that kind of atmospheric build-up before—in the cyclone season. With all the focus on the fallout from the plane crash, no one at the station had bothered to listen to the weather report.

The Bell Sioux droned smoothly onward. It was forty years old, regularly serviced and carefully flown. It was also a bit of a rarey—powered by a Continental Turbomeca turbine engine that was better suited to dusty conditions. Don was a stickler for thorough pre-flight checks and had trained his son to be just as vigilant. They'd found the transponder under the cabin air inlet when they were checking that the grill was clear of dead insects.

'O...kay,' Owen had said, '... no flies on that lot—as it were. They've got us well and truly covered. I guess you're not going to meet Cate Blanchett after all, Dad.'

Don gave a rueful click of the tongue. 'Their loss, Owie. I could be a diamond in the rough...'

In half an hour they were above the hut. They settled the chopper down on the river bed, making sure there'd be enough room for the other helicopter to land. It seemed unnaturally quiet after putting up with the shriek of the turbine.

Owen and his dad walked up to the hut and did a casual inspection for anything that needed repairing.

When Don was a youth, the hut had been an integral part of the mustering—a central place that the teams operated from when they were far away from the station. When heli-mustering was introduced, the stockmen operated differently and could stay in isolated places for longer, being resupplied by the chopper. The hut was now a relic from a bygone era, but still visited with fondness now and again by the family.

It wasn't long before the heavy beating of a powerful helicopter reached their ears. It loomed suddenly above the cliff face of the waterhole.

Owen lent forward with one foot on the sliprail.

... up to their old tricks again...

The big 139 put down neatly in an uninterrupted spiralling arc.

... good pilot...

The side door slid open. With a sweep of his hand, Martin Connelly indicated that the Lucas's should enter the machine.

Father and son slipped through the rails and walked towards the helicopter.

Owen was surprised at how little apprehension he felt.

... go for a ride in the chopper... show them where the case is... probably get dumped... walk back. Easy—be home for afternoon tea...

The two men instinctively bent low as they came within reach of the thudding blades. A step had materialized from beneath the doorway which made it very easy to enter. Connelly was sitting closest to the door, facing rearward. Next to him was the woman. Brecks was in the front with the pilot.

Connelly waved the Lucas's to the two rear armchairs.

Owen entered first and sat opposite Gina Wu. The leather almost sucked him into the seat, it was so plush.

When Don was seated, the door automatically slid closed. Instantly, the cacophony of the engines and the swirling blades ceased. The cabin became as still as a lounge room. The new arrivals couldn't help but look at each other in astonishment.

Connelly laughed out loud. 'I bet you wish you could do your mustering in one of these, huh?'

With a pensive look out of the window, Don murmured, 'If I had this chopper for mustering, I'd sell it and retire.'

Owen gave an obsequious grin—*no point in confronting these guys*. Aggressiveness was not in the family nature, and they both stood to gain from generating a degree of trust. 'You'd let me have one fly but, wouldn't you Dad?'

Wu smirked. Connelly guffawed. Then he held up his hand with a pointed finger. 'Hey, Don... seriously, we appreciate your cooperation in this matter. I've got something for both of you.'

He pointed to the base of the armchairs. 'If you reach down there and pull out the drawer... go on... just pull it out...'

After the surprise from the cooler bag, Owen's face revealed his doubts.

'No body parts, Owen!' Connelly laughed. 'Go on!'

Don and Owen did as they were instructed. Inside each drawer was a small, metal case.

'Open them up, boys.'

The two stockmen flicked open the latches of their respective cases and lifted the lid.

Connelly beamed. 'There you go! One hundred thousand dollars in used fifty-dollar notes, each.'

In his peripheral vision, Owen saw his dad quietly lift out one of the bundles of notes. He did the same. After a moment, he said, 'So, does that mean you're definitely not going to shoot us?'

Connelly slapped his thighs. Wu's smirk transformed into fascinated derision.

'No, no... come on, fellers!' Connelly held out his arms in appeal, '... we're just glad to be getting the case... back—getting it back. We *are* getting it, aren't we, Owen?'

Owen nodded obediently.

'Great... great...' Connelly looked genuinely pleased. Don put the bundle of bank notes back into the case. 'Thank you,' he said very simply, looking up at the man opposite him.

Owen put his money back into the case. 'Yes, thank you very much—we weren't expecting... well, this.'

Wu spoke suddenly. 'It's nothing! Really, to us, what we're giving you is nothing... not compared to what we're getting in return. But you don't need to know about that. Now, Owen, if you would be kind enough to look out of your window and inform us of where we should land, we'd be very grateful.'

Owen looked out of his window. They were sitting about two hundred metres above the water hole. He had not even noticed that the helicopter had ascended.

'If you follow the river north... about two kilometres... you'll see a big, rocky section as the river bends right. You'll be able to land on that. The case is in a little cave, sort of overhang, not far away.'

Wu turned to the pilot to see if he'd heard, but he was already pitching the craft forward.

They sat in silence as the Augusta Westland came in over the shelf of rock and landed.

For some reason, Owen felt a sudden nausea.

... what if the case isn't there?

He hadn't thought of that eventuality. It had only been a bit over forty-eight hours. But, what if the case wasn't there? He and his dad would be in serious trouble.

'You look a bit anxious there, young Owen!' Connelly had his hand on the door lever and was giving him a doubtful look.

Owen forced himself out of the chair and ducked across to the door. 'I'm okay.'

Connelly put his hand on Owen's shoulder. 'Now, just before I open this door—a few instructions. You guys jump out and get the case and bring it back here. We're going to stay with the machine—okay?'

Owen nodded.

'Oh,' Connelly added, '... don't forget your cash.'

Owen's dad passed him his case and held his own case in the other hand.

... so, we are getting dumped...

The door opened. The onslaught of noise was quite frightening.

Don followed Owen out of the chopper to the ground. Their shirts flapped in the maelstrom of downdraft.

... obviously aiming for a quick exit...

Owen scrambled away from the Augusta to a ledge of rock, onto which he put the case. His dad did the same.

Without looking back, the young stockman led the way between the rocky outcrops to the overhanging ledge a little higher up. To his immense relief, he could see the metal briefcase, just as he had left it, lying in the shade on the sandy floor of the little cave.

As he reached in, he happened to notice some movement amongst the trees on the other side of the little knoll on which they stood. He pulled the briefcase clear and hefted it under his arm. He squinted against the sunlight. There had definitely been something moving through the trees—too high to be a beast—too big to be a bird.

Don took his son by the arm. 'You okay, mate? You're not thinking of running off with it, are you?'

Owen shook his head.

'Come on then, let's get this over with... I assume we're walking back.'

Owen followed his dad downward back to the helicopter.

Connelly had alighted and was standing just outside the door looking up at them, shading his eyes with his hand to his forehead. Brecks had left the front seat and was standing next to him, leaning against the aircraft body with one foot on the rear wheel.

The Lucas's reached the last thin rocky plateau and were about to jump down when the two men at the helicopter suddenly galvanised into action.

Brecks hurled himself through the doorway into the cabin. Connelly sprinted forward with an intense look on his face.

Brecks reappeared at the doorway, but his time with a weapon in his hand. He fired a short burst from the hip in their direction, then lifted the gun to his shoulder and fired again.

To Owen and his dad, in the act of moving forward and jumping down from the little ledge, it happened so unexpectedly that they were taken completely off guard. Owen landed and flung himself flat to the rock. The briefcase left his grip and skidded towards Connelly, who was running towards him in a crouched position. He could see that Connelly was yelling at him, but Owen's focus was on the long white flashes from the machine gun, and the incredible noise it made.

Connelly reached the case, grasped it, and scampered back to the chopper.

Brecks, still firing in Owen's direction, had jumped out of the doorway and was intent on assisting Connelly in some way.

With his chin pressed to the rock, Owen could feel the shockwaves coming from the machine gun.

... when are the bullets going to hit me?

He saw Connelly reach the helicopter—he saw Brecks turn around and pull the spent magazine from the gun. Almost at the same time, Wu threw a new magazine out through the doorway. Brecks caught it one-handed, knelt to the ground, reloaded and recommenced firing in one incredibly smooth motion.

The Augusta began to wind up. Dust and leaves swirled through the air.

Connelly got one foot onto the step and suddenly straightened. He turned around with an astonished look on his face. He pitched slowly forward and landed head first.

The inside of the cabin was lit up with a stark, white light. Wu was firing a machine gun through the open door.

Owen felt his father roll into him. They exchanged a brief look then turned to the helicopter.

Brecks reached forward to pick up the briefcase, firing continuously. He grasped the case and turned to the doorway. With his left hand, he commenced to fling the case inside—but, he too, pitched forwards, the case leaving his hand and sailing in an arc towards the doorway. Brecks fell flat out onto the rock. The case landed on the footstep of the ascending helicopter. Wu was kneeling inside, firing short bursts.

The helicopter lifted off.

Owen tucked his face down in his arms and covered his head with his hands to protect himself from the whirlwind of debris. He endured the blasts of air and listened as the sound of the turbines and thrashing of rotors was joined by a high-pitched whirring. Still the gunfire raged, accompanied with the occasional whine of a ricocheting bullet just above him.

... above me!

He turned over and risked a peek through his hands.

About ten metres above him was a giant, black drone. Like a fat spider with eight propellers, it was the size of a car and it hovered unsteadily above Owen and his dad. Underneath the drone was a turret with a single protruding barrel that recoiled with every shot. Sparks flew off its dull surface where Wu's machinegun fire struck.

Owen swung his head around and saw that the Augusta had risen to about the same height as the drone and was climbing quickly. The drone began to ascend at the same rate.

Some part of the drone exploded away from it, the remnants falling down and clattering to the rock metres away from the two men. Its pattern of flight became unsteady—it yawed left and right in progressively greater arcs. Then, it broke away from the firefight and veered towards the ridge on the other side of the river.

Completely bewildered, the two stockmen watched as the drone resumed a wobbly hover and began firing at the other side of the helicopter. The chopper pilot quickly spun the machine around so that the open door once again faced its attacker. Inside, Wu let the drone have another salvo of machinegun fire.

By now, the two aerial combatants had attained more than a hundred metres of altitude, and still they gyrated about each other as they sought a favourable position.

Don grabbed at his son. 'Let's get out of here—if they crash, it could be on top of us!'

The two men quickly negotiated their way across the rocky ledges and took shelter behind a stone outcrop near the top of the knoll.

Above them, they could see that the incapacitated drone was now attempting to ram the Augusta. After one unsuccessful pass at the helicopter's rotor disc, the drone deviated so far from its target that the helicopter had the chance to nose down in the opposite direction and run for it. It passed above the two men, engines maxed out and rotors at full tilt. Something dropped from it. In an angled trajectory, the briefcase fell through the air and crashed through the trees not far from the rocky outcrop.

Owen turned around. The drone was reeling violently in the sky. At the top of one uncontrolled loop, it suddenly flipped upside down and drove itself at great speed straight onto the rocky plateau. Its carapace shattered, and bits of propeller whined through the air nearby.

Then, apart from the diminishing throb of the departing helicopter, it was quiet.

The two men clutched at the rocky surface. Finally, they allowed themselves to relax.

Don let his head drop and took some big breaths.

Owen looked out over the view below. 'Good thinking, Dad,' he said, nodding at the place where only moments before they had been squirming for cover, and where now there were fragments of titanium skin and twisted wire.

Don looked across at his son. 'What the hell have we got ourselves into, Owie?'

Owen shook his head.

Further out onto the rock plateau, the bodies of Connelly and Brecks lay face down and unmoving.

'Should we go down and see how those two blokes are?' said Owen.

Don settled down and lent with his back against the rock. 'Not really… we'll just let them expire completely, if they haven't already. I don't particularly want to nurse either of them back to good health.'

Owen had another good look. 'I think they're both dead… they haven't moved a muscle.'

'Good, son. Now, let's just sit here for a minute and plan our next move. What do you suppose happened?'

Owen slid down against the rock next to his father. 'Well, that drone was a surprise—although, I know now, that it has been stalking us, or that chopper, since the plane crash. I saw it hovering between the trees two days ago, and then again when we reached the top of the rise here. I just didn't recognise it as a drone.'

Don gave a little nod. 'Obviously, it was after the briefcase as well— but just like the crew from the chopper, whoever is operating that drone, had to wait for you to retrieve it.'

'And when I did, they pounced almost immediately.'

'That's right. It must have followed the chopper at ground level to the bend and then hid itself amongst the trees waiting for you to collect the case. And,' continued Don, '… because the drone was unable to retrieve the case itself, the drone operators had to take out the chopper. That was what those two saw as we approached them—the drone coming at them from over the hill.'

'I thought they were shooting at us!'

'You *and* me, mate. I thought we were goners for sure.'

The noontime air was still and breathless. The only sound was some soft crackling noises from the wrecked drone.

Owen looked into the distance, remembering the flashes of the machinegun. 'That drone did a pretty good job of taking out those two blokes.'

'Sure did. My guess is that its first few shots can be fairly accurately placed. It probably has some sort of target recognition software that allows it to re-aim very quickly. But when the scenario changes, it becomes difficult for an operator, because of the time delay, to find the target.'

'That, and the fact that it was being shot at—did you see all the bullets hitting it?'

'No, I didn't, son... I had my head down, as you should have.'

Don put his arm around Owen's shoulders. 'What we have to consider is... how far away is the operator of that thing?'

Owen thought for a moment. 'Let's go and have a look at it.'

'Why?'

'Because, if it has electric motors, I'd say the operator would be relatively close... but if it has liquid fuel, it could have a range of hundreds of kilometres—it's quite big.'

'Good lad... okay, we've got to pick up our loot anyway... before someone comes along and changes everything.'

As they scampered down the slope, Owen could see that the cloud front was just about upon them. At one point they both froze in their tracks, thinking that they could hear the approach of a helicopter— but it was in fact thunder. It looked very much as though they were going to be hit by a massive storm—or a cyclone. With all the drama that had transpired, neither of the two had realised just how much the wind had suddenly picked up.

When they reached the lowest ledge, they grabbed the little cases with the money and stopped to have a look at the wrecked drone. There was a lot of thick, black liquid that trickled away from the crash scene into the cracks and crevices of the rock platform.

Owen pulled a face. 'That thing looks creepy... like a squashed insect.'

Don grabbed Owen by the arm. 'Steer clear of that stuff, Owen... that's a special fuel of some sort... probably highly carcinogenic... c'mon, let's go.'

Owen pointed up to the knoll. 'What about the case?... it fell from the chopper.'

'Bugger the case, Owie!' Don yelled against the rising wind, '... we've got to get back to the chopper.'

Both men took one quick look at the two bodies about fifty metres away, then turned and strode off towards the hut.

Fat raindrops splashed onto the stone. Owen could feel the temperature dropping. If it was a cyclone, then the entire rocky platform would go under in a rush of floodwater. Next dry season there would be nothing left to show that there had been a battle here—no drone—no bodies.

Chapter Four

The 'Press Gallery' in New Farm used to house a printing press. Over the years, most of the industry had moved out of the area; being close to the city, the suburb had become gentrified, and old and inefficient businesses had gradually made way for up-market residential high-rise. Industrial warehouses were renovated into luxury condominiums.

Don and Gail bought the building when they were newly married. They'd begun a life on the station at Yappar River, but they both knew that they wanted more; the times had changed and it was no longer necessary, nor desirable, to slog away the whole year in such isolation.

Growing up in North Queensland, Gail had established a network of creative friends, many of whom went on to live on stations and remote towns. Their art became a fundamental part of their self-expression in an often tedious life.

The idea of having a gallery where they could show their art came to fruition when the Lucas's decided to establish a base in Brisbane. The old printing house offered austere accommodation in a converted storage space upstairs, but it had the exciting advantage of being ideally suited to conversion into a gallery.

Each wet season, when work at Yappar ceased, the Lucas's would decamp to the gallery and arrange massive working-bees with all the potential exhibitors. Gradually the Press Gallery came into being—just at the time when the surrounding suburb was being colonised by new money.

The gallery hit its stride straight away; local residents were always passing by—strolling, biking and walking their dogs. When Don and

Gail invited a friend to set up a coffee shop in return for managing the gallery, the formula was complete—business compounded. The Press Gallery was *the* place for new arrivals to visit when they wanted to decorate their new abode.

As the years went by, Gail spent more and more time at the gallery—not so much because she wanted to, or needed to, but mainly because operations at Yappar Station were changing, and the old homestead was becoming redundant.

Heli-mustering, cattle trains, live export, the workforce drain to the mining industry—all these factors contributed to a different style of station management. Gangs would fly in, work for a few months on particular tasks, and then fly out again. 'Station life' was becoming a memory.

Living at either end of the state suited the Lucas's—Don still needed the 'bush' and Gail was thoroughly engaged in the city. After thirty years of marriage, they still looked with longing for each other as the queues streamed from the arrivals gateway.

Owen tugged at his bowtie. The bloody thing was throttling him. He put down his champagne glass, looked at his tanned reflection in an art piece on the wall, and checked that his tie was still straight and his hair flicked the way he liked it.

By the opposite wall of the gallery, engrossed in an earnest conversation with a party, his mother raised a furtive eyebrow in his direction.

... don't worry, Mum... I think I can stay composed for another hour or so...

He took his glass and resumed mingle mode.

It was crowded; that comfortable crush that offers both refuge and encounter according to one's mood. He drifted into conversations and drifted back out, without obligations and without offending anyone.

But his mind was elsewhere. During his time at university, he'd developed a turbine engine concept that he'd been slowly piecing together as time and finances allowed. Now, a year after the incident at Yappar waterhole, and with the money that he and his father had acquired, the proof-of-concept prototype had been built. It was this project that consumed Owen. Any thoughts of the battle over the briefcase were quickly sidelined by the demands of the research. With his trusted team looking on, they had tested the engine in a shabby workshop on the outskirts of an industrial precinct. The motor had surpassed everyone's expectations. It's simplicity of design enabled the machinists to find, through a series of trials, the optimal proportions for each of the working parts. The final prototype achieved good power over a wide rev range, and it did so smoothly and efficiently. It was a triumph. But the path to commercialization was a whole other matter; the motor had so much potential that it required very careful consideration about how best to release the intellectual property.

'Owen?... would you like me to refill your glass?' Linh Vuong smiled up at him.

'Oh, hi, Linh... no thanks, I'm only good for one drink.' He placed his empty glass on the tray she was holding out. He immediately regretted that he hadn't accepted the offer of a refill when he saw the tiniest hint of disappointment in the young woman's face.

Without faltering, she cast back her head and smirked, 'I thought you were a rowdy, hard-drinking stockman? Is wine too effete for you... would you prefer a beer?'

Owen laughed. 'No, sorry to disappoint you, but I'm only good for one beer too.'

The Vuongs had opened an Asian grocery store in the Valley at about the same time that Owen's parents had started the gallery. He'd seen Linh now and again when, as a teenager, she worked casually at the gallery coffee shop. She still worked there now that she was at uni.

'Sorry, Linh... but somehow I seem to have remained ignorant of what you're studying.'

Linh's lovely smile widened. 'I'm graduating next month!' She placed the tray on a nearby table and moved closer to him.

'Oh, wow! Good on you—in what?'

'Archaeology, management, education... sort of hybrid thingy... you know...'

'Uh huh... work in a museum, putting together educational programs and stuff like that?'

'Oh, I hope so,' she clasped her hands fervently. 'Or, get a job in a Vietnamese museum... there are a lot of discoveries being made in the jungles with ground penetrating radar... ancient civilizations... that sort of thing...'

Owen nodded with genuine delight; it was such a surprise to him that Linh, to whom he had barely paid attention over the years, was developing such a fascinating future for herself.

He was about to respond, when she drew back with a composed smile and glanced over his shoulder. He turned. Facing him was a woman who was appraising him with unsettling candour. Before he could overcome his astonishment, she held out her hand.

'Hello, Owen,' she said, her lips pouting ever so suggestively, 'I'm Francesca—I don't want to intrude, but I would like your expert opinion on a piece that I'm fairly serious about... when you have a moment...' She ran her fingers over his hand as she turned away.

Owen took a step after her. 'You've come to the wrong person, Francesca... I don't know the first thing about art.' Owen was pleased with the steady authority of his voice.

She turned her head to him, dragging her curls across her shoulder. 'I'm not talking about art, Owen... I'm talking about a turbine.'

For a moment, Owen was unsure of what he'd heard, but there was no mistaking the level gaze of Francesca's grey eyes. He looked around for Linh, but she had discreetly moved away to serve other guests.

When he turned back to Francesca, she was moving purposely through the crowd towards the foyer. Feeling suddenly a little nauseous, Owen followed her.

The turbine project had been kept very secret; the few people involved in it were all trusted and knew that the best road to financial success was to keep it that way. In fact, outside of the team, there wasn't a single soul aware of the turbine being developed.

With a pale, bejewelled arm, Francesca leaned against the heavy timber and glass door that led to the courtyard outside.

Owen leapt forward to give assistance. '... you must have me confused with someone else.'

Francesca clutched at her swinging handbag and strode into the open. 'Owen, we're not confused.' She turned to face him and seated herself on a bench against the raised garden. She patted at the space beside her. 'Sit down and tell me everything you know about the briefcase.'

Owen felt his knees weaken.

... oh, god... here we go again...

He moved towards her and sat down. 'I don't know anything about the case. It fell from the helicopter into the bush... we never went back for it. Then, after the cyclone hit, we were too busy to even think about it. The hangar lost its roof, and the chopper copped some damage. It's only just been fixed, but we won't be flying it out to the station until the new season starts in a month or so.'

'You say the case fell from the helicopter?'

'That's right. The chunky guy tried to throw it into the chopper, but it landed on the step. Then, after the dog-fight, the chopper escaped and the case fell into the scrub.'

'Why didn't the drone go after it?'

'The drone? It was lying on its back on the rocks—smashed to bits.'

Francesca casually swatted at a mosquito. The movement revealed a piece of shining technology deep in her handbag.

Owen sighed. 'Are you recording me?'

'Of course, I am, Owen,' Francesca laughed, '... and profiling you for the truth as well.' She pointed to an ornate clasp on the side of her hair. 'Now, just confirm for me... the drone was shot down was it?'

Owen couldn't help himself from peering at the clasp. 'Yep... got shot down and crashed.'

'Well, well... you see, we didn't know that. We always assumed that the drone had recovered the case. It wasn't until the best part of a year had elapsed that we began to suspect that the ah... material was still out there, in the um, *scrub*. We sent out a team of course, but the flood had wiped the place clean... of everything...' she looked pointedly into Owen's eyes. 'I assume you witnessed Connelly and Brecks being killed?'

Owen stared at the flagstones and recalled the two bodies lying unmoving on the stone shelf. He nodded.

... was that their names!

Francesca raised an enquiring eyebrow. 'Ah... and the drone?... you saw it crash?'

Owen nodded again.

'And you saw the helicopter make its escape?'

Another nod.

'*Then* what did you see? Face the camera, Owen… how will I be able to tell if you're lying?'

Owen sat up and looked directly at Francesca. She was wearing only the lightest make-up and he would have guessed her to be in her late thirties… only because she *actually* looked twenty-five. She smiled at him with lovely lips but kept her distance with her eyes. Her face came close to his and she whispered in his ear.

'Sometimes I use this technology when I'm dating… you know, to reveal a man's true motives. Waste of time, of course… men only have one motive. I sometimes wonder why I bother.'

'And what would *your* motive be, Francesca?… to find someone dedicated to your well-being?… someone loyal and selfless? I should think that you'd be more than capable of looking after yourself.'

For a fleeting moment there was a flicker of hurt in her face, and her lips never resumed the same sardonic curl that there was before.

Owen couldn't believe he'd said something so hurtful. He lifted his hand and gently gripped under Francesca's forearm. 'I'm sorry, that was wrong of me. I shouldn't have said that.'

Francesca's gaze softened. 'You really are one of a kind, aren't you, Owen.' She slid her hand back so that she was holding his. 'It really is the worst luck for you that you were riding out there in the back of beyond on that day… because none of this should be happening to you. However,' she withdrew her hand and looked towards the entrance doors.

Owen followed her gaze.

Linh was standing inside the foyer looking at them through the glass door. She quickly averted her eyes.

Francesca looked at her retreating form with renewed focus. She spoke without looking at him. 'We want that case, Owen… simple as that… simple as that. And we know enough about you to make it happen. Now, are we going to get it?'

Owen stared without expression across the courtyard. '… yes…'

'You know where it is?'

'I know roughly where it is.'

'... roughly?'

'If the flood didn't come up that high, then, yeah, I should be able to find it.'

'Good... good. There's just one thing...'

Owen looked up.

'... we are in a race against, well... our opposition, who have doubtless also come to the conclusion that the material is in limbo, and so we fully expect them to resume the search.'

Feeling a sudden boldness with the knowledge that he was so integral to this affair, Owen spoke up. 'Is it in any way possible for me to know what is in that briefcase?'

Francesca shook her head slowly. '... you mustn't know—you don't want to know, believe me...'

'Why has it taken almost a year for you guys to work out that "the material" is still out there?'

With a little pout of consideration, Francesca replied. 'We can tell by the activity on the commodity futures market, Owen... that's all I can say. Now,' she stood up and ran her fingers through Owen's hair, '... we have to move, post-haste. You won't be needing anything—we've got everything covered. I want you to be at New Farm Park within an hour. Walk... no lifts. You can manage that can't you?'

It was only about a kilometre from the gallery. He'd have plenty of time for a quick goodbye, a garbled excuse for leaving and to change into something appropriate for the bush. He nodded.

'There'll be a helicopter... they can't wait. And don't attract attention.'

Francesca put her hand on Owen's shoulder. 'You're doing the right thing... let's get this over with.' She turned and walked out of the courtyard.

Owen sighed and looked at his watch. 10:25pm. He strode to the entrance door. People were beginning to leave the exhibition. He stood for a while with a tight smile, holding open the door. Then he ducked inside and wound his way around the corridors and displays, loosening his tie as he went. He needed to find his father and avoid his mother. The whole Yappar incident was unknown to her—what with the cyclone, damage control at the station and the fact that she had happened to be in Brisbane at the time, meant that an appropriate moment to discuss what had occurred didn't eventuate until two months had elapsed. By then, it was agreed that mother need not be troubled with that information for the moment.

'Owen!'

He abruptly turned. Linh was facing him with a look of curiosity.

'… everything okay?'

Owen leaned casually against what he thought was a wall but was instead the back of a display cabinet. It slid marginally away from him. 'Whoops!' He grabbed it and slid it back. '… yeah… all good. Hey, Linh, have you seen Dad?'

Linh's dark eyes searched his. 'He's putting out the garbage.'

'Oh, great… thanks…' Owen brushed Linh's hand with his then turned to the kitchen.

His father was sorting aluminium cans into a bin.

'Dad… a quick word outside.' He held open the screen door as Don carried out the bin.

It was cool and quiet at the back of the gallery.

'Ah, sudden development vis-a-vis the waterhole incident,' Owen began, '… they want me to retrieve the briefcase from where we saw it fall.'

Don Lucas put down the bin, gave one nod and looked away.

Owen continued, 'They're going to pick me up in a chopper at the park in about an hour… less…' He studied his father's impassive face. 'It'll be okay… I know where it is… they don't want trouble… they just want the case.'

Owen's dad was quiet for a moment. '… and there's nothing we can do, Owie… except to find that blasted case and give it to them.'

Owen gripped his father's shoulder. 'I've got to run…'

Don covered his son's hand with his. 'You better, mate. Take care…' He drew Owen near and hugged him.

'Oh, and, Dad… they know all about the turbine… but don't go looking for any spy cameras until I get back… okay?'

Don nodded slowly. '… make this all go away, son… find the case.'

Owen gave his dad a squeeze on the shoulder and turned to the kitchen door. He quickly made his way to the steps that went up into the loft and ascended three steps at a time. Once in his room, he pulled out a large drawer and began to change.

In two minutes he had on jeans and joggers and a heavy long-sleeved cotton shirt. He had neither elastic sided boots nor his usual hat at the gallery.

... this'll have to do. Okay, let's hustle...

He halted at the top of the stairs.

...don't attract attention... No problem...

Owen turned around and went to the gable end wall of his room. He opened up the heavy wooden double doors that allowed entry into the loft from the back lane. The gantry crane, with its block and tackle lashed to a brass cleat, overhung the footpath. It was the only way to get furniture into the loft and, when Owen was a teenager, he and his friends would use the hoist to get into his room. Only now, the Jacaranda had grown so much that he could easily leap from the threshold into the tree and lower himself in seconds.

He hit the pavement silently and glided in the shadows to the road.

Even at this hour, there were still people about, enjoying the cool night air. He lengthened his stride. His thoughts turned to the turbine project.

... seriously, these people are in a totally different league... they must have had me under surveillance for some time...

The road came to an end at the Powerhouse, and Owen crossed the carpark to the riverside walk that led to the entrance of New Farm Park. The noises of the suburb faded as he ventured further along the treed laneway. He looked behind him. Someone was walking through the shadows in his direction—a woman.

... have a bit of sense, girl... what's wrong with sticking to the streetlights...

The laneway circumscribed the park and, in a clearing at the centre, Owen could make out the dark silhouette of a silent helicopter.

... okay, so they definitely weren't expecting no for an answer... this chopper has been here for a while...

There was enough urban glow for Owen to make his way around

the garden beds towards the rendezvous. He checked behind him. Now there were two people. One seemed to be assisting the other. Not wanting to involve innocent citizens, Owen jogged towards a darkened patch under a huge fig tree and waited. The two figures crossed the grass straight to him, one of them aiding the other in the most unusual manner. A man's voice called out.

'Come on, Owen... to the chopper.'

Owen hesitated. There was something very odd about the way these two people were engaged... as though...

The sudden beam of light was blinding. Owen averted his eyes.

'Hurry up, Owen... I won't say it again.' The voice was right beside him now. The light went out. Owen walked on obediently, his night vision completely spoiled.

When they were near the helicopter, there was a muted hum as the door slid open. A soft interior light lit Francesca's face. 'What's this?' she demanded, looking over Owen's shoulder.

'She followed him', said the male voice from behind.

Owen whipped around. Just metres from him, a man in a tracksuit was holding Linh tightly by the shoulders. 'Linh!'

The man shoved the young woman forward so that she collapsed in Owen's arms.

Owen helped Linh to her feet. 'Why did you follow me?' he implored close to her face. Then, directing his attention to the thug, said, 'Steady on, mate... she's got nothing to do with this...'

'She does now,' he spat.

Owen turned to Francesca. 'She doesn't know anything... she's...' but he couldn't think of an adequate way to describe the woman he was holding.

'She's your guardian angel, Owen—by all appearances.' A sly smile spread on Francesca's lips. She waved them on board with an imperious flick of her wrist. 'Get in, the two of you, hurry up.'

The helicopters engines began to spool up.

At one point, Owen thought about the possibility of not getting on board. He turned around. Mr Tracksuit had his pistol resolutely trained at Owen's mouth.

Francesca huffed, 'It's alright, Owen... no one is going to get hurt, but we obviously can't let your girlfriend go for the moment. Sit over there.' She pointed to the two armchairs against the rear bulkhead. 'Anyway, she can make herself useful looking for the case—it'll be fun. Now, buckle up. What's your name?'

'Linh—L-I-N-H.' After having anglicized her name during her school years, it had become a habit for her to spell out her name now that she had reverted to the original Vietnamese.

Francesca's eyes lit up. In the distinctive nasal inflection, she said, 'Thật là một bất ngờ ... bạn vẫn nói ngôn ngữ của bạn?'

Linh's mouth gaped just a little. She nodded with an admiring pout. 'It's more of a surprise to hear *you* speaking my language so well.'

Francesca laughed and held out her hand. 'Well done... I'm Francesca.'

There was a moment of awkwardness as the passengers dealt with the helicopter's stomach lurching ascent from the park. The lights of the Valley scrolled by the windows, and Owen estimated that their altitude could be only a few hundred metres.

... staying well below the GA zone... must have some clout though— no one flies a rig this size so close to the airport without a few eyes being discreetly averted... heading straight over Nudgee and then the bay— and off the radar. This baby won't really benefit from altitude, even with twin turbines... at 300kph—1200k... plus at least two refuels... be five hours minimum...

Owen sighed and re-entered the social realm to find that Linh and Francesca were garrulously chatting away, both in English and Vietnamese.

...curiouser and curiouser...

Once again, the seats seemed to suck him in, and he felt a sudden weariness that surprised him.

...I'm probably being drugged... so what!... Linh's taking it all very calmly... hasn't got a clue what this is all about... I wonder what scenarios are going through her mind... must ask...

Chapter Five

Owen woke up because the hushed drone of the engines had ceased. The side door was open and the cool night air was wafting into the cabin. Francesca's voice carried clearly from outside.

'... I could have worked as an academic or in the corporate sector... but I like too many things. I'm a consumer—not just materially, but of people as well. It's not particularly noble of me, I know, but I can't help being what I am... I mean, why are we fulfilled by beauty and excess?... even when we know it's all artifice... we want to attach ourselves to anything triumphant... extravagant. Well, I do... that's why I'm on this gig—excellent money and, well... just *very* good money. And as long as I get what I want, everything's fine, but if anyone gets in my way...' There was an ominous silence.

Owen ducked his head through the door opening and looked out. The two women were in the act of adjusting their clothing in the gloom of light coming from the helicopter's cabin.

Francesca waved a finger at him. 'The boys' loo is on the other side, Owen.'

Owen pulled a face. 'Couldn't you go just a *little* bit further afield?'

'Look, you might be perfectly comfortable with waving your willy about in the wild, but Linh and I are urban creatures, and we prefer to *see* where we're squatting.'

Owen sighed and rolled his eyes. '... good god...' He sat down and called out, 'Are we refuelling?'

Francesca and Linh stepped back into the cabin. 'The boys have just gone to get the truck... won't be long.' She passed Linh a box of moist tissues and the two of them wiped their hands.

Intuitively recognising the development of a conversational hurdle, Owen eased himself out of his seat. 'Oh well, may as well take advantage of the opportunity.' He excused himself and ducked out into the night air. He walked around the aircraft and stood serenely studying the night sky. In the distance, a truck engine started and headlights arced across the paddock. In no time, the beam trained on the helicopter.

'Oh, you're kidding me.' Owen hastily completed his mission and zipped up. At the window, two faces pressed against the glass. A burst of laughter came faintly through the soundproofing.

... I don't believe it... two hours together in an armchair and they're as thick as thieves...

The tanker drove up just as Owen climbed back into the cabin. He didn't dare to look at Linh. This was all Francesca's doing.

She smirked at him. 'That's what you love about the outdoors, isn't it, Owen... it's just one big toilet.'

'Ha, ha... very funny. Excuse me if I don't feel like contributing to on-board cheer, but not so long ago, someone was pointing a gun at my teeth.'

Francesca smiled contritely. 'How did you two meet?'

Outside, a pump started, and the sound of voices intruded faintly into the cabin.

Owen looked into the distance. Something was changing. He was suddenly, unambiguously aware that the person seated next to him was occupying a space in his life that no one had ever before.

'Owen?'

His voice was soft and low. 'We've known each other since we were teenagers. Linh used to work at the café.' In his mind's eye, she moved gracefully around the tables, wearing a pale-yellow blouse and with her hair in a tight bun. He smiled... then frowned.

... we're being kidnapped! Now would be a good time for a reassuring gesture...

He slid his hand across to the armchair beside him and found Linh's hand, upturned and awaiting him. Owen looked across.

Linh regarded him with an expectant gleam in her eye. She squeezed his hand.

Owen had a sense of displacement, and his field of vision narrowed ever-so slightly. *Oh, no... not now... my heart is supposed to be beating faster!* He took a deep breath and returned Linh's squeeze.

Francesca clapped her hands. 'Oh, my god!... this is priceless,' she squealed. 'You see what I mean, Linh? This is what I live for—to see a man suffused with emotions.'

Linh's face softened. She gazed into Owen's eyes. 'I see exactly what you mean, Francesca... it's a wonderful thing... knowing that it's for me.'

Francesca clapped and squealed even louder.

Mr Tracksuit appeared at the door. 'We're ready to go.' He shot a disapproving look at Owen's hand holding Linh's. He and the pilot stepped into the cabin and edged their way to the flight cabin.

Owen was suddenly self-conscious of his proximity to Linh. He lifted their clasped hands and looked her in the eye. 'Is *this* why you followed me?

Linh held her head coyly to one side. 'Put it this way, Owen—if it had been someone else that was introduced to a stranger and, within seconds, had followed her outside so that he could sit by her and hold her hand, only to be abandoned, and who then rushed to get changed into work clothes and leave secretly by the back lane... well, I probably wouldn't have followed them no matter how odd it all seemed...'

Francesca leant forward and pressed her hands onto Linh's knee. 'Oh, Linh... you are exceptional.'

Owen's mind reeled, but he had to agree—Linh was exceptional.

Francesca sat straight and produced a superior look. 'I should tell you though, Linh, that Owen's swoon has a less than romantic origin—he's prone to fainting because of his extremely low blood pressure.'

Owen glanced heavenward. 'Oh, yes... and how is it with techno-lady?'

'Gina Wu, you mean? Haven't a clue, Owen... although she did write a very replete report on you.

The helicopter rose with a steady acceleration that caused the three passengers to sag in their seat.

With elegant fingers, Francesca reached for a console at the end of the arm rest. Her chair tilted and laid out. With her eyes closed, she said, 'Well, children… it's very late, and we should try to get some sleep. Hopefully it won't be a long day… but it could be.'

Linh placed her other hand over Owen's, leant her head close to his ear and whispered, 'We're doing well… I have no idea what's going on, but it's very exciting—I'm loving it.' Then she kissed him softly. 'Goodnight.'

Francesca stole a peek with one eye and grinned. She reached beside her and switched off the cabin lights.

The turbine whine seemed accentuated now, although it was not at all intrusive. Owen laid out his chair. Beside him, Linh, with her slight frame, had managed to curl up and looked as though she was already fast asleep.

…loving it!… my god, I'd better find that briefcase…

When Owen awoke, the horizon was aglow with the rising sun. Linh was still asleep and so was Francesca. It was too dark to see the landscape, but he guessed that they must be well into the channel country by now—cattle country. What was it that Francesca had said?… something about commodities… futures. He knew zip about the stock market, but his father had spoken on occasion about futures— the trading of prospective crops not yet planted. It sounded bizarre to him, and he didn't try very hard to grasp the concept. What was in that case that had to do with futures?… an algorithm that foretold the, well, future? Everything could be explained by algorithms these days, it seemed. Maybe shares, stocks, bonds… securities?… he had no idea about any of them. But whatever it was, it could in some way affect the future, because it had taken a year before the interested parties realised that it hadn't been, what… activated?… sold? And some poor bugger had met a gruesome death. Images of the severed hand appeared in Owen's mind.

Mr Tracksuit squeezed between the two forward passenger chairs and loomed over Owen. His amber eyes reflected flecks of the orange dawn. He pointed a finger into Owen's face.

'Find the case… don't think about running… or, I'll have to put some lead into you, which, believe me, I'll enjoy doing.'

With tiny nods, Owen hoped that he was conveying sufficient

sincerity to convince this idiot that he had no intention of escaping. Where was this guy expecting him to run? It was almost as though he was provoking him. Truly, a psychopath if ever there was one.

Francesca's voice came menacingly. 'Get back in your seat, Nigel.'

... Nigel! Who's called Nigel nowadays? Surely, they're playing good cop—bad cop...

Nigel pushed himself away from Owen with a painful grip above the knee and turned to the flight deck. 'We're landing in five minutes.'

Linh writhed into a sitting position, blinking and rubbing her eyes. She flicked Owen a hopeful smile, then stared out the window at the rim of sun emerging above the horizon.

Francesca stared solemnly ahead, obviously absorbed with the final details of her mission.

Trees panned past the windows.

... here already... obviously saved the coordinates in their GPS. At least it'll be cool this early in the morning...

The machine lurched mildly as it came to rest on the shelf of exposed stone near the rocky outcrop. There was just enough light now to make out the terrain. The rotors started to wind down and Francesca reached for the door switch.

... not wasting any time...

A swirl of cool air entered the cabin. Francesca leant forwards. 'Okay, you guys know what to do... or, at least, you do, Owen. Linh, you may as well go with him... another set of eyes.' From her handbag she extracted what looked like a metallic business card and passed it to Linh who was closest. 'It's on... just talk into it when you need to. How long do you think you'll be?'

In his mind's eye, Owen saw the briefcase fall. He recalled his orientation atop the outcrop. 'Give me an hour. Hopefully I'll have found it by then.'

Francesca nodded. 'Good. We have other technology available to us and, to be honest, if we'd known about the demise of the drone, we'd probably have tried that option first. But even so, we weren't aware of the approximate location so... you're still the most cost-effective means of retrieving the case. I'll park myself on a high spot somewhere and keep an eye on you with these.' From her handbag she pulled a streamlined set of what looked like swim goggles.

The rotors had wound down to a lazy spin. Francesca let herself out. Linh and Owen followed.

Ahead of him, Owen recognised the little ledge that he and his dad had jumped from just as the shooting started. He looked at his feet. This was about the spot where Connelly and Brecks had ended up— shot in the back by a drone. He glanced downstream.

... wonder where their bodies are now...

'Come along, Owen... no time for reminiscing.' Francesca gave him a little shove in the back.

'It's up here.' Owen began the climb to the knoll.

When they got to the top, Owen showed Francesca the little rocky overhang where he had initially hidden the briefcase. Then he swept his hand towards the bush on the other side. 'The case fell out there somewhere... shouldn't take me that long.'

Francesca looked around for a comfortable boulder to sit on. 'You won't mind if I leave you to it?... I have a bit of a thing about wandering about in the wilderness.'

'Me too,' Linh declared, '... but I feel perfectly safe with you, Owen. Let's go.' She began the descent.

Owen grinned and shook his head.

...the wilderness!... the only thing to be scared of in the bush is other people...

He headed towards the likeliest spot, all the while reimagining the trajectory of the falling briefcase. The cyclone had dropped about 400mm of rain on its path inland, but just looking at the vegetation, Owen could tell that the flood waters hadn't come this high. The scrub here wasn't that thick, but there were a lot of stony outcrops that could easily hide an object. Linh trod softly behind him. He liked the way that she kept her balance on the irregular ground.

'The most dangerous things you'll encounter out here will be a hive of feral bees in summer. No kidding, they will attack in one, unrelenting cloud of anger. I've seen cattle run almost to death by the little bastards... not that they'd be killed by any venom or anything... it's just that they're trying to escape the pain. Not that we're likely to run into any now... too early.' Owen was pleased with the reassuring tone of his voice. 'When they're in dangerous mode, you can hear them from fifty metres away...'

They'd come to a slight rise in the terrain where a disjointed ghost gum stood proud of the surrounding vegetation. The tree fitted with Owen's vision of the falling briefcase. 'It's bound to be here someplace. Let's have a little scout around... I'm usually pretty good with spatial awareness things... y'know, reference points and angles...intuitive trigonometry I suppose...'

Owen turned around with a disarming smile.

Linh walked straight into his arms and raised her lips to his. She pressed to him and kneaded his mouth with hers. Owen ran his hand from her waist, upwards to the nape of her neck. They balanced with closed eyes underneath the ghost gum. Linh lifted her hands to Owen's biceps and probed lightly around his mouth with her tongue.

A tiny, distant voice intruded. 'Ahem... young lovers, I don't want to spoil the moment, but you *are* on a mission.'

Linh extracted the transmitter from her skirt pocket and put it near her mouth. 'We've found it.'

Francesca couldn't hide the excitement in her voice. 'Oh, well done... well done. Okay, straight back to the helicopter, don't dawdle.'

Linh looked up into Owen's startled eyes.

He mouthed, 'Where is it?'

Linh's eyes refocused above and slightly to one side. Owen turned and looked up. There, suspended in the twisted branches of the ghost gum was the silver briefcase with the manacle.

'Oh, you little beauty, Linh.' He gave her shoulder a squeeze.

She coyly raised an eyebrow. 'It was my pleasure.'

Owen closed his eyes and let his forehead settle onto Linh's. He wrapped his hands around her small waist. This moment merged so naturally with the past—why had he never really noticed her? He'd been so caught up in... stuff. Now, he knew, there would be another dimension to his life that was going to make everything just so much more fulfilling.

... everything will change with this girl...

He asked, barely above a whisper, 'Can you climb trees, by any chance?'

Linh looked askance at him. 'Try me.'

'Okay... if I give you a leg up, do you reckon you'll be able to get up to that first fork?'

'In my skimpy waitress dress?'

'Oh, right...' Owen cast his eyes around for some alternative.

'Of course, I can get into the fork, silly... but you'll have to promise not to look up my skirt.'

A tantalizing image crossed Owen's mind, and that fraction of a second was ample time for Linh to make up hers. She bent down and slipped off her flats. Then she unclipped the waist band of her skirt and deftly flung it over a fallen branch.

'There, now you won't be able to look up my skirt, and I'll have a bit of room to move.'

'I could have restrained myself, you know,' Owen said indignantly, as she stood before him in her underwear.

'I hope not, Owen... I'd have been very disappointed.' She moved to him and hugged him with her head to his chest.

Francesca's disembodied voice issued from the fallen branch. 'For god's sake you two!... get a move on. What's the problem?'

'No problem, Francesca,' Owen called out, '... the case is up in the tree, but we've got it covered,' he looked at Linh, '... sort of...'

'Okay, well hurry up, or I'll send Nigel down.'

Owen lent towards Linh. 'Can you believe that?... Nigel?'

She giggled silently. 'No wonder he's so angry. C'mon, hoist me up.'

It took very little exertion for Owen to assist Linh up into the tree. Her lithe body stretched to the fork, and she effortlessly clambered out towards where the briefcase was snagged. Owen found a stout stick and lofted it to Linh's waiting hand. With that, she could reach the case, and with a few pokes, it came free and fell to the ground.

Linh looked down. 'I'm going to drop from here.' She grasped a thin branch and lowered herself so that she hung suspended with her feet about three metres above the ground. 'Think you can catch me from here, Owie?' she called down.

'No worries. Keep your arms and legs together, okay?'

On the count of three, Linh let herself drop. Owen caught her easily and together they fell to the ground. For a moment they lay in the leaf litter, he with one hand on Linh's breast.

She reached up and stroked his mouth with her thumb. Their heads came together and they kissed once more.

'Right, that's it! I'm sending Nigel down...'

Owen lifted his head. 'Francesca, can you actually see us with those goggles?'

'Yes, I can. They're just super powerful binoculars with very good image stabilization... you're in line of sight... nothing that amazing. Now, get your hand off her tit and hustle back here... we've got to get going. Don't forget the briefcase.'

Owen looked down at Linh.

She said, 'Owie, I need a little bit of resuscitation—can you give me a squeeze?'

Owen bent his head and kissed softly and squeezed delicately, then kissed delicately and squeezed softly.

'Owie,'

'... hmmm...'

'I think I'm being attacked by angry ants.'

The two of them hastily got up and brushed themselves.

'Can you check me for ants?' Linh turned her bottom to him.

'Oh, yeah... here...' he brushed at an imaginary ant, '... and here...'

They started laughing. Owen hugged her from behind. 'C'mon... we'd better be getting back.'

He retrieved the case while Linh put on her skirt.

They were back at the knoll within ten minutes, trying to keep a straight face at Francesca's disparaging looks. She snatched the case.

When they commenced the walk back, Owen had a thought. 'Francesca...'

'Yes,' she answered without turning around.

Owen looked down at the helicopter. '... just be careful. This is the point where the drone attacked...'

Francesca clambered steadily down without breaking stride. 'There aren't any drones, Owen. Last time was different—the crash was fresh. This time... well, this time we're the victors.'

Nonetheless, when it came time for the helicopter to lift off, Owen scanned the horizon with great care.

But nothing surprising happened—apart from the fact that they were dropped off on the Cloncurry/Normanton highway with just a case full of fifty-dollar notes amounting to one hundred thousand dollars, and a bottle of water each.

'It has to be like this, kids,' Francesca had said, '… sorry. Really enjoyed your company though.' And then to Linh, 'Tôi rất ghen tị với bạn, Linh … chia tay.'

When the helicopter had become a speck in the sky, and not a single vehicle had come past as they stood expectantly by the side of the road, Linh turned to Owen with a little sadness on her face and said, 'She told me that she was envious of me and wished me well.'

Chapter Six

Owen held Linh close and looked out to where the road met the horizon. In the far distance, he could see a road train coming their way.

Linh's hand brushed over Owens back pockets. 'Owen!' she exclaimed, '... your phone?'

Owen's face was set in a grimace of indecision.

Linh put her hands to her mouth. '... you left it on board on purpose? Oh... you've got "find my phone".'

Owen's mouth puckered and pouted and his eyes roved to all points of the horizon.

She placed her hands on his chest. 'Is that wise?... what would you benefit from it?'

Owen absentmindedly caressed Linh's shoulders. 'Actually, it really did fall out of my pocket in between the seat cushions when I was sleeping. And then, I thought about what I'd do when I realised it was missing—locate my phone with the app—so, I pushed it deeper into cushions. It was an accident... I lost my phone... it happens. I was thinking of retrieving it just before they dumped us here, but when I saw the direction we were going, it made me curious. They are headed into the dead-set never-never.'

Linh arched a curious brow. 'Where's *that*? Don't forget, I'm an utterly urban, Asian immigrant.'

Owen grinned and kissed her forehead. 'Ok, well, there's nowhere that's so remote any more. There are drilling rigs dotted like the measles all over this country, and you can get a soy latte at the end of the most brain rattling dirt road to the back of beyond, but, originally, the most uninhabitable and dangerous country that a man could venture into was... that-a-way...' and he pointed across the road.

'... that-a-way?'

'Uh huh... western gulf country... the Roper river... screaming hot one minute and six feet under water the next, with nowhere to run. Sound romantic?'

'Not particularly.'

'It isn't... and a hot latte wouldn't make it any better... believe me, I've been there.'

Linh looked distantly across the road. 'Don't people go wandering out there in their four-wheel drives towing caravans and stuff... for fun!'

'Sure, they do... but they never stray far from the comforts of their rig.'

Linh turned at the sound of the approaching road train. 'Should we wave him down, Owie?'

'Don't worry, he's slowing down for us.'

'He is?... he's miles away... how can you tell?'

'He'll stop for us... he's got about twenty gears to run through *and* it's going to cost him the best part of ten bucks.'

'Ten bucks?'

'Yeah, that's how much extra diesel he'll use getting back up to highway speed after he's picked us up.'

The old Mack, hitched with four empty cattle trailers, finally rolled up and stopped, with a lot of squealing and hissing, in the middle of the road.

Owen took Linh by the arm. 'C'mon.' They walked up to the offside door, with the frightening roar of the engine right next to them. With practiced dexterity, Owen jumped up onto the fuel tank steps and reached for the grab rails. He clambered to the door and stood wide as he opened it.

The driver, dressed in industry standard shorts and flip-flops, flung back his head upon recognising his passenger. 'Owen Lucas!... what the bloody hell are you doing out here, mate?'

'Lionel!... mate, am I glad to see you,' Owen yelled back over the din in the cabin.

'Who's your friend? C'mon, get in...'

For a rig the size of a wharf, there was only one passenger seat. With Owen's assistance, Linh climbed up and looked over the threshold into the cluttered cabin. A tangle of coiled CB leads hung from the roof and a cluster of gear sticks sprouted from the floor.

Lionel pulled his esky off the seat and jammed it between the backrests. 'How are ya, love...I'm Lionel. There you go—plonk yourself down...'

Linh scrambled onto the seat and held out her hand. 'Hi... I'm Linh...'

'Sorry, love... can't hear ya... you'll have to speak up.'

'I'm Linh!'

Lionel delicately took Linh's hand. 'Nice to meet you, Lee.'

Linh had an awkward moment of intimacy with Lionel as she held herself poised over the gearsticks while Owen seated himself. He then took her by the waist and sat her down on his thigh.

Owen and Lionel then commenced a painfully loud discussion using that uniquely acquired sharpness of voice that manages to cut through all manner of industrial clatter as the truck was nursed through its entire range of gears. The engine noise swelled and waned with each change and the heat from the firewall was intense. Lionel listened attentively as he wrenched at the gear levers and stomped on the pedals.

Linh much preferred the helicopter. The trade-off was that now she had Owen's arms around her. She managed to catch a few words and picked up that Owen wanted to get to an airport as soon as possible.

Lionel grabbed for one of the CB handsets and began an exchange that was completely incomprehensible to her, and that ended with him giving Owen a cheery thumbs-up.

At a top speed of 70kph, the day drew on. The landscape remained unaltered and the sun gradually shifted from shining in their window to searing the driver's window.

Lionel pulled down a blind and bawled, '... be in Cloncurry in about half an hour...'

His two passengers, by now with their feet up on the hot dash sill, closed their eyes with relief and anticipation.

When the engine finally ground to a stop at the roadhouse just out of town, the silence was so overwhelming that the two young hitch-hikers felt completely unbalanced. They carefully climbed out of the cabin and swayed into each other, breathing in the oily air next to the motor.

Lionel appeared and leant against the massive bull bar. 'Let's grab a drink. Then I can drop you at the airport. Got the use of Dot's car.' He hefted his flip-top phone to Owen. 'Make your calls with that. See you inside, and you can tell me your story.' He canted his head with a knowing look.

Linh didn't have her phone—it was in her bag at the gallery. But there was an important call to make because, whilst Owen's dad knew what was going on, he didn't know about Linh.

Owen handed Linh the phone. 'You be okay?... I'll go in and sort out our trip home. One of my school buddies works for a grazier out here, and Lionel says for the sort of money that I'm waving at him, he's all set to go—company plane.' He squeezed her hand and headed to the roadhouse.

Linh had the two middle seats of the Cessna 206 Stationair all to herself, and whilst it was still cramped and uncomfortable, she couldn't fight the weariness that enveloped her. After watching the runway drop beneath them, she had a last bleary look at the flat horizon and fell asleep.

Owen was too excited to sleep.

His friend, Travis, had been happy for Owen to take the controls right from take-off. 'You've got a fair bit of time on fixed-wing, haven't you?' he enquired as they walked to the plane.

'A bit. Only the 150 we used to have on the property... nothing like that,' he'd pointed at the 206.

Travis did all the flight checks and radio protocols and let Owen steer the plane out to the runway. With intermittent advice from his friend, he was airborne and turning lazily to the south in minutes. Once they reached a cruising altitude of 10,000 feet, Travis engaged the autopilot. 'So,' he breathed ominously, '... is it terribly inconvenient that the first two people you meet, after mysteriously appearing out of nowhere, happen to know you?'

Owen snorted softly. 'Bloody lucky, actually. But, yes, a bit inconvenient.' He gave a sidelong glance. 'Do you remember that jet that came down a year ago over our place?'

'Only because I'm in the industry. Never a mention of it in any of the papers and stuff... telly... very odd...'

Owen nodded deeply. 'Yeah, weird, hey... and, to add to the mystery, there is no wreck, because it was washed away in the flood. Although, I bet if I flew the chopper downstream, I'd find bits of aluminium wrapped around a tree here and there.'

Travis looked steadfastly ahead. 'Okay... that's news. So, you saw it?'

'Saw it... yep—too closely.'

'Drugs?... weapons?'

Owen sighed suddenly and tried to clear his mind. He'd probably said too much already. 'Listen, Trav... I honestly can't tell you more about this whole thing... because the people involved are ruthless— very well equipped and ruthless. They have enough clout to be able to make a jet disappear... and that's much harder than making a human disappear. So, I'm really glad to have finally gotten rid of this crowd. And yes, I was caught up in something dangerous, through no fault of my own, but now it's finished. I really don't know what it was all about... honest.'

Travis gave a resigned grimace. 'Wow!... so, it's all good now?'

'Mate, I hope so... I gave them what they wanted... and they kindly abandoned us by the side of the road...'

'With a shitload of cash...'

Owen's mouth opened.

Travis laughed. 'Hey, c'mon... who goes hitch-hiking on the Normanton road with just a custom made slim-line briefcase, and then offers me ten thousand dollars to fly them to Brisbane?'

Owen smiled ruefully. 'Okay, fair enough.'

Travis pointed gun fingers at his passenger. '... but I hear what you're saying, and I don't want to know any more.' Then he harked back his head and said, '... although, she's cute!'

Owen turned around and looked at Linh.

... yeah, she is cute... and smart... and brave...

He let his head rest on his arm as he surveyed her.

...she kissed me!...

Travis made a scheduled radio call. When he finished, he patted Owen on the shoulder. 'Get some sleep, mate... we've got a while to go yet.'

The return to Brisbane was uneventful. Considering the anxiety that followed Linh's sudden absence, affairs had been settled remarkably smoothly, and it was all due to Owen's dad having a very tense discussion with Linh's parents in the early hours of the morning. The most he could do was to pinpoint Linh's disappearance with the time Owen left for his rendezvous with the helicopter and deduce that she must have followed him. When her call came in the afternoon, there was a collective sigh of relief. The Vuongs had been fully informed and sworn to secrecy. There was no other way—it was all too bizarre.

They dropped Linh at her house without even getting out of the car.

It was a surreal moment for Owen. Linh jumped out of the back seat and quickly leaned into the passenger window to bid the Lucas's goodbye. She said nothing—just a meaningful nod to Don and a discreet squeeze at Owen's shoulder. Then she turned and walked through the gate.

Don did a careful U-turn. 'Now, Owie... as you know, having spent most of my life in the saddle, I'm not terribly well equipped to read the finer signs of body language... but I assume, from Linh's mysterious disregard towards you, that the two of you have got something going... am I right?'

Owen grinned. 'Ah, you don't miss much, Dad.' He gave his father a gentle shove on the shoulder. It felt good to be able to talk about Linh instead of ruminating about the "conspirators".

Don lifted his fingers from the steering wheel in an apologetic gesture. 'I mean, I assume that's why she followed you in the first place—because she likes you.'

'Yeah... she saw that something wasn't right when I was talking to that Francesca chick that they sent down to get me, and then, after I'd spoken to you and disappeared upstairs, she must have decided to keep one eye on the old gantry door just in case I decided to slip out. Then she followed me.' Owen furrowed his brow at a recollection.

'You know, I remember one time climbing down the gantry with my mates, and seeing Linh looking at me from the courtyard when she was waiting on tables... it must have been when she first started at the gallery.'

Don slowed the car and turned into the laneway behind their house. 'Well, I hope she hasn't complicated matters too much.' He switched off the engine.

'I shouldn't think so, Dad. They've got what they want and, well... that's the end of it. Actually, Linh and Francesca got along really well—they could both speak Vietnamese.'

Don nodded absently then looked at the case in Owen's lap. 'And they gave you more cash!'

'Yeah, and two bottles of water!'

'These people dole out money like it's, yeah... cheaper than water!'

They both laughed.

Don's phone burbled in his pocket.

'Wow!... Dad... you're actually receiving a message.'

It was a family joke that Don was way behind the times when it came to modern communication technology. He insisted on keeping his trusty flip phone even though it was almost a decade old.

Don looked at his phone... for a long time.

'What is it, Dad?'

He passed it across to his son.

Owen read the message. *Hello Don, just need to tell you that your son's phone has been posted back to your home address. That will save him activating any tracking app which would have caused a lot of bother and would have placed him in very serious trouble. Phew... tell him to be more careful in future. G W*

Owen nodded. 'That's Gina Wu... the woman with the machine gun in the back of the chopper, remember? The way she texts, is the way she must run the show.'

Don opened the door but stayed in his seat. 'I suppose it was worth a try. Dangerous people to play games with though.' He slapped Owen's thigh. 'C'mon, let's go grab a coffee—your shout,' and he flicked a glance at the aluminium case.

Chapter Seven

Life for Owen quickly re-established its routines. One difference was that, for the first time, he did not go to Yappar Station for the mustering season. It was agreed that he should put all of his energy into the turbine project in order to bring it to a workable prototype as quickly as possible so that they could present it for evaluation by a CSIRO panel. If it was deemed worthy of further development, well and good, but if it failed to attract interest, then Owen would abandon it and find another direction.

The other thing that changed for him was that Linh was now so much a part of his life. They spent as much time together as they could. Each had exciting things to relate to the other; Owen with his engine research and development, and Linh with her passage through to a career in anthropology.

'Sometimes I just can't believe my luck,' she said one morning, seated at coffee shop two doors down from the gallery.

The café owner arrived with their drinks and smiled broadly at the two lovers who had eyes only for each other.

'... you know that field position thing at the ministry of antiquities that I was telling you about?'

Owen took his eyes off Linh and gave the waiter a friendly nod.

'... well, I was accepted... even though they preferred a masters and a few years' experience! I got it.'

Owen pouted and looked miserable.

'What?'

'Does that mean you're going to Cambodia?'

Linh looked disconsolately at the table. 'Yeah... but only for a few months at a time. I don't exactly know what the time frames are...'

Owen reached out and clasped Linh's hands in his. 'I'm only joking. That's fantastic news and it's exactly what you want and what you're good at. We're part of that whole global dynamic thingy that dazzling young people are caught up in. It'll be fun—me visiting you in exotic locations... you visiting me in the bush...' He cradled his coffee cup in both hands and lifted it to his lips.

Linh air swatted at him.

Owen laughed and changed his grip on the cup to one hand with a prominent pinkie. It had become a habit over the years of camping for Owen to clasp his mug in both hands. He wasn't aware of his social faux pas until Linh had drawn his attention to it.

On another morning, at a different coffee shop, just a week before Linh was to leave for Phnom Penh, they sat together studying a map of Cambodia.

'Apparently the site is here somewhere, near to the Laotian border,' Linh pointed with a slender finger, '... it's not far from the Mekong River... apparently... I'll find out soon enough.'

'And what's the attraction here? Have they found the remnants of a city?... like Angkor Wat.'

'I don't know, Owie. It's all very secret... competing institutions... museums, very precious about their projects. I honestly don't know. That's why I'm a little bit amazed that I landed this position.'

'Maybe they're looking for particularly ignorant people,' Owen said with a thoughtful frown.

'Oh, thank you, Owen Lucas, for your insight,' Linh knuckled his nose.

A chair scraped nearby.

'... they probably just want someone overawed, underpaid and too afraid to rock the boat.'

Owen became serious. 'Have you checked them out?... is it all above board?'

Linh stroked Owen's cheek. 'It's fully endorsed by the university. But, I know that if I get into trouble, you'll come for me like Indiana

Jones.'

A man eased himself up to their table with a chair in his grip. He sat down.

Owen recognised that complacent air of authority. He looked steadily at the man's face without saying a word. Linh had the same reaction.

In his fifties, urbane and perfectly attired, he clasped his hands in his lap. His voice was low and silky. 'Ahh... I see that you are already acquainted with my type,' he smiled tightly. 'My name is Alasdair.' He casually reached inside his coat and pulled out a slim envelope. 'By way of introduction, I'd like you to see these,' and he pulled out two photographs that he carefully placed onto the table.

Without touching them, Owen studied the colour prints. One of them was of him, riding towards the camera on Stella, with huge cumulonimbus formations glowing orange in the distance. The other was of him and his father standing atop the rocky knoll. He was holding the briefcase, again, with giant storm clouds pressing down.

Owen lent back and took a deep breath. 'So, you're with the drone outfit, I take it.'

Alasdair gave a curt nod. 'That's correct, Owen.' He placed his hands on the table edge and steepled his fingers. 'I gather, from your demeanour, that you have resolved everything regarding, ah, the location of the briefcase.'

Linh shifted her eyes between the two men.

With an implacable look, Owen lent forward in a small gesture of assertiveness. 'We have given them what they want—they, in turn, have been generous—we are quits.'

Alasdair studied his hands. 'Thank you... that is what we concluded. We were convinced that our rivals had obtained the case. Our drone was so badly damaged in the firefight that we lost communications with it. We placed all our hope in the ability of the drone to continue fighting autonomously without our input. We immediately initiated a retrieval operation but, as you know, the cyclone moved in and made everything impossible. About a week later, even though it was still raining heavily, we got a helicopter out there, but the place was unrecognisable—water everywhere.'

Owen allowed his face to relax into the tiniest smile.

Alasdair capitalised with a rueful smile of his own. 'Yes... we should have realised, but we had to try. When the floods subsided, after about a fortnight, we went out again and, as you would be perfectly aware, the place had been swept clean. We searched downstream, but it was impossible to see anything amid the huge tangles of debris. We had high hopes of recovering the drone and its video footage but couldn't find a signal from the transponder anywhere.'

Owen raised his chin. 'Where was it positioned?'

Alasdair leant politely forward. 'I'm sorry?'

'Where was the transponder positioned on the drone—its location on the fuselage?'

Alasdair paused to think. 'Oh, I believe it was located somewhere on the top of its carapace... out of the way of ground fire... crash protection... that sort of thing.'

Owen allowed a degree of affability to reveal itself in his body language. There was something likeable about this guy; he was polite and he was divulging a hell of a lot more information than anyone else had. 'Well, there's your answer, Alasdair...'

Alasdair leaned back and smiled in anticipation.

'... the drone got shot up so badly that it lost its ability to control itself. It ended up trying to ram the chopper...'

'Trying to ram the helicopter!' Alasdair interrupted, suddenly much more animated. 'That was the autonomous program, you know... it did that of its own volition! We'd lost communications by then. Incredible! Sorry, go on.'

Owen couldn't help but grin at Alasdair's obvious elation. 'Well, it tried to fly into the chopper's rotors, but after the second pass, and all the while copping a hail of lead from the machine gun, it went into a steep climb, turned upside down, and drove itself into the rocks below. It missed us by about forty metres.'

Alasdair, nodding continuously, listened intently.

'So, I reckon that the transponder, being on the top of the body, got smashed to bits. Then, when the rains came, the drone would have been washed away for miles.'

Alasdair stroked his jaw and looked into the distance. 'So, it did end up in the river... we were never certain. We were worried that it might have tried to fly home and that it ended up crashing somewhere where it would be discovered... even though it was programmed to avoid populous areas. Wouldn't do to have some grey nomads come across it,' he smiled disarmingly.

'You're not wrong!... the thing's creepy as hell.'

In the moment that Owen and Alasdair were engaged in their thoughts, Linh asserted herself.

'You said that you *were* convinced that your rivals had obtained the case. Did you mean, that you believed that they actually *had* the case, or, that after a period of time, you realised that they in fact *didn't* have the case.

With a deferential gesture, Alasdair acknowledged Linh's question. 'Well done, Linh. Yes, by *were*, I meant, as you said, that after a period of time, we realised that our rivals did *not* possess the case. Our unsuccessful retrieval operation was based on the hope that our drone had downed the helicopter and that we might find the wreck... and the case.'

Owen gave Alasdair a critical look. 'So, you didn't see the blond guy hoik the case onto the step of the chopper?'

Alasdair snorted softly. 'It may come as a surprise to you, Owen, but our technology let us down at that point. The barrel flashes from the machine guns were so bright that they disrupted the light sensors of the camera. We could just make out Brecks hurling the case, but we could not identify much more. We assumed it landed inside the cabin. That was his name, by the way—Melvin Brecks. The other chap was Martin Connelly. And the woman is Gina Wu—avoid her at all costs.'

Linh put down her coffee cup. 'So, the case fell back to earth, but each party erroneously assumed that the other had acquired it. Then, upon some critical event, it became apparent that the case, or rather, the information that it contained, was still lost somewhere in the outback. Then, one group quickly mobilised and rushed off to find the one person who might have some clue as to what happened to the case... an innocent young stockman—masquerading as a shonky art dealer,' she wrinkled her nose at Owen.

With hands clasped, Alasdair put a knuckle to his lips and examined the couple in silence.

Inside the café, the commotion of new arrivals signalled the transition to the corporate lunch hour as parties began to claim tables.

Alasdair fidgeted and scanned the room with his peripheral vision. He reached out and collected the photos from the table. 'Is there somewhere we can go to that is a little more private?'

'And more comfortable,' Linh added, as she adjusted her position on her chair.

Owen rose from the table. 'Follow me... I've got just the place.'

Five minutes later, the trio were in the showroom of the gallery overlooking the courtyard. Except that it wasn't a showroom any longer, but rather a den and store room for the gallery's most coveted art works.

'Sorry about the clutter,' Owen began as he closed the door. 'We tried to create a corporate environment at one stage... you know—posh buyers being wooed with wine and... whatever. But it wasn't Mum and Dad's style. Anyway, most buyers purchase online nowadays when they're probably sitting at a kitchen table in their underwear for all we know. But the lounges are still here—please, be seated.' He moved to a small cabinet against the wall. 'We've got a bottle of Scotch here that's been here so long that it has probably aged very nicely. Would you like a drop, Alasdair? There's ice and soda.' He opened a small bar fridge.

Alasdair settled himself slowly in an armchair and crossed his legs. 'You know, Owen... I'm beginning to like you more and more. Thank you, I'd love a Scotch... no soda, just ice.'

Owen set about wiping a tumbler and extracting ice from a tray.

'Am I the only one having a drink?' Alasdair enquired.

''fraid so. Linh and I don't drink much... often... habitually. C'mon, Linh... help me out here.'

Alasdair laughed, then said gravely, 'I think I need a drink, seeing that what I'm about to tell you is known to very few people on this planet.' He reached out and took the glass from Owen. He lifted his drink in salute. 'Be aware that you are hearing this with the full knowledge that, should you ever attempt to divulge this information, we will be able to thwart you at every turn—and worse... if necessary...'

'Cheers,' said Owen falling back into his armchair.

Alasdair took a sip. 'Well, it's quid pro quo—we put you in the picture and you help us to build a bigger picture.'

Linh spoke up. 'Hang on... you are about to tell us a supposed world-wide secret, and then you expect some service from Owen?'

Alasdair gently swirled the Scotch through the ice. 'I am about to tell you a significant truth... and I don't expect anything from Owen in return.'

Linh looked a little crestfallen. 'You don't?'

'I don't. I'm not here to impose on Owen. As it happens, I'm here to impose on you, Linh. But, we'll come to that shortly... well, maybe not shortly, because this is a big story. Are you ready?'

Owen and Linh nodded.

'Alright then.' Alasdair put down his drink on a side table and settled back. 'The information that was in the briefcase had to do with the planet Venus. It contained masses of data—historical, cultural, scientific, even mythical and social interpretations about our nearest neighbour—the planet of love. Apart from the moon, Venus has been more closely studied than any other celestial body—and there is a good reason. Venus affects our planet in a way that has become critical for humans ever since they became agrarian, and megalithic people demonstrated that fact in the most empirical and unambiguous way possible—they built vast structures with one simple intention... to observe Venus.

'Now, you might well ask, what was so important about this one planet that justified so much time and labour in creating an observatory. The answer is—rain. Ancient civilizations came to understand the relationship between the position of Venus and high rainfall events. In other words, they could, to a certain extent, predict the climate. Now, at the time of the building of the huge megalithic structures, this knowledge must already have had immense significance; one obvious example being that communities were given notice about forthcoming droughts and famines so that they could prepare themselves accordingly. Just as important, they would have had advance warning long before neighbouring tribes began to be affected by the failing rains and could thus prepare themselves for the inevitable starving hordes that would descend into their countryside. Renaissance artists have bequeathed us fanciful images of priests conjuring the heavens, but believe me, the individuals responsible for the design of the structures and the interpretation of the findings were outstandingly resourceful and pragmatic people, considering their limited means.

'Over the aeons, the knowledge of Venus was both built on and dissembled. The hard, useful facts remained in the hands of a small number of initiates at the centre of powerful empires, whilst, at the same time, in order to disguise the obsession with the study of Venus, there proliferated a whole range of pseudo-cults that promoted Venus as the goddess of love—Ishtar in Mesopotamia—Isis in ancient Egypt. Venus became responsible for procreation, fertility, health—which was kind of true in a way—as well as, in the case of the Mayans, portending the arrival of war—which was also kind of true when neighbouring tribes were forced to go on the rampage because of famine.

'As our civilizations developed, the true effects of the planet Venus on the planet Earth became mired and hidden in occultism and fairy stories.'

Linh suddenly rose from her armchair and walked to the bar fridge. 'So, are you able to tell us how it is that Venus affects the rainfall on Earth?' She extracted a bottle of water and screwed off the top. She offered Owen a sip before settling in her chair.

Alasdair smiled indulgently. 'Indeed, I will, Linh. But first, I must ask you to lay your phones on the table and to take out the batteries. I'm sorry...'

Linh and Owen quickly complied.

'Thank you,' Alasdair said. He took a sip from his glass. 'The reason why Venus affects the rainfall on Earth is because Venus' upper atmosphere, which is mostly water vapour, is being stripped off by the force of the solar wind and blown into space where, every now and again, the Earth, being further from the sun, runs into this cloud of gas, where it is absorbed into our own atmosphere. This produces a higher than usual concentration of water vapour in the atmosphere which, over a period of time, produces increased precipitation.' He paused with an expectant look. 'There!... that's all there is to it. Not much really, when you consider the wars that have been fought for possession of this secret.'

Owen stared out into the busy courtyard where lunchtime diners busily devoured their meals. 'No... not much of a secret, but one that would be worth billions if you were a futures trader.' He looked across at Alasdair.

'Touché, my boy. That is exactly why this information is so valuable. And, I'll tell you another thing—the whole history of futures trading was instigated by the people that were in possession of the secrets of Venus—like gambling with a stacked deck.'

Levering himself out of the armchair, Alasdair went to stand in front of the window. 'I can't begin to tell you how sought after this knowledge has been over the years, but I will give you some examples from our recent past. Tell me, either of you, why Captain James Cook became famous.'

Linh looked at Owen for his response—which was to make a nodding movement at her as an indication that she should field the question. She rolled her eyes. 'Well, Captain Cook explored the East coast of Australia... um, yeah...'

'Indeed, he did, and naturally, that makes him quite prominent in our history. But did you know that exploring Australia was not the most important reason for his trip, and that he only reluctantly went there with a very peeved and disagreeable crew? He had been given sealed orders that he was to open only after he left Tahiti. After the joys of female hospitality in the islands, the crew were hoping to continue their explorations in the South Pacific, but no, the orders quite specifically stated that they were to head home as safely as possible via New Holland—which everyone knew was a desert inhabited by lice-ridden nomads—follow the coast north until they came to the straits of Torres, and head west again until they were in the spice islands, then home. There was no mention of a prolonged exploration of, what eventually became Australia; the Royal Society, who sponsored the trip, wanted the Endeavour back in Portsmouth as soon as possible. Why? They further insisted that Cook not deviate from this route, as they had determined that this was the safest way back to England. They were not to go around the Horn... far too dangerous. And Cook would have complied with that order if it wasn't for the fact that they bumped into the incredible islands of New Zealand and decided, correctly, that the Royal Society would probably want to know a bit more about this verdant paradise discovered more than a hundred years previous by Abel Tasman. So, they spent a month or so circumnavigating it and mapping the coastline. Then they continued on their safe passage home, striking Australia somewhere near Eden. They resolutely refrained from making any landfall until they came to the amazing harbour of Botany Bay, where, upon Joseph Banks' insistence, they made a quick recce and determined that, yes indeed, the place was inhabited by savages, and whilst it looked a damn sight better than what the Dutch had described, it wasn't lush and there were no spice trees growing. So, they jumped back in the longboat before the aborigines got their aim in and sailed two thousand miles up the coast before an annoying puncture forced them to go to shore again. The rest of the voyage was reported as pretty uneventful, and they arrived safely in England.'

Linh interjected. 'Why the emphasis on safety?'

Alasdair leant against the window sill. 'The Endeavour was carrying very valuable cargo—information. The Royal Society was sweating on the safe return of the data, gained in Tahiti, of the transit of Venus across the disc of the sun. Now, modern scholars will tell you that the astronomers on board were trying to establish the exact position of Venus in its plane of orbit. Well, Edmund Halley had worked out to perfection the orbit of a *comet* over fifty years previously, so the orbit of Venus was a no brainer. No, what they were hoping to observe was some evidence of the solar wind's load of gaseous water being blown off the Venusian atmosphere. Of course, there were no cameras in those days, so the scientific party had to describe, in the most eloquent detail possible, what they witnessed as they looked through special lenses directly into the oncoming cloud, propelled by the rays of the sun.

'You see, for quite some decades, the predictable rains from Venus had begun to fail. The conspirators became worried. What would happen to their position of power if they couldn't predict times of abundance and times of famine? Their first chance of a look directly at Venus with the power of the sun behind it came about in 1639. Using a *camera obscura* effect, the astronomer, Jerimiah Horrocks, believed he was able to see a cloudiness surrounding the image of Venus. As transits of Venus across the sun are always associated with subsequent wet weather, the coterie of scientists in the know realised that this was probably evidence that water was being transmitted from Venus to Earth. If they could determine the strength of such an event from the observations of the transit, that information would be even more valuable. Only now are we beginning to understand why the megalithic observatories were so massive; we've always assumed that they were used at night so that, from inside the tunnel sanctum, the object under observation would appear brighter because of there being no background light from the stars. Now, we realise that these astrolithic structures were used during the day, and were designed with a small opening, a long tunnel and a vestibule deep inside where, we think, the ancients held up a finely polished slab of limestone to act as a screen onto which could be seen the image of Venus along with the shimmering contours of the clouds of water vapour on their way to Earth.'

Owen looked stunned.

Linh was mesmerized. As a student of anthropology, this revelation was astounding. She could barely speak. 'Does that mean... that most of the, as you say, astrolithic structures, from around the world are dedicated to the study of Venus?'

'Well, now here is an interesting thing. Typical astrolithic sites appear to have arisen with great focus and commitment at just one time during the era of the relevant civilization; they didn't continually build structures; we don't find scattered examples of megalithic observatories all over the place. Usually, it is just one significant site, built at great expense, and used for only a short while. This points to Venus observations, because Venus transits are rare—only two couples, eight years apart, every two hundred and forty-three years, and much fewer for any one particular place of Earth. The sites that remain to us are truly mega in size—and scarce; the ancients seem to have known when the time was upon them to begin construction;

knowledge that was handed down by priests versed in the geometry of the sky.'

For a moment, Owen thought that Linh was going to cry.

She closed her eyes and hugged herself. But then she unleashed a look at Alasdair. 'I still don't see why the ancients needed to build time consuming constructions if they already knew about the relationship between Venus and rain.'

Alasdair walked back to his chair. 'They didn't need to... absolutely didn't need to. But, if your community has a priesthood that accurately foretells the seasons, year after year, decade after decade, and then announces one day that they would like to construct something special that will bring the whole community together, and that their edifice will serve as a reminder for centuries to come of the wonder of their deity—their God... then, you'd probably end up with a lot of enthusiastic volunteers. I mean, they must have!... the structures exist.'

Linh closed her eyes again and let her head arc backwards. Her voice was soft but strong. 'Ye cannot behold the face of God with thine natural eyes...' She opened one eye and peered at Owen, '... because if you look at the sun, you'll go blind!'

'But, they were looking at Venus!'

'*Crossing* the sun...'

Alasdair laughed and slapped his leg. 'Bravo, Linh... bravo.' He stood and walked over to the cabinet and poured another drink. 'Have you got the stamina for one more story?'

Linh's eyes lit up. 'Oh, yes please!' She hugged her knees.

Owen smiled and went and sat beside her on the arm rest, draping his arm over her shoulder.

'Just before I do though, can you see that couple at the table near the gateway?'

Owen and Linh peered out the window.

Owen tut-tutted, 'Sad to say, they are doing what so many people nowadays shouldn't be doing—spending too much time on their phones.'

Alasdair chuckled to himself. 'Yes, it's brilliant, isn't it... twenty years ago, the surveillance team would have had to hide their monitors and pretend to be having an engaging conversation. Now, they can ignore each other and scroll from one camera to another and no one thinks anything of it.'

Owen looked at Alasdair. 'You've got cameras planted here?'

Alasdair gave a little gesture of surrender. 'Only for today—they're flying cameras... miniature drones. We'll collect them all before we leave.' He took a slow sip from his glass. 'Now, we go forward a few years... to the 1960's,' he cast a look of challenge towards the couple. 'What was the most significant event to occur in that decade?'

They looked at each other for a second. 'The moon landing!' they replied, almost in unison.

'Very good, yes... the Apollo moon landing in 1969.'

Owen rubbed his hands together in exaggerated glee. 'Oh, great... you're going to tell us how it was faked!'

Alasdair laughed. 'No, no... I can't reveal everything! I want you to do your own research on that one—your own logical deductions.'

Owen gave a little pout of disappointment.

Linh gently pushed his lips back in with her finger.

With his elbows on the armrests and with steepled fingers to his chin, Alasdair began his story. 'It was the time of the cold-war; two emergent powers wrestled for supremacy in an age of burgeoning technology. But, it was as much about actual advance as it was about propaganda. All the resources available were poured into projects that would both increase the technological advantages of the respective country as well as to promote the image of success and progress. John F. Kennedy famously intoned that the United States would put a man on the moon before the end of the decade. The space race was under way; people looked up at the moon and imagined that soon a rocket would land on its surface. What was less well known was that, three months before Kennedy's speech to congress, the Russians had managed to perform a fly-by, not of the moon, but of the distant planet Venus.

'Oh, they didn't neglect the moon; in fact, they had flown past it within six thousand kilometres, and had already crashed a probe on its surface before the end of the fifties. But their focus was on something more important than coming back with a pocket full of moon dust. Six months before the famous flight of Apollo eleven, two

84

Russian Venera probes, launched from Earth three days apart, drifted down through the Venusian atmosphere and sent back some very disturbing information—the reserves of water vapour in the upper atmosphere were almost depleted. What were left in Venus' deep and dense atmosphere were the heavier molecules of carbon dioxide and sulphuric acid. The time of rains that the ancients had mysteriously divined for thousands of years, was coming to an end. The clouds of vapour that reach the Earth have become patchy and thin. That is why we are experiencing such uneven rainfall around the globe at the present; deluge in one place, drought in another.'

Owen cleared his throat. 'But, if the transits only occur four times in two hundred years, how does that make a significant impact on our weather?'

'Well, the reason is that, whilst a visible event is very rare, the Earth frequently runs into cloud streams from Venus. Its plane of orbit is only a few degrees different to Earth's, and its period of orbit is quicker, so there are many opportunities for this to occur. And, I should point out, it's not as though Earth gets all of its rain from Venus—far from it. The Earth has its own systems and, let's face it, it is covered in water. The Venusian exchanges act as a catalyst to existing weather cycles; they significantly compound natural rainfall events. You can imagine though, how valuable it is to be able to predict the vagaries of the weather, not just for agriculture, but in wartime too.

'Anyway, it's interesting to note that, whilst there was so much to be gained from winning the race to the moon, so much prestige in the age of television, the Russians directed about half of their space budget, and the cream of their scientists, towards Venus. That alone indicates how vital it was for them to gain a better understanding of our nearest neighbour. Since that time, the Russians have made twelve more missions including soft landings on the surface. But, the main focus has always been on sampling the atmosphere and trying to work out whether there were hidden reserves of water vapour, or whether there was the possibility of chemical transformations occurring that produced water. Nowadays, there are any number of European, Japanese and other satellites orbiting Venus. Why? What sort of information do we need about a place so remote and so hostile? The answer is; atmospheric data. Every country wants its own access to the secrets of Venus.

'The moon, on the other hand, is virtually a forgotten frontier and no attempt has been made, in almost fifty years, to go back—even with all the advances made in technology.'

'So,' began Owen, '… what was in that briefcase?'

'Ah, yes… the briefcase. It contained all sorts of photographic and numerical data, all stored in solid state, about everything we've just talked about and more.'

Linh interjected. 'Then, why are you after that case if you already have the information?'

Alasdair swirled his drink. 'We have a good overview of what we call, the "Viride" project—that's "green" in Latin—but we don't have all the hard data at our fingertips. Only one duplicate of the distilled knowledge was made, and it resides in a very secure place that we, in theory, have access to, but that would require an inordinate amount of grovelling, not to mention an admission of negligence on our part, and we were hoping not to have to go down that path. One electronic copy of the original documents was given to us, stored in solid state, and it came down in the plane along with our courier. We were in the midst of a relocation of our operations centre and we were ambushed. We'd still like to get back that material.'

'But,' said Owen with a shrug, '… now that the water vapour on Venus has virtually dissipated, the information is not as relevant any more, surely. Would that be true?'

'Very astute of you, Owen. The accretion of vapour on Earth is so patchy now, that it's anybody's guess as to where the rain might fall. Still, there's money to be made in other nations' disasters if you can reasonably predict them. Also, if the Earth is going to experience a global drought, it will be extremely advantageous to know when and where it's going to be most devastating.'

To Linh, Alasdair suddenly sounded tired. With a wan smile on his lips, he seemed to slump. She took a deep breath. 'Alasdair… would it be too rude of me to ask you how old you are?'

'Not at all, under the circumstances,' he said, directing a little salute to her with his hands in prayer. 'I am eighty-six years old.'

The young couple showed obvious surprise. 'You don't look anywhere near that old, Alasdair, said Linh softly.

Alasdair rubbed his eyes. 'Sometimes, I feel it, though. I have been a conspirator since I was in my early twenties. I was recruited at a university, as most conspirators are, and I have worked anonymously, secretly and without credit or glory since that time. One benefit that I took advantage of—and not all conspirators do—was to avail myself of the best nutritional regime possible, the best physical lifestyle and, well... a fair bit of medical input, which has even included a bit of surgery here and there,' and he framed his face with his hands. 'Well, the longer one lives, the longer one has to put up with one's reflection in the mirror.'

Linh came nose to nose with Owen. 'Will you still love me when I'm eighty-six, Owie?'

'Sure... if you can put up with me when I'm ninety!'

From outside could be heard the sound of diners speaking over the top of each other as they bade their farewells.

Owen framed a question with a puzzled look. 'So... I gather, you came to the conclusion that the case was still unclaimed when the activity you were expecting on the stock room floor didn't eventuate... or wherever it is that you do futures exchange stuff...'

'That is exactly correct, Owen. If our opposition had in fact obtained the material, even allowing for a reasonable amount of time for them to digest the information, we would have seen a particular kind of bidding for certain commodities after about six months. But we didn't—so we knew it was still out there.'

Linh rested her arm on Owen's thigh. 'And, now we've given the case to the other side...'

Alasdair turned up the palms of his hands. 'You had no choice. Owen saw first-hand how rough these guys can play—our courier was very attached to his mission, wasn't he, Owen?'

'Don't remind me.' Owen said, visualising the hand being pulled out of the bag.

There was a contemplative silence as each of them dwelt on their own thoughts.

Linh ventured a question. 'You said earlier on, Alasdair, that your main reason for coming here had something to do with me—what is it?'

'Ah yes.' He laced together his fingers and looked up at the ceiling. 'We are in the habit of keeping abreast of anything that is new or that might create change in the world. We have to; not to do so would put us at a severe disadvantage in terms of interpreting the world and maintaining control. We are continually playing catch-up with emerging technology and trends. So, we have agents everywhere. Now, most of these people don't even know that they are working for us—probably ninety-nine-point nine percent. And most of our agents, for want of a better term, only work for us just the one time in a seemingly innocuous capacity. They might be part of an organisation that is a bit like a guild, or a brotherhood. They might be, let's say, an electrician who might get a job repairing a fault in the house of someone of interest to us. In the course of his work, he might be asked by a superior in the brotherhood to secrete a device somewhere in the house—no questions—just the intimation of securing some lucrative jobs later on—nudge, nudge, wink, wink. Our man does his job—and we have successfully installed a monitoring device without raising any suspicion.

'Many of the societies that previously only admitted solicitors and bank managers and the like—and *only* men—now open their doors to tradespeople of both sexes—*gardeners* supplementing their unemployment benefits! The pool cleaner!... Because, they are the ones who possess gate combinations, door keys and have access inside the house, or office or institution. An appropriately nuanced request for information... a subtle hint for an exchange of favours... an appeal to an ideology or family values... is all that it takes for us to achieve our mission.'

'Jesus!' exclaimed Owen.

'Oh, yes... the status quo has changed considerably over the years.'

Linh spoke up. 'Is that what you're doing to us?... priming our confidence in you?'

Alasdair nodded and looked away. 'Yes... yes... I can't deny it. My only defence is that I want the two of you to be in the bigger picture—without compromising your safety.'

'So, you want me to be one of your agents in the nether regions of some Asian jungle.'

Alasdair smiled to himself. 'More interesting than that—I want you to be a double agent.'

The room was quiet again as this piece of information was being processed.

Linh lifted her chin. 'Oh, I get it... I've already been recruited... that's why I got the job...'

Alasdair studied the floor. 'We had a perfectly suitable candidate set up for this assignment—unbeknown to him, of course. But he was overlooked. When we saw that you'd been appointed, we did a background check and lo, we came across the Owen connection. From there, after a bit more research, we arrived at the conclusion that you would be just the sort of person who might be able to help us.'

'As a spy!' Linh retorted. She had a think about this. 'I was made aware of this position through my supervisor...'

'Yes, yes,' interrupted Alasdair, '... of course you were. There would have been a chain of wishes trickling right down from the head of the faculty to your supervisor... and you wouldn't have been the only student to get that information... it's just that I doubt that the other applications even got past the first desk. But your submission was brazen—how dare you apply for this job without your post grad and without any field experience—and yet, you speak fluent Vietnamese and are comfortably assimilated into an English-speaking society *and*, you are an immigrant—no time to have created partisan alliances. You obviously ticked a lot of boxes, and our man missed out. There!... my invitation in its entirety.'

Owen looked worried. 'But, Linh doesn't even know exactly what her job entails yet.'

'No... but I do...'

With round eyes, Linh asked, 'They're not smuggling opium out of the golden triangle, are they?'

Alasdair looked briefly at his watch. 'No, no... nothing as mundane as that. No... the situation is that an exploration crew from a mining company came up with some interesting results from their ground penetrating radar surveys. We know that much. Naturally they are keeping their cards close to their chest but, strangely, they're not deploying the sort of gear and resources that one would expect from the discovery of a mineral deposit. Our mole in the ministry of antiquities alerted us to the fact that they intended to recruit some staff with the sort of qualities that led us to believe that they have found something of archaeological or anthropological significance that will need subsequent *contextualising*,' and he indicated inverted commas with his fingers, '... by a suitably qualified person, naïve enough not to know the difference, and young enough to be bullied— and totally comfortable in an English-speaking milieu.'

'That's me!' exclaimed Linh joyfully.

The two men laughed.

Alasdair continued. 'I'm pretty sure there's nothing sinister here... but there are a few strange anomalies. Anyway... you've got a job to go to... and I have sent you an electronic package that is hidden in your phone. If for any reason you need assistance, you will be able to activate it. Just ask for me.'

Owen and Linh exchanged glances.

'Would you like to have some lunch, Alasdair? Believe me, it's no trouble.'

'I'd very much like to, but I can't. I have to leave you two lovely people. I do hope that one day soon I will see you again.' He stood up and straightened his clothes. He held out his hand. 'All the best with your motor, Owen. If you don't have any luck through the usual channels, I'd be happy to have a look at it.' They shook hands. He turned to Linh. 'Good luck, my dear. Don't get caught snooping—but do stay alert. Stay very alert.' He shook her hand. 'I will make my own way out if you don't mind.'

Owen held open the door. 'Not at all. Fare well, Alasdair...'

Alasdair showed great delight at this. 'Thank you, so much, Owen... that is very nice of you.' He slipped through the doorway and disappeared around the corner.

Owen turned to Linh who was standing at his shoulder. He hugged and lifted her gently.

Linh threw her arms around his neck. '... mmm...' she groaned, '... it certainly is exciting being around you.'

Chapter Eight

The last message that Owen received from Linh was a hurried text proclaiming that she had finally found the hangar that housed the charter company that was to fly her out to Krong Stung Treng. From there, in the northern corner of the country, she was to go by road further north towards the Laotian border.

But, now, it had been two weeks without any communication.

Gail Lucas set a cup of tea in front of her son. 'Well, it *is* in a remote part of the country, Owie.' They were perched on stools at the kitchen breakfast bar. 'She's probably hard at it and completely enjoying the experience.'

Owen looked wistful. 'Yeah, probably.'

It wasn't as though Owen was pining for her because he had too much time on his hands; quite the contrary. His team was in the final stages of fine-tuning the latest iteration of the turbine engine—this version utilising an adaptation that eliminated the need for an ignition mechanism. Instead, the combustion timing process was triggered by the fuel pulses. This made the design even simpler than it already was, as well as allowing the motor to operate at much higher revs.

The technical challenge occupied Owen's mind to the exclusion of just about everything else. Just about. Linh was a residual memory. And there was one other thing; ever since the meeting with Alasdair, Owen had become hyper-conscious of the possibility of miniaturised surveillance drones spying on the turbine development. They had screened all the windows of the workshop and had built a double door entrance. They searched everywhere and vacuumed with the greatest care. As far as they could tell, the place was spotless and camera free.

Owen had even gone through the delicate process of interrogating the other three members of the team with the objective of finding out whether there was any reason at all for someone to be dissatisfied with the project. The answers were that, all of them were totally committed and understood perfectly that any meaningful remuneration would not be happening until a long way down the track.

Then, one day, Owen received a message on his phone that simply said: your workshop is clean—Alasdair. He didn't know whether to be relieved or more anxious.

News from Linh came most unexpectedly—on television. He'd received the tip-off on his phone: SBS—9:30 tonight—A.

The item concerned a solar energy installation somewhere near the braided streams of the Mekong River. The solar-thermal generating plant would produce enough electricity to service the nearby town plus any small industry attracted by the cheap power. The initiative was funded by Aura, an international development conglomerate, whose aim was to create renewable power in order to protect the environment and its incredible biodiversity. Images of the townscape panned across the screen as Owen listened to the eerily familiar voice of the narrator.

'... the residents of Krong Stung Treng rely extensively on wood for cooking fires. The town's electricity supply, for lighting and refrigeration, is supplied by an antiquated diesel generator that, more often than not, is silent for lack of fuel or because of breakdown...'

The item cut to an image of the narrator standing beside a dormant generator inside a dilapidated shed.

Owen felt his heart surge. Linh looked poised and confident; yet... there was something unreal about her composure. He immediately recognised her vulnerability; something that usually did not concern her; she was always happy to declare her ignorance about an issue and never resorted to bluff and pretence to master a situation. But now, she postured unconvincingly.

'... the nearby hospital that services the region will benefit greatly from a reliable power supply, and administrators are already proposing to install more advanced life-saving equipment...' She walked towards the camera, wringing her hands as she spoke, 'Aura has confirmed that the solar installation is nearly complete, and that power will be available before the end of the year. The array is two hundred metres in diameter and will comprise some three thousand heliostats. The reflectors will track the sun and focus the light onto a central boiler tower which will provide steam to run a generator...'

Owen had the distinct impression that Linh was reading from a script. For a moment he felt an overwhelming affection for her because he knew full well that she was not naturally interested in mechanical technology, but that she always gave her undivided attention whenever he spoke about his turbine research.

Linh signed off, and the program returned to the presenter, who concluded the story with a salutation to the responsible approach of first world nations to industrialization in developing countries.

Owen felt a surge of relief; this looked like a great assignment for Linh; not *exactly* in her field of training, but definitely a project where she would get valuable experience.

The morning after the program, he was driving to the "Facility", as they called the turbine lab, when his old Volkswagen Beetle suddenly lost power and he was forced to duck into a convenient road siding.

The old "Bug" had been owned by his grandfather who bought it for twenty pounds when he rescued the occupants who were entrants in one of the great 'Around Australia' rally's in 1963. He'd pulled them out of flood waters with his ex-army Blitz. It took days for the waters to recede and by then, the contestants had had enough of roughing it, and decided to cut their losses. Grandfather hosed out the car, rebuilt the starter motor, and never looked back. It was a most reliable vehicle for years and years. Eventually it ended up in a machinery shed and languished there with a tarp over it. Owen discovered the Beetle when he was twelve years old. He'd climbed inside and sat at the steering wheel. He dusted the emblem on the hub and it gleamed like new. In his young mind, he figured that if all it took was a bit of dusting to resurrect the old car, then this was the project he'd been looking for. With his grandfather's help, he restored the Volkswagen, completely rebuilding the engine and converting it to twelve-volt electrics. Being a country car, it had no rust, and the upholstery was completely original. Owen loved it.

The car was on its third engine rebuild—but now it was stopped by the side of the road.

Owen got out and walked to the rear. He opened the engine bay and bent down with his hands on his knees. He was pondering whether it was fuel or electrics when he heard the crunch of gravel behind him.

It came to him surprisingly quickly—breakdown near a siding—visitor pulls up within the minute. He inspected the distributor. Attached to the thin wire from the condenser he found what he was looking for.

'Found it!' he called out loudly enough so that the person approaching him would hear. Without turning around, he examined the wire—and the cut-out module clamped to it. The shoes came to a stop right beside him. 'Okay,' he breathed without looking up, '... do *I* have to get this thing off, or do you disarm it, or whatever? It's radio controlled, right?'

'I can see why Alasdair has a high opinion of you,' a woman's voice cheerfully replied.

Owen looked beside him. She was wearing gym shoes and stretch pants. 'Ah, Alasdair. That was going to be my next question. What is it with the women thing, anyway? Don't you have men spies?' He heard the slap of rubber gloves being slipped on.

... is she going to kill me by the side of the road?

She hunkered down next to him. A faint scent of perfume wafted his way. Her blonde hair was tied back in a pony-tail. With gloved hands, she reached into the engine bay and grasped the module between her fingers. With a deft twist, she pulled it away from the wire.

'Good to go,' she said and turned to face him. She had the sweetest smile. 'Let's just have a quick chat first.'

Owen was a bit thrown by her nearness. He rested his arm on the bumper.

'Alasdair is wondering whether you'd like to go on a little assignment to Cambodia... nothing intrusive or dangerous... just to check first-hand what is happening in the town. We don't have anyone to do this job for us. Whoever is orchestrating this has been very clever; Cambodia has open borders, yet, because of the complexity of the language, it is difficult for foreigners to travel in remote areas without drawing attention. We have some nationals that we could recruit, but the country doesn't have the same degree of social flux that would allow people to travel inconspicuously to its farthest reaches.'

'But me, a hundred and eighty-four centimetres tall, without a word of Khmer, will blend in like the local hog merchant.' Owen raised a doubtful eyebrow.

The woman threw back her head and laughed. She covered Owen's hand with hers. 'Well, no... but here's the thing; you have a reason to go. You will draw attention to yourself no matter what you do, and that itself, will confuse the surveillance. We want to know what Aura is doing in that part of the world. Our sources inform us that Aura is not what it seems. You don't have to record anything incriminating—you are a hopelessly love-torn tragic trying to unite with his girl—and in the process, we'd like to avail ourselves of your engineer's mind and report to us anything unusual.' She canted her head and smirked triumphantly.

Owen retrieved his hand and rubbed his brow. 'Do you have a name?'

'Yes... it's Cassandra.'

'Really?'

'No.'

'O...kay, Cassandra. Now, tell me one thing—is Linh in any danger?'

Cassandra shook her head. 'No. She is doing a great job up there. They needed a spokesperson for their project—not an easy brief—and they got it. She's articulate, cultured, pretty... and she has a workable understanding of Khmer. This is the thing that has aroused our interest. They could have gotten any bimbo for their press releases. Why choose an anthropology graduate with passable Khmer? We're completely at a loss.'

Cassandra scanned the road. 'Think about it, Owen. I know you're very busy, but the mission can't be that long because no one wants to stay in that area for any length of time. And you'll get to see Linh.'

They stood up.

'I didn't know Linh spoke Khmer...'

Cassandra peeled off her gloves. 'Her mother is Khmer. Her family migrated to Vietnam when she was a girl. She preserved some of the language in stories and songs... just enough for the kids to be familiar with the sounds. That's as much as I know.'

Owen needed to know one more thing, 'Is Aura associated with the, y'know... briefcase crowd?'

Cassandra nodded. 'Yes... one and the same. They're ruthless, Owen, as you know... but we truly believe that you and Linh are in no danger. Have you heard from her recently?'

'No... not since she left Phnom Penh.'

'Well, it's nothing to worry about... there's no micro-wave up there, so she can't use her phone. Even land-lines are dodgy. All the more reason to want to visit her, hey!' She held out her hand. 'Send your answer to the number that Alasdair used to contact you. See ya!'

Cassandra walked back to her car—a hybrid Lexus.

Owen admired its newness.

... no wonder I didn't hear it sneaking up on me.

He turned to his VW and closed the engine bay lid.

He got in. It started straight away.

Chapter Nine

The heat was like nothing Owen had ever experienced before. Summers out on the station could be pretty intense, and just before the monsoonal rains it became very oppressive. But here, in Cambodia, on the road to Kampi, the heat had extra weight—it burdened him like a blanket.

The old bus had pulled over at a tiny shop where the proprietors had virtually blocked the narrow road with a shady umbrella and upturned boxes for seats. Owen had walked straight past the al-fresco arrangements into the more solid shade of the tin roof. He seated himself carefully on a crate of chickens and took out his water bottle. The heat radiating from the corrugated roof was ridiculous. He felt weak—in fact, he knew he was weakened.

For the past few days he had lived on nothing but fruit, much of it not yet fully ripe, and some— because in this part of the world things matured to the point of decay as you held it in your hand— over-ripe. The sudden departure from his normal diet resulted in an upset stomach which, though not catastrophic, added to the sense of displacement that was already acute.

Owen pondered the fact that some people were just not suited to travelling—not so much travelling—after all, he liked nothing better than to range far and wide in the outback—but imposing on the people of another country.

... I don't belong here—belonging is fulfilling your rightful place—in society, in the landscape... I don't fulfil any need here... I am extraneous...

a burden...

His newly acquired hunger was altering his mind. That, and the heat, was causing him to hallucinate—he was sure of it.

Owen took some deep breaths and another swig of water. A little boy came and stood by his side, holding out a bottle of Coca Cola. Owen smiled. He pressed together his hands and, from his seated position, made a small bow. He indicated as best he could that he didn't want the Coke and that he was happy with his water. Quite impassively, the boy turned and went back inside the dwelling.

From within drifted the smell of frying oil. It was just the restorative that Owen needed. He got up and moved further inside the shop. One of the other passengers of the bus walked past him with a bag of what looked like dumplings. The man offered Owen a closer look at the food and chattered and pointed excitedly to where a woman was hunkered beside a wok. Despite his sense of disorientation, he realised that he was at a crisis point and that, if he didn't eat something substantial, he could end up swooning in one of his familiar fainting spells. And where would he be then? At the mercy of Scar-face—the guy that he'd seen on two occasions after landing in Phnom Penh, and who now occupied the entire rear seat of the bus even though it was quite crowded and the passageway was filled with baggage.

Owen bought the dumplings.

They'd been following the Mekong River northwards for two days now in a bus that never exceeded fifty and stopped at the most unlikely places even when there was no one standing by the road. Now, about halfway to Krong Stung Treng, the sealed road was steadily disappearing, and dust seeped inexorably into clothes and hair. The driver, who was very short and wore platform shoes in order to reach pedals, had the annoying habit of looming up to prospective passengers at full speed and coming to a sudden, dusty stop as though he'd just re-entered from space. The passengers would board, bathed in fine loam, and their baggage would puff red clouds as it was thrown into convenient spaces. Owen came to the conclusion that the driver was bent on exercising his control over the vehicle just to spite the fact that it was so slow.

He had obviously caught the wrong bus. Not that he was expecting a

Greyhound; it was just that the route had been inexplicably circuitous and seemed to offer the most intimate shuttle service to the locals. And, the driver kept asking him for more money with each leg of the journey.

As the afternoon wore on, Owen could see in the rear vision mirror that the driver was becoming drowsy. His eyes would droop for seconds at a time. Owen cleared the baggage from his lap and prepared to leap for the steering wheel should the need arise.

In a state of readiness, he nibbled on his dumplings and refrained from looking at what was inside. It occurred to him that *he* was the one that was out of sync. It was all a matter of perspective; he would slow down and celebrate each instant for what it was.

There was something truly ghastly inside one of the dumplings. He spat it carefully into the paper bag.

He began to feel a burgeoning euphoria that he hoped was due to his brain receiving much needed nutrition, and not due to him relinquishing his mind or, worse still, having his dumpling spiked. He'd heard about that—coffee shops that laced their drinks, thereby gaining a devoted clientele. He smiled at the thought. He turned around as though to embrace his fellow travellers. Most of them were fast asleep. Scar-face wasn't. Through dark glasses, he seemed to be looking straight at Owen.

It was the reality check that Owen needed. He faced the front and sighed heavily. He was getting further and further away from any chance of assistance.

Leaving Brisbane had been very uneventful—expedited, was probably more precise. Visas, tickets, even boarding passes, dealt with by unseen hands, were made available most opportunely. Even a rail ticket had been provided, which was odd, because the airport is not far from New Farm. It meant that, on the day of departure, Owen walked to Brunswick Street station carrying the backpack that had arrived by courier from an undisclosed source.

He was not an experienced traveller; not like many of his friends. The only trips he'd made abroad were to New Zealand. On quite a few occasions he'd visited engineering facilities, initially to gain experience in machining technology and engine research, and later, to take advantage of the unique innovation abilities that so many New Zealanders possess. Travel, as such, wasn't as much of a priority for him.

He'd boarded the train and found a double seat and had barely balanced his pack on the seat when a woman in the aisle announced pre-emptively that she would like to sit there. There were plenty of vacant seats.

Owen looked up. Cassandra smiled expectantly.

'Ah,' Owen grunted, '... what was I thinking... leaving without a last-minute briefing.'

Cassandra sat demurely beside him as Owen hefted the pack to the seat in front.

'Do be careful with that backpack, Owen,' she said as she extracted a package from a tote bag. 'The fabric is a solar panel—you can charge your phone from it. Just put it in the sun. Now, this is for you... local money—quite a bit of it. You are familiar with the exchange rate?'

Owen nodded. 'About ten thousand Riels to a dollar—frankly, I don't care. I'm happy to pay extra...'

'Yeah, good for you ... but we don't want you to be any more conspicuous than you already are.'

Owen looked out the window. 'Like that's possible.'

'There's also a special shirt with water-proof pockets in the shoulder that will hold a fair bit of cash... a credit card with the PIN already on your phone... and a whole heap of stuff on your phone that you'd be advised to read before you arrive in Cambodia. It'll self-delete, so you don't need to worry about that. We can't give you anything else—it would compromise you... you understand?'

'Yep... I'm a love-struck loner without a clue in the world.'

Cassandra blew him a kiss. 'Listen—Cambodia is a great country to visit, but where you're going it's a tad isolated, and English speakers are thin on the ground. But you'll manage. Also, there is a secret aspect to your trip which we would like to keep that way. So, make sure that whatever you do, you can explain away through innocence or stupidity.'

She briefed him on a few other issues, and then wished him good luck with a surprising amount of emotion in her voice. She stayed on the train when he got off at the international airport.

As he waited in the departure lounge, his eye settled on the small pocket in the front of the backpack. In view of the nature of the trip, Owen had taken a few precautions of his own. With a soldering iron, he had carefully melted a hole through the synthetic material of the smallest pocket. When he placed his phone in the pocket, the camera lens lined up with the hole.

...but now I've burnt a hole in my solar panel... hope it still works...

When he arrived in Phnom Penh, he sat down at a café, put his phone on record, and placed it in the pocket. Then he walked through the airport and caught a taxi to his hotel.

A short time later he sat on his bed and reviewed the video. That was the first time he saw Scar-face—following him with an insolent self-assurance.

On subsequent excursions from his hotel, he had other tails—people who would stalk him with an unwavering focus but assume a picture of innocence as soon as he turned around.

Owen's smugness soon turned to anxiety when he saw just how many people were keeping an eye on him.

He filmed one of his tails browbeating a clerk at the ticket booth where he'd just purchased a bus ticket to Krong Stung Treng—all the while standing with his back to the action immersed in reading travel posters on a wall.

That was probably why Scar-face had lurched wide-eyed onto the bus as it left the terminus—Owen was on the wrong bus. His actual tail was on the express. Scar-face had gone into damage-control, booking himself a chicken-class passage along the Mekong so he could be near his quarry.

Late that afternoon, the bus finally arrived at Krong Stung Treng and manoeuvred into a compound. Owen was tempted to use the interpretation app on his phone to ask about accommodation but decided against it. The trouble was that the Khmer words are so difficult to pronounce that the average non-speaker makes less progress than they would with sign language, with which the Khmer people are generally very patient.

As it turned out, the town was very tourist orientated and it was no problem communicating in English. Soon, Owen was stretched out on a bed in a comfortable hotel on Sixty-Three Street. A quick check on his phone confirmed that there had been a shift change with his surveillance. A lot of resources were being directed into monitoring his movements—that was obvious.

After a commendable meal of fried rice in a nearby restaurant, he returned to his room and began disassembling his backpack. That was the last instruction remaining on his phone—to assemble a camera drone—and he had to do it before the directions were automatically deleted.

The backpack was built with a thick plastic sheet as its main frame. Owen located the zipper that allowed the sheet to be slid out. Following the instructions on his phone, he peeled away the plastic coating on the front and back of the sheet. This revealed that it was actually made up of three thin sheets of carbon fibre, each with incised, press-out shapes. These formed the skeleton of the drone. In addition, the aluminium handle and framework readily came apart at scored intervals to become bracing and brackets. The plastic reinforcing in the base of the backpack turned out to be four carbon fibre propellers. Each of the four fat castors came apart with a special tool to reveal an electric motor. The electrics clipped together with natty little couplings.

For one moment, Owen had a horrible feeling that he'd made a mistake. With an audible sigh of relief, he realised that the rectangular space that he was staring at was where his camera would go. This was a relatively fat unit that Cassandra had given to him with instructions to take some holiday snaps. There was something in the way she'd pressed it into his hands that prevented him from making a disparaging comment about it. Now he understood; the thing was mostly battery and it clipped nicely into the drone body.

According to the instructions, an operating app would appear on his phone when he arrived at the appropriate coordinates. He checked his phone—*yep, downloaded.*

He placed the drone on the floor and put his thumbs over the virtual sliders on the phone. The mechanism had a soft-touch feel to it and pushing the sliders all the way up enabled only enough thrust for the drone to begin to hover. It was surprisingly quiet, given that Owen was in the confines of a room. The instructions stated that he could release his fingers on the phone without it winding down, and that resuming sliding from the bottom would enable more power to be applied. The centre slide was for attitude control—forwards and backwards.

Owen switched off the drone and tucked it into his now floppy rucksack.

... all set to go—just don't have any idea where...

Chapter Ten

Being so close to the mighty Mekong River, there had often been talk of developing hydro power for the region. The trouble is that most of Cambodia is flat and there are not many good sites for dams. Since the disastrous civil war of the eighties, when the small amount of infrastructure in place was left to run down, there had been attempts to harness the power of the river through micro hydro-electric units. However, the economies of scale were not favourable even though the source was free. Only a few systems were in place, and very often not for long, before they were washed away in floods.

Early in the morning, Owen walked along the new concrete bridge across the Mekong. It was over a kilometre to the opposite bank. From its tall spans, he could clearly see just how flat the surrounding countryside was.

When he got back to his hotel, he enquired whether there was anyone with a vehicle of some sort who would be prepared to take him sight-seeing. When he saw the manager hesitate for just a moment, he realised what was going on. Undoubtedly, the heavies had made it known to the manager that his guest was of special interest, and that anything the manager could do to expedite matters for them would be greatly appreciated.

'I ring... driver...' the man faltered, bowing repeatedly as he backed up to the old phone on the bench behind him.

'Thank you very much,' said Owen. He watched as the manager extracted a piece of paper from his pocket. He studied it closely as he dialled.

... yeah, right... like he always has that scrap handy in case someone wants a ride...

After the call had been made, Owen was instructed to make himself comfortable at a rickety metal table on the footpath. The manager gave him a Coke out of the fridge that he opened slowly so that it hissed conspicuously. Owen nodded his thanks and went to pay, but the man declined with smiles and bows and returned inside.

Owen rolled the cool bottle against his forehead and contemplated the streetscape. Across the road was the Central Park whose stunted greenery looked rather out of place in a town where it appeared no one had time for the aesthetics of nature; everywhere, people were eternally bound to livelihoods and families. The roadway itself was broken so badly that it had become virtually a gravel road. In the middle of the park was an enormous advertising billboard on a pedestal that looked totally out of place amidst the modest hoardings fronting the shops. Rising above the rooftops of the buildings on the other side of the park were two tall communications towers replete with microwave transmitters.

Owen scowled.

...totally integrated into the twenty-first century here... why haven't I heard from Linh?...

Above him, electrical wires drooped from pole to pole. This is what he needed to evaluate—just how much power was being used by the city?

The town was surprisingly large in area but, in many respects, it was like a huge village. Most of the electrical power was used for lighting—a relatively small draw. Only the larger hotels and public buildings had electric stoves, refrigeration and water heaters. Most residential power needs were met with gas, diesel and wood. The small amount of cabling and scarcity of transformers in the centre of town indicated to Owen that the electricity needs of Krong Stung Treng were very modest... and needed mostly at night.

A solar thermal generator would only supply power at night if it had a heat transfer system built into it... and that was expensive.

A scooter pulled up at the curb and the rider signalled with his head for Owen to jump on.

... a tad rude... he doesn't even know what I want...

Owen walked over. 'Hello, are you able to drive me around the town?'

'Yes, I take you where you want to go,' said the driver in very respectable English.

'Good-oh,' Owen climbed on the back, 'No helmet for me, then?'

'We go past friend... he give you helmet if you want.'

Owen decided against it. '... probably wouldn't fit me...'

'Okay... we go then.'

The scooter zoomed off and joined in with a posse of other scooters wending their way along the boulevard.

...be interesting to see where he takes me...

They turned into Street Twenty-Two and sped along. The driver seemed to be speaking and Owen leant forward to enquire. His answer was a sharp push in his face with the heel of the driver's hand. It was then that Owen realised the driver had a helmet with a headset; he was communicating with someone.

'Hey, listen buddy,' Owen yelled at the helmet, '... would you mind telling me where we're going?'

The man lifted his right hand to his shoulder, formed a pointed knuckle fist and drove it down hard onto Owen's thigh.

It was a well-executed strike that produced a surprising amount of pain in Owen's taut leg.

...okay, here we go again... don't ask questions and all will be revealed...

They came to the intersection of National Highway Seven and turned north, crossing the kilometre wide Tonle Kong River just above its confluence with the Mekong.

Owen thought about how he might strangle the driver from behind without coming to grief himself. Eventually his outrage subsided, and he allowed himself to lean back with a tight grip on the rear baggage rack.

The countryside sped monotonously by. The flat landscape had been cleared of the original forests centuries ago. In its place thrived regrowth which itself was periodically cleared for various crops. The road verge was a scrappy confusion of shrubs and grasses beyond which lay the cultivated acres of farmland, although what exactly was being grown he couldn't determine.

The land was monotonously level.

...perfect for building a solar thermal installation...

Farmhouses and little hamlets panned by and still the road led resolutely north towards the Laotian border. Owen could feel the sun stinging his arms, and he wished that he had worn a shirt with long sleeves. On occasion, he could see in the rear-view mirror that there was a car some distance behind them. He thought nothing of it until, after a good many minutes of straight road, the car showed no sign of wanting to pass. The scooter, out on the open road, was severely lacking in power and they could only have been doing about sixty kilometres an hour.

They'd gone about twenty of thirty kilometres, in Owen's estimation, when the driver braked and turned into a narrow side road. It was obviously a construction thoroughfare and not a farm track because wheel ruts spanned the whole roadway. The scooter bumped along and Owen caught glimpses of the car behind them.

...why am I not surprised?...

Ahead, the roadway curved around a copse of tattered trees and, when they rounded, Owen was suddenly in view of a vast extent of heliostats. From his low vantage point, they seemed to gleam and stretch to the horizon. The scooter came to a stop. The driver harked back his head and barked, 'Get off!' Owen stretched his legs and calmly backed off the seat. The car crunched to a stop next to him. The back door flung open and Linh jumped out. She ran into Owen's arms without a word.

Owen closed his eyes and hugged her close. He swayed with giddiness and disbelief.

'It's been a long time, Owen,' said a woman with a strange but familiar accent. For a second, he was standing on the scoured surface of Pepper Knoll. Owen didn't want to hear her... he didn't want to be docile and obedient... answering the questions for her lie detector. He opened his eyes.

Gina Wu leaned on the car door and smiled at him. He had never seen her smile before. She looked even more threatening.

Then Linh was reaching up and kissing him on the lips. Before he could respond, she pulled back and regarded him with wide eyes. 'What on earth are you doing here?' She laughed with amazement, 'I can't believe it!'

Wu unwound from the door. 'I told you it would be a big surprise.'

Linh turned with a querying look. 'Have you two met before?'

There was a charged silence before Wu responded. 'Have you been keeping me a secret, Owen?'

Owen didn't know what to think. First and foremost, he was here on a covert mission... but Linh was fully aware of the reasons why she was chosen by Aura... she'd just never met Wu before... and Aura was obviously familiar with Linh's role in the retrieval of the briefcase... so where did that leave him?

Linh squeezed Owen's arm. 'Owen?'

Wu laughed. 'I'm just joshing with you, Owen, I don't want to make it any harder for you than it already is.' She strode out a few paces and surveyed the array of mirrors. 'I was on the first recovery mission, Linh... at Yappar River. Has he ever told you about it?'

'... um, a little bit. Oh, where are my manners. Owen, this is Gina Wu... she is the project manager for the solar power installation...'

Owen felt the buzzing in his ears. Too much sun... and no hat—that's what it was... and half an hour on the back of a bike with a psychopath. He closed his eyes.

...I might just avoid saying anything at the moment... couldn't be any worse than blurting out something indiscrete... even if I look a complete dill...

'Owen is spying on us, Linh!'

...oh, great!... she knows...

Linh held him at arm's length. 'Spying!... Owen?... I don't think so,' she giggled, '... but, whatever the reason, I'm so glad that you're here.' She hugged him tightly.

...Linh, what's going on? I don't remember you being so vacuously bubbly...

The driver of the car walked around and opened the boot. He reached inside and lifted out a backpack—Owen's backpack—the one that he had placed in a locker in the foyer of the guesthouse and padlocked with a Yale... and which he had then extracted again when he knew the manager was engaged somewhere else and hidden behind the air-conditioning unit outside his window.

'Recognise that?' Gina turned and pointed at the backpack.

Owen's mind cleared. It was the unexpected that sometimes overwhelmed him—but now, he knew exactly what he had to do. 'Yeah, okay... it's mine. It's got a valuable drone in it and I didn't trust the guy in the office, so I put it where I thought it would be safe. Thank you for retrieving it for me.' He walked up and snatched the backpack from the driver.

Linh produced an indulgent pout. 'Owie... did you come fully prepared to look for me?'

She moved towards him and kissed him tenderly on the cheek, 'I know I've been a bad girl not writing to you, but I've been busy, and communicating is a bit problematic in this part of the world.'

Owen allowed some exasperation to creep into his voice. 'Well, how was I to know what was going on? I had no idea what I might have to resort to to find you... I thought a drone might be the best way to scour the countryside for solar plants... I don't know...'

Gina squealed with delight. 'Oh, stop it, you two... really, you're priceless... you are,' she dabbed at her eye. 'Linh, come here, I want to show you something—bring the rucksack.'

Linh and Owen followed Gina to the bonnet of the car. She held out her hand and Owen handed her the backpack. She placed it on the bonnet and unzipped a tiny, hidden pocket from which was retrieved a thin electrical cord. She took out her mobile phone and plugged it in.

'Look!' she pointed to the screen, 'it's charging my phone.'

Linh gasped. 'Wow, Owen... that is so amazing!'

Owen was looking anything but amazed.

'Oh, this is a pretty amazing bit of kit alright, Linh... you know what else it can do?'

Linh looked from Gina to Owen and back again. '... no...'

'When it's plugged in like this, it also becomes a fairly powerful transceiver.'

Owen sighed heavily.

'... powerful enough to send and receive a coded message from a satellite. Bet you didn't get this at a camping shop.'

Linh's brow creased ever so slightly.

'And *this*...' Gina opened up the main zip and pulled out the assembled drone, '... is like nothing you'll get at Toys R Us or, for that matter, in Q Branch,' she chuckled at her little joke. 'Why don't you fly it for us, Owen?... I'm curious to see how well you go.'

Owen sighed again and delved into his pocket for his phone. He activated it and puzzled at the screen for a moment. Gina cranked her head beside Owen's shoulder and pointed with an elegant finger at the icon that had mysteriously appeared the previous evening. He tapped it. The flying controls appeared immediately. With the drone sitting on the centre of the bonnet, he pushed the sliders up. The drone hummed into life. Owen increased the revs and the drone rose smoothly into the air.

'Now, I want you to take some pictures, Owen... do you know how?' Owen tapped another icon in between the sliders. The slider graphic vanished and a visual appeared of the ground view beneath the drone. The controls still operated normally and Owen flew out over the expanse of heliostats. He looked at the screen for the photo icon. One tap produced a still shot that lingered on the screen for a few seconds. Pressing the video icon showed that the camera was recording. Another icon activated the camera's orientation which was controlled by tilting the phone in the appropriate direction.

'Is this yours, Owie?' Linh's question was barely above a whisper.

Owen kept his eyes on the screen. 'No... well, yeah... I've got the use of it while...'

'... he's spying on us,' Gina finished the sentence.

The drone was about one hundred metres in the air. By zooming out, Owen could get a picture of the entire array of mirrors.

Gina leant against Owen's shoulder as she watched the screen. 'Go around the perimeter, Owen. I want you to get some unequivocal shots—no computer-generated ambiguities... just the real thing... because that is what we're doing—we are building a thermal solar electricity generating plant... just as we said we would.'

Owen concentrated on circling the vast installation. The drone was almost out of sight as it hovered over the furthest reaches of the system.

'... and I *do* want you to take back this information. If getting Linh to present an entire segment about this project on national television doesn't convince people, then perhaps your holiday snaps will do the trick.'

The sun was almost at its highest point and it was becoming unbearably hot. Owen returned the drone across the middle of the array and landed it a few metres away from where they were standing.

He walked out and retrieved it. 'Well,' he said decisively, '... I've accomplished my missions—I've got some footage of this place, and I've confirmed that Linh is being well looked after. So, I guess it's all good.' He gave his best smile.

'And we've accomplished our mission,' Gina replied with an odd emphasis, '... so, yes... it is all good.'

'Excellent,' Owen drawled, as he carefully stowed the drone into the backpack, '... but, it will bug me monumentally, if I didn't at least enquire about the nature of your mission... because I assume you are not referring to the solar plant as such.'

'Of course, you would... but I should warn you—don't outsmart yourself. You two are a lot of fun and we wouldn't like it if you became inextricably enmeshed in something terminal... you know what I'm saying?'

'Okay... I get it... don't get too smart, and I won't get rumbled.' He went over to Linh and held her gently.

Gina approached them with a pointed look on her face. She placed her hands on Owen's shoulders and adjusted the collar of his shirt. 'You see, Owen... even the smartest of operators can come undone. Your man—I've no idea what you call him...' she raised a searching eyebrow at him.

'Alasdair...'

'Alasdair!... hmmm, okay... well, Alasdair tried to get inside our project. He put up an eminently unwitting candidate—who we were about to hire, because, as you know, it's good to keep your enemies close—but then, in light of our little adventure in the bush, and then finding out about Linh, we had a better idea. It's such a rare occasion when one can predict the future. We realised that, by offering the job to Linh, Alasdair's minions would eventually find you, and then certain connections would be made and so on and so forth. In short, we knew where he would be and what he would want—priceless information to us, because we can make some very profitable extrapolations from that. We intimated that we were after gold, then timber, then anthropological projects blah, blah, blah, and all the time we staked out the relevant places. Suffice it to say, Alasdair's network is extremely compromised—and I don't mind at all if you inform him... I would expect you to.'

Linh spoke up. 'It was profitable for me, too. I don't feel bad about being used.'

Gina gushed and hugged Linh. 'See!... that's why I don't want to see you guys get hurt... you're both so very, I don't know... reasonable! Not like the manipulative, ravenous brats that I have to deal with most of the time.'

'Would it be too unreasonable to suggest that we find some shade?' Owen asked lamely.

Gina became suddenly business-like. 'No! Haven't got time. I've got to be somewhere much more important, and you lucky children are going to make your own way home on... guess what?... the scooter!' She turned and spoke sharply to the scooter driver, who opened the petrol cap, peered inside and gave a curt nod in return.

'All set to go. Remember, we are building an infrastructure out here that, whilst it is not *entirely* altruistic, will do much to assist development and prevent environmental damage—and we used you guys so that we could get to know our 'competitors' a little better. So, there you have it—nothing sinister. Unfortunately, your work with us terminates here, Linh. I hope you understand. You will have gained some valuable experience working with our team, even if it was a bit outside your area of interest.'

Linh came up and hugged her. 'Thank you, Gina, it was a good experience... I enjoyed it all.'

Owen held out his hand. 'Hey, thanks for the bike... is there a little case of money that comes with it?'

Gina gave him a look.

'... no?... that's okay, we'll manage. Right then, we'll be off...'

Gina quickly got into the car along with the other two men. It reversed into a space, then spun the wheels as it accelerated away.

Linh looked at the scooter. 'Do you know how to drive one of these, Owie?'

'I bloody hope so... we'll cook if we stay out here much longer. There's a little shop thing just down the road... we'll go there. We need to talk.'

As Owen examined the scooter to find out how to start it, Linh wrote with her finger in the dust *BUG IN COLLAR*.

Owen nodded and sighed. 'I should have guessed!'

Linh regarded him with some apprehension.

'... it's a kick start... I was looking for a starter button.' He winked and smiled, 'C'mon, jump on. Once we get going, we should cool off.'

Chapter Eleven

On the way back to Krong Stung Treng, taking advantage of the noise of the wind and the scooter, Linh thoroughly examined Owen's collar. There was no bug. Even so, when they got back to Owen's room, they were mindful of what they said. They changed and rode out in the late afternoon towards the airport where the accommodation for the solar project administrative staff was situated. Linh had to walk past security by herself. She collected her things and was back on the scooter inside twenty minutes.

It was so pleasant to ride through the countryside, that they decided to ride the scooter back to Phnom Penh. They stayed one more night at the guest house, the two of them in an abominably narrow and squeaky bed, taking it in turns to be on top, drawing out their lovemaking with the slowest movements possible, and finally falling asleep soaked with sweat.

The next morning, they took it in turns to steer the scooter and to snooze on the back. They took the river road because it was more populated and because there were frequent stalls and cafes. The journey was taking forever. They left the river at Kampong Reang and rode through the late afternoon to Khnar where they found a guest house to stay for the night.

Being able to speak some Khmer, Linh immediately endeared herself to everyone they met. Also, she was infinitely better at procuring food, and she knew what dishes would appeal to Owen. Surrounded with the unfamiliar, they explored each other totally. Each new experience revealed something exciting about the other. They were infatuated with each other—selflessly and sincerely.

In a previous attempt to learn some Vietnamese, Owen had come across the word, tốt, which means, good, favourable and beautiful. Now, was the first time that he used it as an endearment for the one he loved.

That night, in the light of the candles, languidly sprawled over the double bed that they'd managed to score, they felt brave enough to promise to love each other for always. A short while after that, they were both asleep.

The next day was a dash for Phnom Penh—offload scooter with the flower seller in exchange for enormous bouquet—catch taxi to airport—offload bouquet to helpful booking receptionist—spend three hours in plastic chair with head in hands waiting for flight to Singapore. The next flight wasn't until very early in the morning.

The departure lounge was empty. Linh rested her head on Owen's shoulder. 'Do you think this is a good time to talk about what we saw up north?'

'Are you kidding me?... this is the very place that will be bugged to the max... we shouldn't even be thinking about what we saw. They're probably reading our lips as we speak... literally...'

'Well, that's what lip reading is—the reading of lips...'

'... do you think we're hallucinating?'

'Maybe... kiss me...'

They kissed.

'... no...'

'No, what?'

'No, we're not hallucinating. That kiss felt very real to me.'

They both laughed and then sighed simultaneously. The threat of being spied on and the immediacy of travel over the previous few days, had kept them in suspended tension. Their only release had been their intimacy. Now, at last, the landscape seemed clear of danger.

They turned to each other, ready to debrief.

'... you go...'

'No, you go, Tot... I've still got to hear about everything you got up to when you arrived.'

Linh straightened in her seat. 'Well, as you know, they flew me up in a chopper—just me! … in this executive machine—and set me up at the headquarters. I'd been given stuff to read, but it was all sort of generic stuff about current archaeological projects and government policies and what have you… nothing really specific, and nothing that gave me any idea what I was up for. I was introduced to Gina the next day—very affable and charismatic lady—although I did accidently see her getting up one guy for some booboo that he'd made, which wasn't pretty—anyway, she told me that my job was to be the PR person for the solar thing—no explanations… I was to get tarted up, get alluring and informed and report to the camera team the next day. We did pretty much the same report day after day, just from different locations in town.'

'Did you ever go to the actual site?'

'Not once. That was the first time I saw it—with you.'

'Odd.'

'The whole thing was odd. It was only because of our chat with Alasdair, that I could make some sense of the whole arrangement… but I didn't want to let on that I wasn't disappointed, so I did some token whinging about not being able to fulfil my skill set and was suitably indulged and promised that things would change. And they did. The film crew disappeared, and I was left pretty much to my own devices.'

'Was Gina there the whole time?'

'She was either at the site or in, what they called, the lab… which was another curious thing. The lab was a whole wing under the strictest guard. There were really tall communications towers and antennas and dishes and stuff all over the place… and I suspect that some of it must have been underground because one day, just after we'd had a lot of heavy rain, there was water being pumped out for hours and hours.'

'… and you weren't allowed in?'

'No way! As soon as I came near, the guards would flick me a 'get lost' finger.'

'So, all that stuff about gaining experience when we said goodbye to Gina was just a lot of rubbish…'

'Yep… I just went along with what she wanted… I just wanted to get out of there as quickly as possible.'

'... whilst maintaining the illusion that you thought you had a long-term career with Aura.'

'Precisely... although, I don't know whether we managed to fool her.'

'Well, you heard what she said—about using us as bait.'

'She's probably glad to get rid of us... something doesn't stack up about that place.'

Owen was staring distantly at the observation panes. The interior lights reflected in all directions, creating annoying glare in places.

Linh searched his face and massaged his knee. 'What are you thinking, Owie?'

Owen remained silent. His mouth had a grim set to it, and his pupils were so focused that they didn't move.

'... Owie?'

The colour slowly drained from his face and his breathing deepened.

'Owie, what's wrong?'

Owen's mouth barely moved. 'I know what they're doing.'

'Are you okay?... you look very pale.'

Owen nodded minutely.

'What are they doing?'

Owen looked at Linh with dread in his eyes. 'They were heliostats, right?'

'... r...ight...'

'... not solar electric panels...'

'Okay... yeah...'

'So, they are designed to focus sunlight onto a tower, where water will be turned into steam...'

'... as I understand it, yeah...'

'But there's no tower...'

'Not yet... that's to come apparently.'

'But, there's no pathway through the array of mirrors to get to the centre.'

'Does the tower have to be in the centre? Couldn't the mirrors be angled to a place on the perimeter, where the tower could be built?'

'But then why build a circular array? And there's no provision for transmission of the power. There is no turbine, no generator, no heat storage... in short, what they have built, first up, is the most fragile part of the whole system—the heliostats—and they're going to sit there for months and months, probably years, while the rest of the infrastructure is built? And why so far away? There are untold acres of flat ground within a few kilometres of the town.'

Linh shook her head. 'I don't know...'

Owen was focusing on an imaginary place. 'The pedestals for the heliostats all had conduits going into the ground—which is fair enough; that supplies the information to operate the electric motors that angle the mirrors. But did you notice the tower way in the distance? Presumably the information for each individual heliostat comes from somewhere remote, to the tower and then underground. But why remote? It's just another expensive complication!'

'Owen, your voice is rising... be careful...'

Owen took a big breath. 'It all makes sense, Linh. The site was complete—the trucks had come and gone—the road had weeds growing in the cracks—all of the fabrication facilities had been dismantled. The dongas trailered out. It's ready to function.'

'What are dongas?'

'Temporary construction sheds.'

Linh looked very worried, not so much about the picture that Owen was painting, but more for Owen himself. 'What is it ready for?... are you sure about your deductions?'

Owen reached down to his backpack. It had resumed its previous dimensions—the drone was in pieces throughout the pack. He retrieved the camera unit and switched it on. Then he took out his phone. With a few swipes he had the images folder on the screen. He pulled up the video and trawled through it at high speed until he came near to the end. He held the phone so that Linh could see it.

'Check this out... tell me what you see.'

He started the video at normal speed. The drone was flying across the array back to the group. The upturned mirrors reflected the blue sky. They were not all synchronised to the same angle, and some of them flashed at the camera as they caught the sun overhead. At one point, the flash was so intense that the screen went black. The auto-aperture soon regained control and the video continued until it was switched off by Owen just before it landed.

Inside the fluorescent lit lounge, it was eerily quiet. Even the music had been switched off. At the far end, a cleaner with a back mounted vacuum cleaner wended his way between the rows of seats.

Owen raised an eyebrow in his direction then dismissed him with a shake of the head. 'Not a good cover for a spy... with a noisy machine on his back.'

'So, what was I supposed to see?' Linh whispered harshly, '... it was a bit difficult with the glare.'

'That is exactly what you were supposed to see.'

Linh made a look of appeal. 'Sweetie, I'm not an engineer... help me out here.'

Owen looked hard into Linh's eyes. 'What you saw out there is a weapon... a satellite destroyer. Each one of those mirrors can be individually aimed to a point in space. If all of those mirrors were aimed at a satellite, it would be fried within minutes, even if it was hundreds of kilometres above the earth. Now, a lot of spy and military satellites are in fairly low orbits—get good triangulation data that way—and they would be the obvious targets.'

Linh was thinking fast. 'But it would only work during the day—a clear day!'

'Yep. No matter though... the low orbit satellites go around the earth a couple of times a day. At some point they will be above the site in daylight hours.'

'Yeah, okay... but it's not a very reliable weapon though, is it? You can't deploy it at a moment's notice.'

Owen softly kissed Linh at her temple. 'I love the way you think!' He scanned the area. The cleaner had gone. 'It's not meant to be used as a regular weapon—ambush is its specialty! One minute the satellite is working perfectly and the next minute it has failed...'

'But couldn't the operators see where the attack was coming from?' Linh interrupted.

'No! No, that's the beauty of this thing—it sends out a destructive beam, in what frequency?... the visible frequency! If it were any other frequency, there's a good chance that the gear on board would triangulate its origin before it failed. But light!... what do you see?...

a *blinding* flash... it's in the visible spectrum... overload... you see nothing... no chance of detecting its origin... the cameras are blinded.'

'So, you're saying that it could disable a satellite, and no one would know why, and then, it could disable more satellites, one by one, and there would be no smoking gun.'

'Exactly... apart from the fact that each event took place in the same place in the orbit. And as you say, no smoking gun—no missile trail... assuming that there are missiles that will go that far.'

Linh furrowed her brow. 'Are you sure that the mirrors could generate enough heat to melt a satellite?'

'They don't have to melt it... just disable the circuitry.' He held her hand. 'Have you ever focused sunlight onto your hand with a magnifying glass?'

'No!... why would I do that?'

Owen rolled his eyes. 'It's a boy thing. It gets bloody hot! All the light from the area of the glass gets focused into a dot about one hundredth of the original size; therefore, a hundred times hotter than sunlight on your palm. Same with the array. You said two hundred metres wide? That's pi times one hundred squared... about thirty thousand square metres... into say, a ten-metre square focal point... that's *three thousand* times the heat of the sun on the surface. Can you imagine, on a day like we had out there, how much heat that baby could throw into space?'

'Okay, well here's a thing; wouldn't the rays become dispersed, or diffracted or whatever it is?'

'Very good, Linh... they would, but not as much as you think. The earth's atmosphere thins out very quickly with altitude. About *half* of our atmosphere is below ten kilometres... once you get past that mark, very little diffusion will take place—the beam will pretty much retain its shape. It's not a laser by any means, but it makes up for that in sheer size.'

Linh wriggled in Owen's direction. 'You're really quite excited by this, aren't you?'

'Well... excited and appalled at the same time. And here's another thing—as I looked at the array, something didn't seem right. Now I know what it is. The heliostats are way too close to each other to effectively aim at a solar tower. They're virtually touching. If they had to angle towards a tower, the rear unit would shine its light into the back of the one in front of it. Even given the site's relative proximity to the equator, during winter the sun's angle would have to be about thirty-five or more degrees off the vertical which would require significant spacing. There's no doubt about it—they are meant as a weapon—to reflect directly into space.'

'So, they could annihilate everything in space?'

'Oh, no... no way. They could only get the satellites that have an orbit that comes within, oh... about, I don't know... say, two hundred kilometres either side of the site.'

'What!... that's not exactly a *Star Wars* weapon, is it?'

'No... but, like I said, it's like a booby trap... it sits there and disables everything that flies over... and a lot of satellites will *eventually* orbit over that site...'

'And no one will suspect anything... because it's a solar plant—even if it isn't hooked up.'

'And it's miles away in a place that's not at all a secret but is rarely visited. And who knows how many more sites like this they are building?'

Linh pawed at Owen's shoulder. 'Do you want a coffee?'

'Do I ever.'

'Come on... there's a machine over there. What are we going to tell Alasdair?'

Owen leant against the coffee machine as Linh fed it coins. He looked drawn and tired. 'I hope we never get to see Alasdair, I really do...'

'But, we have to tell him... or someone—they're building a space weapon out there!'

'Don't worry... he'll make contact with us. I just have to wait for my car to break down or go for a ride on the train.'

They ambled back to their seats, trying not to spill the overly-full cups.

Linh sipped carefully. 'Do you suppose there's a quiet war going on the whole time, between these groups of... of...'

'... conspirators.'

'... yeah, do you?'

'I guess so. But you, being a student of history, would know better than most people that sometimes, the battle grounds and conflicts we see around the world are in reality proxy wars between invisible foes fought by nations manipulated into impossible situations.'

'Wow!... Owen, are you channelling some long dead historian in your exhausted state?'

'Must be... or they've put something in the coffee.'

'And what nationality do you suppose these conspirators are?'

Owen shrugged. 'Probably doesn't matter. They're most likely international entities... y'know, with no signature nationality... harder to trace.'

Linh leant away from Owen and looked him up and down. 'You've thought about this before, haven't you?'

'No,' Owen replied with a blithe smile. He sipped his coffee.

'Yeah... I suppose you're right— just because Alasdair is an Aussie, it's hard to imagine that Australia would be at the pointy end of any significant conspiracy.'

Chapter Twelve

A week after arriving back in Brisbane, things had pretty much returned to normal. Linh had developed a cold and had spent two days at home in bed. When Owen visited her, Linh's mother probed about how she could have caught such a nasty cold when she had been instructed to take all the dietary precautions and home tonics to prevent just such a thing occurring. The two lovers caught the other's eye, each recalling a few hot, sweaty nights when they had fallen asleep with the ceiling fan on at full revolutions and waking up cold and chilled.

Progress at the Facility had been amazing in Owen's short absence. The turbine engine had been set up on a test stand and connected to a planetary reduction gear. In lieu of a dyno, the team had simply connected a propeller to the output shaft and had measured the revs against another motor of known power. The performance figures were very encouraging, but what was even more promising was that simple adjustments to the intake and exhaust timing produced noticeable increases in power. As well, because the parts could so easily be machined on a three axis mill straight from the CAD files, they now had two identical motors that could be reconfigured in parallel so that the incremental steps towards higher performance were never allowed to go backwards.

Once again, Owen became completely immersed in the delight of a technological challenge, and thoughts of the adventure in Cambodia hardly entered his mind. He'd wondered why he hadn't been debriefed and thought once or twice about activating the number on his phone but decided that it was probably better just to wait for a summons.

Linh was busily applying for jobs in her field of anthropology/education/administration but had missed out on the busiest part of the employment season because of her stint in Cambodia. She was beginning to seriously consider whether or not there might be some "position" available with Alasdair's network where she could combine her work with a role as a spy—after all, the world needed to be protected against the agencies engaged in nefarious weapons development—and Gina and Francesca seemed to have pretty good jobs...

Cleaning a table, Linh stilled in mid-wipe. She had been given extra shifts at the Gallery, which she gratefully took. This was a perfectly practical arrangement for everyone, but of late, a tiny resentment had begun to grow. At lunchtime, the garrulous smart set would fill the café, and she could see how easy it would be for her if she worked for the conspirators. But then she would come out of her daydream and feel ashamed for having contemplated the notion.

In many respects, Owen was living the privileged life of the typical Gen Y age group—building on a career while living at home. Don and Gail were more than happy to free him from any domestic responsibilities whilst he focused on his project. This arrangement was a fortunate outcome of the times and of the family's circumstances. Both parents knew that their son was a sincere and hard-working young man who would prosper from the particular advantages he was given. His only duty was to pick up the café supplies from the provedore at Eagle Farm. This was a regular, leisurely Wednesday trip in the Gallery's little van to the warehouse complex in the industrial area.

Two months after returning from Cambodia, Owen was in the provedore office finishing off the paper work. He flirted indulgently with Vanessa and Helen, who were the same generation as his mother, and headed off to the van, congratulating himself on how tactful he'd become at handling situations like that.

He hopped into the driver's seat and saw that he had a passenger. The man wore a cap low over his brow and was unshaven. 'Drive to the service station on the corner,' he said matter-of-factly, '... and park front-on against the hedge.'

Owen hesitated for only a second. '... yeah, no worries...' He drove the few hundred metres to the station at the intersection and parked in front of the high hedge that bordered the car park. He switched off the engine and looked across. His passenger looked about fifty, a bit scruffy, overweight but not fat. In fact, if it wasn't for the obvious fatigue on his face, he could have been an executive on holiday.

'Thank you, Owen,' he said with obvious gratitude. 'We don't have that much time... if you would be so kind as to buy me a pie and a cup of coffee, I would be greatly obliged...'

'Sure,' Owen said.

... of course, he knows my name...

He climbed out and walked to the entrance, pulling his wallet from his pocket.

When he got back, it looked as though his passenger had fallen asleep—or died. But, he caught Owen's eye and nodded.

'Thanks,' he said, '... climb in and let's make it look as though you've stopped for some lunch.' Then he held out his hand.

Owen jumped in, handed him the bag and put the coffee in a pull-out cup holder.

'My name is Darren.' He nibbled at the edges of the pie. '... haven't eaten since last night... thanks for this.'

'Not a problem, Darren.'

Darren smiled at the pleasure of eating. 'It's funny how appetizing something as simple as a pie can be when there is nothing more to live for in life.'

... whoa... might settle in here... this could be a long story. Owen wound down the window.

Darren sipped his coffee. 'Do you read the papers much, Owen?... watch the news on TV?'

'No, not really... just snippets here and there... headlines.'

'Uh huh... typical of your age group.' Darren gave a tired grin.

'Did I miss something?'

'No!' he waved his hand dismissively. '... it's just that there was a story about a week ago of a terrible crash on the border... family... driver fatigue... terrible...'

'Oh, yeah.' Owen had caught snatches of the reports of an awful accident. It was on all news bulletins. 'A mother and three children... all of them...' He couldn't finish the sentence.

'All of them killed, Owen... all of them dead... my family... my family, gone in an instant.'

Owen knew he had to get this right. 'I'm very sorry, Darren... I'm sorry that has happened to you.'

Darren took a big bite of the pie now that it had cooled a bit. 'Oh,' he said with a full mouth, '... you needn't be sad... not for me. I never loved my wife—she was a grasping, vain and disloyal woman incapable of affection. And my kids were spoiled rotten... I mean, they were *really* rotten... in that they would never have been able to redeem themselves in adulthood. They didn't have an ounce of empathy... for person, animal or plant... they were utterly selfish. Seriously, the world is a better place for their demise.'

Owen felt that weird sense of displacement that always presaged a fainting episode. The leaves of the hedge rippled and pixilated. He took a deep breath and rested his head against the door.

'Are you shocked, Owen?'

Owen nodded. 'Yes... I am.'

'Oh,' said Darren, with what sounded like genuine remorse, '... I didn't mean to upset you... it just happens to be the truth.'

Owen opened his eyes. 'So, why are we here?'

Darren cleaned his hands with the paper bag. 'I've come to tell you my story, Owen. I want to tell just one person... just one good person— and, going on your reaction just now, I know you're a good person— one person that will hear my story and make a judgement accordingly. Then I can go to my death knowing that one soul at least knows the truth. I will feel a lot better for having opened my heart.'

'You're not going to kill yourself, are you?'

Darren laughed cynically. 'No! No... others will very efficiently do that for me.'

'What?'

Darren held up his hand as though to discourage any more enquiry. 'When I finish here, I will go to my secret place, freshen up and have a shave, put on some outrageously expensive clothes and catch the train to city central. I will walk in full public view towards the plaza in front of the Town Hall, and by the time I get there, they will have put someone in position to kill me.'

'Shoot you?... in broad daylight in a crowded place?'

Darren snorted with mirth. 'No, no... I will have a heart attack. It'll be quite quick really.'

Owen spread his hands with incredulity. 'But you don't look as though you're about to have a heart attack.'

'Actually, Owen,' Darren leaned across suddenly, '... my last medical revealed that I'm a prime candidate for one,' he chuckled. 'In any event, my seizure will appear quite natural.'

'... but it won't be.'

'No. If you ever get hold of the CCTV footage, and I advise you not to try, you'll see a person coming towards me with dark glasses and a longish package under their arm. That'll be my killer.'

'I can't believe we're discussing this... but seeing as we are, how do they, y'know...'

'Kill me? Easy... by using a powerful sonic pulse straight to the heart. That's what the dark glasses are for—infra-red aiming. It'll feel like someone has thrown a brick at my chest... drop me like a bag of shopping. People will gather around... undo my jacket... the killer will hover nearby and administer another, fatal pulse from close range. Well-meaning citizens will bang away at my chest and effectively seal my fate.'

A cool breeze fanned through the car, but Owen was finding it impossible to reconcile nature's pleasant elements with Man's machinations. 'Why does anyone want to kill you?' he asked at last.

Darren sighed heavily. 'I'm a liability now, Owen. My family no longer exists... I have no one to protect any longer, and some might think, nothing to live for—which couldn't be further from the truth, actually... but anyway, in their eyes, I'm out of control. They don't own me anymore... and if they can't rely on me to preserve the *wonderful* life that they have created for me, then there's no knowing what crazy thing I might do to expose them... so I have to die.'

'What did you mean about *not* having *nothing* to live for?'

Darren brushed pie crumbs off his lap. 'Man... I have the largest fly-bridge cruiser in the harbour... I have membership to all of the best clubs... I live in a bloody mansion on the river... I've got the international, jet-setting lifestyle that people dream about—so why would I want to give it up? I don't care that I will never see my family again—I never saw them anyway! Nothing has changed for me! I would continue with my life and keep doing what I'm good at. But... *but*... maybe I *have* changed... maybe circumstances have changed enough for me to re-evaluate my life. They don't know... and *they* can't take the chance.'

Owen looked at Darren's soft, white hands. 'What are you good at?'

'Achieving nothing, Owen... achieving nothing. I'm a professional at it.'

'Sorry, I don't understand.'

'This is the story that I need to tell you... so I'll begin right away.' Darren propped himself in his seat. 'I've always been pretty much invisible, right from my childhood. Not below average—no... such people will attract attention in any number of ways. No, I was a good student, but unspectacular—a middling sportsman with no special attributes—socially unimpressive, but not shunned—people assumed I had friends, but I didn't... people assumed a lot of things about me, really—that I had interests, ambitions, a love life. Indeed, I had all of that, but what I seemed to lack was passion... don't know why. My family lacked passion—they were all grey—they were all subdued... I inherited that, I suppose.'

Owen observed his new acquaintance closely.

...what am I?... his confessor?...

'I did a business degree. As usual, I did well enough, and I observed the changing times from the sidelines. But, no sex, drugs and rock an' roll for me... well, a timid flirtation that neither blew nor expanded my mind. My passions remained in limbo.

I was encouraged by one of the lecturers to join the student council, so I did. Hardly opened my mouth at any of the meetings—everything was either too new-age and radical, or too political, or too anti-social... I voted with the majority each time. One day, I got to talking to this guy at some community meeting that I'd been relegated to, and he let me know that I would be able to access funds for any of the proposals put forward by the student council. At first, I felt too intimidated to suggest that I might be able to assist, but then an issue came up where a bunch of students were looking for publishing opportunities for some compilation of extremist literature. No one on the council had any idea how to go about it, so I consulted my new friend. No problem! A publishing deal was arranged, promotions on radio and telly, funds for the print run... a *fait accompli*!

'My stock seriously rose at subsequent meetings. I became an indispensable middle man—and a social saboteur.

Owen massaged his brow. 'How did you become a saboteur?'

'This is how—I was instrumental in funding things that drew attention *away* from any activity or venture that would promote strong social relations... generate greater diversity in the community... instil individual independence—not the reactionary, self-centred strain ... but the cohesiveness that unlimited variety engenders. No, my masters didn't want that—they wanted a compliant and indentured community... citizens who would spend decades paying off their worthless higher education loans. They wanted to break up the rigour and organization of subjects. They fragmented the timetable so that students were in and out of the place at all times of the day, eroding student bonds and stretching a barren curriculum into many years. At the same time, the institutions wrote their own textbooks and delivered more and more stuff online, thereby promulgating vacuous theories and destroying the sense of continuity and relevance in vast bodies of knowledge. I helped to create much of that.'

'And for that you think you deserve a death sentence?' Owen was getting tired.

'That, and much more. I was well looked after, Owen. I acquired all the material things... things that I didn't even want! A fly-bridge game-fishing boat? I hate fishing, and I get sea-sick. Jet-skis? I've got about half a dozen, I think. Hate them! They scare me. Fast cars, luxury cars, vintage cars, ATVs... I never drive them, except for the Austin Healy, which I really do like. And I acquired a trophy wife. It was all part of the narrative that I conformed to—not that I minded! Not a bit of it—at last people acknowledged me. In fact, there was a mysteriousness about me—people wanted to know more about me instead of overlooking me, as I was used to.

'I began to work at government levels, achieving all those banal initiatives that promote hollow, nationalistic zeal... that support a heightened sense of entitlement and moral right... that perpetuate the illusion that we are a smart country... a deserving country... a country engaged in preparing for the future. Yeah... I fanned those embers... people who want to belong and be different all at once... communities that praise individuality whilst rewarding conformity... blathering on about one trivial thing after another... political parties fatuously brawling with each other and slowly self-destructing. I was on film boards, making sure that only "worthy" projects about societal injustice received grants, which would invariably flop at the box office and only end up firming the divides of inequality in the community. And, we'd promote the "triumph of the underdog" type of film which is an essential opiate that diffuses any real attempt by those who are disempowered to correct any wrongs in the order of things.'

Owen felt he needed to clear his mind. 'But surely, Darren, even if you wanted to blurt all of this on TV, or even on social media, you'd never get a look in... those in power would just shut you out. So, what are they worried about?'

Darren massaged his face with both hands. 'Good point. But I forced their hand when I went to ground, because now the police think that I had something to do with the crash. For me to suddenly surface would be too messy. I'd be in the media spotlight—a prominent citizen standing on a very powerful platform. A heart attack is the best solution.'

Owen took a big breath. 'And, may I enquire about which side you are working for?'

'Side?'

'Yeah, um... Cassandra?... Francesca?... Gina?... no?...'

'Sorry, mate... don't know them—and I'm not just saying that. I believe you have met other operatives, but I don't know them by those names.'

'How did you get my name?'

Darren looked directly into Owen's eyes. 'You're on a list that falls within my domain. You have *newcomer* status—I don't know why. My job was to get to know you and to gradually work my voodoo on you. But then, there was the accident. I heard about it on the news not long after it happened. I knew what it meant straightaway—the essential equilibrium of my position had become upset—the kind of pledge that they expected from me could only be honoured if I became dead. And to tell you the truth, Owen, I was ready to, not so much die… but to stop living. I haven't been living all my life… I wouldn't know how to… so why would I want to keep doing this? I don't—I'm ready to stop. But, I just wanted to tell someone who might care. When I read your file, it seemed to me that you might be someone who would care.'

The afternoon sun had moved to the other side of the hedge. The front compartment of the van was shaded.

Owen felt a great sadness for his passenger. 'I'm sorry, Darren, that there wasn't more passion in your life… something or someone that really inspired you.'

Darren nodded sightlessly. '… so am I… so am I.'

Owen's phone rang. He'd been through all the stages of having personalised ring tones and grabs of music; now he just wanted something that cut through the miasma of audio pollution.

'Hi, Mum… no, nothing… just got caught up in something… won't be long… yep… see ya…'

Darren looked at him askance. 'So, what have you been up to that got you involved with…'

'The conspirators?' Owen added helpfully.

'… okay, yep… that's us. There are lots of people involved with any number of subversive agendas, it's just that the great majority of them don't realise it.'

Owen spread his hands and sighed. 'I was in a very remote place where a jet was brought down, and I found something that I shouldn't have.'

Darren affected a taken-a-back look. 'I'm surprised you're still around.'

'Are you?… oh. Well, maybe I got lucky. Everything's been sorted out now, though.'

For a moment, the two men appraised each other.

Darren nodded and smiled. 'Well… it's been nice to just talk with someone without having to direct the outcome. I don't want to know anything about you, Owen... I just wanted to talk— needed to talk, without anything getting in the way. You've been a good listener, and I thank you for that.' He held out his hand.

Owen shook his hand, surprised at the weakness of Darren's grip. In an instant, he realised that he knew more about this man than anyone ever had. His vision tunnelled; the person next to him was an empty entity—someone who had clung to the material world and would vanish from this realm without a single comforting thought.

But, there was nothing that Owen could do, except to say, 'Thank you for telling me your story, Darren. It will help me... help me to make my life better.'

Darren looked away. He seemed happy enough with that. He opened the door and slid from the seat.

Owen watched him in the side mirror as he walked towards the footpath.

Chapter Thirteen

About a week later, Owen told Linh about his encounter with Darren. They were lying together in the late afternoon sunlight on, what Owen called, his day bed. The loft was so big that there was ample room for such a luxury. It was where Owen would crash when he needed to unravel some mechanical problem. He'd told only his mother about this habit, and she half believed that it actually worked. To Owen, it was like meditating—but without the rigour. Somehow, ideas would fall into place after he'd collapsed face down on the bed.

But now, entwined skin to skin with his lovely girl, Owen was hoping that his story might alter a train of thought that he sensed Linh was pursuing.

'So... I don't know,' Owen concluded, 'Maybe we were lucky... but Darren definitely thought his time was up.'

'I haven't heard anything on the news at all,' Linh deliberated close to Owen's ear.

'Guy has a heart attack!... big deal. No matter how public it was, it would hardly rate as a news item.'

Linh nuzzled closer. 'Are you telling me this as a cautionary tale?'

Owen had long ago worked out that the art of suggestion was not his strongest suit. 'Yeah.' He stroked her arm. 'I know that it's frustrating not being able to find what you're looking for but, hey, you've found me!'

'I know,' Linh whispered. She sat up and absently massaged Owen's chest. 'I guess our little adventures had more of an impact on me than I realised. Maybe it's the knowledge that there's another level entirely where people do exciting and stimulating work...'

'Like assassinations and sabotage.'

'True... but, maybe there is other stuff that they do that is well, more wholesome.'

'Maybe.'

'Owie, I have to get some new clarinet reeds in town. Why don't we go past the Town Hall and see if anything happened there... at all... vis a vis your recently deceased passenger.'

Owen groaned and frowned.

Linh appealed with wide eyes. 'Aren't you curious? Don't you want to know whether or not he really was murdered?'

Owen groaned louder.

Linh grabbed Owen's head with both hands and made him nod repeatedly. 'Yes, Linh... that is an excellent idea... I have been consumed with curiosity all week.'

Owen laughed and tickled Linh in her ribs. She hastily brought her arms to her side and collapsed in a fit of giggles with her face to his.

'I've got an idea,' she said after a while, '... it'll be exactly a week tomorrow when the incident would have happened, if it happened at all. There will probably be the same security guard on duty, so...'

The last rays of the sun stole through the jacaranda onto the bed as Linh outlined her plan.

The next day, with her phone to her ear, Linh stood in front of the Town Hall and conspicuously searched the plaza area. Her conversation with Owen was, to all intents and purposes, completely authentic.

'... how far away are you?'

'... just about to cross Adelaide Street, if we ever get a walk signal...'

'You sound all puffed out...'

'... well, I've run all the way from the bus station—oh, here we go. See you in a sec.'

Owen jogged up to Linh, who had positioned herself close by the security guard at the bottom of the flight of steps.

'... hey, Sweetie... phew, I'm stuffed...' Owen gave Linh a quick peck on the cheek then bent down with his hands on his knees.

'Owie, your face is all flushed. You're not going to have a heart attack, are you?'

Owen looked up at the security guard and grinned. 'Nah, I'm not about to make a spectacle of myself by dropping dead in public.'

The guard, who had half a smile on his face, pointed to a place on the plaza. 'You wouldn't be the first, mate. Bloke carked it right there about a week ago. Dead as a maggot.'

Owen straightened with concern on his face. 'Fair dinkum? Was he very old?'

'Nah! He was in his fifties or so... really well dressed. Nothin' they could do for him. The crowd was all over him, trying to resuscitate him. Even had a doctor handy but, no good... carted him off in the ambo.'

'How sad,' said Linh with her hands to her mouth.

'At least it was quick, love. I had to attend to some of the paperwork. You see it all in my job.'

The trio conversed for a little while longer. Then Owen and Linh said cheerio, and walked off, hand in hand, towards the picturesque Uniting church across Ann Street.

In silence, they climbed the stone steps to the entrance and went inside. It seemed like a natural thing to do. Inside it was cool and quiet. They slid into a pew and stared solemnly towards the sanctuary and the stained-glass window beyond.

Neither of the lovers was religious. Linh rested her head on Owen's shoulders.

'All the best, Darren,' Owen said softly, '... we won't forget you.'

'... all the best, Darren,' Linh whispered.

They held hands, their thoughts dwelling on other people's mortality.

Later, when they emerged, blinking and frowning into the sunlight, Linh suddenly exclaimed, 'Well, I'm cured... no more hankering for a job with the conspirators.'

Owen stopped in his tracks, spun Linh to his chest and kissed her lingeringly on the mouth. He ran his fingers slowly from her neck, through her hair, up the back of her head. He had a way of slowing down the movement so that Linh's consciousness was focused on the pleasurable sensation and the fact that it seemed to last forever.

'I love you,' he said, at last.

'... why?' Linh breathed softly.

'... because I do... and I should. Because I'm alive and lucky to have you.'

Linh looked up drowsily. '... and I'm so glad that you love me... I feel that I am something much greater because you love me... like the individual me is just a part of what I am...'

Owen nodded. 'We have created, from nothing, something intangible yet most highly desirable. I wonder whether we will be able to take it with us when our time comes?'

Linh wrapped Owen's cheeks with her hands. 'Owie... you've been really moved by all this, haven't you?'

'You'd be pretty stupid not to learn from an experience like this,' he replied. 'Shall we get a fruit smoothie for lunch?'

Linh reached up and lightly kissed Owen on the lips. 'I love the way you're always thinking of my tummy.'

When Owen returned to the Gallery later in the afternoon, after having walked Linh to her house, there was just one person enjoying a coffee in the courtyard. At first, he took no particular notice. He pushed open the doors to the foyer and paused.

A lone woman, fifties chic, swing skirt, glamorous and independent...

He turned and walked towards her.

'Hello, Francesca... how unpleasant to see you.'

Francesca made a face. 'How ungallant of you to say so, Owen.'

Owen pulled up the chair opposite. He sighed heavily. 'I was under the distinct impression that we were all square now; you got what you wanted and I got what I wanted—to be left alone.'

'You don't want to be alone in this world, Owen, believe me.'

That had more of an impact than Francesca could have imagined, given Owen's experiences in the past week. 'Okay then,' he replied, '... how about I just don't want to have friends like you.'

'Ohh... harsh!' Francesca looked away. 'Come on, invite me inside where it's warmer because I want to tell you something that I hope will be of great interest to you.'

Owen rubbed the bridge of his nose with an exaggerated gesture.

He got up from his chair. 'Come on then.'

With a sullen look, Francesca folded her arms and turned away. 'You're not making me feel welcome at all, Owen!'

He eyed her sympathetically and put out his hand. 'Come on, Francesca. Let's go inside where it's warmer...'

Francesca grudgingly placed her hand in his.

With a languid smile, he helped her from her chair and, as she attained her balance next to him, he gently put his arm around her.

'Do you have a boyfriend, Francesca?' he enquired gamely.

'I have lovers, Owen... lots and lots of lovers.'

'Ahh,' Owen mused, '... so it's not about love then.'

Francesca pressed her breast into Owen's bicep. 'You are absolutely right about that. I'm far too selfish to be considering another person's needs.'

Owen didn't move away. Instead, he put his other arm about her and drew her close to him. Francesca let her head rest on his shoulder.

'Ahh, Francesca... what I couldn't tell you about life...'

'... would fill a terabyte of memory,' she said into his collarbone.

Owen chuckled. '... you're lovely, Francesca... I do hope that you'll find someone that you want to make happy.'

Francesca put her arms around Owen's waist. 'You need to have had appropriate modelling to become like that. My parents were both actors... each too self-absorbed.'

They moved towards the foyer entrance, Owen with his arm around Francesca. They settled into a booth partially hidden by a floor installation of sculpted textiles and looked at each other with bemusement.

A young waitress appeared. 'Hi, Owen. Can I get you anything?'

'No thanks, Emma. Oh, on second thoughts, a G and T might be nice?' He appealed to Francesca.

'Lovely, thank you.'

'Two gin and tonics then please, Emma,' and he held out one horizontal finger and then three horizontal fingers.

Emma signalled that she understood.

Francesca cradled her chin in the heel of her hand. 'You have a nice way with people, Owen.'

'I had different modelling,' he shrugged his shoulders. 'So, what's this fascinating piece of information that you want to tell me?'

Francesca lent back with her hands in her lap. 'First of all, I need to put you into the picture. Then, I hope, you will be a little more sympathetic to my proposal.'

'Okay, shoot.'

'At present, the world is in a state of flux. I have been briefed to tell you only that the global play for power is, as yet, unresolved and is likely to get messy. To that end, the faction, if you like, that I represent, is preparing, in whichever way possible to, if not triumph in the mêlée, then at least to prevail pretty much intact. To achieve that will require ingenuity and cunning. Now, much of the global order of things may change—particularly in manufacturing. One of the strategies used by those seeking global supremacy is to weaken the manufacturing base of their competitors. This is an age-old strategy that has become particularly relevant in an ever-shrinking world...'

Emma arrived with their drinks and placed them on the table with a look of angst. Owen took a quick sip then gave her a smile and a thumbs-up.

Francesca continued. 'One of the most highly evolved systems of manufacture is, as you will doubtless be aware, in the manufacture of engines. Motors of today are made to incredibly fine tolerances with astonishing degrees of reliability. To suddenly have to become self-reliant and make our own engines with the same high levels of perfection would be impossible. The networking of design, tooling, fabrication and whatever else, could not be achieved even in decades.'

Owen was nodding slowly. 'I think I can see where you're going with this.'

'Can you, Owen? I do hope that you can grasp the seriousness of the situation.'

'You want to develop my turbine because it is simple to manufacture... it doesn't require anything more sophisticated than the sort of tools you'd find in a high school technics department. Am I right?'

'Absolutely right. Although, you have kept us in the dark ever since you installed flyscreens. Who would have thought that something as simple as that could thwart the best exponents of espionage in the world?'

Owen snorted. 'Glad to hear it.'

Francesca leaned forward. 'We can help you to develop the motor, and we would pay you and your team very well to...' she hesitated with an urgent look.

'Keep it under wraps.'

'Yes... for the time being.'

Owen took a sip of his drink.

Francesca looked at hers, took it delicately and drained the glass. 'I hope you don't employ Emma behind the bar,' she said with difficulty, '... she'll send you broke. That's got to be half gin!'

Owen grinned. 'Actually, speaking of rocket fuel, that's one of the other features of the turbine—it'll run on just about anything, because it naturally vaporises the fuel... which, in the scenario you were putting to me, would be a very useful thing.'

Francesca acknowledged this meekly. She studied the table. 'Owen... I know that this is asking a lot of you. My only defence is this—when the time comes for you to commercialise your engine, it will cost a fortune to protect it, and because it is so simple to build, you won't be able to control unauthorised production. I mean, you'll still be able to make a lot of money from it, but you will be disappointed at how quickly you will lose control of your baby. It's inevitable... the world is a big place.'

'And, the benefits if I sell to you?'

'Actually, Owen... we don't just want to buy your intellectual property—we want you to work for us.'

Owen slumped. 'You know, I can entertain the idea of you paying me to shelve my engine... but working for you... 'fraid not.'

'Why?'

Owen leant back in his seat and looked up at the ceiling. 'I suppose it's because I don't know enough yet to take sides... know what I mean?'

'Of course, I do, Owen... and, I understand that.'

'One of the things about my life that I really like, is that I am in a position to make up my own mind on so many issues.'

Francesca smiled broadly.

For the first time, Owen detected a wistful compassion.

She raised a shrewd eyebrow. 'Although, we are surrounded by many illusions... sometimes it's advantageous to listen to those who have been monitoring the progress of the world for centuries.'

Owen's eyes widened. 'Centuries?'

'Oh, yes... many centuries... millennia in fact.'

A frown creased Owen's brow. 'You are part of an organization that goes back millennia?'

Francesca nodded.

'Well, in all that time, haven't you learned that it's not nice to murder people and commit acts of sabotage?'

Francesca's eyes fell away. The chic, the panache that she conveyed so well, seemed to have abandoned her. She looked alone.

Chapter Fourteen

Owen looked at his watch. It was almost four o'clock. He rose and stood next to Francesca. 'I take what you're telling me very seriously. Let's talk some more where it's more comfortable.' He held out his hand. Francesca smiled up at him and graciously accepted his offer.

Owen led the way upstairs to his room. The winter sun angled through the windows and cast a warm glow over everything. He indicated two heavy, leather lounge chairs. Francesca settled into one of them while Owen searched through his bar fridge.

'Um, I've only got ginger beer... would you like a ginger beer, or would you like me to make you something else downstairs?'

Francesca held out her hand. 'A ginger beer will be lovely... thank you.'

Owen handed her an opened bottle and lowered himself into the other armchair. 'Cheers!'

They clinked bottles.

...now, let's see if I can take control here...

Francesca looked about the room. 'Very nice, Owen. When I was a child, my bedroom was a loft... though much, much smaller than this. It was above a theatre... one tiny dormer window that looked out to a warehouse across the road. My parents were obsessed with making the playhouse profitable. For a time, it was a great place to be a kid. My friends and I would do our make-up in front of the lighted mirrors, and stage little performances with all the wigs and costumes. But they all went to different high schools and my teenage years were quite lonely. I used to get thrust into roles whenever there was a part for me, or if someone couldn't make it—that's where I learnt to act—to carry a part. Eventually the theatre closed. Mother and Father did shift work in factories. I would come home and let myself in through the glass doors into the foyer, then walk through the dark theatre to the stairs behind the stage. There was no electricity because the building had been condemned. We basically squatted there. My room was ridiculously small. I used to do my homework by a gas lamp. I was good at languages—my dad is Russian, and my mum is French. I would take the lamp down to the stage and recite all sorts of stuff in all sorts of languages. I speak six languages well enough but like to dabble in a bunch of others.'

'Vietnamese being one of them...'

'Oh, yes... well, you see... my mother was brought up in Vietnam.'

Owen nodded agreeably. 'How did you start in this job?'

'I was chosen... multi-lingual... good looking... good actor—I had all the prerequisites to be a spy.'

'Did you know that you were becoming a spy?'

'... hmmm... sort of. I knew that what I was doing was deceitful on various levels, but hey, show me a job where you don't have to sell your soul.'

'True. So, your life changed dramatically!'

'You have no idea.'

'And your parents?'

Francesca's smile was touched with sadness. 'They still run the theatre. They're bohemians... eccentric... very aged now, but they love what they do.'

'I thought you said the theatre was condemned?'

'Owen... I was making a lot of money that I didn't need to spend, because every luxury is provided for me. I wasn't in contact with my parents, but I always kept an eye on things, which in my position is not at all difficult. I found out that a developer wanted to build units on the theatre site. That was the stimulus I needed to pour hundreds of thousands into the building, and to restore it to its former glory. I had it designed so that it was multi- functional. That way, Mother and Father could make a living from it again. That's what they do... strut along the café strip by day, and host cultural events by night.'

'But you've never gone to visit them.'

Francesca shook her head.

'Because your life is ridiculously busy... and you're waiting for that time when it won't matter anymore that you've been away so long.'

Francesca took a shuddering breath. Her voice laboured with emotion. 'God, Owen!... how old are you? You shouldn't be able to manipulate me like this.'

Owen's voice was soft but strong. 'I'm not trying to manipulate you, Francesca... it's just that I've discovered something about you that I really like. That's a beautiful thing that you did.'

'Yeah!' Francesca cried, '... the place is worth millions because it's a bit like this joint—it's become gentrified over time—*and I own it!*' She lowered her head to her hand.

Owen knew that he didn't want to save her with pity. 'Bloody hell, Francesca!... that's great!... that's great. You've produced an ideal solution—your parents are happy, and you won't be out of pocket... nothing wrong with that!... nothing wrong with that at all. Although... if you really want to complete the circle, you probably should pay them a visit. After all, they did help to create someone who is pretty amazing.' He levered himself out of his chair and sat on the armrest next to her. He hugged her to him. 'Don't be upset... you have created something wonderful... much, much better than still living with your parents because you can't get into the housing market.'

Francesca laughed and spluttered simultaneously. She dabbed her face on Owen's jeans.

The sunlight had gone and the room was becoming grey.

'C'mon,' Owen said, with a squeeze of Francesca's shoulder, '... why don't I turn on a few lights and order us some dinner.'

Francesca looked up out of the corner of her eye and shook her head with dismay. 'Wow!... and I thought *I* was living the high life.'

With a chuckle, Owen separated and switched on some lamps. 'On occasions like this, I pay for my meal... and I'm a good tipper.'

'Occasions with Linh?'

'Yep... that's right.' He arranged two chairs around a drop-side table and rummaged around for a table cloth.

Francesca strode to a wall mirror and inspected herself. 'Is she available tonight? I'd really like to see her again.' She blotted at her eyes with a tissue.

'What?... so that the two of you can have fun at my expense again?'

'No,' Francesca plumped her bodice, '... I've got an assignment for her that I think she would be good at.'

Owen paused as he inspected the contents of a drawer. 'An assignment?'

'Yes. It won't be a hardship, I assure you. Have you ever heard of Amanoi Resort in Vietnam?"

Owen carefully draped a tablecloth that he'd found, over the drop-side. 'No, can't say that I have. Is it nice?'

'Nice?... yeah, it's nice. It's the most exquisite, coastal resort in the country. You have to see it to believe it.'

'Sweet!... so, you want her to check up on the staff... make sure they're not stealing the toilet paper, y'know... stuff like that.'

Francesca sat down at one of the dining chairs. She shot Owen a belaboured smirk. 'It will be a bit more challenging than that.'

Owen swiped at his phone. While he waited for an answer he scrolled through some playlists on his computer. Soon, the cascades of Chopin's Etude Op. 25 infused the shadowy loft.

'Hey, Linh,' he murmured into the phone, '... were you practising the clarinet?... thought you must have been. Hey, something's come up—would you like to have dinner with me tonight... an old friend of yours... Francesca... yeah, we've got the lights turned down low and a nice red from the cellar... okay, I'll see you in mere minutes then... see ya...'

He scrolled up another number. 'Hey, Jenna... so *you're* on tonight?... cool. Hey, listen, special favour for your big brother—can you bring up a tapas selection for three?... what?... well, a woman, if you must know... no, not beers... bring up a Moss Wood Cabernet Sauvignon... it's a red... wine! Hell's bells, Jenna!... bill it to one of the tables... 'cos I don't want Mum to know... I know it's expensive, I'll pay cash when you bring it up... Jenna, please! I've got guests that I'm trying to impress and you're not helping... thank you...'

Owen turned around. Francesca was standing in front of the speakers, trance-like with closed eyes. Her slender fingers trembled to the pulse of the piano.

He sat down at the table and watched as she absorbed the music.

Without altering her contemplation, Francesca said, 'There was one more thing that occupied me on the dark stage. There was an old piano. I'd had lessons since I was about five... my father was a very accomplished pianist. I can play all of this.'

The passage climbed imperiously to a momentous crescendo.

'You're a bit of a dark one, Francesca...'

The piece trailed off like falling bells.

'*I'm* a dark one! You're the stockman listening to Chopin and ordering a one-hundred-dollar Moss Wood.'

Owen laughed. The subdued lighting accentuated her sculptured face. She looked more alluring than ever—and ever so dangerous.

...serious trouble there... although, it doesn't hurt to like someone for the things that they're good at...

Francesca eyed him knowingly. 'You're not attracted to me, are you?'

Owen shook his head. 'But I like you... there's something about you that I like... maybe it's your pure selfishness. In a way, it's an admirable thing... you know yourself... completely.'

Francesca came towards him, straddled the chair and rested her elbows on the table. She faced him with her chin in her hands. 'I imagine love to be like, when you let yourself fall backwards and expect someone to catch you... y'know?—you have utter faith that that person is going to be there... that they *will* catch you... that they are there for *you*. And, when you can let go your fear and allow yourself to fall with the most blissful confidence, then, you are not falling, but you are in heaven... it would be rhapsodic... and it's only when you crash into the ground, that your world collapses.'

Owen reached across and enfolded her elbows with his hands. 'Is that what stops you from falling in love, Francesca? The fear of crashing?'

The two of them searched each other's eyes. 'You know what, Owen... I'm going to answer that question truthfully, because I think you deserve it. My curse is that I don't have to make-do... I can have whatever I want. And that's all well and good with material things...

but not with love. We tend not to know what we need... and we make all the wrong choices. But, please don't feel sorry for me. I'd rather be unlucky in love and have endless affairs, than to have whatever else people make do with.'

'Sounds like fun, Francesca!' Linh said brightly from the doorway.

Francesca turned. 'There you are!... hello...' She stood up from the table.

Owen rose. 'Hey, Tot... you caught me playing handsies with Francesca.'

'So, I noticed!' She approached Francesca and shook hands warmly. Owen directed her to his seat while he found a little stool to sit on.

Jenna appeared at the door holding a large platter. In one hand she gripped a wine bottle. 'Oh, hello,' she exclaimed with mild surprise, '... only *two* guests tonight, Owen?... that's unusually intimate. I might actually get some sleep tonight.'

Owen rolled his eyes. 'Francesca, this menial is my sister, Jenna... just put it down over there, thank you. You're dismissed.'

Jenna put the platter on the table then wrapped her arms around Linh. 'He's narrowed it down—it's between you and Francesca. Good luck.'

Linh returned the hug with a laugh. 'Ah, Jenna... you make it so easy for me to be with your brother. Someone has to be there for him.'

Jenna reached across and shook hands with Francesca. 'It's nice to meet you.'

'Lovely to meet you, Jenna. I'm so relieved to see that Owen doesn't get *everything* his own way.'

'No way!' Jenna turned and held an upturned palm at Owen.

'What?'

'You owe me a hundred and fifteen dollars.'

Owen groaned and strode to the dresser next to the bed and grabbed his wallet. He searched for the correct amount as he walked back. 'Here, it's the closest I've got. You owe me five bucks.'

Jenna took the notes with her head canted in query. '*I* owe you five dollars—*you* owe *me* five dollars...'

'How do you work that out?'

'My tip! Ten percent of the wine, plus you should really be tipping me a little something for bringing up the food.'

Owen lunged at his sister and, after a brief scuffle, managed to subdue her in a headlock and march her out of the room. He closed the door and turned to his guests. Linh and Francesca regarded him with alarm.

Owen drooped with a woe-be-gone look. 'Oh, great!... you two have been together for less than a minute, and already you've ganged up on me.'

Francesca surveyed the selection of tapas. 'Really, Owen... you can be so melodramatic.' She winked at Linh.

Linh smiled sympathetically. She put her arms around him and rested her head on his chest.

Owen happily nuzzled the top of her head.

Francesca popped an olive into her mouth and daintily licked her fingers. 'While you two get reacquainted after your hour-long separation, I might just powder my nose... if that's okay?'

'Sure, Francesca... on the left as you come down the stairs.'

'What?... no ensuite?'

'Unfortunately, no... I have a potty under my bed.'

Linh looked up. 'Really?'

'Of course not!... I open up the loft doors and pee out into the street.'

Francesca walked past the couple. 'I'm leaving...'

Owen and Linh laughed, and sat down at the table.

There was a little crease of worry on Linh's brow. 'Owie... what's she doing here?'

Owen covered Linh's hand with his. 'She's got a job for you.'

Linh's frown deepened. She regarded the platter with unfocused eyes.

'Are you thinking about not accepting?' Owen queried.

'Owie... you know what we talked about. Do we want to get mixed up in this?'

Owen massaged Linh's hand. 'She made me some sort of offer for the turbine... at this stage I have no idea exactly what she's proposing. But what I am getting a sense of is this; there seems to be a blurred boundary between those who unknowingly work for the conspirators and those who are admitted into their secrets.'

Linh put a finger to her lips and looked over to where Francesca had been sitting.

Owen waved his hand dismissively. 'It's okay... I've had a look under the table and I don't think she's planted anything elsewhere... I kept my eye on her.'

Linh nodded thoughtfully. 'So, you think we will be better off being recruited?'

'Not me. I'm going to stick with developing the motor. I don't want to be paid off just so it can be shelved. Anyway, I've got another avenue to see this thing through to commercialization that she doesn't know about. No, I was thinking more about you. You are incredibly young and, all things being equal, you will develop a career for yourself in good time. But even so, if you *were* to work for Francesca's outfit, you would be operating at the highest levels of management. She obviously sees potential in you. You would be groomed,' he laughed, '... literally, to become part of an organization that has tremendous resources. It would be very exciting.'

'And, I could end up like Darren.'

'He was different—he was needy, and they took advantage of him. You wouldn't want what they gave him... you would be much more in control.'

Linh lifted Owen's hand to her mouth and kissed it softly. 'Thanks, Owie... for allowing me to take the job. It would be very exciting... but, I'll stick with our original plan—no joining the conspirators!'

Owen grinned, leaned over the table and kissed her. 'We can make our own conspiracies,' he said, with their lips touching.

Sounds on the steps hinted at Francesca's approach. Owen got up and scoured a shelf for some wine glasses.

Francesca slipped into her seat. 'Has Owen told you the news?'

'That you have a job for me?'

Francesca nodded. 'Are you interested?'

Linh took a big breath. 'I am... I am... but I've decided that I'm just going to pursue the usual career avenues... boring as that may be.'

'That's not boring... not at all. But, my job offer is not a permanent one... not yet. I thought of you when my team and I discussed this assignment—you'd be well suited—but I have just made an executive decision to make this job more attractive.'

Owen set out three different glasses and poured the wine.

'Thank you, Owen. May I state my offer before we toast?'

'Certainly, Francesca,' Owen said as he perched himself on the stool.

'Well, originally I wanted Linh to work at the resort to do some spying for me on the side. But now, I realise that she would be much more flexible if she was in fact a guest... staying at the resort with her very appealing husband... um, that's you, Owen.'

'Oh, right!'

'Oh, I can't wait to try this wine. Here's to a very charismatic couple—cheers.'

The trio clinked glasses.

'Thank you, Francesca... that's very kind of you.'

'Thank you,' said Linh with a lovely smile.

Francesca sipped from her glass with a practised motion. 'Ahh... you can understand why those who can afford to, will only drink expensive wine.'

Owen gave an indifferent shrug of his shoulders. 'It's okay, I suppose.'

'You'd prefer a palette of campfire ash and mosquito wrigglers, would you?'

Linh laughed as she selected something from the plate.

'Anyways,' Francesca continued, '... let me outline the mission. Just a reminder first up—this is for your ears only—you must not discuss this with anyone... clear?'

'Clear,' the couple answered in unison.

'Good. Okay, the action centres around a tiny coastal town called Vinh Hy which is in the bottom third of Vietnam. There is a small fishing harbour and a well-developed aquaculture industry, but apart from that, the area is surprisingly remote. This is because it is surrounded by a large national park. The main coastal road passes inland of the park, so not many travellers make their way along the winding road to Vinh Hy. However, there is one other feature that the town boasts—the Amanoi Resort. This super luxury get-a-way for the very well-heeled is built on a promontory with natural vegetation and all-round views to the sea. This is where you'll be staying. So, all in all, a delightful destination, far removed from the usual bustling tourist dives. Even the village around the harbour is abnormally calm and restrained. Why then, I hear you ask, would we have any interest in such a place?'

Francesca languidly cut a croquette in half and popped it in her mouth.

'Well,' she said, whilst fanning her mouth, '... ooh, that's still hot... there is another feature about this place that makes it very interesting. It is the closest point of land to the Spratly Deep—an oceanic depression that gives access from the South China Sea to the North Pacific Ocean.'

Francesca dipped a slice of sausage into an aubergine Mirza Ghasemi. 'This is truly delicious. Do you guys cook this all here?'

Owen was jolted out of his thoughts. 'Oh, no!... no, we get a Turkish restaurant down the road to make it for us. We haven't got the staff for this kind of thing. We get a lot of our specialty foods made elsewhere. You'd think it would be too expensive, but people don't mind paying for a wide selection of food, as long as everyone at the table is happy. The other restaurants are so close by, we just text through our order and pick it up when it's ready.'

'Ingenious... so, people come here for the ambience.'

'Yeah... all the art work... comforts... privacy... so, what—the harbour is actually a submarine base?'

'Not yet... the fact is, the harbour is much too shallow. However, not far off the coast the water is very deep and, about one hundred kilometres out, the continental shelf falls away to a wide, abyssal plain that is many thousands of feet deep.'

Linh leaned forward. 'When you said the Spratly Deep, is that close to those islands that everyone is fighting over?'

'Absolutely—the Spratly Islands... nothing more than sand banks at the very top of huge oceanic mountains...'

Owen raised a quizzical brow. 'So, this whole thing is about submarines, then?'

'We think so. Our intel informs us that just off the promontory, about half a kilometre out to sea, there is a huge concrete structure being built that is most likely an underwater base for submarines—

deep enough to be out of sight but not so deep as to make it impossible to build. The pre-fab components are floated to the site by specially built tugboats disguised as trawlers. The activity so far hasn't created any suspicion as far as we can tell. The local trawler industry is a bit bemused by the fact that these new boats seem to be intent on fishing so close to the shore when the best fishing is just off the continental drop-off, where there is a nutrient upwelling that supports a lot of marine life. But, apart from that, things seem pretty quiet.'

'So, what... you want us to paddle out one day and see what the deal is?'

Francesca laughed. '... well, if you have the opportunity... but, no... your job is to find out how they are co-ordinating this operation from the resort. We know for a fact that there are operatives working there and we're very curious about why something as relatively simple as a docking station should require a land-based team.'

Linh spoke up. 'Don't you have people that can do this sort of thing?'

'Plenty... but the thing is that today, with face-recognition technology and the massive number crunching ability of modern computers, the great majority of our operatives would be data matched to other fields of service and would become instantly compromised. We need fresh faces... innocent faces.'

'Do you know who is behind this mission?' Owen asked.

'We're not sure, but we suspect the Japanese.'

'The Japanese?'

'Uh huh. You see, the world's powers have finally stalled—there are no more frontiers... only borders. For hundreds of years the Europeans expanded from the west to dominate new parts of the globe—and the Chinese expanded from the east. The Arab nations controlled trade— mariners sailed further and further over the horizon until they were back where they started. For a few hundred years, nations eyed each other distrustfully and shored up their defences, each convinced of their own supremacy. There were fights, sure, but even the First World War went unreported in the East, as China battled its own demons. The Americans embraced their emerging technologies and Australia gained a very real independence. And most countries chose to ignore their neighbours and live in splendid delusion. Well, now the real powers behind the super powers are jockeying for position, each knowing full well that it is a life and death struggle. Japan is one of those powers. Just one hundred and fifty years ago, Japan was a curiosity on the world stage—a nation of sword wielding samurai warriors and impoverished farmers. The Europeans decided to take advantage of the warlike nature of some of the inhabitants and allowed them to develop, in just a few decades, the world's most advanced navy and the world's most advanced industrial technology.'

'Why?'

'So that Japan could be the strong-arm in the east. The Europeans knew that they would never be able to control China, so they cultivated the Japanese warrior classes to become the best exponents of warfare. They were trained in England, Germany, France and the United States. They were shown how to make the latest in military technology. Just after the turn of the century, the Japanese navy annihilated the Russian fleet on more than one occasion. The Japanese were encouraged to attack Manchuria so that they would have a base on the mainland. Thus, the European powers kept both the Russians and the Chinese under control.'

Linh interrupted. 'I've heard it said that the rise of the Japanese on the world stage has never been adequately explained...'

'Absolutely correct, Linh—it was achieved by the European powers... who built their warships and trained their soldiers... virtually for free—after all, what sort of trade could the Japanese engage in to pay for all of this? It would take a lot of silk to pay for a battle ship.'

'So,' continued Linh, '... the Western powers deliberately created a police nation in the east—one that they knew they would be able to control if they ever got too big for their boots...'

With a chicken wing to her mouth, Francesca nodded vigorously. '... yes, well that is exactly what transpired during the Second World War—one of the many agendas was to rein in the quickly developing Japanese...'

'... because of their imperialist intentions?'

'Actually, no. We are taught that the Japanese had those ambitions, but in fact, they were forced to expand in order to secure resources that they would need for the conflict that they knew was coming. They realised that with the massive, world-wide acceleration in technology, their place in the east as a strong arm for western powers would be short-lived.'

Owen topped up the wine glasses. 'Wow!... I'm actually glad I didn't do history at school—at least I don't have to unlearn stuff. But, how does that all tie in with our sub base?'

'Okay,' Francesca replied, '... it's like this... after the war, Japan courageously reinvented itself. But they have always been mindful of the fact that they are alone... uniquely alone. Other countries have shared heritage—there's a sense of ancestry. We are blended communities. But the Japanese have been isolated by geography and by decree for many, many centuries. They have no bonds with any other nation. As well, after their forays abroad, they have been vilified the world over. So, they retreated into themselves and focused their unique skills to become the world's most superlative technologists. In effect, the entire nation has become one of the handful of global conspirators. The Japanese agenda is to look after itself... which is fair enough. And the way they achieve this is by staying on top in the technology race.'

'Are you saying that the Japanese are one of a group of conspirators that are vying for supremacy?' Linh offered.

'Yep, that's right. They do it out of necessity—not like the other conspirators, who do it out of covetousness.'

Owen and Linh looked at each other. 'Which group are you with?' they managed to get out almost simultaneously.

Francesca avoided their eyes and took a sip of her wine. 'I'm with the group that's looking after your interests.'

The couple pondered this piece of information for a moment.

'So,' said Owen with a sigh, '... getting back to the mission... what's with the subs?'

'Well, we don't know anything for certain. What we do know is that there seems to be a Japanese connection—don't ask me for the details because I don't know—and that the structure being built may be for submarines.'

'Why don't they build their base closer to Japan?' Linh responded.

Francesca eyed the two with a steely intensity. 'Remember... you are sworn to secrecy. This is very, very confidential material that no one would believe if you blurted it to the world and would very likely result in your demise.'

Owen massaged his brow. 'Do we *have* to know this?'

'It doesn't matter if you know... as long as you keep it to yourselves.'

Linh shifted closer to Owen. Owen gave a small nod of assent to Francesca.

'The reason why the base isn't being built in Japan is because their enemies know all the best locations on the Japanese coastline for that sort of thing and they are keeping a close watch. Whereas, the coast of Vietnam is regarded as benign... there's no surveillance by anybody. It's just that we have made the association between some very big construction projects in the area—bridges, buildings, roads—and the import of enormous quantities of concrete and steel—plus the unusual activity off the coast. That's what someone in our organization was paid to do—connect the dots.'

Linh rubbed her eyes. 'So, you want us to be guests at the resort, keep our eyes open, innocently snoop around and... connect some more dots...'

'Yes—but don't think of this as some sort of junket. I want you to be imaginative and daring. You have the benefit of anonymity—you should be able to get away with a lot...'

Owen and Linh exchanged looks.

Francesca arched and stretched. 'I don't expect you to commit to this straight away. But do keep abreast of the news... there'll be something that will rouse your interest in the next few days. But, for now... it's time for me to leave you enchanting people.' She rose from the table. 'Thank you for a lovely evening and a very agreeable wine...'

The trio chatted as they wound their way down the stairs. Francesca shook hands very warmly then let herself out through the glass doors of the foyer.

Chapter Fifteen

Francesca's visit to the Gallery occupied less and less of Owen's mind as he focused on important final stages of the turbine development.

However, the visit continued to prey on Linh's mind as she weighed up all that had been discussed that evening. She especially paid attention to the various news media but noticed nothing of particular significance. The usual political intrigues prevailed... and crime, fires, accidents... pop gossip, sport and superficial bulletins covering world events. There was one story though that, whilst not well fleshed-out, retained traction over a number of days. It concerned the interception of coded signals by ham radio operators around the world who were finding that certain restricted wave bands were being heavily utilised by powerful transmitters, and all amateur operators were being notified to cease monitoring those bands. This story developed initially in Iceland where outraged amateurs, who weren't fully familiar with the rules, managed to get their grievance covered by the national radio broadcaster. The story was dumped pretty quickly, but due to the global networking of the ham radio fraternity, it was picked up in other parts of the world and continued to feature as a curiosity piece in mainstream media bulletins. Predictably, those stories fizzled out until the thread could only be followed on underground, conspiracy blogs.

Linh was curious. She and Owen sat up in bed one night and Googled everything they could find on restriction of the short-wave frequencies. In one of the forums there was mention of the fact that the amount of traffic on the military frequencies was reminiscent of the Cold War days of the sixties. They discovered that regulation of these wave bands had relaxed a lot ever since the military began using microwave frequency satellite communications. Then, with advances in transmitter technology available to amateurs, more and more began to broadcast on these uncluttered airwaves—until now. Interspaced with the jumble of code, there were very clear announcements stating the penalties that would be imposed on those infringing the restrictions.

The young lovers turned to each other.

'Are you thinking what I'm thinking,' Linh said, softly.

Owen slid back and wrapped his arm around Linh's waist. 'I hope so.'

'No... focus for just a little longer, and then you can let Libido off the chain.'

'Oh, right... well, it did occur to me that the reason the military is using shortwave so much is because their usual satellite channels have broken down.'

'And why would that be?'

'Well now, that would be because the satellite overflew a certain spot in Cambodia and got fried... is that what you're thinking?'

Linh slid down alongside. 'Owie, do you think that is what happened?'

'Hmmm... in view of what Francesca said about paying attention to the news... I'd say, probably.'

'Does that mean... war?'

'There's always a war on... it's just not always visible, and more often than not, it's not reported.'

'Wow... you're sounding like a long-time conspirator.' Linh spooned into a comfortable position. 'What does it all mean for us, though?'

Owen absently nuzzled Linh's neck. 'Don't know... don't know. But one thing I have worked out, is that these organisations rely a hell of a lot on casual operators. I mean, in a way, you could be working for the conspirators if you are a teacher... following a prescribed curriculum that propagated a particular world view, or a loans officer issuing housing loans to people who can't afford it in order set up a market crash.'

156

'... on which the conspirators cash in.'

'Exactly.'

Linh pressed into Owen. 'Are you creating an excuse for us to go on a holiday to Vietnam?'

Owen sighed. 'I'm just wondering whether it makes any difference.'

'As long as we're not responsible for kicking off World War Three.'

'There won't be a World War Three.'

'Why not?' She turned and looked into his eyes.

Owen's stare transfixed somewhere distant. 'The various conspirators have got too much to lose if they upset things. They need thriving nations... even with the attendant pollution and racial scuffles and all that... they need strong industries to make all their BMWs and mobile phones... they need vigorous farms and fishing fleets for their fancy foods. What's the point of creating a wasteland? No... there won't be a confla... confag... conflig...'

'...conflagration...'

'...that. Not to say that it won't get nasty at the cutting edge, as it were, of the battle for superiority. I mean, I've seen that first hand.'

'We don't even know which side she's working on. What about Alasdair? Whatever happened to him? We've heard nothing since we came back from Cambodia.'

The two of them were quiet for a while. Outside, cars hissed softly by. In the subdued lighting, the massive beams of the pitched roof looked like the fingers of a protective hand.

'I guess,' Owen said at last, '... we have to decide on whether or not we want to take advantage of any possible, well, advantages that the likes of Francesca can offer us, and then use those benefits in the most ethical way... or, do we cut ourselves off from the people who, let's be honest, have given us some pretty significant insights.'

'Will we be able to resist their manipulative ways?'

Owen suddenly shifted in bed. 'You know what?... I don't think that they actually try to manipulate people. No—they couldn't be bothered! They just plain *buy* them! They've got so much money that they just say, "Do this, for this much money!" and people go, "Okay, sure."'

'... and everyone's a bit player so their conscience is never strained.'

Owen looked dejected. 'Now you're making me feel bad about

accepting the offer.'

They lay in silence.

'Mind you,' Linh mused, '... there are a lot of people who would *love* to be struggling with this matter—whether to accept an offer to holiday at one of the world's premier resorts.'

'Yeah, you're right... let's just do it. Surely there can't be any harm in keeping an eye out for the occasional submarine... or whatever it is we're supposed to be looking for.'

Linh suppressed a wicked smirk and pressed herself against him. '... no harm at all.'

By the morning, a message had appeared on Owen's phone—an "F" followed by a mobile number.

He and Linh showered and dressed and made their way up the street to a coffee shop.

'So,' Owen breathed, after they'd taken a seat in the sunlight, '... are we in?'

Linh nodded with surprising assurance.

'Okay then.' Owen took out his phone and commenced composing a message. When he finished he looked up to see Linh looking at him with an odd intensity. He raised his brow in query.

Linh leant closer. 'Do you feel different knowing that you're a spy?'

Owen rolled his eyes. 'I have no intention of going out of my way to do any spying. If something should fall into our laps, well and good. Otherwise, if they are prepared to send two novices on an expensive vacation in the hope that they'll uncover the vital clue to an international conspiracy, well, too bad... we're not going to do anything rash.'

They had muesli and fruit salad for breakfast and had just been served their coffee when a van pulled up at the kerb. Francesca stepped out of the sliding door. The van drove off.

Owen took a big breath. 'Here we go...'

Francesca looked fresh and lovely. She pulled up a seat without a word.

'Seriously, Francesca,' Owen demanded '... are you camping in that thing? How did you get here so quickly?'

'Ah, yes... sometimes it takes all of my skills to maintain the illusion of glamour. However, I can't dilly-dally. I take it that you are still committed to the mission?'

The two of them nodded in unison.

'Good... the travel details will be sent to your phone. Any questions?'

Owen took a moment to answer. '... ah, well... I was wondering whether or not we are allowed to know where these disguised trawlers are coming from.'

Francesca stood and placed her chair against the table and said in a low voice, 'Sorry, guys... just for the moment, see what you can discover. Oh, by the way... the monitoring crew at the resort appear to have left some time ago... don't really know if there's anything significant for you to do there, but anyhow... keep alert. And, you two are very up-market—you'll be flying in by helicopter from Ho Chi Minh City. Try and look the part. My team thought that a stratospheric superiority complex might be just the excuse you need to get you out of any indiscretions that you might make. Think, spoilt brats... that should do the trick.'

Owen and Linh exchanged apprehensive looks.

'... anyway... have fun.' The van had materialized, double parked, just near their table. Francesca twirled around and strode to the sliding door which had automatically opened. She stepped in and the van silently pulled away.

Linh gave Owen a measured look. 'I don't know whether to feel elated or deflated.'

Owen slowly shook his head. 'This is crazy. Oh, well... let's enjoy our coffee.'

Vườn Quốc gia Núi Chúa, or The Mountain Lord National Park, at about two hundred square kilometres, is a tiny remnant of what Vietnam must have looked like hundreds of years ago—before the forests fell to farmers' axes... and the defoliant, Agent Orange. The Sikorsky S-76 D took about four minutes to traverse the width of the park before it was hovering over the grassy landing area adjacent to the Amanoi Resort administration buildings. From their elevated position, Owen had just enough time to see that the resort was at the head of a small natural harbour, and within a shallow bay created by two capes. He moved forwards so that he was just behind the pilots.

'Go out to sea a little way. I want to take a photo of the resort from the ocean side.'

The pilot, who looked every bit a grizzled veteran and, for all Owen knew, may actually have been a combat pilot here in the early seventies, turned slightly to answer. 'No way, buddy.'

Owen raised his voice fractionally. 'Why the hell not!'

'No-fly zone,' the pilot returned evenly.

Owen grasped the back of the chairs. 'I just want to get a picture of the resort... surely that can't be a problem?'

The pilot made preparations for the landing. 'Sorry, son... civil aviation designated area... can't fly out in the bay.'

Owen allowed a petulant edge to creep into his voice. 'You must be joking!... there's nothing out there. Who's going to know if you overshot the mark by a few kilometres?'

'Rules are rules, buddy... and the flight recorder never lies. Now, sit back down before you make me crash this thing.'

Owen hastily withdrew and scowled at the pilot's eyes looking at him from the cabin mirror.

After the smoothest of landings, Owen and Linh strode off towards a lush knot of trees, each waving their arms about in exaggerated appreciation of their surroundings. Very shortly, stifled cries emanated from a nearby building and, when they turned, they saw a heavy-set gentleman jogging after them, calling their names. They stood still and allowed him to catch up.

'Hello, Mr and Mrs Lucas,' he gushed breathlessly, '... we are honoured to have you as guests...'

'We're thinking of going for a swim,' Linh pronounced, '... where's the pool?'

The man clutched his hands. 'Certainly... certainly,' he laboured between heavy breaths. 'I am the manager. May I introduce myself— my name...'

'Is someone taking care of our luggage?' said Owen sharply. Then, with a gentle swat at Linh's bottom, '... not that we're planning on wearing anything in the pool. We *do* have a completely private pool, don't we?'

'Oh, yes, absolutely,' the man cooed reassuringly, '... yours is the deluxe pavilion with...'

'Deluxe!' protested Linh, 'That's a bit kitsch, isn't it... nowadays *everything* is deluxe. We were expecting something vastly superior to deluxe, isn't that right, Owen!'

Owen's brow creased. 'The pilot *has* taken us to the right place, I hope?'

The man bowed obsequiously and wrung his hands. 'Yes, yes... you are in the grounds of the most exclusive destination in South East Asia—Amanoi Resort. My name is...'

'Do you know what, darling,' Owen placed his arm around Linh and directed her back towards the helicopter, '... I'm thinking that a refreshing cocktail might be just the thing to have pool-side. What do you think?'

Linh giggled as Owen hugged her near. She looked over her shoulder. 'Your website claims to have an excellent bar—is that true?'

'Mrs Lucas, have no fear... our staff are trained to answer your every wish...'

Linh made big eyes and turned away. 'Well, that's a relief because, frankly, that's what I'm used to.'

The man scuttled up beside them. 'If you wouldn't mind coming through reception, we'll hand you your keys and complete a few formalities... if that's not too much trouble.'

Owen looked blithely ahead. 'No, of course not... my name is Owen Lucas, by the way. What's your name?'

'My name is...'

'Oh, look, darling,' Owen pointed, '... there are the tennis courts.'

Amanoi Resort delivered on its promise. The two lovers looked out over the edge of the infinity pool towards the ocean's horizon. Nearby, a floating tray held their cocktails. The temperature of the water was perfect. And they weren't wearing their swimmers.

'Have to maintain appearances... as it were,' Linh had said with an apologetic shrug as they exited the bungalow. 'Anyway, you're used to skinny-dipping.'

161

'Yeah... but that's about fifty kilometres away from the nearest human being!'

Now, the setting sun cast a golden hue on everything, and the sea looked like mercury.

'I feel terrible about the way we're behaving, Owie.'

Owen arched and floated on his back. 'To tell the truth, I'm actually enjoying it. I can't believe we're doing it, but I'm enjoying it.'

'That was clever of you to talk to the pilot.'

'It was, wasn't it. Well, at least we've found out about one restriction without having to make a formal enquiry.'

Linh swam up to Owen and squirted water onto his face. 'There is one slight problem though.'

'What's that?'

'Well, the pavilions are all relatively private. There's no way that we can monitor them without being conspicuous.'

Owen grabbed the metal edge of the pool and rested his chin on his knuckles. 'I'm not interested in the resort. Anyway, Francesca said that the operatives seem to have left. What I'm more interested in is what's happening out to sea. And this is the perfect place to do some sustained snooping.'

'Francesca said that the next flotilla will more than likely arrive tomorrow... every ten days on average.'

'Yeah... what we have to do first up is to get some idea of their speed—with a load and without. We also need to pinpoint their position and how it varies between visits.'

'Sounds like we'll be here for the long haul.'

'Yeah... like that's going to be a hardship. Can you see that boat out there with the mast light?'

'Uh huh.'

'That'll be their marker boat... it stays there to make sure no one runs over the construction site.'

'What's a submarine base, anyway, Owie?'

'I have no idea. Francesca's the one who mentioned it. I would have thought a dry dock would be much more useful... or a surface ship for replenishment purposes. No idea.'

'But, there *is* something out there. How far out is it?'

'Don't know,' Owen looked around, '... but we'll soon find out. Is there anybody about?'

Owen pushed off underwater and glided to the stone pool edge. He propelled himself out of the water and went inside. Moments later he reappeared with binoculars in his hand. He dived towards Linh and surfaced next to her.

She wrapped her arms around his broad shoulders. 'You are such a show-off.'

Owen adjusted the binoculars and peered into them. 'I can't help it if my every movement is an affirmation of a superior being.'

Linh splashed at his face. 'Oh, my god! You've been here one hour and you've become insufferable.'

The light had almost gone. The surface of the pool flickered with dim reflections.

Owen handed the binoculars to Linh. 'Don't you love having conspirators for friends... check it out—waterproof, night-vision, self-focusing, range finder, GPS *and* it takes photos. Pretty cool huh?'

Linh located a water-proof toggle switch on the body. '... *and*, a digital zoom.'

'No way! Give us a look.'

The evening meal in the magnificent communal dining room was a triumph. They were served wonderfully spiced seafood with delicately composed salads and crispy fried sweet potato laced with sweet chilli sauce. Seated in privacy behind screens of intricate wooden lacework, they laughed quietly as they attempted to assess the qualities of the six-hundred-dollar 2010 Lucien Le Moine Chevalier Montrachet they were sipping.

Linh forbad Owen to display any obnoxious behavior. 'I think we've established who we are... let's just become invisible instead.'

'Can't I have a little go at the waiter?'

Linh reached out and tightly gripped Owen's hand. '*Never* upset the waiters! They'll spit in your food.'

Owen raised an eyebrow. 'Is that what *you* do to horrible customers?'

'No, I don't!' Linh studied the desert menu. 'Let us never become rich, Owen... you'd be unbearable to live with.'

Owen studied Linh's face as she perused the card. It was the first time that he had ever seen her even the tiniest bit upset. He gently raised her hand to his lips and kissed her tenderly.

'I've never been a spy before,' he said softly, '... who would you like me to be... Sean Connery... Jason Bourne... Johnny English...'

'I'd like you to be Owen Lucas being Owen Lucas and not taking this adventure too seriously, as you said you would.'

'... hmmm... not too seriously—Johnny English it is, then.'

Linh looked up with a doleful smile. 'I am not sharing that gorgeous bedroom with Johnny English...'

Owen grinned broadly. He steepled his fingers. '... ah, about that...'

'What?'

'Spending the night together.'

'What?'

'It won't be in our comfy, king-size bed, unfortunately.'

'You're not thinking of spending the whole night floating naked on an airbed in the pool, are you?'

Owen laughed, 'No. No, we're going to be sitting on a rock, hugging each other for warmth. It'll be very romantic. We'll bring a bottle of Lucien the Man, or whatever.'

Linh appealed to Owen with an exaggerated pout of displeasure. 'Do we have to?'

'Yeah,' he said, looking serious, '... the boats are due very early in the morning, and we need to be as close to them as possible so that we can gauge their speed... get some idea of their set-up.'

'Are we going to go *hiking*?... at night?' Linh looked aghast.

'Yeah, it'll be ok... you speak the language... and we have night vision goggles.'

'We *have*?' Linh put her hand to her mouth. '... we have?'

Owen casually looked around. 'I'm pretty sure we have. That snorkeling gear that they've kitted us out with is completely unnecessary... all the gear is supplied here. I bet when we have a good look at it, it'll be full of surprises.'

Linh gazed into Owen's eyes. She drew his hand to her and kissed it. 'Have you made up your mind yet?'

'... about?'

'Dessert.'

'Oh, yep... let me have a little look... hmmm...'

'... because I'd like to try the Eggnog mousse with almond Dacquoise, but I'm going to order the café liégeois with Chantilly cream...'

'Excellent choice.' Owen dipped his eyes lovingly at his girl.

Chapter Sixteen

The southern cape that they walked to was only about five kilometres from the resort, most of it via the main road. From there, a track led down to Bãi Hỏm, or, as Linh translated, Turtle Beach. A further scramble of half a kilometer over the moonlit white boulders brought them to the promontory that Owen had decided would make a good position for surveillance.

The initial plan had been to walk along the coast, but after seeing the height of the hills and ridges and the extreme ruggedness of the forested shoreline, Owen quickly determined that that would be impossible. Linh commented that in many ways the cragginess of the landscape was reminiscent of the Aegean seashore. Taking the road was definitely the easier option.

There was hardly any traffic and they'd only had to jump into the bushes a few times to avoid detection. Once they were on the path to Turtle Beach, they donned the night-vision goggles that Owen had correctly guessed were disguised as snorkeling gear, but when the half-moon came up, there was enough light to see by. When they crested a huge rock dome on the promontory, they could see the lights of a cluster of ships a few kilometres out to sea.

'Okay, let's get happening,' Owen breathed heavily. 'We'll park ourselves against this boulder... that'll make a solid reference point... and we may as well sit and be comfortable. Got your pad ready?'

'Affirmative, sir,' Linh replied, '... setting time... now.'

'Well done, corporal.' Owen raised the binoculars to his eyes. '... ready to mark one... mark—one three five point six eight... mark two—one three six point zero five…'

There was a light breeze blowing from the south and they could hear the surf on the rocks below. As pre-arranged, they would do a sighting every five minutes.

Linh shivered and hugged herself to Owen. 'What if they're fishing boats?'

Owen opened his jacket and enfolded Linh. 'Oh, well… it'll be good practice.'

'They *are* very close though.'

'Sure are. We'll know within a couple of readings if they're our target.'

'Target!' Linh scoffed, '… this really is a Boys Own fantasy, isn't it?'

'Better,' Owen kissed Linh's forehead, '… we've got six-star accommodation and I get to go to bed with the communications girl.'

They laughed.

'Mark coming up,' said Linh.

They spent the next four hours monitoring the four ships, travelling in what looked like a square formation, until the sky began to pale ahead of them. Then Linh said a curious thing.

'This rock is beeping…'

Owen turned to her. '… beeping?'

'I've been lying with my head against it between marks, and I can distinctly hear an electronic beeping sound.'

The dawn was gathering quickly. Owen stood back and inspected the boulder. It wasn't very large, but it was handily positioned for them on the top of the rock dome. As well, it appeared unusually slab sided which had made it convenient to lean against. He tapped it lightly. There was a degree of reverberation that would not have occurred with a natural boulder.

'Well, well,' Owen murmured, '… an artificial rock. Now why would that be?'

Linh ran her hands over the structure. 'It's very well done, isn't it… the colours and the lichens. Obviously, it's got something to do with the sub project.'

Owen managed to clamber on top. 'There's a lift point up here. It must have been deposited by helicopter.'

Linh looked out to sea. '... so, it's a communications beacon.'

'Of a sort,' grunted Owen as he jumped down, '... I bet it's a positioning device... to help the ships place their load in exactly the right spot. There'll be another one of these on the cape up there,' he pointed northwards, '... allowing the ships to triangulate their position.'

'Why don't they just use GPS?... that's accurate enough isn't it?'

'Especially military specs... but maybe that's not secret enough for them... so they've set this up... no risk of eavesdropping. I bet that's what the technicians were doing here—coordinating the lasers.'

The sun was about to rise. In the intensifying light, Linh scrutinised the uneven surface of the structure. 'You're right, Owie... there's a little aperture just here...'

Owen had a quick look at the spot. '... hmmm... c'mon, we'd better get out of here. This place will be lit up like stage in a minute.'

They made their way over the piled boulders back to Turtle Beach and commenced the climb back to the road along the narrow track. Just before six o'clock they were walking past the tennis courts on the way to their pavilion.

A voice from behind hailed them. 'Good morning, Mr and Mrs Lucas!'

The couple turned around.

Linh clutched at Owen's arm. 'Oh, my god—it's him! Be nice, Owen.'

The manager approached with a jaunty stride. 'Ah, you have been out already... how good for you to have the exercise.' He looked with mild surprise at the rucksack on Owen's shoulders.

Owen looked over the top of the man's head. 'Yes, we photographed the sunrise this morning from a more natural setting... without all the shacks and clutter getting in the way.'

The manager looked vaguely alarmed at the mention of shacks and was about to defend his establishment when Owen cut in.

'Would you mind sending down some breakfast... croissants... cream and coffee... some fruit... that sort of thing.'

The manager convulsed with a little bow. 'Of course. I will attend to it straight away.' He was about to dismiss himself but remained examining Owen's face.

Owen was regarding the manager in a most avuncular manner, his eyes creasing with the sincerest of smiles. He held out his hand, and when the manager took it, he bowed slightly. 'I'm sorry, but I haven't allowed you to introduce yourself.'

The manager straightened. 'I am Abelino Dinh. My father's family have lived here for many years—my mother's family is from China.'

Owen gently shook Abelino's hand. I must apologise for my rudeness, Abelino, but we were playing a little game that, well, went beyond a joke.'

'Aha... I am glad that you tell me this, because we were going to poison you on the last day of your visit.'

Owen guffawed half-heartedly. Linh looked appalled.

Abelino's grin transformed to a full-throated laugh. 'I, in turn, must apologise,' he snorted between breaths, '... for telling a joke that has gone beyond a joke... is that correct?' He clapped a massive hand on Owen's shoulder and gently spun the two of them in the direction they'd been travelling. 'Do not let me uphold you... breakfast will be down directly... and I will personally taste each component just to be sure.' Again, he hooted with laughter then waved his arms dismissively, '... another joke!... another joke...'

On their way past the pagoda lake, Linh hissed, 'See! That's what comes of being rude and impolite... you could end up being poisoned.'

Owen took Linh gently by the shoulders and turned her to him. 'I haven't kissed you yet, today,' his voice caught with emotion, '... may I?' He brushed a few stray strands of hair from her eyes and touched his lips to hers. They lingered in a caress, feeling the warmth of the morning's rays on their skin.

Linh draped her arms over Owen's shoulders and lifted her mouth harder against his. He had been such a boy when she'd followed him to the helicopter that night. It seemed like a long time ago. It was different now—just as exciting, but there was so much that she loved about him, and it troubled her that outside forces might change things between them. When he stopped to appreciate her in moments like this, she felt reassured that he would always see things from the best perspective.

She dug her nails lightly into the back of his head. 'We're having fun, aren't we?' she whispered.

Owen hefted her off her feet. 'We sure are,' he grunted with satisfaction. He lowered her to the ground. '... you know what we should do?'

Linh clasped Owen's head between her hands. 'I know what we'd *like* to do—have breakfast then jump into bed... but what we *should* do is set up the monitoring gear on the terrace and *then* have breakfast.'

'... and maybe pull up the sun lounges so we can do the readings in comfort.'

'Now you're talking! Actually, I am really hungry. Can't wait for a croissant.'

As they ambled to their pavilion, Linh asked, 'Why did you suddenly decide to be nice to Abelino?'

Owen shrugged. 'I just realised that there's no need for us to monitor anything in the actual resort... so, we don't need a cover. I didn't want give him any more grief.'

The rest of the morning was spent lazing on the terrace and falling into the pool when they got too warm. The boats had obviously reached their destination, about four kilometres off the shore, and, still in a square, were positioning into a new heading. They took pictures every ten minutes and documented the range. As well, Owen had worked out that the speed of the fleet had been around three kilometres per hour as it passed them at roughly ninety degrees from their position on the cape. This had made the calculation very simple.

'That's slower than walking pace,' Linh remarked.

'Yes... it is *very* slow. They must be towing a huge structure. But, if in fact it is made from concrete, as the intel suggested, then it would be far too heavy for four ships to carry.'

'... unless it has its own buoyancy,' Linh ventured.

'Very true. Whatever it is, it's completely submerged, and creates a lot of drag.'

Linh licked the cream off a strawberry. 'Maybe the thing has pockets of air in it—I don't know, just a thought.'

'You're absolutely right, Linh... very large pockets of air. Let me see... where's that pad?... the specific gravity of concrete is about two point four... that would mean that for a concrete object to have neutral buoyancy...'

'I'm going to make a green tea.' Linh rose from the recliner.

'...uh huh... neutral buoyancy, would be, one divided by two point four...' Owen scribbled on the pad, '... equals about point four. So, sixty percent of the structure has to be hollow... that's a *lot*.' He drew a circle on the page and then a smaller concentric circle. '... let's see, take a radius of, say ten... area equals ten squared times three point one four two... three hundred and forty-two... now an inner circle of say... uh oh... this requires... Linh!' he called, '... can you bring my phone when you come out?'

'I thought we weren't going to use our phones.' Linh replied from inside.

'Oh, no... calculator.' He continued to scribble until Linh came out with the tea.

'What are you working out?' she said as she handed over the phone.

'Well, I've calculated that for the concrete structure to float just on the surface, about sixty percent of its volume would need to be air spaces. Now, I'm just going to see what dimensions that would translate into if it were a circular structure... let's see...'

Owen tapped away at his phone while Linh gazed out over the rim of the infinity pool to the boats in the distance.

'It's strange,' she mused, '... that they are building this structure in full view of a whole bunch of tourists with nothing better to do than to gaze mindlessly out to sea.'

'... mindlessly, being the operative word... probably ideal, actually...'

'... hmmm... probably...'

Owen held the note book out for Linh to see. 'Look... say the object was fifty metres in diameter, a flat cylinder... which I think might be close, given the tightness of their formation ... then, with an inner circle of forty metres, completely hollow, the structure would have neutral buoyancy...'

'... it wouldn't sink...'

'Correct... but the flat sides would need to be covered... waterproofed... in order to create the air space...'

'It would be easier to create lots of little air spaces I imagine... sort of like a tessellation of geometric shapes...'

'Hell's bells!' Owen exclaimed, '... *I'm* the one that did engineering... but you're perfectly correct. Nowadays when they pour foundations for houses, they position Styrofoam blocks in strategic places in order to use less concrete but still maintain the strength. They could have done the same thing here.'

Linh sighed heavily. '... and the day started out so romantically.'

Owen moved over the recliner and wrapped his arms around her legs. '... and it will resume its romance as soon as we nut out this problem.'

Linh produced a satisfied expression. 'Alright then... so, what are we tackling?'

'Well, first thing... the likely shape of the object, given that the boats were pretty much in a square formation.'

'... um, a square, I suppose?'

'Yep. And a circle.'

'... a cross...'

'Uh huh... and basically any other irregular shape, bearing in mind that it has to have sixty percent air. But if we assume a uniformly geometric shape so as to maximise the air pocket ratio, it comes down to a square and a circle...'

'... and you favour?'

'... the circle... because it's stronger... and somehow, makes more sense.'

'... like for an underwater dome... it would take the pressure better.'
Owen nodded solemnly.

'Wow!... you think they're making an underwater habitat?'

Owen stared vacantly beyond the pool.

'Owie?'

Without altering his countenance, Owen nodded. '... they *are* building a habitat... a moveable habitat... commonly called, a submarine.'

Linh's brow creased. 'A submarine?... out of concrete?'

Owen regained his composure and quickly scanned the area. He moved nearer Linh and spoke in hushed tones. 'I just realised that a whole lot of hollow circular segments could be joined together, right... to make a long, hollow tube. All you'd have to do is make a suitable nose and tail piece, and you've got yourself a sub.'

Linh had a look of doubt. 'Is it really that simple?'

Owen smiled. 'Well, no... all you'd have would be a shell—a very big shell... but then there'd be the fitting out... to make it rise and sink in the water and to propel it forwards... even to steer it!... and that's without any weapons or defensive equipment.'

Now Linh had the distant look. '... unless it was being used in a different way.' She looked intently into Owen's eyes. 'I imagine that a sub like that, with a thick reinforced concrete skin around it, would be able to resist a fair bit of pressure.'

Owen stared back. 'I take your point.' He rose, grabbed the binoculars, and walked to the edge of the terrace. In the distance, the boats had realigned themselves so that the diamond square formation pointed to the horizon.

Linh came and put her arms around him. 'Do you remember what Francesca said about the abysmal plain, or something?'

'Abyssal plain... yeah, thousands of feet deep and right in the middle of the most hotly contested bit of real estate on earth.'

Linh hugged him tighter. 'Owie... do you think we should get off this terrace?'

Owen nodded slowly. 'I've got an idea... just in case we *are* being watched from one of the boats, let's do something that would give them the impression that we are oblivious of their surveillance and completely uninterested in what they're doing.'

'... hmmm... what did you have in mind?'

He turned towards her and spun her so that her back was to the sea. '... well, this for starters,' and he deftly unclipped her bikini top.

Linh reached up with her mouth. 'Owen Lucas,' she murmured, '... I don't recall Johnny English doing something like this.'

Chapter Seventeen

Owen and Linh spent the next day loitering around the resort, playing a bit of hit-and-giggle tennis, having a spa, a massage and aromatherapy—the benefits of which they probably negated by having a couple of cocktails afterwards. At sunset, as they sat in the "pagoda of serenity" and contemplated the changing colour of the sea, they both realised they'd had enough luxury and that it was time to leave.

'... might keep it a surprise though, just in case Abelino hasn't told the cook about the change of plan,' Owen voiced, as they walked along the cliff tops back to their place.

'Well, we could use the resort as a base... but I'd rather just cut loose, maybe make our way up to Hanoi. What do you think?'

Owen had his arm around Linh and squeezed her near. 'I wouldn't dream of it... unless I was doing it with you.'

Linh made a little sound of pleasure.

Once inside the pavilion, they were at a bit of a loss. They refused to watch television or scroll up a movie. Their bellies were completely full so they didn't feel the need to snack. They'd agreed that it was fatuous to play cards in a place like this, so they sat on the couch with the note pad and commenced designing the house that they would like to live in.

Both of them had arrived at the same philosophical conclusion— that the happiest home was a small one. Having seen how some of their wealthy friends and acquaintances had achieved their dream of owning a big house and having observed how the huge spaces effectively separated the family, they'd concluded that a cosy home—in fact, a minimalist home—would be the most pleasurable living environment.

Linh recalled a visit to a big house, where they spent the entire time perched on stools in a kitchen big enough to service a restaurant, while the host doled out take-away that they ate while watching a game show on the second television.

'... and big houses are expensive to heat and cool... all that glass.'

'... and how can you shut away your baby in a room of their own?'

Yep, a small house sounded exciting.

They were having a good time.

Linh stretched and yawned. 'You know what I might do?... seeing as this is our last night...'

Owen scratched her back. 'What might you do?'

'Ooh, that's good... lower... I might stroll up to the bar and get us a glass of port to help us sleep.'

'We'll get it sent down...'

'No... it's just up the path... and there are fairy lights the whole way.'

Owen absently turned to the page with his calculations for the theoretical submarine. 'Oh, okay... I'll be waiting for you.'

Linh kissed him on the cheek and slid off the lounge.

The idea of a concrete submarine seemed absurd. How would you power such a thing? It was massive. If it was fifty metres in diameter then it could easily be four times as long.

... two hundred meters! You could create an ecosystem inside it... but where would the energy come from deep down in the ocean... ocean vents! Super-heated water could be an energy supply... if you put steel tubes into the vent—a radiator—heat exchanger... that could run turbines for electricity... lights for photosynthesis, electrolysis of water for oxygen... and hydrogen... for fuel... how would you use the fuel? Explode it in a chamber of water and jet the water at the stern... steerage as well!...

Owen stood up. The explosion of ideas unsettled him. Would it all be possible? He looked down at the note pad again. He saw something that he'd completely missed—the page with his calculations had half of the perforations ripped. He picked it up and examined it closely.

They'd been very careful with the note pad—it contained all of the observation data that they had collected the previous day... not that it would make any difference now—they'd worked out what was going on. But the rip!... why? And only on the concrete calculations. He was certain that the pad had been carefully replaced in the front pocket of his back pack. He'd wanted to keep it neat. And now the page was half torn out... as though someone had changed their mind at the last second...

Owen ran for the door and sprinted up the lighted path. The pavilions were spaced well apart for privacy, and theirs was the most remote one—right above the cliffs. The bar pavilion was a good three hundred metres away—a charming stroll when one had nothing better to do, but a hell of a long way to sprint. He thought of Linh—he thought of a person who knew why they were here. Why hadn't they taken the page? Why hadn't they taken a photo? Were they coming back? What would be the advantage of taking Linh? Where would they take her? But it was just a whim... to get a drink... they can't have planned on it. But *someone* had looked at the pad. *Someone* was onto them.

His chest burned but he felt strong. He'd always been a good runner. The rough concrete was ripping up his feet.

Where would she be? Close by? In a car on the road? Please, no... they should never have taken this assignment.

Where would she be? There were no proper roads in this part of the resort... just paths big enough for golf buggies. The entrance was a good kilometre away. If he could get to the admin building, there was no other way out. How long had she been gone? He'd been too absorbed in his stupid submarine theory...

He rounded a hairpin bend and struck out the last fifty metres to the bar. It was well lit and quite busy... and he was wearing nothing more than pyjama shorts. He burst through the door.

Linh looked at him with incredulity and nearly dropped the two dessert glasses of port. She hastily put them down at someone's table as Owen leapt to her. The hubbub of conversation ceased—only Owen's gasping of air broke the silence. He hugged Linh awkwardly then bent double with exhaustion.

She whispered in his ear, '... is everything alright?'

Owen nodded and panted. He grabbed her by the hand and led her to the door.

The barman came and stood by them. 'Is everything alright, Mr Lucas?'

Owen leant against the door and sucked in a few deep breaths. '... yes... everything, despite appearances... is absolutely perfect... absolutely perfect...'

Linh stroked Owen's arm. 'My god, Owen... what happened?'

He placed his hands on her shoulders and his forehead against hers. '... I thought I'd lost you...'

'Lost me?'

'... yeah... to drink. Were you really going to down two glasses of port?'

Linh looked at the staring faces. She pushed Owen through the doorway. 'Very funny.'

They commenced walking down the pathway. Owen was now very conscious of the rawness of his feet—but nothing could intrude on the relief he felt at having Linh by his side. He moaned softly with the emotion and took some extra big breaths.

Linh steered him to a bench set amongst the shrubs. 'Owie... you're all clammy. What on earth happened?'

They sat down. Owen slumped with his elbows on his knees, holding tightly to Linh's hand. At last his breathing began to settle. He raised Linh's hand to his mouth and rested it there. The night breeze eddied through the garden and rustled the leaves.

Linh held herself close to him. 'You'll get chilled, Owie... we'd best go inside.'

That was good advice, and Owen smiled and looked up in acknowledgement.

He was about to explain his behaviour when the sound of voices issued from further down the path. The two of them stayed still and quiet, out of a desire for privacy, more than any other reason. A man strode suddenly past their hidden alcove. He was speaking intently into a small walkie-talkie and passed by without noticing the couple. The distorted reply from the radio faded as the man receded into the distance.

Linh put her hand over Owen's mouth. The moonlight was enough for him to see the fear on her face. He looked at her with bated breath. Now, *she* was becoming informed of their predicament.

'They're looking for us,' Linh whispered. She withdrew her hand from Owen's mouth.

'Vietnamese?' Owen queried.

'No... Japanese. I picked up, "he ran off after the woman." That's all...'

'You know Japanese?'

'A bit... I did it in high school... did an exchange for one term.'

'You never told me that.'

'Owen, we're being hunted! Is that why you ran after me?'

He nodded. 'They found the note pad. They must be from the ship... must have seen us taking sightings. Now they've sent a posse after us.'

Linh's eyes were as round as Owen had ever seen. 'What are we going to do?... I'm in a singlet top and you're in shorts decorated with little surf boards.'

Owen rubbed his face with both hands. 'Well, at least we're hidden.'

'We can't go back to our place, can we?'

He shook his head.

'All our stuff is there... we won't even be able to make it through the country... we'll have to steal a boat. God! I'm going to be a boat person again.'

'You were a *boat* person?'

'No... I'm just letting you know that I haven't lost my sense of humour.'

Owen snorted with laughter.

Hurried footsteps approached them from up the path. The two of them withdrew deeper into the shrubbery. A portly gentleman marched past.

Owen leapt out from behind the bushes and whispered hoarsely, 'Abelino!'

The manager halted and spun around... to be confronted by Owen standing half naked in the garden with his finger to his lips.

Owen beckoned the manager to join him in the shrubbery.

'Mr Lucas?'

Linh popped up above the shrubs. Both of them signalled for silence.

Casting a quick glance up and down the path, the manager joined the couple in the garden alcove. 'This better not be another joke that has been taken too far,' he warned.

Owen protested with both hands. 'No, no, no... Abelino, we are in serious trouble. We have been involved in something,' he held his breath with indecision, '... and now there are people after us.'

Owen and Linh could not have hoped for a better response from the resort manager. He looked furtively around, then ushered them further into the concealment of the bushes.

Gone was the affable host. Abelino Dinh leaned forward like an admonishing teacher. 'So, *you* are the reason for their presence... it all makes sense now. They came in one of the ship's tenders earlier today. Some of our staff reported them lurking about. We searched for them but they eluded us. Then we had another report about an hour ago, that they come by road. Now, the barman contacts me and tells me that you are behaving strangely. I was just heading down to your pavilion to see what the matter was.'

Linh held the manager's shoulder. 'Thank you, Abelino... we are in a lot of strife.'

He gave a prolonged sniff. 'Are you, indeed?' He eyed them both doubtfully.

Owen tried his best to appear composed. 'We need our gear, and a way out of here... is there any way that you can help us?'

The manager stroked his moustache. 'I can arrange something. I will bring the linen buggy past here... you will be able to hide under the sheets. I will send someone down to get your luggage. Will they be in any danger if they enter your pavilion?'

'God no!' Owen blurted, '... it's *us* they want.'

Abelino made no move to leave. 'And why is it that these sailors would want so desperately to meet with you?'

Linh looked anxiously at Owen.

He could see no value in dissembling the truth. 'We've been asked to monitor what is going on out to sea... with those ships. We must have been seen while we were observing them from our terrace. Now they want to find out what we've learned.'

The manager's eyes glinted in the moonlight. In the shadows of the garden, his bulk seemed to be accentuated... and not all of it was benign.

Owen suddenly remembered the size of his hands when he'd finally allowed the manager to introduce himself.

'And, may I enquire about what you have learned?' asked Abelino.

Owen raised upturned palms. 'Well, *nothing* at this stage,' he declared, '... we've plotted their position, but honestly... I have no idea what's going on. Somebody at the office suggested that they might be setting up an oil rig... I wouldn't know...'

'Your wife works for the same company?'

'No!... no, no. Linh and I are just making the most of this assignment.'

'Just a couple enjoying some casual espionage.'

Owen had never felt so helpless in his life... being interrogated in his pyjamas.

The manager laid a heavy hand on Owen's chest. 'I choose to believe you, Mr Playboy... who arrives in a helicopter and drinks six hundred-dollar wine. You have stirred up these no-good sailors who have invaded my domain, so I, Abelino, will assist you to flee.'

Owen gave a resigned sigh. He'd never been a convincing liar.

Linh whispered, 'Thank you, Abelino.'

The sound of running feet galvanised the manager. He deftly stepped out onto the path and commenced walking. Two of the Japanese crewmen almost ran into him. They looked with suspicion towards the alcove. One of the men made to enter the garden. The manager pulled him back by the collar and kneed him in the small of his back. Anticipating the attack from behind by the other sailor, Abelino lashed out with a back-handed clout that landed square on the side of the man's head. He fell senseless to the ground. The other crewman had twisted painfully to confront his assailant and promptly received a thudding punch to his nose. In mere seconds, the two of them had been stretched out unconscious on the grass.

Abelino reached into his pocket and retrieved a two-way radio. He spoke into it in Vietnamese. Then he returned the radio and rubbed his knuckles.

Owen and Linh raised their heads above the shrub they'd hidden behind. Neither of them could think of anything appropriate to say.

Abelino stepped over one of the men and approached them. 'I have called for the buggy,' he said in a low voice, '... as well as some handcuffs.'

Owen made a helpless gesture. 'You handled yourself extremely well, sir.'

Abelino smiled distantly. 'Yes, it's been a while.'

'A while?' Linh probed.

The manager moved nearer to them. 'I took on this job when I retired as police chief in Da Nang.' He reached out and clasped them both on the shoulder. 'What say we get you on a flight back home as quickly as possible? I can deal with this,' and he waved his arm towards the two sailors, '... but I can't promise you protection if for some reason the hunt for you gets more serious. At this stage, it's just a ship's crew... who knows who they'll send tomorrow.'

Chapter Eighteen

They'd been away for less than a week. Everyone was surprised to see them back so soon. It was no secret that they were destined for Amanoi Resort—it was all part of establishing credibility just in case they were investigated.

To add to the speculation, the two lovers seemed very subdued. Had they argued? It seemed very out of character for either of them.

Owen had told his dad the whole story, even his speculation about the submarine construction.

Don spent a lot of time shaking his head in disbelief. 'Makes you wonder, doesn't it, Owie... where the world is headed. When are you going to be debriefed?'

'Dunno, Dad... no doubt Francesca will appear out of nowhere at some time.'

'I have to say, mate... that was a pretty spectacular bit of deduction that you made...'

'Yeah... it *is* a bit of a leap. But, just thinking about how the boats formed up later in the day, makes me even more certain that they were progressively flooding some of the compartments and allowing the section to flip into a vertical position. They probably have some huge jig on the sea bed that aligns the segments to the growing sub... probably has massive hydraulic jacks powered by a compressor on the ship that pushes the segment against the previous one...'

'... tapered alignment holes... that sort of thing...'

'... exactly. And, bear in mind that they can maintain neutral buoyancy the whole time. It's not as though they have to deal with the massive weight of the thing... it's just suspended in the water...'

'It's bloody brilliant, mate... it's mind boggling actually. And you reckon they could use hydrogen to propel the thing?'

'I think so... hydrogen and oxygen... in a water-filled chamber... combing in a massive explosion to create a jet of water. The only thing I'm not sure of is whether the reaction creates a net vacuum as it cools and condenses.'

Father and son ruminated on this for a moment.

'Probably does, son... but the thing would be to continue adding hydrox to the mix and convert the condensation into steam.'

For the first time since his return from Vietnam, Owen's face lit up. 'You're right, Dad... you're right. *And*, the contracting gas will help to draw in water on the intake cycle!'

Don shook his head in wonderment. 'You are a dead-set inventor, aren't you,' he slapped his son on the leg, '... anyhoo, a bit closer to home and everything mundane—the engine demonstration stand is finished ... we can think about making a few presentations.'

'That's great, Dad... yeah, we've got our own secret project to focus on...'

However, Owen found it very hard to marshal his thoughts. He felt depleted... unconnected. He told Linh.

'You're feeling used... that's what you're feeling,' she said matter-of-factly. 'I felt the same way. Think about it—we spent five short days living the high life as international spies... like Abelino said, drinking six hundred-dollar bottles of wine... we think we have uncovered a secret plan to build the world's deepest diving submarine... we were the target of a pretty intensive manhunt... we escaped only by incredibly good luck... we can't tell a living soul, apart from your dad, about our adventure... and you're wondering why you can't pick up where you left off...'

Owen knew then that he would never be able to negotiate the complexities of life without this wonderful woman. 'You're absolutely right, Linh... you're absolutely right.'

They were lying on the day bed. Linh cradled Owen's head in her lap. 'It's not your fault that you haven't worked that out... you've got so much to think about and plan for at the moment. But I've been waiting on tables... I've had plenty of time to think,' she stroked his forehead, '... you are experiencing the malaise of the conspirator—an inability to make meaningful connections... theirs is a life of perpetual disassociation.'

The sound of Linh's voice almost brought Owen to tears. He loved her so much.

He told her.

Linh lowered her head and kissed him. '... and you know that I love you, Owie... very much.'

Owen turned his head and kissed Linh on the thigh. Her skin was so real... her leg was so comforting. He had never felt so close to her.

A few days later, the turbine team were sitting around the scarred and stained dining table in the workshop, brainstorming the best way to market the motor. Everyone was in favour of actually producing the engine in a product, mainly because it would continue the hands-on involvement that the team was used to, rather than negotiating licensing agreements, which could take years and still expose the invention to predation by faceless multi-nationals. Incorporating the turbine in an everyday product would unequivocally establish their right to the intellectual property over any other claim. As well, the marketing benefits of being the first to launch such a product would be that they could create a generic identity before any competitors had time to promote themselves. The marketing expert that they had on board referred to "brand privilege" and "pre-emptive loyalty" and other mind-bending axioms.

This was all fascinating stuff to Owen, although he freely admitted to himself that his strength lay in design. He began to daydream.

The problem with turbines was that they had a limited rev range. They revved very high, sure... but the difference between say, forty thousand revs per minute and fifty thousand revs—ten thousand extra revs per minute!—was only twenty-five percent. Not that much extra power. A car engine, on the other hand, produced useable power at two thousand revs and, if you increased that by just another two thousand revs—a one hundred percent increase in revs—you'd have massive extra power. This was one of the reasons that turbines had failed to make it in automotive applications—the difficulty of developing suitable gearing for a high-speed motor in a vehicle that went from standing still, to fast.

His turbine, on the other hand, could idle at a few hundred revs and reach maximum power at twenty thousand revs in a few seconds. However, despite the low rotational speed for a turbine, the power curve was squished right up to the maximum rev end, with no meaningful power below that. There had to be a way of...

It was then that he conceived the ultimate iteration of his turbine motor.

Owen rose from his seat and went to the whiteboard. The others stopped in their discussion and followed his progress.

From a distance, Don examined Owen's blank face—he'd seen that look before. He waved the others back to the discussion. 'Leave him... he's alright,' he said.

In the days after Owen's epiphany, there was a noticeable change in his demeanour. His vitality returned and he became his engaging old self again.

He didn't restrain himself from celebrating around Linh; at first, he'd been very conscious of the inspiration that he was experiencing compared to the frustration that she was experiencing.

But she had set him straight. 'No, no... don't think like that. Our circumstances are very different... life is not all equal. You *must* celebrate your successes... your genius. Not to do so would be bad for you. *You* celebrate your successes, and *I* won't hold it against you... how about that?'

Not that Owen had *actually* experienced success—he just had an idea. But typically, an idea was worth more to him than tangible progress or reward. He couldn't help himself from describing the workings of his new concept to Linh and was continually amazed at her ability to interpret mechanical relationships.

And she felt a growing satisfaction at her ability to understand the subtleties of the physics involved. She applied her critical thinking to contesting Owen's assumptions about the performance of the motor, challenging him to support his claims.

Owen took it very seriously. He brought her to the lab.

Wearing earmuffs, he showed her the portable demonstration stand and fired up the turbine. She operated the throttle and watched in fascination as the needle climbed on the rev counter. Now she could feel a connection to the project. She assessed the virtues of the turbine with a revitalised objectivity; what, in fact, would be the best way to market the motor? ... how would a woman respond to this new technology? ... which domestic, everyday gadgets would benefit from reinterpretation with turbine power? ... could it be miniaturised?

They had a cup of tea and tossed around ideas, reaching across the old table every now and again to hold hands. Owen was thoroughly enjoying the moment.

They switched off the lights and closed the security screens and walked out into the sunlit carpark. A large white sedan was parked in front of the workshop. The front doors opened and two men in suits stepped out. In unison, they adjusted their coats and stood holding their hands loosely in front of them.

'Let me guess,' Owen sighed, '... you're from occupational health and safety and you've come to check that we've been wearing our earmuffs... am I right?'

'Get in the car, Owen,' the passenger said with peculiar clarity.

The driver walked to the boot of the car.

Owen shielded Linh. '... ah, no... it's okay, I've got my own car,' and he pointed to the Beetle parked two spaces away.

'Get in the car,' the man said again, '... or we blow up the workshop.'

Owen frowned with disbelief. 'Oh... *blow up* the workshop... with what?'

The second man stepped from behind the open boot with a grenade launcher levelled at his hip. The other one opened the rear door.

It was a Sunday—the carpark was empty. Owen did a quick scan. The industrial area was deserted. These blokes would probably get away with it.

... if this is Francesca's idea of a summons, she's being a bit theatrical... she doesn't need to operate like this, after the relationship we've built. So, who the hell are these guys?

186

The second man lifted the launcher to his shoulder and spread his stance.

Owen couldn't wait any longer. He turned and pressed the car keys into Linh's hand. 'You go home, Tot... I've got to go with them... we have no choice...'

Linh gave him a level look. 'I can't call for help... if they become trapped, it'll end badly for you.'

Owen nodded. They kissed.

One of the men called out, 'Give your phone to your girlfriend!'

He did as he was told, then turned and walked to the car.

The car drove swiftly through the suburbs into the heart of the city. Owen sat in the back seat and weighed up his options. There were none. His two abductors, who looked like corporate bouncers, obviously felt no threat from him by leaving him unrestrained. If he leapt out at the traffic lights, they would just come around again later and make sure it didn't happen again. He asked them whether they worked for Francesca and received no reply. The car turned into a private underground carpark in Edward Street. Owen sighed and slumped. He didn't know what to think.

The car stopped in a bay and the two men unbuckled. Owen let himself out and stood by as the men got out. They motioned him towards a service lift and waited in silence until the doors slid open. They stepped in, but Owen hesitated.

'Get in!' one of them barked.

Owen closed his eyes and moved slowly into the lift. He began to pant.

'What the hell's wrong with you?'

Owen dismissed the question with a curt wave and remained standing with his eyes closed.

'He's got claustrophobia.'

Owen nodded weakly. '... yes... but I'll be okay...'

If Francesca had anything to do with this, then he had to prepare in whatever way he could. She knew that he was prone to fainting... why not add to the embarrassing list of weaknesses.

The lift doors opened. Owen was the first one out. The place looked abandoned. There were no business plaques on the walls and no signs on the doors. The men led him down the corridor to the end door. They opened it and beckoned for him to enter. The room was quite large with no windows... and absolutely bare except for two steel tube chairs. One of them was obviously for him because one of the men indicated he should sit. In the other chair sat Francesca, poised and smiling. Diagonally behind her stood a rather severe looking woman with her arms folded in front of her. He heard the door being locked behind him. Then, the two men walked to opposite corners of the room and faced him.

... well and truly covered...

Francesca looked quite gorgeous, with her dark hair piled rather whimsically, and wearing a short dress with black stockings and gold strap heels. She sat upright with her hands in her lap.

Owen tried to look bewildered. 'Francesca... how unexpected...'

'Owen,' she articulated, '... how are you?'

'I'm okay, now,' he said a little feebly, '... the lift... you know...'

'Oh, my goodness!... you really are a delicate creature aren't you... I should never have sent you on that assignment.' She exaggerated a frown. 'However, you did very well, didn't you?... you and your little sidekick. I'm sorry it's taken so long to get back to you... I've been tied down with other business.'

The woman behind her made a movement and glanced at one of the men in the corner.

Owen waved away the apology. 'To be honest, I hoped that you'd given up on us, seeing as how we returned early with just a page full of observations that you could have gotten from a satellite.'

Francesca laughed abruptly. 'No, you did much better than that.'

Owen spread his hands in an apologetic gesture.

... I have lovers... lots and lots of lovers...

She leant forward and put a knuckle to her mouth. 'I'm told that you have made some astonishing deductions from your poolside vantage point... why don't you tell me about them.'

Is that how they trapped you, Francesca?... you got picked up in some high-class bar...

'Owen?... you are obliged to give me a debrief, you know.'

'Yes... sorry, I was just thinking about what it might have been that gave you the impression that I was in possession of more information.'

'Well,' she said with a hint of hesitation, '... it's this,' and she looked at one of the men in the corner. He came forward and pulled a piece of paper from his breast pocket. He unfolded it and held it for Owen to inspect. It was a photo image of his calculations from the note pad.

So, someone was about to tear the page out when they realised that a photo would be better.

'You see, Owen,' Francesca continued, folding her arms suddenly, '... these gentlemen—and I might add that that is a very generous appellation—have come to the conclusion that your scribblings about buoyancy ratios and so forth are very close to the mark. We just aren't quite sure what that mark is. We were hoping that you would tell us.'

I would have told you, you know that. I would have told you everything... why bring these thugs into it? And your make-up? You're always so immaculate...

'Owen?... are you alright? You seem very distant.'

'No, I'm okay...' he pulled at his collar, '... it's just that...' he clutched at his throat, '... I need...'

I need to distract these guys so that I can have a really good look at your ankles to see if they are in fact zip-tied to the chair leg... because, despite a fair amount of animation, you haven't moved your legs once...

Francesca appealed to one of the men. 'He's doing it again... having one of his fainting spells. He's hopeless... it's certain types of stress... that's what it says in his file.'

Owen rose unsteadily to his feet. He moaned softly and held his head in his hands. 'Sit down, buddy! Sit down,' one of the men shouted.

But Owen didn't sit down. He remained in the same spot and began gagging. His body began to spasm. With a stricken grimace, he looked directly at one the men in the corner and gaped alarmingly. He wobbled on his feet and lurched towards Francesca. The two men leapt out of their respective corner to intercept him, but not before Owen, crying and dribbling, had stumbled into the woman behind Francesca. The two men tried to pull him away, but all four of them toppled towards the wall. The woman lashed out at Owen with her fists, but he shoved his foot in behind her leg and she fell to the floor. Owen landed heavily on top of her, making sure that his knee plunged deep into her belly. She screamed and scratched at his face. All the while he gurgled and hissed and flailed his arms about. The men had a good grip on him by now and attempted to reef him into an upright position, but Owen clung tightly with one hand to the woman's clothing so that the men fell towards him again.

At the same time, Francesca was yelling, 'Don't kill him, he's got the information!

Owen's tongue came out. One eye looked into the distance, the other at his nose. He twisted to face the men, gargling loudly and clutching at their clothing. His face was raked with scratches. For a moment, they stared with indecision as he pleaded with his eyes for help, all the while groping at their lapels. In his peripheral vision, he could see Francesca raising the chair and driving it down. The moment it crashed into the skull of one of the men, Owen's fist came up from the ground and rammed into the other man's nose. His head pitched back. Blood spurted in an arc... but his grip on Owen slackened only briefly. Owen tried another punch, but his opponent anticipated it and ducked most of the impact, although Owen did manage to follow through with an elbow to his forehead. The man closed in, his face rubbing against Owen's and his fingers searching for his throat. Then he head-butted Owen in the nose, but immediately sagged on top of him. Francesca had smashed the chair into the back of his head. Everything was suddenly still... no movement... no noise. A pair of hands reached from behind him and gouged at his eyes. Owen twisted out of the way and swung his elbow back into the woman's jaw. There was a nasty crunching sound and she went still underneath him.

'Well done, Owen!' Francesca stood triumphantly above the huddle of bodies. She didn't linger. With swift movements, she searched the two men and relieved them of their weapons.

'She's armed too, you know,' she said to Owen, pointing at the body he was lying on.

But Owen was incapable of moving. He just needed to reattach to the real world. Just for a time there, he *was* a person suffocating because of some phobia. And then there were all the hands reaching for him with intent to harm. He suddenly felt revulsion at being so intimate with these hateful people. He pushed his unconscious assailant away from him. Francesca held out her hand. She helped him to a sitting position. Then, she went over to the woman and retrieved a Taser from her clothing.

Owen got up and sat in the chair he'd occupied only minutes before. His face hurt.

Francesca came over and knelt beside him. She looked so incongruous in her party attire. She was without her sandals now. On closer inspection, Owen could see just how much her make-up was smudged and worn. There was still a trace of a spicy perfume.

She put a hand on his knee and looked up at him. Softly she said, 'Oh, you brave, brave boy. You saved my life tonight... you saved my life.'

The room was deathly quiet. Owen felt miserable. His face *really* hurt.

Francesca stroked Owen's knee. 'You made all the right decisions... you were incredible, Owen... I am so, so proud of you.' She looked away. 'You deserve much more than this... I'm very sorry... but it's the way things are... and there's very little that we can do about it.'

Owen turned to her. 'Were you ready to die, Francesca?'

A hidden anguish surfaced just for a second. 'Yes... yes. I have never been so ready. All I can say is that it's a big relief to still be alive... that's got to be worth something.' She looked as if she was about to cry.

Owen put his arm around her. 'Hey... you were amazing... you *are* amazing. *I'm* glad that you're alive too.' He pointed to her feet. 'You still have the zip-ties around your ankles—just in case you're thinking of re-joining the party.'

Francesca sat on the floor and tried to slip the ties off her feet, but they wouldn't go over her heel. 'Is that what alerted you to the situation? That I was dressed like a floozy.'

'Not a floozy, Francesca... just dressed to enjoy yourself.'

'You are so sweet, Owen.' She crooked her arm on his lap and leaned against him. 'Yeah, that came as a surprise. I'd seen him before... took a fancy to him... had him profiled... he came up squeaky clean—well, not *squeaky* clean—I do like a bit of beast in my men. But they must have got to him... to do a job on me. We got into his car, and *they* were there,' she flicked a finger in the direction of the unconscious threesome.

Owen massaged the nape of Francesca's neck. It was his natural response—to comfort.

She rested her head on her arm. 'How did you know that I'd be able to free myself?'

Owen tried to remember the tumult of thoughts that he had when he first entered the room. 'Well... I still wasn't sure how you were positioned in all of this. It struck me as odd that you would resort to abduction to hear what I had to say. Then, when I saw how you were dressed, I immediately realised that you were not there of your own free will. And then, there was the school deputy standing behind you. I figured that they wanted to make it *look* as though you were conducting the interrogation, because there'd be a better chance of me telling what I knew. Plus, you very cleverly conveyed, through your movements, that you were in fact tied to the chair.'

'Oh, Owen... you have no idea how desperate I was.'

'I can well imagine. I thought how clever it was that they only had to restrain your legs to the chair and stand by with a gun—or better still, a Taser, as it turned out... and you were completely immobilised, but still able to conduct a debrief as though everything was normal. When I stood up, I could see that the ties were probably loose enough for you to easily slip them off the bottom of the chair leg. Then I tottered towards you as though I might be setting up to attack you... which drew madam closer... and I just continued straight on into her. I knew I had to take her out—discreetly... and then?... I just hoped to god that if I kept the two blokes busy dealing with a frothing madman, you would come to my rescue... and you did... although, you did cause the second one to head butt me on the nose.'

'Sorry 'bout that.'

'Not a problem... I'm more worried about these scratches.'

Francesca massaged one of her ankles. 'I reckon I was in that chair for about four hours. I really need to pee.'

Owen tapered off his massage to Francesca's shoulder. 'I shall avert my sight.'

'You shall go home, Owen.' She levered herself off the floor and turned to face him. She ran her fingers through his hair. 'I have to take care of a few things up here. This episode ends here. Those guys were special mission... I don't know where from—yet. They were waiting for your details before making a report. It was me that they linked to the mission... you and Linh were identified as possible candidates based on face recognition on your return to Australia. So, they just picked you up and put you in front of me to see what happened. They warned me that, if I spoke first, they would be extra unpleasant with you.'

'Another reason for making it *look* as though you were in control.'

'Precisely. You inadvertently gave away that we were connected. It's not your fault.'

Someone in the pile of bodies moaned.

Francesca picked up the Taser from the floor. 'You have to go now, Owen... we can't wait. Go home and tell Linh that you're okay... she'll be beside herself with worry. Go!'

Owen nodded and held out his hand. 'Well done, Francesca.'

They shook briefly.

'Wait!' said Francesca. She handed Owen the Taser. 'Cover me with this. Come closer.'

They moved to the bodies.

'If he moves, just pull the trigger. I'm going to get the key out of his pocket.' At arm's length, she reached into a side pocket of the coat and extracted the keys. The man remained motionless.

They walked to the door. Francesca unlocked it and swung it open. As Owen passed by her, she reached up and kissed him lightly on the cheek. 'I'll be in touch,' she said. Then the door closed with a heavy click.

Owen walked down the stark corridor to the lift. He pressed the down button. The doors slid open immediately. He got in and contemplated the control panel.

Should he go down to the basement carpark?... or maybe the ground floor?... would the doors of the foyer be locked?... was there anyone else in the building?...

He heard a muted bang. He poked his head out of the lift. Another muted bang... followed shortly afterwards by a third.

He felt the familiar nausea overwhelm him. The roaring commenced in his ears.

... oh, god... not now... after all I've been through...

Owen sank to his knees and backed up into the lift. The control panel swam before his eyes.

... go the ground floor... probably the best bet...

He reached up and tried to aim his finger to the "G" button. The roaring became a din and blackness engulfed him.

He came to, staring up a woman's dress.

... could be worse... who is she? I hope she knows I'm here... it'll be embarrassing if she suddenly sees me lying here...

'Hey there, Owen,' Francesca said playfully, looking down at him. She pressed the door open button. 'Are you ready to come out?'

Owen issued a prolonged moan. He sat up against the lift wall. 'Ohh... why does this always happen to me?' he said thickly.

Francesca squatted down beside him. 'Will you be able to walk okay?' They were in the basement carpark.

'Come on, I'll help you up.' She stood back and offered her hand.

Carefully, he allowed himself to stand. He was recovering surprisingly quickly.

Francesca steadied him. 'I'll give you a lift home... come on.'

'... you've got their keys?'

'Yes, Owen... isn't that lucky.' She pressed the fob. The car unlocked with flashing lights.

They settled into their seats. Francesca adjusted hers and then backed out rather carelessly, straight into a rubbish skip. Without the slightest bit of concern, she drove up the ramp to the roller door.

'Don't you love driving other people's cars,' she gushed.

Clutched in her hand was a remote that she activated with a nippy press of the button.

'Thank you, Mr Deverill,' she said gaily, '... or whoever you really were.'

The roller door clattered slowly open.

Owen looked across. 'Did you shoot them?'

Without looking at him, Francesca waved a warning finger.

With barely enough room to clear the door, she edged the car out onto the footpath and accelerated down the street.

PART TWO

Chapter Nineteen

Yappar River never changed for Owen. Not that it remained the same the whole time—far from it. Every flood and every drought transformed the wend and flow of the water. The banks could be a lush tangle some years and a rocky jumble in other years.

What never changed for him was the peace he felt when he was out by himself. He couldn't explain it... there was something so nourishing about being in the bush... and it wasn't the food. Eating fried fish garnished with native plants, such as the charmingly named scurvy weed and prickly lettuce, gave him a heightened appreciation of sustenance, but left him perpetually hungry. On a few occasions, he had gone through the laborious process of grinding the nardoo sporocarps and rinsing out the poisons, just as Vern, the old stockman, had shown him. Sometimes he made Johnny cakes out of the doughy mess, and it would cook to the size of half a scone. If he was lucky he might come across a patch of native plantains which would cook up into a pretty decent meal, but one had to be careful of eating too much of the bush food. So, he always had a big container of muesli mix with powdered milk already stirred in. Most people found the quietness scary, the isolation boring and the long nights tedious.

This is just what Owen needed—time to heal.

A horse snorted behind him. He turned with a ready smile. Linh was riding Stella. She grinned back and gave the reins a gentle flick in the hope that it might motivate her horse to walk. Good old Stella obliged and clacked lazily towards him. Barra sat nearby, squinting and panting happily.

Owen was on Champ, his father's horse. He couldn't remember when it was that he began to feel as one with his mount. There were pictures of him in the album at age two riding Gordon, a retired stock horse. He'd been on and off horses so frequently throughout his life that he barely made the distinction between riding and walking.

'It's beautiful, Owen,' Linh breathed, as they surveyed the view from the high bank.

'Yeah?... do you like it?'

'Truthfully?... if I were here by myself, I'd hate it. But I'm with you, so I love it. It *is* very tranquil... and I'm glad to see you so happy.'

'And, I'm glad that you've made friends with Stella.'

They laughed as Linh leant forward and patted her horse.

Owen lifted the binoculars to his eyes—the same ones they'd been given in Vietnam—and scanned the river below. 'My god, Linh, these *are* worth their weight in gold,' he murmured.

'Can you see anything?'

'Nah... some places are such a tangle you could hide the entire drone in there.'

Linh dismounted and walked up to Owen. She held onto his leg. 'I won't mind if we never find any parts of it...'

Owen put down the glasses and held her by the shoulder. 'I know.'

This was the fourth day of their trip. There was no particular agenda. Owen just wanted to be out in the bush. The old hut at the water hole held many happy memories for him, so they headed there first. The nights spent in the corrugated iron structure were wonderful. Sharing his swag with someone as lovely as Linh was beyond what he could ever have imagined. In the morning, they would look out of the doorway at the cliffs on the other side of the waterhole and watch them go from a deep red to gold, as the sun came up. Linh wore nothing but socks and a beanie, and he held her silky skin close to him and kissed her persistently. She made him so happy.

They were on their way to the site of the jet crash. Out of curiosity, Owen had periodically scanned the river for evidence of the drone. Now, with Linh resting her chin on his thigh, he knew that even if he came across something likely, he wouldn't want to look at it anyway.

Linh remounted and they continued the trek. They stopped on the rise where Owen had first seen the smoke. Looking through the binoculars, Owen was surprised to see that the aft section with the engines was still there, pitched into the ground at a steep angle.

'I'd have thought that the flood would have carried it away... but there you go, it's still there.'

Linh looked mesmerized. '... to think that this is where it all began,' she uttered. 'Are we going down?'

Owen swung Champ's head back to the direction of the camp. 'No way... no way.'

Barra seemed pretty happy with this decision. He barked once and bounded ahead in the way that dogs do to show their pleasure.

There had been another, very compelling reason for Owen and Linh to drop off the radar after the events of his abduction.

On his return home, Owen had stayed in bed for two days, partly to allow the wounds to his face to heal but mostly because he felt too disordered to deal with his daily commitments. He was happy just to lie against a pile of pillows and occasionally look out of the window to watch Linh waiting on tables. She would frequently come up to the loft to cheer him up and to dab herbal tinctures wherever it was needed. The scratches were surprisingly deep in places and a doctor friend of the family had recommended, in addition to antibiotics, extracts of lavender and ti-tree and other unguents that caused Owen to smell like an old-world apothecary.

One of Owen's school friends, Braydon, had happened to drop in one day, and the two of them spent some time playing darts from the day bed. Braydon was a journalist working independently for an online news service. He mentioned that he had contacts at the various police stations. Owen asked him to quietly find out about any recent deaths in Edward Street. A few days later, Braydon got in touch to inform him that there had been no incidents reported, but that the contact for that area had been instantly posted elsewhere for enquiring. The only other slightly mysterious death—mysterious because the authorities were keeping it out of the media—was the apparent death by drowning of a woman. This came from one of the other contacts who thought Braydon might be interested in the item. With a terrible sense of foreboding, Owen asked his friend to see if he could get some more information. Not long after, a text with an attachment came to his phone. He had to sit down before he could open it. It was a photo of the unidentified woman. Owen burst into tears—there was no mistaking it was Francesca. He recognised the dress. He couldn't linger on her face—it looked stark and forsaken.

Linh was very worried about him when she came up. They sat together on the bed. She waiting patiently for him to reveal what was on his mind.

At last he told her. It was a terrible shock for her too. They folded into each other's arms.

Linh recalled the time of the helicopter ride to retrieve the case when, despite the tense circumstances, she had made a real connection with Francesca—speaking a foreign language and talking about boys. Francesca had welcomed her into the complicated realm of womanhood. Okay, maybe she wasn't totally admirable... maybe she saw things for what they were. Who could judge? She played in a dangerous game and lived at a level of alertness that would overwhelm most people. And now, she was gone. What a waste.

When Owen's mum came up to see what had happened to her waitress, she took one look at the mournful couple on the edge of the bed and went immediately to the office. Through a satellite link, she got through to her husband, who was out in the field, and informed him that it was time to send Owen back to Yappar Station.

Two weeks later, they arrived. They'd driven up in an old van that they'd bought privately. Don had made the stipulation that the two of them should be as inconspicuous as possible, and that meant no flights and no hotel accommodation. The van allowed them to sleep in council sites and off the road. Taking the inland route, they at first drove with intent, but quickly found that it was so much fun to stop off at swimming holes and to camp at places of beauty, that the journey took its time. And then, the radiator had a complete meltdown at Muttaburra, halfway between Barcaldine and Hughenden. With the help of the local blacksmith, Owen rigged up a truck radiator on the roof, with pipes going in front of the windscreen to the engine.

Linh thought it looked like something out of *Mad Max*. Fortunately, by this stage of the journey, they were travelling on pretty isolated stretches of road.

Through third parties, they would relay coded messages back home just to let everyone know that all was well. Linh's family thought it was wonderful that "the children" were doing a road trip, and happily bestowed their blessing. Owen knew that Linh felt guilty about not being able to tell her parents the whole story... but what was to be gained from it? The situation was impossibly complicated. Even Linh and Owen had difficulty coming to terms with it.

When they got back to the waterhole, Owen revealed the big surprise that he had been promising his girl. With a plastic tarpaulin under his arm, he led her down to the sandy end of the waterhole and triumphantly showed her a large, shallow hole he had dug.

Linh produced a look of dismay. 'Is that my grave, Owen?'

'Oh, god, no,' he lifted her up and swung her around, '... it's our hot tub!'

'Really?'

'Yes!... look...' He took the tarp and laid it in the hole. Nearby was a pile of wood to which he knelt. Striking his flint, he soon had a waft of smoke rising. 'Now all we need to do is heat up some water,' and he pointed to a galvanised tub and two plastic buckets sitting some distance away.

Linh waved away the smoke. 'That's ingenious... hey!... can I make a shaped seat to sit in?'

Owen flicked the tarp out of the hole. 'That's the spirit... improve on centuries old bush tradition. What's your pleasure—side by side or facing each other?'

Linh dipped her head and threw him a knowing look. 'Facing each other.'

They scrabbled about with the buckets and produced the desired contours, and then they sat in them to check for comfort. When they were happy with the shape, the tarp went back over.

'How long before bath time?' asked Linh.

Owen picked up the buckets and went to the water's edge. 'Oh, after dinner...'

'After dinner?... it's not even dark yet!'

'Well,' Owen walked back with full buckets, '... we have to fill up this tub and the gal one, and we have to wait for the fire to settle... then, when we're making dinner, we'll cycle the water on the fire... it'll take about two hours.'

'Wow... we'll *need* a bath by then,' Linh smirked.

During dinner, Owen would go down to the tub, pull out two buckets of water, empty the hot water from the gal tub into the big tub, stoke the fire, pour the buckets into the gal tub and put it on the fire.

'Is that *really* an old bush tradition? said Linh dubiously.

'Yep, sure is. I remember one time when our hot water system broke down, Dad put a tarp in the trailer and filled it up from the bore. Then we spent a good while shuttling water in and out from the fire until the bath was ready.'

'... and the whole family got in?'

'Sure did... and that water went on to make the best hooch north of Cloncurry.'

For a split second, Linh imagined the Lucas's as a bunch of lawless hillbillies. As she settled into the hot tub, she thought it was ironic that, living in the city, she had never been in a hot tub, and that now, in the "back of beyond", she was enjoying the bliss of a warm bath under a starry sky. Owen had tied together twitches of ti-tree that he put in the heating water and which secreted the distinctive zesty scent.

This was what they both needed to restore their spirits, although, as Linh had remarked, it was difficult for the two of them to reference themselves now that they had been introduced to the scale of global machinations by hidden powers. It would be much easier to follow a conventional career path in all of its relative simplicity. It was as though their choice now lay between seeking a meaningful relationship with the conspirators or dropping out of mainstream society and becoming self-sufficient hippies.

They stayed in the tub for hours. The night became very cold, but every now and again, they would get out, fill a bucket each with water from the tub, tip the hot water that was on the fire into the tub, fill up the gal tub and put it back on the fire. Returning to the hot water was beyond bliss.

Linh had her mouth just above the water. 'Owie... I will remember this bath for the rest of my life,' she said, kneading him with her foot.

Owen had placed an old horse blanket next to the tub so that when they did finally get out, their feet didn't become sandy. The long immersion had produced a euphoric disorientation, and when they towelled off they swayed and hung onto each other for balance.

Draping a doona around Linh, Owen hugged her near and, with Barra trailing behind, they made their way back to the hut.

It was one of those static winter nights when it seemed that the silent trees were waiting for a change in the weather. Occasionally the curlew's mournful whoop travelled from somewhere distant. The only other sound came from the thin squeak of the hut as it rocked rhythmically on its stilts.

At some time in the early morning, Barra growled softly. Owen was immediately awake. Being careful not to disturb Linh, he slid out from under the doona and crawled to the open door. The sliver of moon didn't throw enough light for Owen to see far. He wouldn't use the torch because it destroyed his night sight and would reveal his position to whatever menace might be out there. The dewy cold settled on him as he waited. But there was nothing that he could detect. Barra could do the sentry duty—he was going back to bed.

When the kookaburras started their racket at first light, Owen woke with bleary eyes. For once, he wasn't looking forward to getting a fire started and preparing for the day. The long time spent in the tub had drained him, so he rolled over and went back to sleep. He was on holiday—he was allowed a sleep in.

Much later, he awoke to hear the wrens chattering outside the hut. Stretching with contentment, he ventured out to the top of the steps and climbed down. The bare earth glowed in the morning sunlight... and in the pebbled creek bed, dull and menacing, sat a drone.

Owen tensed with shock. The thing looked completely out of place... foreign and dangerous ... and it was pointed straight at him. There was nowhere to run... no *time* to run... actually, no *need* to run. If it had wanted to annihilate the two of them, it could have done so when it arrived before the dawn. There was another concern—he had nothing on. He turned and trotted lightly up the stairs, grabbed his shorts and hastily slipped them on.

... nothing like being prepared to face the enemy...why is it here?

He stepped back down with a wary eye on the distant machine.

'Good morning, Owen,' came a voice from directly in front of him.

Startled at the proximity, Owen quickly scanned either side. There was no one to be seen except Barra, with trembling hackles raised.

'It's all right, don't be afraid. It's me, Alasdair.'

... Alasdair!... after all this time? Now what am I in for? And we were just starting to relax...

Owen couldn't help reaching out to see whether or not the conspirators had invented invisibility.

'Grab one of your camp chairs and come down to the drone... I want to show you something.'

It was so surreal that Owen consciously breathed extra deeply just in case his mind had intentions of deserting his body. He walked slowly towards the drone, picking up one of the camp chairs near the fire on the way.

The drone was big—about as long as a car, with swept back wings and long, spindly legs. It looked like a cross between a cockroach and a moth—only massive. As he got nearer, Owen could see that at the root of each wing there was a large ducted fan.

...okay... VTOL capability... interesting. That explains the shock absorbent legs...

Underneath the nose of the drone, a small hatch popped open.

'Inside the hatch are two small tripods, Owen. Pull them out and set them up on the ground where I point with the laser.'

Owen extracted the tripods. On the top of each was a black, optical ball.

'Pull the legs out all the way... that's right.'

A small green dot traced its way erratically over the ground and came to rest a few metres away from the drone. Owen walked over and positioned the tripod over the dot. Then he followed the dot to another position so that the two tripods made a triangular formation with the nose.

'Well done. Now take your chair over to where I'm pointing and make yourself comfortable.'

Owen followed the dot to a place about three metres away from the front of the drone and seated himself with a big, expectant sigh. He explored a few ideas.

... the voice must be produced by some sort of bi-focal wave projection to create an audible sound wave right in front of me... and I fully expect that now I'm about to see a hologram of Alasdair...

Owen was not disappointed. Even though it was a sunny morning, a nebulous flashing suspended itself above the ground and instantly formed into a holographic image. Alasdair sat before him in an armchair, relaxed and smiling.

The voice that Owen heard, conformed with his visitor's position and distance.

'I'm sorry that it's been such a long time, Owen... things have been a little crazy, to use the modern parlance.'

Owen couldn't believe how clear and solid the image seemed.

... not excessively bright... no shimmer... it's as though I could shake his hand...

Alasdair looked taken-aback. '... um, you *can* speak to me... I *will* hear you.'

'Oh, yeah... sorry, Alasdair. I was just spun out with the reality thing... it is *very* cool.'

Alasdair laughed. 'Oh, just a parlour trick... used to impress people to come and work for us.'

'Is that what you want me to do?... us?'

'Yes,' he sighed, '... but I won't coerce you, because I'm hoping that I won't need to.'

Owen half nodded in assent.

'We had a difficult time finding you! We checked this place on a few occasions but it wasn't until you lit the bonfire for us that we could pin-point you from one of our satellites.'

Owen looked over to the little sandy beach. The fire was still smouldering. 'Oh, right... yeah, I made a hot tub for the two of us last night. Didn't expect to be perved on from outer space.'

Alasdair guffawed and slapped his leg. 'No chance of that... the heat signal was way too strong to pick up any suggestive silhouettes.' He had one more chuckle. 'Is Linh still asleep?'

Owen nodded. 'Why?... does this concern the two of us?'

Alasdair pulled a grim face. 'Put it this way... the two of you together, will work well on this mission.'

'Mission!... sounds serious.'

Alasdair stood up and walked around... except that he stayed in the same position relative to the river stones. 'Ah, everything is serious of late, Owen... very, very serious. I don't know where to begin, apart from saying that the technology explosion—of which you are literally witnessing an example—is creating a battlefield the likes of which we've never seen before.

'What I mean is that, apart from the *means* by which we engage in battle, even the motives and rationales are obscure. It used to be easy— we'd fight over material things. Then we fought over the abstract notion of power—which very quickly becomes anything but abstract. Now? I don't know what we're fighting for... and, paradoxically, it doesn't matter for as long as the battlefield is an abstract one in cyberspace... which is where most of the conflict occurs.'

'Until someone "accidently" drowns... or has a "heart attack" in a crowded plaza...'

Alasdair displayed genuine shock. 'I'm sorry, Owen... I'm not familiar with those circumstances.'

Owen felt suddenly angry. He leant forward in his chair. 'You sent Linh out on a mission for which she was completely unprepared. They twigged to her, and to your organisation! Then, you sent me out with enough kit to totally compromise me. It was a disaster! We could easily have ended up in some godforsaken ditch in Cambodia. And then, you didn't even debrief us! Just left us to get on with our lives, even though every other conspirator on the planet now has a "file" with our names on it.'

Alasdair had seated himself. With a finger to his mouth, he was looking very contemplative. He looked askance at Owen and pointed the finger to indicate a spot behind him.

Owen turned around. Linh was standing close by with a chair in her arms.

'Is it okay if I join you guys?' She put a hand on Owen's shoulder.

Owen reached around and opened up the chair for her. 'Good morning, baby,' he murmured.

Alasdair indicated with his hands that the two should sit closer together. 'I could use the speakers on the front of the drone,' he said, '... but they sound so impersonal. I prefer to use the audio projection technology, but it only has a small field. Hello, Linh... it's very nice to see you again.'

Linh had her arm around Owen and her head right near his. 'Hello, Alasdair... do you often go camping like this?'

He laughed. 'The fact is, I do. Not camping as such, but travelling and sightseeing. We've developed such good virtual reality that, when you combine it with a treadmill, you can go for a stroll along the Great Ocean boardwalk or tour the Louvre... lots of places. Crowds are problematical—we're still trying to perfect that. I do it because of my age and the fact that I'm a bit limited in where I can go in public nowadays.'

There was a moment of silence as the two lovers visualised the concept of virtual tourism.

Alasdair coughed lightly. 'I must apologise for disturbing you here in this idyll, but my need is rather pressing so I took the liberty.'

Owen pointed rather rudely. 'We were told that you, and whatever outfit you're with, were finished... defeated by some other crowd?'

'Ah, yes... the Cambodia affair. That wasn't our shining moment... we were rather compromised in a number of ways. But the realm of the conspirators has many dimensions. We regrouped in a different space and were soon able to reassert ourselves. Also, I don't know whether you've been made aware, but some of the, shall we say, powers at large, have recognised the need for unity in order to prevent certain disastrous outcomes from befalling our world, and so there has been a heretofore unprecedented level of cooperation between them.'

'Glad to hear it,' said Owen.

Alasdair guffawed heartily. 'Of course, you are, Owen!... of course, you are. Ah, I wish my life could be as uncomplicated as yours,' he suddenly leant forward with a look of concern, '... not that you don't have significant difficulties in your life, m'boy.'

'You don't know the half of it.'

Alasdair conceded that point by bowing his head. 'It's just that I am staring at the possibility of worldwide destruction, and it's not doing me any good at all. I can't tell you how much I enjoy talking with the two of you—you are both such excellent listeners,' he chuckled indulgently.

Linh spoke up. 'So, you'd like us to save the world, then?'

'If you'd be so kind,' Alasdair mimicked.

The morning's bird-song had subdued by this time. The sun on their necks was becoming uncomfortable. Owen pulled out the large bandana that he always carried in his pocket and draped it over Linh's neck.

Alasdair continued. 'Look, I won't impose for any longer. What I'd like you to consider is to come and visit me. I have a very nice place that I'm fairly sure you'll like. Then we will have a chat about the mission. What do you say?'

'Where is your place, then?' asked Owen.

'Well, I can't tell you exactly where it is, but I can tell you that if you continue your tour around Australia—anti-clockwise—I will tell you when to stop... though you'd probably want to get something a bit less conspicuous than that weird van you are presently driving.'

'I thought you said that time was pressing?'

'It is, Owen... but I can wait until you come to me. However, I'd prefer you not to dawdle.'

The couple exchanged a look then nodded in unison.

Linh spoke. 'Will our lives deteriorate if we don't help you?'

The old man in the hologram sagged with defeat. 'I believe so, Linh... the whole world is at risk of deteriorating.'

Owen parted his hands. 'And we're the ideal candidates to prevent this from happening?'

'We could get others... but you two are the perfect combination for our particular needs.'

'Is it dangerous?'

Alasdair stared pointedly at them from his hover above the pebbles.

'It'll be dangerous if we fail.'

Owen felt compelled to protect the two of them. 'And, you're absolutely sure that we are the best fit for the ah, mission?'

'So our computers tell us!'

'Your computers?'

Alasdair settled back and ran his fingers through his hair. 'If we had to rely on a panel of analysts to make these decisions, nothing would get done. We have biometrics for the both of you, as well as psych profiles and a whole bunch of other stuff that I don't concern myself with. When we punched in the relevant details for this assignment—and that in itself is a monumentally complex task—we waited a day or so, and out popped the answer... and it was you.'

'Us?' they said in unison.

Alasdair gave a shrug of indifference. 'Well, naturally we gave it the personalised treatment, and in the end, we had to agree... the complexities of this mission could best be negotiated by Owen Lucas and Linh Vuong... bad luck for you maybe, but good luck for humanity.'

The two of them looked totally bewildered.

'What on earth is so special about us?' Linh queried.

'I'll tell you,' Alasdair sat forward again, '... you are a young waitress who happens to speak fluent Vietnamese, and you are very close to a young man who is a very gifted engineer, and who happens to have an uncanny resemblance to a marine mechanic, who we are going to nobble, in order to get our man onto a mega-yacht, where the two of you will have a massive communications advantage, because all of the staff on board are strangers to each other, and are deliberately chosen on the basis of speaking incompatible languages...' Alasdair sucked in a big breath. 'There! That is what the computers came up with... ingenious actually!'

Owen looked perturbed. 'But, I don't know the first thing about marine engines.'

'Don't you?' Alasdair said slyly.

Owen ejected himself out of the chair. 'Bloody hell! So, you *have* been spying on us!'

'Calm down, Owen,' Alasdair put up his hands, '... we haven't spied any more than any other organisation that has an interest in perusing internet searches and patent searches. And based on that information we know that your team is investigating the possibility of applying your turbine design for marine applications. Isn't that the case?'

It was true. Marine power looked like being one of the best applications for the turbine concept. Large luxury power boats and ships tended to have diesel piston engines—super yachts and military vessels went for straight turbine or turbine/electric hybrids—mega ships went back to diesel piston engines—units that were four stories high, weighed well over a thousand tonnes and did about two revs per second. At first the team could not believe that their turbine could compete with a behemoth like that, but after carefully considering the build difficulties, they realised that the turbine would not only be much cheaper to build, it would also make much better use of the fuel, and therefore be cheaper to run—which is the parameter that is most important. Not that the team was intending to build a ship's engine straight away... it was just another option for further down the track.

Owen sat back down. The reminder of his turbine project left him suddenly agitated. His work as a designer and problem solver was a refuge where he felt totally capable and empowered, and to have that taken from him left him emotionally vulnerable. Luckily, he had his passion for the outback, and sharing this time with Linh satisfied him beyond expectations. But, just for a moment, he regretted not being at the lab.

Linh stroked his neck.

'Yeah, okay... we've been looking at marine engines, but that doesn't mean I know anything about conventional motors... or whatever is in that mega-yacht.'

'I know, Owen... I know. I'm sorry to have annoyed you. Look, if I can just explain your role in this—you will be taking the place of a low-ranking mechanic whose job is utterly mindless. He is paid very well to examine the operation of the motors, the desalination plant, air-conditioners and generators.'

'Hardly mindless.' Owen interrupted.

'Hear me out. He simply cruises throughout the ship's belly listening and looking for *any* sort of anomaly...'

'Like rats.'

'Very unlikely. The thing is, every mechanical device on board is monitored electrically—there is no need for someone to be down in the engine room. Nonetheless, he is there as a back-up. That is his only job. He does it six hours about with another person... endlessly walking, checking and occasionally wiping fingerprints off the handrail... because apparently, the engine room is professionally cleaned about twice a year.'

'So, the only person he ever gets to speak to is his patrol buddy?'

'Not even her. She only speaks German, and he only speaks Finnish.'

'Finnish! How's that going to work?'

'Extremely well, according to the security contingent on board. They love it if no one speaks.

'Her?' said Linh in her best sulk.

'Don't worry, Linh. They got her off a fishing trawler in the North-Sea... she looks like Rosa Klebb... you know, from James Bond?'

'And the other guy? What was his gig before they shanghaied him?'

'Miner. Good understanding of machinery and ever-so-ready to do something else. He does a two-year stint for which he is generously remunerated. Most people get cycled out in that sort of time frame. Wouldn't want them to become too familiar.'

'And I just swap places with him on his way to work one day?'

'Ah, not quite. You see, the various crew members tend to stay with the boat for the duration of the cruise—wherever and however long that might be. They have accommodation on board.'

Linh spoke. 'Where is this cruise taking place?'

'It's in the Mediterranean, but I can't tell you exactly where just yet.'

'And my job?'

'Linh, you are with the wait-staff. You will be positioned in a queue, and we will slot you in at the appropriate time. Wait-staff are turned over frequently. You won't have any trouble following the routines. You come from Hai Phong and you speak only Vietnamese. You have been chosen because you are an excellent menial. You will be surrounded by other awe-struck girls with no language in common.'

'Sounds promising.'

The winter sun was at its highest point by now. Owen and Linh were both perspiring freely.

Alasdair stood and placed his hands behind his back. 'I will go now. Think about what I've proposed... I don't involve you lightly... both of you have so much to offer our world... but you also happen to be our best chance for success in this mission. I leave it in your hands. Don't stand too close to the drone when it takes off... it could fling out a stone. Owen would you replace the tripods when I have disappeared? Sounds so dramatic, doesn't it... we still have to come up with a suitable sign-off for holograms.' He waved and the hologram went out.

Chapter Twenty

Owen was still feeling out of sorts when the drone finally took off. Linh sensed his fragility and suggested that they stoke up the fire and cook up a nice breakfast.

Owen had a better idea. He brought her close and looked at her with weary eyes. 'I'm sorry, Linh' he said, '... the day started off so well. But I know what will make me feel better... come with me.'

They walked to the gal tub which was sitting on the embers of the previous night's fire. The water was hot. Owen took one of the buckets and filled it from the waterhole. He poured some into the tub and swirled it around with his hand.

'That should be just right.'

When he looked up, Linh was already taking off her top. 'Excellent idea, Owie,' she said.

They trickled water over each other in the vibrant light and washed away the drear of the morning's visit.

When they were towelled dry, and dressed in fresh clothes, they made damper with soda water and cooked it in the ashes. Owen showed Linh how to tap the ash off the crust when he lifted out the golden baked bun. They ate it with plenty of butter.

'Tot, the thing about camping,' said Owen with his mouth full, '... is that there's very little to do besides swimming and eating, so camp food should be engaging... like this—thick crusts that will keep you amused for a good while.'

Linh nodded her agreement as she gnawed at the end slice.

The next morning, they began the two-day return trip to the homestead. For each of them, something had changed. There were longer periods of silence as the horses poked along. Alasdair's proposition had entered deep into their conscience. The world was at risk—and they were the ones who could save it. That would be enough to occupy anyone—especially if they were serious about getting involved.

They made camp in a dry river bed, but it wasn't until nightfall, when they were snug in each other's arms, that they could talk about their dilemma.

Owen drew the doona over their heads. 'How's your bum?'

'Sore.'

'Do you feel like saving the world?'

'Not today... I'm too saddle sore.' Linh nuzzled into Owen's neck. 'Where do you think he lives?'

'West of us somewhere... he said, travel anticlockwise... doubt it would be in Queensland... probably in the Northern Territory... there are any number of hidden places there.'

'Can't be too far away, if time is of the essence.'

'No... he intimated that he lives there most of the time, so it wouldn't be a humpy in the long grass.'

'The long grass?'

'Yeah, the Blackfellers in the NT make their home in the long grass... it grows to way over your arm's reach. Makes a protected space and not a bad bed.'

'You've slept in the long grass?'

'Sure have... it grows just over the range. Been droving there on occasion.'

'Are you allowed to call them Blackfellers?'

'Yep... when you talk about Blackfellers, you're referring to their way of life... their culture... an original people who live close to the land. Sure, their skin colour is an obvious feature that we've used to conveniently distinguish them from the other mob... called Whitefellers... but the *real* distinguishing feature is their way of life. And the *really* real distinguishing feature is their different values... that is the thing that separates communities more than anything else—values.'

'Okay... give me an example.'

'Well, my grandfather, who lived during the time of some pretty serious racial divides, pointed out to me that, over the years, there were plenty of Aboriginal people that were welcome in any white neighbourhood. In the eyes of the Whitefellers, they were the successful ones— in sports, acting, politics, the arts... whatever... they were sought after for radio, television, newspapers... the white community flocked to them just as they would to a white celebrity.'

'So... there was no racial issue?' Linh murmured.

'No! If people were die-hard racist, they wouldn't want anything to do with someone from another race no matter how popular or influential they might be. But people aren't racist. Grandad used to tell me that people are *culturist*... that they get a bee in their bonnet about the *way* other people live... their *values*. For instance, think about all the... what's the word?... bad labels...'

'... pejoratives...'

'... yeah... used to describe people's values... like, Greenies or Ferals and Bogans and Yuppies... the super-rich. Even 'middle-class' can be used as a pejorative... like, if I said disparagingly, that you had such middle-class aspirations. I mean, you only have to rock up to a polling booth and you'll find middle-class people from the same suburb of the same racial pedigree standing opposed to each other because of some perceived difference of values. I mean, really, people are very sensitive about their values, and they'll happily embrace anyone, no matter what their skin colour, if they see eye to eye on certain issues.'

'Owie, you're getting all hot.' Linh lifted the doona. '... you must have had some good conversations with your grandad.'

Owen ran his fingers through his hair. 'Yeah, we did. He was a good bloke. He used to say that, out in the bush, a conversation is a rare and sought-after occurrence—not to be spoilt by discussing the meaning of life.'

Linh shook with silent laughter.

'Fair-dinkum!... sometimes we'd be camped under the stars and I'd be waiting patiently for a morsel of wisdom, and he'd just sit there looking into the fire. After an hour he'd say, "That fire has burned down nicely, hasn't it, Owen"... and I'd be thinking, "Well, that's bleedin', bloody obvious..." but I'd say, "Sure has, Gramps... burned down real nice."'

Linh laughed as Owen mimicked his grandfather's voice. '... but he *did* give you some pearls of wisdom?'

'Oh, yeah... we'd be riding alongside each other and he'd say, "... you don't need that many pointers in life, son... just look at where the sun rises in the morning, and where it sets in the afternoon... you should be pretty right in the meantime."'

The bush was quiet around them. A pygmy glider scuttled up a paper bark nearby, then drifted in the night air to the base of another tree. Linh followed it with her finger.

Owen pulled her closer. 'There used to be stacks of gliders floating about all over the place. But now there aren't nearly as many. Don't know why.'

'Maybe the climate is changing.' Linh ventured.

'... maybe...'

'I wonder what the issue is that's threatening the world?'

'Who knows... like he said, the technology is racing ahead faster than we can control it.'

'Mankind has never done a particularly good job of controlling technology.'

'No... it always gets directed towards war.'

'... and medicine...'

'... true...' Owen yawned mightily, '... got to get a new car too... van...'

Linh stroked Owen's forehead. 'Good night, my darling. I *so* want to be with you in the morning,' she whispered.

They arrived back at the homestead in the early afternoon. The horses were brushed and given an extra ration, then let out in the paddock. There was no one about. Don and the boys were working on another station for a few days, so Owen and Linh packed the van, fuelled it and went to bed early.

At first light they drove out over the cattle grid and headed north along the track to Normanton. It was very easy to get lost in the vast flood plain with its criss-crossing tracks and trails. There were very few distinguishing topographical features, but Owen had been on this route a few times before and pointed out to Linh the little stone cairns that had been erected to help travellers find their way.

'Trouble is, the terrain can change so much from season to season, that even the locals can get bush-wacked,' he informed her.

Linh could see that her stockman boyfriend was clearly enjoying the drive. 'Do you like driving out in the never-never?' she asked.

'I absolutely do,' he replied with a wide smile. 'I don't know what it is... maybe the sensation of movement because the trees and everything are so close... or maybe it's the softness of the surface—the give and the falter as the wheels skim over the dirt... or maybe the wending and winding and off-camber corners... don't know, really...'

Linh burst out laughing. 'My god, Owie!... you sound like a poet.'

Owen threw back his head and joined in the laughter. 'Tell you what, though,' he said with a pointed finger, '... the first person who writes a book called, *Best Dirt Roads of Australia* will be on a winner, because anyone who's spent time on the dirt will know exactly what it's about—the connection between driver and car. Mind you, there's thousands of kilometres of corrugated dirt road that everyone does their best to avoid.'

Owen came to a stop in the middle of the road. 'Here, you have a go.'

After hours of driving, they finally came to the braided beds of the Norman River—and still had eighty kilometres of undulating, stony crossings to travel.

The arrival of the strange, hybrid van in the tiny township of Normanton was met with a few raised eyebrows.

While they were filling up at a petrol station, a young man approached them and engaged them in conversation. He said that he had a van for sale, and that it was particularly well suited for travelling anticlockwise around the country. Owen and Linh looked at each other and said that they might be interested. The van, a late model, four-wheel drive, Volkswagen Trakka, was parked around the back of the petrol station. It looked in great condition and had all of the handy facilities that make bush camping more convenient. When they poked their heads back out of the vehicle after a look inside, the man presented them with already completed paper work.

'The keys are in the ignition,' he said, '... when you've transferred your things out of the other van, I'll take it off your hands for you.'

The two of them nodded hesitantly and asked about how much he wanted for the Trakka.

'Nothing,' replied the man, '... it's all been taken care of. The tank's full.'

So, about an hour later, after a quick shop for groceries, Linh was driving west along the Burketown Development road, while Owen was flicking through data sheets on desalination plants, marine engines, air-conditioning and generators that had been thoughtfully left in the overhead rack.

They followed the unsealed highway, at the very bottom of the gulf, to Burketown, where the horizon is so incredibly flat and barren that visitors become overwhelmed by the extent of the sky; they tend to feel overly exposed. The drive continued for two hundred and fifty tedious kilometres across the border to Booroloola and the landscape never varied.

For Linh, sitting in the passenger seat, the scope of the isolation began to make her feel anxious and restless. She tried to relax with her head against a pillow, but she couldn't escape the uneasiness that she felt.

Owen looked across. 'Are you not feeling well? Do you want me to pull over?'

Linh nodded and reached out to Owen's shoulder.

When she got out and walked away from the car, she had to sit down for fear of falling over.

Owen sat with her on the yellow dirt. 'If you're feeling crook, you might have to lie down in the back of the car until we get to a clinic.'

Linh rested her arm on Owen's thigh. 'No... I'm okay, Owie... truly. I'm just trying to come to terms with what's making me feel like this. Give me a moment.'

The afternoon was wearing on. Owen stretched out on his back and let Linh rest her head on his tummy. They hadn't seen another car for over an hour. Not many people needed to travel up in this corner.

'Owie,' Linh said distantly.

'... mmm...'

'This part of the world makes me realise that we're living on the very surface of a huge planet that's lost in the void of space.'

'... and you were laughing at *my* poetry.'

Linh crooked her arm to fondle Owen's chin. '... but I had another thought, and that had to do with where I come from, and where we've been in South East Asia... those incredibly beautiful parts of the world that are so rich in life and diversity... and comparing it to here, where it's so desolate. I guess I was having a kind of culture shock—being from the city and all.'

Owen stroked Linh's breast. '... do you think this will help?'

Linh closed her eyes. '... yeah...'

No sounds at all reached them. Looking up at the endless sky, it really was as though they were on the fringe of space.

'... and then, I thought about the countless multitudes in other parts of the world, and it suddenly dawned on me that, one day, when we have vastly different technology, this unending plain might be completely transformed... like those futuristic images of cities on other planets... y'know, with twin suns and stuff.'

'... and that was making you feel woozy?'

Linh laughed. 'Yeah... I feel a lot better now... but don't stop what you're doing...'

Owen stroked Linh's forehead with his other hand. 'I'm glad you feel better. You're not the first person to be overwhelmed by the space out here. There are plenty of accounts of explorers feeling a sense of doom after months out in the open. Of course, it could have been starvation, constant harassment by the Blackfellers, snake bite...'

Linh put her hand over his mouth. 'Now you're laughing at me.'

Owen shook his head. 'I think it's wonderful,' he said through Linh's fingers, '... that you are sensitive enough to think those things. I love you for it.'

Linh rolled over and straddled him. She kissed him squarely on the mouth—the two of them lying in the dust on the side of the road to Booroloola.

They decided to camp where they were.

'I just never get used to the fact that you can pull over on the side of the road and set up your camp,' Linh expressed from her chair by the fire.

'I know,' Owen agreed, '... it's great isn't it!'

'There's just one thing, though,' she continued, '... you travel for miles and monotonous miles with the objective of reaching a town, and then, when you get there, there is seriously nothing to see... just a petrol station, a pub, a neglected park with a monument to the war heroes of the area... a shop... a few houses... you fill up, grab an ice-cream and drive on. It's so... unspectacular.'

Owen passed Linh a shot-glass of port. 'Well, most of the attraction out here is under the water—the fishing is insane. All that flood run-off each year grows the biggest prawns and the biggest mackerel. That's why the folk out here might appear a little gruff at times—because being on the land is an inconvenience that they're prepared to put up whilst they prepare for getting back out on the water.'

'Really?'

'... might be...'

'Oh, Owen... you're filling my head full of lies.'

'Maybe... but what else would you do out here, Tot?'

Chapter Twenty-One

The drive to Booroloola early the next morning was, according to Linh, uneventful. According to Owen, it was brilliant. The road had just been graded. They'd only been driving for a few minutes when they passed the road gang with three graders in line. The road from then on was dead smooth.

'Out here, my dear... there is nothing quite as exhilarating as being the first to use a newly graded road... it's sublime isn't it?'

'Yes, it's sublime—will they have coffee in Booroloola?'

'Like I said, a long, long time ago... you can get espresso coffee in the most remote corners of the country nowadays... thanks to the Grey Nomads.'

'What are we, Owie?'

Owen didn't respond. His face was impassive.

'Owie?' Linh put her hand on his thigh.

Owen covered her hand with his. 'Sorry... just thinking about what we actually are.'

They drove in silence all the way to the turn-off to the township.

'We won't get fuel here, Tot. There really isn't anything to see. It's one of those places that people shouldn't crowd unless they have business there. Are you hanging out for a coffee?'

Linh shook her head. 'No, not at all. I just wanted to be sure that we wouldn't be driving off the edge of the world.'

Owen laughed. 'We'll get fuel at Heartbreak Hotel.'

'Can't wait.'

At the hotel, Owen made the decision to travel north through the Limmen National Park to Ngukurr, a distance of about two hundred and fifty kilometres. He'd never done that stretch before, and the winding dirt road, through some of the oldest geography on the planet, held a great attraction.

'They reckon the road is pretty good at the moment, and it'll be more interesting than going up the tar from Daley Waters.'

Linh hugged his wiry body. The distances that they had travelled compared to the dearth of settlements they had seen, defied belief. She watched as he let some more air out of the tyres. She held so much trust in his calm demeanour.

At one campsite, on the Roper River, they were walking along massive stone slabs and came across giant imprints of six-toed human feet. At night, the red eyes of the freshwater crocodiles could be seen wherever they shone the torch.

They hit sealed roads for the first time in a month just before they came to Mataranka. Owen took Linh snorkelling to the source of the thermal springs. They got in at the stone steps and wallowed amongst the tourists. Then they donned their masks and fins and swam up through the tangles of fallen trees against the very warm current. On the surface, the place looked very uninviting—a wetland of clumps of reeds with thick scum floating on the water. But under the water, the clarity was so good that vision was infinite. The only places where light entered in the aquatic realm were through circular holes in the scum. Each time they came to the surface for a breath, they had to make sure that the snorkel wasn't caught in a spider web. The maze of deep pools went on and on.

Owen was enthralled at being in this pristine place. 'I reckon we would be one of the very, very few people to ever have done this,' he enthused as they caught their breath in a scum port-hole surrounded by spiders.

Linh stayed close to him and blew extra hard into the snorkel to evict any straying creatures.

When they got to Katherine, they stayed the day in a caravan park and spent a good while catching up with family. It didn't take long to find someone whose phone they could use after the exchange of a few travel stories and a few notes to cover the cost. To add to the complications, they had to ring family friends first who would then make their phones available to whoever the call was intended. They were determined to stay below the radar as much as possible.

'Do you think they know where we are, Owie?' Linh asked when they were lying in bed.

'Are you kidding?' came his scornful reply. 'This rig probably has a transponder the size of a football stuck to it somewhere. As long as it's only Alasdair's mob that's tracking us.'

'So, we were never in any danger of getting lost then.'

'Oh, thank you for the vote of confidence... I knew exactly where we were at all times.'

Linh draped her leg over Owen's thigh and rubbed herself against him. '... mmm, and where are we now?'

'Right now,' Owen drew her closer, 'we're in the middle of Oz and I'm in bed with the loveliest Munchkin of them all.'

From Katherine, the couple headed to Flora River National Park, which was a relatively short trek. When Owen was a boy, the family had camped there and he'd always remembered the incredible beauty of the falls. Though not spectacular in height, it was their broad cascades and the surrounding fringes of vegetation that made an aesthetic impact on his young mind.

He wanted to show Linh. They spent the day exploring the tracks that surrounded the pools, being mindful that maybe, just maybe, a saltwater crocodile had made its way to this remote location.

The camping area was surprisingly busy, so rather than trying to shoehorn their van into an available space, they decided to either find a place off the road or to continue to Victoria River. As it happened, the terrain remained so unvarying and the road verges so exposed that Owen advised Linh just to keep on driving.

'I don't like being too close to the road,' he mused, '... the concentration of desperados in this part of the world is just a bit too high for my liking.'

The Trakka had been fitted with moderately powerful driving lights that cast a useful beam onto the verges.

'That's where the wildlife always ambushes you,' he pointed out, '... straight out of the scrub and into the side of your car.'

'Do you remember that ute at the campsite with the rack of spotlights on the roof? It'd be like driving in daylight.'

'Yeah, but no good for out on the road. You have to dip your lights for oncoming traffic way in advance, and all your night vision is ruined, so you'd be driving blind for a good bit.'

'Well, how about that, hey!' Linh said in her best Ocker.

Owen's phone chimed.

'Didn't think there'd be any reception out here,' he said softly. '... mmm... no ID.'

The two of them exchanged a meaningful glance. Owen swiped to the message.

'Drive on to Timber Creek, apparently. That's what it says.'

'How far is that?'

Owen stroked at his chin. 'Well, we're not that far from Victoria River... probably be one hundred and thirty k's... two hours. We'll get a coffee at the roadhouse.'

Linh looked over. 'What's in Timber Creek?'

'Not much. It's on the Victoria River... got the Keep River National Park on one side of the river, and Bradshaw military training area on the other basically.'

'A military zone?'

'Yeah. O...kay. I like your thinking. You think maybe he lives there?'

Linh shrugged. 'How do you get there if it's across the river?'

'Bloody big concrete bridge! It's a huge, wide bridge across the Victoria River which has got to be at least two hundred metres across at that point, and when you get to the other side you come to a dead stop because there are massive steel gates preventing anyone from going any further.'

'Ideal,' said Linh. 'And does it have a sign saying, 'No Junk Mail'?'

They laughed. Road signs ahead informed them of the roadhouse not far away.

'How big is this training area?'

Owen raised his brow in thought. 'As far as I know, it's very big... used to be a pastoral lease. I think it goes all the way to the coast...'

'What do they do there?'

'Spend obscene amounts of money.'

'Sounds like our man...'

'Yeah, you're right. The only trouble is that every now and again they play with their guns and I would say that things could get pretty hectic.'

They pulled over at the roadhouse. It was quite cold outside. Owen supposed that the tall escarpments that surrounded them probably dropped cold air into the valley and then trapped it there.

Though it was only early in the evening, there was hardly anyone about. Owen thought he'd give their latest theory an airing.

He approached the woman behind the counter. 'What are the chances of having a bit of a squiz at the old Bradshaw station?'

She kept her eyes on the coffees she was making. 'Excellent... yeah, no worries. You'll need to make your way over in a tinny or something, because the bridge is closed. And you'll probably be wanting to finalise your will, because there's a good chance you won't be coming back. If they catch you there... well, you know... it's a military zone... *We were just shooting our cannons and a bomb landed right on him... couldn't find any pieces...*' She looked at them with a mordant smirk.

Owen returned a sober smile. 'Good-oh. Do any of the locals do catering or anything like that out there?'

The two coffees were plonked in front of them. 'They live on rations, love... it's the army... they're on exercises... it's not Club Med.' She rang up the amount on the till. 'Why do you ask?'

Owen made an indefinable noise, 'Just curious... thanks for the coffee.'

The waitress leant with her elbows on the counter. 'Y'know... on first impressions, you two looked like a very sensible couple.'

'We are.'

'Yeah?' She dropped her hand to Owen as he reached for the cups. 'I'd love to hear your story... I'm writing a book... about all the crazy people that come in here.'

'We're not that crazy.'

'No? Then why aren't you snuggled up to each other at some campsite... or even the side of the road. There's nothing ahead worth rushing to. Go on, give me a hint. I'll let you choose your names... for the book.'

Owen released his hold on the cups and enfolded the waitress's hand in both of his. 'Okay... well, I'm Uther and this is my friend, Guinevere, and, after our deaths, we asked the Keeper of the Lake to transport us to a time and place of sublime tranquillity, and we were reincarnated as backpackers.'

'Oh, that's beautiful!' With an emotional sniff, she patted Owen's hand. 'Well, just remember, Uther... out on Bradshaw, they don't use swords and shields anymore... so be careful.'

On the way back to the car, Linh gave Owen a sideways look. 'You know... sometimes, a whole new aspect of your personality just leaps out into the open.

Owen reached for her hand. 'It's a funny thing, Linh... I lived out in the bush for so long... it wasn't until I went to high school in Brisbane that I became more socialised. In year nine, I ended up getting a part in a play, and I really enjoyed it... y'know, pretending to be someone else. My English teacher made me go in two more plays. She said that I carried a role very convincingly. Maybe there's a thespian inside of me waiting to come out.'

Linh unlocked the van. 'Well... you might *need* to carry a role if Alasdair's story is anything to go by.'

They reached Timber Creek about two hours later, and drove straight into the caravan park, which was off the highway. Five minutes later, they were plumping their pillows and wriggling under the blankets, barely able to keep their eyes open.

The sun was well up by the time they slid open the door. Willy wagtails were chattering on the lawn.

A man, sitting in one of their camping chairs, turned to them and said, 'Good Morning, Owen... good morning, Linh.'

Owen nodded and massaged his scalp. 'Good morning. I take it that you will be our lift.'

'Correct,' he replied. 'Dane is the name,' and he flicked off a little salute. 'Best hurry,' he added, '... Alasdair is expecting you.'

Ten minutes later, the two travellers were strolling through the winter sunshine, toiletries in hand, towards a clearing a little way downstream. A dun coloured Robinson R44, so dull that it barely stood out against the beige of the river, was parked on the grass.

Soon, they were flying northwest, over the concrete bridge, towards distant escarpments.

'There's only one way to appreciate this country, isn't there,' Dane called over the intercom.

'Yes,' Owen agreed, '... same as where I come from... you can see the terrain and the geology so incredibly well.'

'Oh, that's right! I'd forgotten you were certified on rotors. Here... have a go. Can you fly from the left seat?'

... unusually well briefed...

'That's where I always fly... my father always takes the right. I'm used to it.'

Owen took the control column and dropped his right hand to the collective pitch lever. Even though it was a bigger machine than he was used to, the controls were very light and responsive. He kicked in a few banked turns and marvelled at the three-dimensional freedom that helicopters produced.

'Very nice, Dane... but I'll let you take over. I'll enjoy the view.'

Dane took the controls. 'You see that green strip up ahead? That's where we're headed... into the gorge.'

The country around them was the typical sparse eucalypt and melaleuca grassland of the Northern Territory. It was only in the protected valleys that palms, figs and other eucalypts grew lush and dense. One such valley opened up in front of them.

In the rear seat, Linh asked a pertinent question, 'So, this *is* the military training zone, right?'

'Correct, Linh... we are flying in a highly restricted area. That's the beauty of having a hideaway in an army exercise range—no one would dream of entering. Alasdair's shack is separate from the live fire sites. The whole place is huge... plenty of room for one hermit with a penchant for conspiracies.' He laughed.

Owen looked up through the bubble canopy at some brilliantly white cumulus clouds. 'It continually amazes me,' he pondered aloud, '... how up-front you guys are about your position as conspirators. Wouldn't it be wise to play down that role just a smidgen?'

Dane lined up the R44 with a particularly narrow section of the gorge—where it became a chasm. 'Ah, Owen,' he sighed as he checked left and right for position markers, '... nowadays you can say whatever you like... politicians do it all the time. They say the most outrageous things—it gets covered every which way on a hundred different media platforms... and then, pfft!... the whole story just evaporates.'

The helicopter was now hovering just above the palms surrounding a large, black waterhole. Slowly, Dane approached the massive red sides of the chasm. 'I'm thinking of creating an app called 'Follow-up' or something... y'know—you mark the news items that you're interested in, and you get all the relevant updates that are available.'

'And when the updates stop?' Linh questioned, looking with apprehension at the sheer rock on either side of them.

'Ah!' Dane punctuated his point with a raised finger on the control column, 'That is when the app marshals the forces of social media to continue the line of enquiry.'

Owen's whole body tensed as they travelled slowly through the ravine. 'So,' he tried to sound relaxed, '... there's no way of escaping what's been said.'

Another chasm appeared on the left, entering the main gorge at a higher height. A thin waterfall plummeted to the jumble of rocks below. At this point, the gorge was wider, creating a very steep amphitheatre.

Dane swung the R44 to face the new opening. 'That's right! Politicians, corporate heads and the like, will be held accountable. And if they cite any so-called facts and figures to support their case, the app will give them time to produce the hard evidence.'

'And, no doubt, will continue to hound them until they do—Jesus!... Dane, couldn't we just have dropped into here from up there?' Owen pointed upwards, '... it *is* a helicopter, after all!'

Dane laughed as he slowly rotated the machine through three hundred and sixty degrees. 'I know... but I wanted you to appreciate just how inaccessible this place is by foot.'

They were once again facing the smaller gorge, a comparatively narrow rift through the flat topography of the land above. Dense vegetation proliferated at the rock-strewn bottom where a creek tumbled until it spilled over the abyss into the main gorge. A curious feature of the ravine was a massive remnant arch or bridge that must have been thirty or so metres wide.

Dane turned to Linh. 'What do you think?'

She shook her head in amazement. 'I've never seen a place so beautiful.'

'No, I mean the app... do you think it'll work?'

Linh laughed out loud and reached forward to give Dane a reassuring pat on the shoulder. 'You might cop a bit of opposition... but god knows, we need something like that.'

Dane chuckled.

The thick stone bridge, craggy and weathered, seemed to have many cave-like apertures in its face. Vines and roots hung down and spread across the openings as though they were protective bars and grills to prevent entry... or, for that matter, exit.

Standing in front of one of the caves was a man, waving. The helicopter climbed to the height of the waterfall and then over the precipice to a large flat rock in the stream bed.

Owen and Linh tried to stay in sight of the waving figure but, by now, the rock bridge was too high above them.

Dane applied all his concentration as he steered the R44 to the rock platform. The machine settled down nicely and the engine was quickly switched off. He took care of the fuel and battery procedures and whipped off his headphones.

'Okay,' he said with a mischievous grin, '... are you ready for the exciting part of this excursion?'

'Oh, my god,' said Linh, '... do we have to climb up there,' and she pointed to the daunting sheer face that rose to the arch above them.

'Impossible!' Dane retorted as he opened his door. 'Come on.' He stepped out and walked towards the edge of the platform.

The two visitors followed Dane along a rough stone path bordered with ferns and shrubs. It led further into the gorge until the massive bulk of the arched bridge blocked the sunlight.

Owen estimated the width of the canyon to be about the same as the height to the bottom of the arch—thirty or forty metres. It was only now that they were in shade that he could see the two thick cables, side by side, that ran from the midpoint of the arch to a platform on the bed of the little creek that they were following. They neared the place where the cables were anchored. It seemed as though they rose out of the ground without any support from above.

Looking up at the bridge formation that spanned the gorge, Owen could see, despite the contrast of shadows against the bright sky, that the bottom of the arch was unusually uniform and smooth. He cupped his hands tightly around his eyes to eliminate the glare.

'... whoa...' he murmured, '... it's artificial... man-made...'

All three of them stood peering heavenward. At a place in between where the cables were attached to the bottom of the arch, an aperture suddenly appeared. From within, attached to the cables on either side, a glass pod began its descent to the canyon floor. Within a minute it came to rest on the platform between the cable anchoring points.

'Going up,' said Dane with a little too much levity. The pod looked big enough for only two people—and it was just a transparent cylinder with no hand holds or rails of any description.

It was in fact two concentric transparent cylinders. This became obvious when the outer cylinder rose about two metres. This revealed that the inner cylinder had an elongated opening large enough to admit a person.

'I'll see you again before you leave,' Dane said, holding out his hand. 'For the moment, it will be just you and Alasdair—and his friend. Be scared by all means, but don't be afraid—the whole structure is way over-engineered.'

They shook hands with Dane and faced the cylinder.

'Oh, Owie... I'm shaking.' Linh took a few hesitant steps forward then looked behind her. 'Hey?... are you coming?'

Owen felt rooted to the spot. Whilst he had no qualms at all about getting airborne in a helicopter, the starkness of the engineering principles involved in the building of this vaulted structure, and the operation of the lift suspended from it, allowed him to fathom the immensity of the forces very clearly. This was an engineering feat that would have presented huge difficulties given the isolation and the need for secrecy. He was utterly awed. He also, unfortunately, had a fear of heights.

It had taken him a long time to come to grips with heli-mustering. Looking out at the horizon was not a problem—staring at the backs of cattle as they thundered over the bare ground always left him feeling slightly unwell.

'Owie?... are you going to be alright?'

'Huh?... oh, sure. Wow, this is amazing isn't it? I can't believe the engineering involved.'

They entered the cylinder. It was very small.

'... I mean, these cables for instance, would have to be under a fair bit of tension in order to prevent the lift from swaying, but not so tight that it would put undue strain on the structure above... which, incidentally, blows my mind...'

The outer cylinder dropped down. The lift began to ascend. They were, to all intents and purposes, standing on a small disc rising above the canyon floor with an uninterrupted view of the waterfall precipice in front of them and the yawning gorge beyond it.

'... I mean, how did they secure it to the canyon sides?... well, they didn't... I bet the frames were a neat fit and that their natural sag would have pinned the sides to the wall... that's what I would have done...' Owen's voice was unnaturally loud inside the cylinder.

The helicopter below seemed like a toy. They were suspended in space.

'... because that's how they would have done it... modular... modular...'

'Please don't faint, darling. Don't faint... just close your eyes... hold me tight... smell my hair... do you like it?'

Owen closed his eyes and let his face drop to Linh's head. He breathed in deeply. Her hair smelled so nice... spices... herbs... lemon myrtle... even when they were camping. She was so clever.

The sounds inside the cylinder changed. Owen opened his eyes. They were inside the arch. With a slight hiss, the outer cylinder continued to rise, opening the narrow aperture. On the other side stood Alasdair, smiling and at ease. He beckoned them to step out.

Linh gave Owen a gentle push.

He exited with a lurch, his hand at full stretch towards Alasdair. 'Hello, Alasdair,' he announced exuberantly.

Alasdair let the hand go by and caught Owen around the chest just as the young man sagged into him. Showing surprising strength, Alasdair hefted Owen towards a bench set against the wall. Linh rushed out of the lift and, gripping Owen's belt, took some of the weight. They laid him out with a scatter cushion under his head.

'Hello, Linh,' Alasdair said warmly, '... I can't tell you how pleased I am to see you both.' He put his arm around her and hugged her near.

'Hello, Alasdair,' Linh replied right next to his ear. 'I do apologise for my man. He becomes a little overwhelmed at times.'

Alasdair laughed heartily. 'He is an amazing man... you are very lucky to have him.'

Linh broke away and held onto the old man's hands. 'I know... I know.'

'Here... take off his shoes and we'll give his feet a gentle massage... that's the best way to bring somebody back to consciousness.'

The two of them administered their treatment, Alasdair sitting on the bench and Linh sitting on the floor.

'Dane is my son,' Alasdair said, 'I noticed that he gave you the scenic tour.'

'Your son!' Linh replied. Then she looked deeply into his eyes. 'That's really nice... I'm glad you have your son here with you.'

'So am I, Linh. He's been one of the best people I've ever worked with... and I choose my staff very, very carefully.'

A low moan from Owen reminded them to focus on his needs.

'Hey, Owie... are you coming to join us?... whenever you're ready, sweetheart... we'll just keep massaging your feet in the meantime... that was Alasdair's idea... good huh...'

Owen opened his eyes. 'I've done it again, haven't I?'

Linh slid over the floor and embraced him. 'Yes, you did. Do you feel better now?'

Owen pulled her closer. '... more kissing...'

Linh happily obliged. '... Alasdair is here,' she said eventually.

'I know. I'm going to make him wait... as punishment for making me go in his lift.'

Alasdair roared with laughter. 'Well, Owen... I have some good news, and that is that there is another way out of here.'

Owen presented his hand without sitting up.

'I'm so glad you've come around, Owen... in more ways than one.' He shook hands.

Linh helped him into a sitting position. 'All the blood back in your head, Owie?'

'Yeah, all good.'

Alasdair held out his hand and pulled Owen to his feet. 'Come on... let's have breakfast out on the balcony—the view is to die for.'

Linh put her arm around Owen's waist and gripped his belt. Together, they walked towards one of the barred cave openings and beheld the sunlit amphitheatre that loomed infinitely from the depths of the ravine to the ragged ridges against the sky.

Chapter Twenty-Two

The balcony was inside a cave, and the tangle of vines and roots that screened the opening were made from wrought iron and acted as a barrier. Potted plants, strategically positioned around the entrance, completed the natural appearance of the construction.

Owen looked closely at how the rock façade was connected to the steel frames.

Alasdair tried to suppress a grin. 'The whole gorge was laser mapped. From that information we made a model on a 3D printer. Then we fiddled with straws and kebab sticks and solder wire and eventually came up with a series of modular frames that could be built elsewhere, then heli-lifted into position.'

Owen darted a wink in Linh's direction.

'... the biggest issue was the shell. It had to look natural... it had to be transportable... it had to be durable, and it had to be waterproof. We decided on modular square sections made from steel and fibreboard with integrated gutters to direct seepage away to proper drains. When the structure was completed, we sat a few hollow boulders and slabs on top, scattered a few cleverly disguised planter boxes about and, viola... a natural bridge and a spectacular home.'

Owen nodded in admiration. 'So, because the whole structure is actually relatively light, you had to put in those two cables to help to spread it against the walls of the canyon... just in case a cyclone came along...'

'Bravo, Owen... that is what I expect from you.'

'Yeah, but who was the genius that thought of the lift?'

Alasdair meekly put up his hand. 'You have to admit though, it makes for a breath-taking entrance.'

Linh hugged her man. 'It certainly took *his* breath away.'

He stroked her leg. 'I'll be okay in that thing now... it was just the whole... grandeur of the place... the amazing construction. It overloaded my low-pressure brain.'

A woman carrying a tray of drinks entered the vast living space and padded barefoot on the timber floor towards the balcony. Alasdair rose from his seat. The visitors followed suit.

'I'd like you to meet my wife, Irena.'

Irena looked about the same age as Alasdair, so she could also have been in her eighties. She put the tray on the table.

The couple came forward and shook hands.

Irena smiled brightly. Her eyes were a vivid green. 'It's very nice to meet you,' she said with a trace of eastern European accent.

Alasdair pulled up a chair for her as Irena chatted and poured the tea.

The foursome watched the light play on the lofty cliffs around them. Owen and Linh could have been the older couple's grandchildren and yet the conversation never patronised in either direction—both generations had important insights to contribute, and each complemented the other's world view.

Irena had a wonderful effervescence. She could draw from the arts, science, history and the esoteric, not in a pretentious way, but rather to colour her stories, often with an ironic dig at the futile aspirations of the modern era.

After they'd had their drinks, they toured the 'Eyrie', as Alasdair called their home. The visitors were shown their room, also with a balcony and an art nouveau type trellis for safety.

'I'll leave you to make yourselves comfortable,' he said, and informed them that there were clothes that they could choose from in the wardrobes. 'Come and have some lunch when you feel like it.'

The interior walls were done in a free-form rendered style to simulate, Linh suggested, the caves of Cappadocia. The room was richly decorated with rugs, vases, wall hangings, sculptures, decorative wooden screens, paintings as well as cabinets and other exotic furniture. Linh looked closely at a leather-bound tome lying on a low table.

She whistled softly. 'Owie... take a look at this... I do believe this is a pretty authentic illuminated manuscript.' She wiped her finger pads on her shirt and carefully opened the book.

The illustrations were in the deepest colour and outlined in gold. The supple pages had a translucent quality. 'I think this is vellum, Owie... it must be very old... like a thousand years old.'

'A thousand years?... then what's it doing on a table like it was a copy of the Readers Digest?... what language is it in?'

'Don't know... Latin I imagine... looks like Latin.'

'I wonder how many other people get to stay here? I mean, if it is a secret place, you could hardly invite people willy-nilly.'

In the centre of the room, hanging from the very high ceiling by a large copper duct was a huge glass dome about two metres across that shone with a pearl lustre.

Owen tried to look up into it. 'Must be a skylight.' He pointed to a ring of vents around the base of the duct. 'See... the sunlight warms the air inside the duct which rises and is exited outside. Cool air comes in through the balcony. I bet in the hot months they put misters on for the plants which also cools the air.'

Linh put her arms around her lover. 'You're so smart, Owie.'

'I'm smart?... you're the one that knows all about velour and stuff.'

'Vellum...'

'... smarty...'

They kissed.

Lunch was a very simple meal that included charred peppers, dates, hummus and Turkish pide bread made from Australian native seeds.

'An unemployed couple that I met many years ago spend their time collecting seeds from Australian grasses for me. It suits them... they travel around Australia, and we get to enjoy some really different bread...'

'At about one hundred and eighty dollars a loaf,' Irena added as she dexterously thumbed crumbs to her mouth.

Owen and Linh exchanged a look and shook their heads in wonder.

'Can I ask you where your electricity supply comes from, Alasdair?'

Alasdair indicated a place above them. 'Up over the ridge is an artificial lake... or dam, really... it's not *that* big. The thing is, it's only about a metre or so deep. About a foot below the surface is an entire array of photovoltaic cells—about ten kilowatts worth. Do you know why they're covered in water?'

Owen nibbled at a date. 'Yes... so they stay cool... but, more important... so they can't be seen from space.'

Alasdair slapped Owen's leg. 'Well done! Got it in one.'

'If the water is clear enough,' Owen continued, '... the reflection losses would be offset by the efficiency gains... especially up here, where the summers can heat up the panels so much they hardly work at all.'

'Very true. Of course, we have the benefit of a small, clear stream that runs pretty much year-round.'

'How do you go in the wet season, when this chasm would have tonnes of water pouring into it every second?'

'We have experienced it many times, and I have to say, that we never get used to it—the noise and the vibration is, quite simply, frightening. We have an observation port that you might care to look at later—you can see straight down. Irena and I sit around it in morbid fascination and watch the roiling water below. We unscrew the main cable connectors so that if a log should drive into a cable, the temporary holder will snap thus preventing any damage to the arch.'

'That would indeed be frightening,' Linh concurred with a shudder.

Irena stood up and began to collect the plates and insisted that the visitors remain seated. 'It is time for you to hear a very disturbing story. I will let Ally tell it... it frightens me immeasurably more than the torrent beneath us.'

Alasdair gave his wife a squeeze on the waist as she walked by. 'I hate disrupting such a pleasant occasion as this, but I'm afraid I can't avoid it.' He leant forward and rested his forearms on the table, steepling his fingers in the manner that the young couple had seen before. 'You would be familiar, Owen with the Hadron Collider?'

Owen nodded. 'The Large Hadron Collider... built to examine sub-atomic particles.'

'Correct. For your benefit, Linh... this is a circular machine that is twenty-seven kilometres in circumference and is buried more than one hundred metres below the ground. It is essentially a track devised to accelerate streams of atomic particles by confining them in an immensely powerful magnetic field. The particles go around and around and gather speed and energy, and then they are directed into other particles. The resulting collision is relatively small, but very intense and, some scientists think that they will be able to recreate the conditions of the beginnings of the universe, or the inside of a black hole or some such fantasy.

'Now, this device lurks under the little French township of Saint-Genis-Pouilly, an inoffensive rural idyll at the foothills of the Swiss border. You would suppose correctly if you thought that digging a twenty-seven kilometre tunnel so far underground and lining it with cryogenically cooled super magnets would be expensive—the whole concern purportedly has a budget of some ten billion dollars... which is a ludicrously insufficient amount. No one knows how much it has *really* cost to build this research facility. A large number of nations have contributed to this project, either financially or with scientists, engineers and skilled labour. The cost of the liquid helium alone was many hundred million dollars. None the less, this unlikely gadget was built with enormous support from governments around the world—governments that scrimp and lie about their domestic budgets and who are constantly juggling expenditure to best achieve survival for their party. You'd have to wonder how they would feel about contributing to a very costly hole in the ground, in a foreign country, so that a bunch of boffins can determine whether or not their theory about a God Particle is in any way a likely thing.

'And that is the paradoxical thing about the Hadron Collider—very few people know about it, even though it has very well-funded publicity campaigns. The trouble is that even people who enjoy science and technology topics are left confused and confounded by the baffling hypothetical hyperbole that most of the scientists engage in to make their purpose sexier. They can't even point to a domestic spin-off for all their research in the way that the NASA space program promoted Teflon and Velcro which, by the way, were in existence long before John Glenn orbited the earth.

'So, without burdening you with more of my cynicism, I will tell you that many people have suspected that the Hadron Collider is actually a weapon—a super laser. There abound many conspiracy theories on this topic, all freely accessible on the web. The problem with this idea is that a ground-based laser has minimal practicality in destroying targets that are also at ground level, and limited ability to deal with airborne attacks and, for that matter, threats from space. The field of fire is simply much too restricted. The residents of Saint-Genis-Pouilly might feel very comforted about being protected by such a powerful weapon, but they would be deluded.

'So, the question remains... why spend so much money on something that doesn't appear to have any social benefits?'

Owen gently intervened. 'As I recall, one of the successes of the collider was to prove the existence of the Higgs boson... whatever that is.'

'Precisely... *whatever that is!*' Alasdair punctuated the statement with a hearty slap on the table. 'I appreciate, more than anyone— because I'm not really *that* technically minded—that a lot of research delves into extremely obscure theory that is incomprehensible to most people, but that does eventually result in a useful product. Take the magnetron, for instance, devised initially for theorists to establish electron mass, then becoming an integral part of World War Two radar systems, and finally, finding a home as the microwave in your kitchen. And solid-state memory drives... I can't imagine how much theoretical conjecture was aired before it became technically possible to build one.

'But the Higgs boson?... quarks?... where are we going with that? And bear in mind that tunnelling for the collider began in 1983... there were no mobile phones then... the first computers were being proudly hefted onto kitchen tables, but you couldn't print anything decent... there was no internet. We lived with the technology that our parents grew up with— ringing from a phone booth. If you think that quarks, gluons and string theory is impenetrable in *today's* world, how *compelling* must the argument have been to go ahead and dig a huge circular tunnel somewhere in France when the Cross-Channel tunnel wouldn't be started for another *five years*!

Linh suddenly put a hand to her mouth to stifle a laugh. 'You're funny, Alasdair,' she said warmly.

Alasdair leaned aside and hugged her. He laughed. 'You know, the best comedy nowadays is the news—particularly from a conspirator's point of view. When you are informed of the reality, the dissembling and deception that politicians engage in is truly laughable. Not that Irena and I go out of our way to be amused by politicians.'

Crows called to each other as they winged over the abyss of the amphitheatre. The afternoon sun produced new highlights on the plunging cliffs and reflected a lovely orange glow towards the balcony.

'I hope you won't mind if I continue my tale... I *am* going somewhere with it.'

Owen nodded respectfully and Linh brought her legs up and hugged her knees.

Alasdair looked into the distance. '... 1983... of course, planning for this project started long before then—it started when the Americans dropped an atomic bomb on Hiroshima. Various powerful cadres in Europe realised that everything had suddenly changed. The emergence of the USA as an atomic power was going to present a whole new paradigm, where conventional battle strategies were instantly outmoded. They needed something new... but what? An atom bomb of their own? No... that was not a defensive measure and might very likely lead to mutually assured destruction. The British and the French did develop their own nuclear devices but sharing a continent with their potential enemy meant that they had to look for something else... something more refined. What then?... what new destructive technology was on the horizon at that time?... what was the ultimate weapon? "I know!" said an assistant research technician reading his super-hero comic book in the stairwell of the laboratory, "A light beam of heat and electrons," or something to that effect... or it may have been Viscount, Faux Pas, lounging in his club and puffing on his Hoyo de Monterrey Double Corona who said, "I'm reliably informed that the creation of a death ray is a distinct possibility. We should expedite the relevant research at all costs."

Linh couldn't help giggling at Alasdair's impressions.

'Whatever the impetus, research accelerated on what would become known as the laser. Now, the laser, an acronym for, Light Amplification by Stimulated Emission of Radiation, was a development of the microwave amplifier, which the British had perfected to a high degree and, despite what the history books say, they improved on that technology and created very deadly beams which they kept very secret.

'But, there was the problem with deployment. The lasers would require prodigious amounts of energy, and they would need to be positioned around the defensive perimeter of the host country, which is not usually where the power stations are. As it happened, all of this stealthy research was taking place just at the time when we were getting serious about launching ourselves into space, and it wasn't long before the cleaning lady, who regularly perused the unintelligible scribblings left on the bench tops, announced one day, "If you put the laser into a geo-stationary orbit, you can charge the gain medium from a laser on earth conveniently located near a power station. That way you'll have an excellent field of fire." This undeniable logic shamed the boffins into making enough improvements so that the cleaning lady couldn't claim a Nobel Prize. They scribbled some more, and came to the breathtaking conclusion that, with the proper infrastructure, they could indeed make the ultimate weapon—an X ray laser.

'Now, a normal laser weapon requires a lot of power, but an X ray laser needs ridiculous amounts of power—so much, in fact, that in order to build up charge in the gain medium chamber, the whole lot would be vaporised before sufficient energy was collected. What to do? Well, another technology serendipitously arrived to save the day—the computer. The experts crunched the numbers and waded through spools of printouts to come to a solution. Rather than bombard the chamber with coherently aligned light, they would select just those aspects of the photons that would deliver the maximum amount of energy with the least amount of heating. Yet again, in the era of exploding scientific knowledge, the answers came from another erstwhile quest—the holy grail of nuclear fusion. In that technology, powerful magnetic fields would suspend matter so that it could transmute into a different state. This is what they needed to create the fundamental particles that would power the X ray laser in space. But where to put it? Well, seeing as how this weapon of defence would benefit countries in a two-thousand-mile radius, they decided to put it in the geographical centre of Europe and encouraged all those countries to contribute, both financially and in spirit, by creating the European Union... but that's whole other story, so let's not go there for the moment.

'So anyway, that's where they began to dig their hole... underneath a little village in France... and a little bit in Switzerland—*what the hell!* Wouldn't the Swiss have something to say about this? They couldn't just move it a few hundred metres away from the border? Apparently not. It had to go right there, and the Swiss were okay with that. Go figure!

'They began to shape their public relations doctrine. In conjunction with our infatuation with outer-space, they commenced *the exploration of inner space*—as though it was vital to the needs of society. They created myths about space and time, reality and consciousness. They commissioned art work to evoke the majesty and mystery of the universe, all to beguile and mesmerize a credulous public. But, the whole time, the emphasis was on developing a defensive X ray laser that would protect Europe from any sort of threat, be it on land, sky or in space, conventional or nuclear... a very old regime was shoring up its defences.

'The last piece of the puzzle was how to get their laser into space. And so, the European Space Agency was formed, *seventeen years after NASA*, despite having all the intellectual and physical resources plus a very good reason to match the Russians in their space program. And what did they do? They sent a telescope into orbit... yes, a telescope... and not just any orbit, no. They put it in a high orbit... a geosynchronous orbit above Europe. Except of course that it wasn't a telescope. It was cylindrical like a telescope, but it was in fact, you guessed it, the gain medium body of the laser. Now all that remained was to wait for the earth laser to begin shooting up some super-charged atomic particles, and the weapon was ready to fire.

Alasdair took a deep breath. 'I think we'll all need a stiff drink after this.'

With a knowing pout, Owen studied the old man. 'But, this *is* only half the story, isn't it?

'*Half the story!*' Alasdair threw back his head in surprise, 'My goodness, Owen... I reveal to you one of the best kept secrets of modern times, and it's not enough for you?'

Linh looked back and forth between the two men, not sure what to make of the exchange.

Owen continued to eye Alasdair.

'Oh, very well, young man... the rest of the story. Well, it goes like this; after twenty-seven years of anticipation, the Large Hadron Collider was finally completed. In 2010, they fired it up and commenced experimenting. Three years later they shut it down. Had it all been worth it? My word it had! They had discovered that the Higgs boson existed... and, as you said, Owen, *whatever that means.* Then they worked on the machine for two years and recommenced their schedule of colliding particles into each other—but only for part of the year, because it is always shut down over winter... wouldn't want those cryogenically cooled magnets to get cold.'

Alasdair gave a deprecatory chuckle. 'I'm becoming facetious. Another curious operational feature is that the machine takes ages to warm up... months sometimes. What I'm getting at is that the machine is only really available for the research scientists for a relatively short time. But then again, how many particle collisions are needed to prove any of these whimsical theories? Most of the time the Hadron collider is ticking over very nicely and sending a stream of high energy particles into space... to the X ray laser that everybody hopes they'll never have to use.

'And then, someone realised that the collider could be boosted to produce even more intense particles to create the *ultimate*, ultimate weapon—a gamma laser. This, believe me, is the most desirable weapon that any country could possess—particularly in this day and age... because, a gamma laser will wipe out stored digital data, and as you know, the world's weaponry is utterly dependent on computers. A gamma laser could be aimed at some institution, government or military, and no one would know about it. It would invisibly scan backwards and forwards emitting rays that will travel through concrete, earth, human bodies and memory matrixes. It will corrupt files to make them completely unusable. It will also cause the employees to age prematurely, but not so that anyone would notice. It truly is an advantageous weapon, particularly if it is only used defensively and its existence is kept very secret. Now, they are a long way away from building the laser body that can cope with the miniscule wavelength of gamma rays, but they're working on it. My understanding is that, because we haven't invented a reflector for gamma radiation—and it's probably impossible—the gain medium body is unable to shuttle the radiation backwards and forwards in order to align the waves so as to make a unified beam. The solution is to make the body very long... *very* long, and thereby create direction for the emerging gamma radiation as the electron layers of the gain medium collapse. So now, the European Space Agency is talking about habitation on the moon—creating a lunar outpost. Is this where they plan to make their super long gamma laser? Why, given all the turmoil and social discontent at the moment, would any government seriously put aside the billions of dollars required to build a space base? And anyway, isn't the moon a bit far from earth? Well, no apparently. Because the gamma laser will be used to insidiously destroy digital networks over a prolonged period of time, it can be focused in a general area and left to do its corrupting work. The fact that the attack is a bit indiscriminate, and that tens of thousands of people will be affected to varying degrees, is of little consequence, and may in fact be a very acceptable trade-off when one considers the alternative means by which a nation might be subjugated.

'Okay, time for an admission on my part—I have no idea what I'm talking about. My information, which I have memorised fairly faithfully, comes from various trusted sources. It is not up to me to understand the physics behind it all, but rather to gain an overview and to implement an appropriate strategy. However, as far as we're concerned, it is immaterial whether or not it is possible to construct a gamma laser, and here is the reason why.

'Weird things are happening in the village of Saint-Genis-Pouilly. For a while now, the inhabitants have been noticing that their wrist watches have been losing time. At first it was just a curiosity. Bear in mind that the township is virtually a suburb of the city of Geneva—the timepiece capital of the world. Residents noticed that when they left the town, their watches were perhaps a few hundredths of a second behind, and when they returned, they would be ahead of the local time. It was only ever a matter of tiny fractions of a second, but in this part of the world, where there is such a pride in keeping accurate time, that was a particularly noteworthy phenomenon. Then, in view of the number of current conspiracy theories doing the rounds on the internet, locals thought that they might investigate this anomaly more rigorously, and came to the conclusion that, yes, there did indeed seem to be a time dilation oddity. Now, you might think that a few milliseconds here and there is not worth worrying about, but I am assured by those in the know, that this represents a catastrophic warp in the nature of things. Time dilation supposedly exists naturally and is caused by differences in gravitational fields. This means that the centre of the earth is actually two years younger than the surface, even though it has been one and the same for billions of years. I know... inconceivable. But now, the crusade to separate the constituents of sub-atomic particles for the purposes of creating a gamma ray energy source, is meddling with the fabric of the universe—we are prying at a chink in the armour of reality. As well, some experts think we are in danger of infecting our dimension with "strangelets", an other-dimensional virus that has the potential to eat up this realm.

'What I *do* know is this—we are not *meant* to escape the dominion of space as we know it—we are not *meant* to interfere with the constructs of our universe. The conundrum of infinity will never be solved by us—we must live with the ambiguity of space and time and enjoy it for what it is. It is better for us to live in an illusion, than to attempt to find an answer we cannot grasp.'

The shadows had lengthened on the hulking rock faces, and it had become noticeably cooler.

Lost in thought, the young couple stared into the abyss. Irena emerged onto the balcony with a tray of drinks which she very quietly set on the table. Alasdair hugged her as she settled into a seat next to him.

'Have you been frightening the children with your stories, Ally?' she probed.

Alasdair smiled wanly. 'Yes... it's not my favourite story, that's for sure.'

Linh spoke. 'So, when you were talking about a global threat, you literally meant the Earth?'

'Unfortunately, yes. It is a very serious, very real threat that has suddenly emerged. As I have said repeatedly, our technology is outstripping our ability to deal wisely with it. I won't say we have a collective wisdom, because we don't. Humans have very rarely demonstrated a collective wisdom. Any of the smart moves we've made in the past have been based on commercial self-preservation. We've never restrained ourselves from capitalising on discoveries, technology and any other opportunity that manifested itself. We are not inherently wise. We are inherently opportunistic and rapacious. And now we are pursuing a technology that appears to offer unrivalled dominance for those in possession, except that it may well wipe out everything.'

Irena handed Owen a tall, green drink. She stroked his forehead. 'This is not a suicide pact. It's a mint julep with Jägermeister and native plum... try it.'

Owen sipped on the straw. An overwhelming essence of herbs and spice laced his palette. 'Whoa...' He blinked as the alcohol in the concoction swelled in his throat.

'Nice, huh,' Irena said tenderly, '... it's to help you recover.'

He reached out and squeezed her hand. 'Thank you... this sure is one heady restorative.'

Linh was cautiously sipping her drink. She grinned and made big eyes at Owen.

Owen pointed off-hand. 'That's a very interesting ring on your finger, Irena.'

Irena held out her hand for Owen to have a better look. 'The eye is jade, set in silver. Some beliefs venerate the eye as the source of what we are.' She held the ring out for Linh to see.

'The source of all knowledge?' Linh queried.

Irena resumed her seat. 'Not so much that... more the place from which we have evolved.' There was a small, teasing smile on her lips.

'Have you ever wondered how the eye evolved?'

The young couple sucked thoughtfully on their drinks in anticipation of an interesting story.

'Well, it was probably one of the very first things to arrive in the primordial soup billions of years ago... sensitivity to light. We're not talking about the fully developed animal eye, but a creature made of just a few photosensitive cells. Then, as the creatures evolved, they never lost the ability to sense light and gradually, through beneficial selection, animals evolved to make better use of the light by focusing it and differentiating the colours. So, really we have developed around our eye.'

'Is that why,' Linh mused, '... we focus so intently on a person's eyes when we speak to them?'

'Maybe,' Irena shrugged. 'We're subconsciously recognising our origins.'

Alasdair acknowledged the point. 'It's like so many things that we are led to believe—we've got it all back to front.'

'Flight, for instance,' said Irena, '... we agonize over how terrestrial beings developed the ability to fly when, in reality, they flew before they could walk.'

'*Really*?' Linh responded. 'How was that possible?'

'Well, when you consider how close the motion of swimming is to that of flying...'

'But you can't *swim* on land,' Linh argued.

'Not now,' Irena countered, '... but a long, long time ago it would have been possible...'

'When the atmosphere was considerably denser,' Owen interrupted.

'Yes, precisely. There was probably a time when the earth's atmosphere was as thick as that of Venus, and the boundary between it and the ocean was very vague and gradual. Creatures that swam, and we're talking about very tiny organisms, began to favour one medium over the other for whatever reasons. They would alight on the land and be very buoyant because of the thick air. Some evolved to exploit the advantages of flight while others gradually adapted their swimming appendages to better negotiate the terrestrial realm. As the atmosphere thinned, these adaptations became more pronounced and exclusive—they had to own a particular niche. Flying fish are an example of a creature that has retained an ability to inhabit two realms just as their ancient ancestors did. But, of course, amphibians and some reptiles still have close ties to the aquatic domain. And some creatures that had made significant adjustments to living on the land, went back to living in the sea.'

'The whales,' Linh whispered.

'That would have been around the time of the dinosaurs,' Irena continued. 'We look at the size of those Jurassic giants and wonder how they could ever have supported such bulk. But, if you factor in a considerably more buoyant atmosphere, then it becomes possible. As the atmosphere continued to thin, the giant creatures had two options—get smaller or return to a more supportive environment... the ocean. There's reason to believe that the earth's atmosphere was still very dense up until some cataclysmic event about sixty-five million years ago. That is why the big dinosaurs died out—the supportive atmosphere was blown away.'

Owen looked at his empty glass. 'Wow... I'm not sure which packs the biggest punch—this or your conversation.'

There was laughter all round.

Alasdair rose from his seat. 'I suggest we have a little rest and reconvene sometime later this evening. How do you feel about that?'

The couple got to their feet and stretched lazily.

'Sounds good to me, Alasdair. We have a fair bit to digest.'

'Good-oh, then. I'm sorry to have burdened you with such dismal news, but...' he shrugged.

Chapter Twenty-Three

Owen and Linh walked to their balcony via an aerial walkway screened with wrought iron branches and leaves. The view from this part of the Eyrie was more to the east. The last rays of the setting sun highlighted the sheer walls of the ravine opposite them, reflecting a salmon hue. The dazzling tones sparkled off every shiny surface inside the room, making it look like a jewellery box. Linh grabbed Owen from behind and thrust him towards the bed. They plumped to the mattress and rolled in each other's arms. Linh's mouth opened against his. They pressed and probed with delicious familiarity and clung with a burgeoning urgency. Linh began to unbutton Owen's shirt.

He murmured close to her ear, 'Do you think it's okay to disport ourselves naked on the bed in the lair of a major conspirator?'

Linh giggled. 'Owie, if we can't trust them, then... I don't know what. I'm sure they will be more than happy for us to enjoy each other in this gorgeous room... what's wrong with this button...'

When at last the winter sun went down, the room ebbed to grey. On the vast bed, the lovers sprawled over the rumpled sheets, each fast asleep. Silently, mesh screens emerged out of the walls to seal the outside openings. A quoll, on her way to the main balcony to dine on the tit bits that Irena always left, paused for a moment with her paws on the screen and looked at the strangers inside.

It was dark and very quiet when Owen woke up. It had become quite cold. He could just make out Linh's shape, huddled like a foetus. He pulled the doona over her and she groaned with pleasure. Feeling the need to visit the bathroom, Owen put his feet to the floor. Immediately, a track of dim fairy lights built into the floor came on and illuminated the way to the bathroom. He realised that they must have overslept their planned evening meeting, but he wasn't concerned about it. It was as though Alasdair and Irena were like indulgent parents who were infinitely flexible and happy to take things as they came. Still, they had a lot on their mind. This gamma ray development was insane. How were he and Linh going to be of any use in disarming this project? And where did this boat or ship or whatever come into the picture?

He walked from the bathroom back to the bed. A trail of lights branched off at one point and seemed to lead towards the main living areas. On an impulse, he decided he would follow it. But first he headed to the walk-in wardrobe which lit up as he entered. He found a towelling gown and slipped it on. He was feeling rather hungry and the thought of perhaps coming across a fridge with some of that native bread and a tub of butter was very tempting. Following the track of lights, he came to the lounge room and from there he detected a glow emanating from, what he assumed, was the kitchen. The tinkle of cutlery suggested someone's presence inside so, with a discreet cough, he ventured towards the opening.

Alasdair was seated at the table leaning back in his chair and looking very reflective. Spying Owen, he pitched forward and waved him in. With a full mouth, he beckoned Owen to sit down and help himself. 'Great stomachs think alike, hey, Owen!'

'In that respect, I think I'm in the genius category.'

Alasdair smiled and nodded vigorously. He pushed a loaf of bread forwards and assembled various condiments closer to his guest.

As Owen sawed off a slice of bread, Alasdair regained his voice. 'I slept in myself... completely out of it. Irena let me sleep, seeing as how you two hadn't surfaced. Now I'm hungry.'

'You've got a lot on your mind, haven't you? Not that you aren't fully occupied with other issues... but I imagine that this crisis would be weighing rather heavily.'

'Toaster is over there if you want to toast it... yes, you have no idea how much of a quandary I, we, are in. The problem is that the rogue elements that are working within the legitimate organisations, such as CERN and the various space agencies, just to name a few, are very securely embedded and observe the highest degrees of discretion. They manage to direct the gamma laser agenda, amongst other things, without ever revealing their complicity or exposing their network in any way. They are being run by the most elite conspiratorial cadre. And we have no idea who they are. And when I say, we, I refer to a number of worldwide secret organisations who have put aside their differences in order to neutralise this obvious threat to our very existence.'

A noise at the entrance made the men turn.

Wearing a plush kimono, Linh brushed a strand of hair away from her eyes. 'I could smell toast.'

Alasdair laughed and pulled out a chair for her. 'I'll cut you a slab... sit down'

Owen rose to retrieve his toast and inserted Linh's slices.

Linh snorted. 'I'm pretty sure that's a girl's nightgown, Owen.'

'Is it?' both men said in unison.

'How can you tell?' Owen muttered as he looked down his chin at his attire.

'Just the cut... and it is rather tight on you.'

'Oh well...' He sat down and commenced buttering toast for the two of them. 'Alasdair was just saying that various groups around the world have come together to try and thwart the crowd that's making the gamma laser.'

Linh put her hand over Alasdair's. 'Sorry we didn't make it to the meeting. We were exhausted.'

Alasdair gave Linh a reassuring pat. 'Not a problem, my dear... I have just confessed to Owen that I slept right through it too. But now is as good a time as any to engage in conspiratorial intrigue—the dead of night!'

Linh gave a melodramatic shiver. 'Alasdair... how are *we* going to be able to help?'

'Okay... first, some more background. The individuals immediately involved in this project are very careful not to incriminate themselves. If you were to trawl through the offices and the computers at CERN, or any of the other organisations, you would find nothing to connect the research being done with the construction of a gamma ray weapon. Nothing! And yet, the research is mysteriously directed to that very end. What is happening is that certain influential scientists are shaping the research to fulfil the requirements of the weapon.

'It is not as difficult to do as you may think. Consider—the research is of a highly speculative theoretical nature—there are hundreds if not thousands of scientists and engineers employed in the various centres, speaking many different languages, as well as being constrained by normal security protocols and abiding by the usual "need to know" practices. In other words, it's a zoo in there. People are very chuffed to be assigned to the place; they are awarded a nice salary and they can live in Geneva—they're not going to jeopardise that by asserting themselves in some awkward way.

'This nebulous state of affairs makes it very difficult for us to divine what is going on. We can't just announce "Stop what you're doing!" because we don't have that sort of authority... we're not positioned to exert political or social pressure at the moment, surprising as it may be to you. The powers behind the laser development are very well connected and have, no doubt, sufficiently compromised those in positions of influence as to render them ineffectual. The scientists who have spoken out about the likely-hood of a cataclysm have been quietly marginalised and ridiculed. *Those* unfortunates we *do* get to chat to because they end up back in their home country looking for work.

'Now, the situation is so dire that we haven't got time to marshal a campaign. We need to engage in something more direct. We need to know the individuals that are directly involved with this weapon program so that we can neutralise them.'

'Kill them,' Linh interjected.

Alasdair shook his head. 'No, no... not necessary. Once we know an individual is engaged in the program, we can employ all sorts of persuasive stratagems to change their mind. But, we have to know who they are first.'

'And how will you achieve that?' said Owen.

Alasdair leaned forward and steepled his fingers on the table.

Owen shot Linh a quick look.

She smirked.

'The alliance, as I will refer to them from now on, meets reasonably regularly, but randomly.

They meet on a boat... an exceptionally fast mega-yacht named *Zeus*.'

'You're kidding!' Linh erupted.

Alasdair produced a look of defeat. 'I know... pretty blatant, huh.'

Owen looked confused. 'What?'

Linh explained. 'Zeus is a Greek god whose favourite weapon was the lightning bolt.'

'And they have the nerve to call their boat, *Zeus*?'

'Yep,' Alasdair replied, '... although, the name isn't particularly rare amongst the ostentatious posers that own big toys, so it's not as though they're giving the game away. Anyway, *Zeus* is a one-hundred metre long piece of gold plated shrapnel, with four MTU diesels giving it a highly classified cruising speed that we happen to know is over forty knots, which it can sustain all night. That is their modus operandi—members arrive by helicopter or speed boat, *Zeus* shoots off to another port in the Mediterranean, picks up some more guests, shoots off to another place, more helicopter and speedboat rendezvous, until the alliance is all aboard. Then *Zeus* zooms to some other unpredictable nook of the Med. We believe that the meetings usually take place in the middle of the sea someplace. Their movements are so erratic and so rapid that we haven't been able to shadow them.'

'If they travel at night,' said Linh, '... isn't there a danger that they could run over another boat?'

'The surface radar on board,' Alasdair continued, '... is so powerful it could fry a pelican at a hundred metres. Now, on board there is a special meeting room that is lined with lead, sandwiched between ten centimetres of balsa. This effectively isolates the room from any sort of electromagnetic and audio eavesdropping devices. The AV network inside is internal only—no outside connectivity possible. The members walk in with just a solid-state memory device which they can open up on a laptop inside.

'These meetings are all about coordinating the weapons program whilst maintaining the illusion of responsible research within the main organizations. The trips take between three and six days, depending on how many of the alliance come on board. You'd think we would be able to monitor helicopter movements to and from the boat but, for every actual delivery trip, there are about ten false charters. As well, the members are picked up in random places, so it is impossible to cover all bases.

'Another security measure, which I have mentioned before, is to employ menial staff from all over the world so that there is no common language by which to collude. Even some of the technicians are employed on this basis. There is a small dedicated crew, but nothing is known about them. Who the principal organiser is in all of this also remains a mystery. I doubt very much that this identity would ever actually step aboard the *Zeus*. The casual crew, by the way, get on board in their swimmers, and the small amount of personal clothing you are allowed to take with you is checked very thoroughly. Uniforms are supplied.

There was a moment's silence as Alasdair munched his bread.

Owen thought it would be a good time to frame the obvious question. 'Surely this alliance is aware of the time dilation phenomenon. How do *they* propose to escape its effects?'

Alasdair sipped on his cocoa. 'They've run down the collider... it's ticking over at a safe rate at the moment and the time dilation episode has disappeared. There's a discrediting campaign in progress that will eventually suppress the whole incident. People will be too intimidated to talk about it... it'll be history by the end of the year. The thing is, they won't need to fire up the collider for many, many years because that's how long the gamma laser will take to build. And, there are many scientists who vehemently dispute that the collider could ever be dangerous in itself, even if it's ramped up to war mode. Nevertheless, it is important to disclose everything about this piece of technology, and not leave it in the hands of a few who might be tempted to take the chance for a conclusive, pre-emptive strike. We may not have as much time as we think.'

Linh spoke through a mouthful of toast. 'And... how are *we* supposed to prevent this thing from happening?'

With a big sigh, Alasdair cast his gaze to the table. 'I don't know that you can, Linh... I don't know that you can. We are clutching at straws here. Our break came when one of our agents tried to enlist a Finnish machine operator to do some work for us. He was all set to go when he told us that he'd been offered a job on a super-yacht that he couldn't knock back. Our agent asked him about this job and filed the information accordingly. When we found out about the *Zeus*, we realised that we had a man in position. However, he was not very compliant, and he probably wouldn't have been able to achieve anything anyhow. But then, after some computer analysis, it turned out that you, Owen, look very much like Heino, that's his name, and that if you were to take his place, and Linh get onto the wait staff, we would have a slim chance of accomplishing our goal.'

'Which is?' Linh probed.

'To strand the boat in the middle of the Mediterranean. If we can keep it in one spot for long enough, we will be able to create some sort of pretext that will require disembarkation from the yacht. Then we will have all of our candidates. That's all we need... to expose the members of the alliance. That will effectively sabotage the gamma ray program.'

Owen walked back from the toaster. 'It's ironic,' he mused, '... that the highly sophisticated alliance is resorting to face to face meetings in this day and age of electronic communications.'

Alasdair nodded. 'Yes, it is... which just goes to illustrate the degree of distrust there is for electronic transmissions.'

'How many of the alliance will be on board for this next cruise?'

'We believe a good many. The treaty that binds the various member nations to atomic research is due for re-ratification soon, and the alliance needs to prepare for the new appointments and protocols that will eventuate—in other words, they have to maintain their network in a system that is designed to purge malignant growths. It's all about putting their people in appropriate positions of power.'

'... and about putting Linh and me in an appropriate position on the boat,' Owen finished.

'Yes...' Alasdair stood up from the table. 'Bring your toast with you... we'll adjourn to the study. I want to show you something.'

The trio padded quietly through the sprawling living areas to a niche set into the sculpted wall. Alasdair beckoned them to sit either side of him on a curved settee. When they were seated, a screen silently enclosed them and they descended to a room below. The décor here was anything but exuberant. Bare, metallic surfaces with switchboards, meters and dials lined the wall. Soft, indirect lighting managed to take the edge off the severity of the fixtures. In the middle of the room was a low circular wall that looked like a wading pool. Its inside surface was as black as a retina.

From a bench top, Alasdair picked up a wand and went and stood by the circular structure. He toyed with some buttons on the wand. The dark interior began to flicker. A three-dimensional shape began to materialise. It was a ship, with angular streamlining, a reverse Dreadnought style bow, elliptical curves, darkened windows and latticed vents and grills. On the sleek foredeck was a helicopter landing area and either side of the angled superstructure were radar domes and assorted antennas. Oval portholes flowed along the length of the hull, interspersed with the outlines for access hatches. The stepped stern incorporated recreational and outdoor-dining decks, sloping away to an adjustable swimming platform.

'Behold,' Alasdair said, '... the *Zeus*.'

Linh tentatively poked her finger into the holographic image. This produced lines of quivering shadows. 'This is amazing, Alasdair.'

'I know,' he chuckled, '... have a look at this.' He inserted the wand into the image. As it dropped down, it revealed the insides of the ship, layer by layer.

'I thought this boat was supposed to be super-secret,' Owen quizzed.

Alasdair pressed some buttons on the wand. Now the image was sliced longitudinally. 'Yes, it is pretty secret... not so much the actual structure—it's hard to keep a three-year build with an army of tradesmen totally secret—it's more about its fit-out... electronics, radar, sonar, that sort of thing. It's kitted out like a state-of-the-art destroyer. Mind you, we had a lot of trouble getting even the construction details out of the Blohm and Voss boatyard.'

Owen peered into the layered image. 'So, what areas are we going to be working in?'

At the press of a button, the image of the engine room became enlarged. Alasdair rotated the space so that it could be viewed from all angles. 'Okay, this is where you will head when you get your signal. Against this bulkhead—that's what walls are called when you're at sea, by the way—are all of the fuel filters.'

'What will the signal be? Just out of interest.'

'The signal will be the *Man Overboard* alarm.'

Owen nodded. 'Okay, good... so you've lined up someone to conveniently fall into the ocean.'

'Indeed, I have, Owen... it's Linh.'

Chapter Twenty-Four

Owen had plenty to think about on the flight to Naples. He felt lost without Linh, but she was in Ho Chi Minh City working as a waitress in an exclusive club and waiting for her escort to take her to the *Zeus*. At times he would have grave misgivings about their involvement in this plot. But Alasdair's proposal seemed completely genuine. Inviting them to the Eyrie had obviously been a strategic move to impart credibility on his behalf. And there was no doubting that Irena and Alasdair exhibited a very persuasive sincerity. He just felt so much concern for Linh's welfare—though it was not an issue over which he had a decisive say. This whole saga may have begun with him, so long ago at Yappar River, but her contribution since had earned her as much right to a say in the matter as he had, and Linh had made the decision to help in whatever way she could—even if it meant falling overboard.

Just the thought of Linh staggering to the rail with a tray in her hand, afflicted with sea-sickness, flu, agoraphobia... it didn't matter... and toppling headfirst into the sea, made him squirm with discomfort.

Linh, on the other hand, found a tray and a plastic picnic set, and got him to critique her performances as she lurched towards the timber rail that they had constructed, with Alasdair's help, to the exact height of *Zeus'* rail. It had been quite hilarious to see her flopping onto the mattress, except that Linh ended up with a severely bruised hip. The actual fall into the water wasn't that far. The lido deck rail was about four metres above the waterline. But, how quickly would they come to her assistance? Most of the crew serving that area would be inexperienced in rescue. Not that she would be in need of rescuing.

He rubbed his face. Linh was resourceful. She would carry it off with aplomb… if that is how you could describe plunging into the water. What about *his* role? Nothing spectacular there—he was simply going to cripple a half billion-dollar super-yacht… with a handful of cooked rice.

Rice! That is what Alasdair's analysts had come up with. At the right moment, while all eyes were on retrieving the fallen waitress, he was to unclip the fuel filter, take out the element and insert a handful of cooked rice. Then he would replace the element and go on to the next engine. Four fuel filters in total. The rice would be sucked into the long fuel line and then into the fuel pump. The fuel pump would mash the rice into fine particles and the engine would probably continue working until the mash got to the fuel injectors. That would be the end. It would take days for fly-in mechanics to replace the injectors. In the meantime, *Zeus* would be drifting helplessly with just the bow thrusters to keep it pointing in a desired direction.

Hopefully, long before the rice was discovered in the fuel pump, the cavalry would come to the rescue. Hopefully. Owen had memorised the passageways to the tender pen where they kept the Zodiacs and other craft. How to open the hatches was yet to be determined. He groaned softly.

The matronly woman in the seat next to him put her hand on his. "Are you feeling not so good?' she said with a strong accent. 'This plane, she fly very good… I fly with it many time… you be okay. I get you bottle water,' and she caught the attention of a flight attendant.

Owen showed his gratitude and chatted affably until the seatbelt signs came on and it was time to land.

He caught a taxi and asked the driver to take him through the centre of the city to the marina. The *Zeus* was moored just off the Castel dell'Ovo, but he had a room for the night at the Grand Hotel Vesuvio on the via Partenope overlooking the sea. He would have liked to be in the mood for sight-seeing, but without Linh beside him, he just wouldn't enjoy it. When they got to the Piazza del Plebiscito, he asked to be let out. He felt like walking the last kilometre. On his back was the tiniest pack with just some underwear and a spare shirt. He would be stripping down to his swimmers at some point in the boarding process, so it was pointless to take anything more. Even his phone would be taken from him and put into a locker. For now, it was guiding him through some seriously narrow streets that switched back on themselves at impossible angles, leading him to fully appreciate the minimalist proportions of the Fiat Bambino. Eventually he came to the fortified Mont Echia, which was just behind his hotel. His jaunt through the dense, urban sprawl left him feeling slightly anxious. The lanes were so narrow that the sun never reached the cobblestones. There was an appearance of decrepitude and despair in the oldness of the buildings. He couldn't imagine living amongst such congestion. When he at last emerged onto the via Partenope, it was a relief for him to relax his gaze to the horizon. Not far off the breakwater, he could see the *Zeus* glinting in the morning light. He walked to the bluff façade of the hotel and entered the foyer.

After the registration formalities, he was shown into a spacious suite with views across the harbour.

He hung his backpack over a chair. Unlike his experience in Cambodia, where his backpack converted into a drone, here he had absolutely nothing in the way of technology.

Rice! He let himself fall backwards onto the bed.

When he awoke, feeling a pleasing hunger, he made arrangements to have lunch on the roof garden. Up there, he imagined, the views would dissipate his fretfulness.

It was a pleasant enough day, but to him, the air felt tainted—just like after a bush fire when still smouldering timber creates a haze. He was seated under an umbrella. There were quite a few diners nearby despite it being mid-afternoon. He felt conspicuous eating alone. He wished that Linh was with him. She would transform this moment into a memorable occasion.

But here he was—a secret agent, on a mission to save the world, dining alfresco on the shore of the Mediterranean Sea. He didn't feel like James Bond. He hoped he didn't look like James Bond. He ruffled his hair. Around him, the chatter of the patrons left him with a sense of dislocation. He wished he was on Stella with Barra searching up ahead.

The waitress caught his eye as she placed food at a nearby table.

With a redolent regard, she moved his way and stood close enough for her skirt to brush his arm. 'Would you like something of me?' she articulated laboriously.

Owen looked up with a big smile. Sure, it wasn't her first language, but that was a deliberate come-on if ever he'd heard one. Now, he had a whole evening to kill and most of the next day, and he was dreading having nothing to do but worry about his assignment. 'Yes,' he replied. 'Do you own a scooter... a Vespa... Lambretta?'

She chewed seductively at her lip and weighed him up. 'I borrow one.'

Owen rested his arm over the back of the chair. 'Are you a good driver?' He didn't want to end up in a hospital just when the world needed saving.

'Yes, I am good driver... it's that I do not own scooter at the moment.'

'When do you finish work?'

'Very soon... I am only rostered for lunchtime shift.'

'Oh, that's great. My name is Owen.'

'Marlene.'

They gently shook hands.

'I'm in room 32, Marlene... if you'd like to call me when you're ready.'

Marlene gave a slow nod of consent. 'I will do that.' She looked at her watch. 'Maybe half hour.'

Owen gave her arm the briefest squeeze. 'I'll be ready.'

'I will choose you bowl of pasta. Ciao,' she said, as she departed.

'Ciao,' he returned, hardly believing the absurdity of him speaking Italian.

About forty minutes later, Owen and Marlene were walking back up the narrow laneways towards her house.

'It is not far,' she said as they hugged the wall to let a car pass. 'I am staying with my auntie while I on holidays... she get me job in hotel.'

Despite the language hurdle for Marlene, she and Owen conversed freely. He was enjoying her company—better than being stuck in the hotel, he thought. He managed to sidestep questions about the reason for his visit, and unintentionally generated a certain mystery

261

about himself. As gently as he could, he made it clear that he would have to leave at noon the next day, to which he detected a hint of disappointment.

Marlene stopped and appraised him for a moment. 'This is my door,' she said, '... you would like to come in?'

Owen told her that he was happy to wait on the street while she got changed. She disappeared inside. He looked up at the tenement house walls, at the louvered shutters some with plant boxes, then at the bare doors with their tiny portico for shelter in the rain. He felt a pang of nostalgia at the thought of the sprawling homestead at Yappar. Would he ever go to live there for a time? Would he and Linh raise children there? Maybe the station was no longer relevant in his life.

Marlene appeared suddenly. 'I was hoping that you still be there,' she said. 'A friend of mine has scooter that I am sure he won't mind to lend to me,' she pointed further up the lane.

Owen fell in beside her. 'I have a better idea. If you could summon a taxi, we will go to a shop and buy a scooter... whichever one you like.'

Alasdair had waved a dismissive hand at the credit card he'd given Owen and told him that there was no limit on it. 'Whereas yours, Linh,' he'd given a contrite grimace, '... has a limit of six million Dong, which, as you know, sounds like a lot, but is in fact only about three-hundred and fifty dollars. We don't want to blow your cover.'

She had replied with a petulant scowl.

Having Linh come to mind caused Owen to slow down on the footpath.

Marlene propped and turned to him. 'You do not mean that?'

Owen picked up his pace and waved her on. '...hmmm? Yes, I do— come on. It's not my money, and I'm determined to be driven around Napoli by a girl on a scooter.'

She caught up with him.

'... and, I want to lick a gelato in a piazza somewhere... and eat spaghetti on the footpath. Oh, wait... that was *Lady and the Tramp*... never mind. Anyway, I want a quintessentially Italian experience, and that means getting you on a scooter. Do taxis come down these alleyways?'

Marlene grabbed his arm and directed him across the lane. 'We will go down here,' she pointed to another side lane, '... then onto main road. Then I will get a taxi.' She withdrew her mobile from her jeans pocket.

Owen was determined to stay connected to his natural persona during the purchase of the scooter. That is why he gave the card to Marlene even before she engaged the attention of a salesman on the floor. He didn't want to do the *sugar daddy* trip—he just wanted to be driven around town, and it was no concern of his how much it was going to cost.

Marlene decided on a lime green retro styled Vespa. The salesman launched into a very animated sales pitch which Marlene cut short with a torrent of words, ending in English with, '... I have not got the all day... hurry up with forms.' She gave Owen a discreet thumbs-up.

It was when they were deciding on which helmets to buy that Owen was gripped with a spasm of guilt that actually wrenched at his stomach.

Marlene was standing in front of him asking him whether they should match the colour of the scooter or go for something else.

She reached out to him. 'Owen, are you alright? You have gone all white.'

Owen rallied as best he could, but there was no denying that this harmless diversion to buy a scooter had precipitated a certain self-reproach—he should have been doing this with Linh.

Marlene decided on the matching helmets, and soon they were zipping through the traffic, with Owen, up close and comfortable to Marlene, as the pillion. He had instructed her to give a running commentary on the sights and scenery—but in her native language.

They drove east and hugged the coast, wending and winding along the smaller roads to avoid the traffic. The whole time, Marlene prattled very engagingly about the countryside while Owen hovered his head over her shoulder, relishing the nuances without any content.

They came to the tiny islet of Nisida which is connected to the mainland by a thin isthmus and parked the scooter by the side of the street. Marlene suggested they stretch their legs and walk to the lookout.

The view into the tiny, perfectly circular bay was lovely. Marlene told the story of how Brutus had his home on the islet, and that he could well have plotted the assassination of Julius Caesar there... and that Brutus' wife, Porcia, a most beautiful woman who had almost become a stud heifer for one of her husband's political allies, killed herself by swallowing hot coals... but that it might have been death by carbon monoxide poisoning. '... not that Shakespeare stop himself from writing about these gory details,' Marlene concluded. She gave Owen a jolly punch on the shoulder. 'Now, you tell me something interesting... tell me about your girlfriend... your wife. A nice guy like you is hooked, right? No, not hooked...'

'Taken,' Owen volunteered.

Marlene responded with a typical Latin gesture of capitulation.

They turned to go back to the scooter. Owen told her about his bout of doubt at the scooter place.

'Bout of doubt!' Marlene guffawed, 'Oh, Owen... we must never lose contact—I want to see how you grow up... oh, not...'

'Mature?' Owen ventured.

Marlene turned to him with a very soft look. 'No, you are mature already, Owen.'

They reached the scooter.

'Are you hungry for gelato?'

'You bet I am, Marlene!'

They returned to the city on the main road. It wasn't nearly as dangerous as Owen thought it was going to be. Most of the late afternoon traffic was going out of town. Marlene managed to pack with other scooters along the way, so that they were never particularly vulnerable. She kept up her discourse in Italian, at times becoming especially voluble. Then, after a long boring stretch of road, where the traffic slowed right down, her tone became surprisingly emotive and impassioned. Her mouth emitted languid vowels, guttural and explosive consonants, and he could feel her rocking on the seat. Then, when the joke hit him, he burst out laughing.

'Yes, yes, yes... talk dirty to me,' he urged at her helmet.

Marlene laughed so hard she could barely keep the scooter on course. 'I have been undressing you for past twenty minutes,' she squealed.

They arrived at Vanvitelli square and stashed the Vespa in a line of other scooters against the footpath. The square, in reality a huge roundabout, had, around its perimeter, at least five gelato vendors. Marlene insisted that they go for a stroll and look at all the displays before selecting a flavour.

'You know why Italians are good at making the ice confectionary, don't you, Owen?'

Owen had no idea and said as much.

'Well, because Roman civilization was so wealthy, many of the citizens could afford to have ice brought down from Alps in hot months of summer. The ice it was flavoured with fruits and compotes as well as nuts and honey. No chocolate in those times.'

Watching the throng, it seemed to Owen that going out for an ice-cream was a national pastime. They ambled leisurely, looking in the windows of shops. It was quite crowded. The summer weather had obviously encouraged the local residents to get a breath of air.

Owen took Marlene's hand. 'Do you mind?' he asked. 'It's just that it seems so unnatural to be out with a lovely woman, and not to be holding her hand.'

Marlene didn't mind. She beamed her pleasure and squeezed his palm.

When they'd completed one circuit, Marlene spun Owen around and held both his hands. 'So, did you see something that you can not live without?'

Owen drew her near. 'I believe I saw a confection that might change my life, yes.'

Marlene pouted with big eyes. 'Lead me… I am curious.'

They wound their way to a pavement stall. Owen pointed out his choice—Armagnac Fig with Salty Caramel.

Marlene pretended to go limp in his arms. 'I will have to have one also—it will prevent us the embarrassment of trying each other's ice-cream.'

Owen chuckled his appreciation at her thoughtfulness.

'... and when you are gone, Owen, I will come here, now and then, to have an Armagnac and Fig gelato, to remember you...'

Owen shook his head. 'Facebook, sweet heart... it's not very romantic, but you won't get fat.'

A couple nearby joined in the laughter.

With their gelatos in hand, Marlene led Owen towards the Parco de Villa Floridiana with its wide walking paths and magnificent gardens. The long summer twilight, shaped shadows and produced corridors of gold. For a moment, Owen thought that he was lost, and when he turned and saw Marlene's unfamiliar profile beside him, the sensation was so pronounced that he stopped in mid-stride.

She squeezed his hand. 'Hey, Owen... I will look after you,' she said, looking at him from under a whorl of dark hair.

When they at last returned to the scooter, it was dark and the street lights were on.

Marlene fitted her helmet. 'I can not let you go to bed on an empty stomach. We will go to my auntie's place and we have spaghetti.'

He sat in behind Marlene and they took off into the roundabout.

Adelina, Marlene's aunt, was in her early thirties, stunningly good looking, and was a concert violinist. This was not at all what Owen had been expecting. He leant back into the sofa and cradled the guitar that Marlene had placed in his lap to keep him amused while the girls set about making supper. He painstakingly shaped a few chords and tried to pitch his hum accordingly. Music was not his forte.

The shutters were wide open and a welcome breeze floated into the upper story living room.

Adelina called out from the kitchen. 'I'm encouraging Marlene to make a determined play for you, Owen. I love the way you can't play the guitar. All my male friends are musicians, and I don't know, but it seems to me that what they've gained in musicality, they've lost in common sense—they're all broke and completely useless around the house.'

Adelina's English was faultless. And her cooking skills weren't too bad either, judging from the aromas that wafted his way.

Owen marvelled at the spontaneity of the furnishing. All of it was practical, but it was so lavishly decorated and embellished, in a way that he'd never seen before. Each tapestry, rug and ornament seemed to celebrate the art form. The room was adorned to inspire.

When supper was ready, they sat at a little round table and focused on their food. The salad was coriander, cucumber and tomato with rasped parmesan to sprinkle on top of the spaghetti sauce. The flavours were so distinct that they naturally inhibited conversation.

'You two are great cooks,' Owen managed to slip in.

Adelina laughed heartily. '*Marlene* is a good cook! Are you sure you don't want to marry her? She's training to be a chef.' She affectionately nuzzled her niece's face.

In his mind's eye, Owen stepped back and took in this charming scene. He felt very fortunate to be at this table with such lovely young women. The familiar sense of translation stole upon him, but not so severely that he was in danger of fainting.

'You seem distracted, Owen.' Adelina searched his face. 'Are you going to tell us why you are in Napoli? Marlene tells me you're being very mysterious.'

Owen carefully wound the last strand of noodle around his fork. Was this tableau the work of conspirators? Two charming girls, intoxicating fragrances, wonderful aromas, a heady wine. No, he didn't think so. 'I'm going to save the world,' he said, with surprising poise.

The two women became absolutely still and regarded him with great seriousness.

'Are you really?' Marlene ventured.

Owen dabbed a napkin to his mouth. 'Yes.'

'Are you a secret agent?'

'Not intentionally... I mean, it's not my day job. It just happened.'

'But you can't tell us what it's all about?' Adelina queried.

'No... but, what I *will* absolutely do, when it is all over... I want to visit you with my partner, Linh, and I will tell you then.'

Marlene suddenly straightened and looked towards one of the open windows. 'Have it got something to do with big boat that comes in the harbour yesterday?'

Owen levelled a steady gaze. 'If you want me to succeed, then you mustn't say anything about me to anyone. It's okay that we've been on trips on the scooter and had gelato in the park—just don't mention it any further—please... not until I see you again.'

Adelina threw up her hands. 'How is she going to explain a brand-new Vespa?'

Owen smiled. 'However she likes—she won it! Rich auntie!'

'That wouldn't be me, then,' Adelina sighed ruefully.

Marlene threw her arms around her auntie. 'Zia, you *are* rich... you have me.' They hugged each other. 'I take Owen to Vesuvio tomorrow. Maybe it go boom, and we die in each other arms.'

The three of them laughed.

Owen checked his phone. 'That sounds terribly romantic, Marlene, but I'm afraid I won't be able to make it... I've just been summoned. Change of plan, it seems. Sorry.' His mouth contorted into an apologetic grimace.

The two women looked very worried. They sat in silence.

Marlene reached out and took Owen's hand. 'In bocca al lupo,' she said softly.

Adelina took his other hand and whispered, '... crepi il lupo.' She looked up. 'Marlene has wished you good luck... but the expression is literally, *in the mouth of the wolf.'*

'... and she say, *may the wolf die.'*

Across the small table, it was easy for Owen to take their hands and put them to his lips. He closed his eyes and delicately kissed each hand.

Adelina stroked the side of Owen's head. 'Wow, Owen... one day in Italy and you've become the godfather.' Then she said in her huskiest Brando, '... time erodes gratitude more quickly than it does beauty...'

They roared with laughter.

Owen had to admit though, that he had never seen *The Godfather*.

'It's our contribution to Hollywood culture,' Adelina said with a flippant wave.

Marlene stood up and went to Owen's side. 'I take you back to hotel. You will get lost if I don't take you.'

Chapter Twenty-Five

The tender that took Owen from the marina to the *Zeus* was enormous—at least ten metres long and styled like a classic ski boat. It was all foredeck and sloping stern with just a small recess with seating for about ten. Everything gleamed—the lacquered timberwork, the brass, the retro dashboard with its analogue instruments. Even the switches reflected the lights around the marina.

Owen sat as close to the driver as he could. It could be very handy to know how to drive this thing sometime in the future. The fuel gauge showed full. The engine sounded like a V8 of mammoth proportions.

... I wonder what the range is for this baby?

There was one other crew member casting the lines, and a young woman who sat very demurely in the back seat and did not look at all as though she was looking for a conversation.

... one of the wait staff no doubt... speaks only Italian...

The driver took the boat up to the plane and it skimmed smoothly on the glassy surface. Within a minute they were approaching the large open hatch in the side of the hull. With a blip of throttle, the boat was gunned just enough to nudge it inside the flooded pen. The other crewman leapt onto the walkway and helped position the boat while the driver remotely activated the cradle that rose up and secured the hull. The driver then aimed the remote above him and the hull hatch began to hum shut.

... not that different from your normal garage really...

Nearby, a pump wound up and the water level began to slowly drop. Without being obvious, Owen watched the driver stash the remote module into the glove box.

No one took the slightest interest in him. The girl was helped out of the boat and was led away by the driver. Owen followed.

Heino had made a fairly extensive list of protocols, locations, duties, on-board routines... enough so that Owen could manage himself without drawing too much attention. Heino was only employed about three months of the year—whenever the *Zeus* was performing high speed runs. For that, he was very well remunerated and gave him plenty of time and the wherewithal to indulge in his hobby of rally driving. Good luck to him, Owen reflected. With the money that Alasdair was flinging his way for abandoning his job, he would have enough to buy an entire rally team.

Owen felt fairly confident about taking Heino's place in the engine room. What concerned him more was whether or not his "new look" would go unquestioned. While Owen had a full head of hair and was clean-shaven, Heino was a skin-head with a massive beard.

'Well, how is that going to work?' Owen had protested.

Linh was equally aghast, 'He's not going to have to shave his head and grow a beard, is he?'

Alasdair had signalled for calm. 'Don't you see? It's perfect. No one has ever seen Heino without a beard... sure, you might get a few comments here and there...'

'Like from Rosa Klebb, who probably has the hots for him,' Linh interrupted.

'Her name is Dora, by the way. Look, the facial recognition program says you overlap in all the critical areas but, seriously, Owen... if it means that you have to get a bit cuddly with her just to smooth things along...'

'... she will hunt me down to the ends of the earth when I ditch her,' Owen responded with a look of dread.

A nervous flutter began in his stomach.

'Entre ici...' came a voice from behind him.

Owen turned. 'Sano uudelleen...' *...oh no... emphasis on the double u's...*

The sessions with Alasdair had been fairly rigorous. This included learning Finnish phrases recorded by Heino, whose voice was lighter than Owen's so, it wasn't as difficult to imitate him. Heino had a reasonable grasp of English which was necessary in his job as the supervisor of the engine room. Irena had coached him to form his mouth into an O shape whenever he spoke in order to achieve an approximation of Heino's accent. Apparently, there was no one else on board who spoke Finnish so that was not going to be a problem. He'd also been informed that the common language on the ship was English, but that there were a few French speakers with whom he'd have to deal.

One of them was probably in the room that the French crewman was pointing to. Owen dutifully moved towards the doorway and slipped inside. A cloth bundle hit him in the face before he could catch it.

'Right oh, usual drill,' said the craggy looking thickset man who'd thrown the overalls at him.

... Mr Kendrick Knowles... and good evening to you, too...

Owen looked about for a change room.

That moment of indecision was all that Knowles needed to become upset. '*Here!*' he bellowed.

Owen quickly stripped to his underwear and was about to get into the overalls when Knowles let rip again.

'*Cavity search!*'

... WHAT?... no one had said anything about that...

Knowles stepped up to him with a menacing expression and stood staring at him from close up. 'What happened to your face?'

Owen couldn't help looking at the man's lumpy nose. His breath was awful.

'*Well?*'

'Nothing... nothing happened to my face.' Then Owen understood. He almost forgot his accent. 'Oh, sorry... yes, my beard. I shave it off... try something new...' He ran his fingers through his hair.

Knowles moved even closer. 'You're actually quite attractive,' he murmured with a ghastly smile. 'I wasn't actually going to give you a search, but now I'm tempted.' His hand struck out and gripped Owen by the wrist.

Owen felt the strength in Knowles' grip, and knew that he would be able to pull him apart like a stick insect. 'No need for search,' he said as resolutely as he could.

Knowles shoved Owen against the wall. '*Bloody hell!* Did you *really* think I would want to search you? Get your gear on and get out of here before I tell Cookie about you... I'm sure he'd like to run his hands over you...'

Owen scrabbled for his overalls on the floor and hopped about as he pulled them on. When he got his shoe stuck halfway down a trouser leg, he leant against the wall and slowly wriggled it free.

Knowles went back behind his desk. 'Which fire extinguisher would you use if the air-con circuit board started smoking?'

'The CO2... red with black nozzle...'

'What colour are the pliers in the tool kit?'

'Green... all of them, the needle nose, side cutters...'

'Which meal do you like?

... which meal?... how was he supposed to know... they hadn't discussed that at all...

Knowles was making some entries in the crew log book. He looked up. '... hmmm... which meal?'

Owen thought hard. What did the Fins like? Fish? Red meat? Reindeer? 'Well, generally I like to have... meat... white meat... or red meat... and vegetables...'

'I'll put you down for no allergies... it's a new thing we have to do. You're not allergic to crustaceans and stuff, are you?'

Owen breathed a sigh of relief. 'No... no... crustaceans are fine... lobster, abalone, scallops...'

'Yeah, don't get too excited.' He finished scribbling and had a quick rummage through Owen's bag of clothes. 'Right, Dora is on board already. You two work out your shifts. Right oh, scram!'

Owen's heart was pounding in his chest.

... holy hell... I'm not cut out for this kind thing...

As he made his way through the narrow corridors deep inside the *Zeus*, he realised that his natural trepidation was probably a good thing—it was so unmistakeably sincere.

He found his cabin and knocked on the door. It was not always a sure thing for Heino to be allocated this cabin. There had been times when he'd been shunted elsewhere. Owen opened the door. The cabin was utterly tidy and obviously not being occupied—and it was the size of a cell.

... squeezy... anyway, so far, so good...nothing to do but work and sleep, obviously...

He threw his little bag of clothes onto the bed and sat down. There was a battery powered alarm clock on the desk and a small box of toiletries, a toothbrush and a bottle of water. He had no shaving kit because Heino had never needed it. Owen thought about requesting an electric shaver but decided that the fewer times he came across Mr Knowles, the better.

...okay, time to introduce myself to Dora... oh, god, I should have taken a Valium...

The engine room was further astern. Owen closed the cabin door and strode purposefully down the corridor.

... might as well look as though I have business here...

He went past the shared bathrooms. The last door, a wheel operated water tight hatch, was clearly labelled in French and English, *Engine Room*, and underneath, *Authorised Entry Only*.

Owen pushed on the door. It didn't budge. With a self-conscious glance behind him, he commenced a fluent rotating of the wheel. When it ground to a halt, he pushed at the door again. Still it wouldn't open. He shoved harder.

... you're kidding me... how does this stupid door work?

There was a vague human sound on the other side of the door. The wheel started to spin rapidly in the other direction. A handle to one side depressed. The door opened inwards and Dora the mechanic stood confronting him with arms akimbo. She unleashed a burst of German before resorting to scolding him in English.

She tapered off with, 'I show you *joke* mister,' and she swung a spanner out of her back pocket.

Owen put up his hands in surrender. 'I am sorry... I get confused. Sorry...'

Dora smacked the spanner into her palm. 'Who are you?'

This bit he had to get right. He'd learnt from Heino's briefing notes that, around Dora, he was a bit of a kidder, mainly because Heino felt it was the best way to disguise his terror of her.

Owen framed himself provocatively in the hatchway. He stroked his chin and grinned boyishly. 'What you think, Dora... I have got better chance with you now?'

Dora took one stride towards him, dropped the spanner at arm's length and swung it up between Owen's legs, stopping just short of touching him. She thrust her face inches from his and stared hard. 'You look different,' she growled.

'I do it for you,' was all that Owen could manage in a thin voice.

'Have you seen the bosun?'

Owen nodded and eased himself out of the hatch frame.

With a suspicious scowl, Dora looked him up and down. 'So, you are Heino's twin, ya?'

... loose and jokey... loose and jokey...

'Ah, well, here is thing, Dora... when Heino tell me about you, I not believe it—I have to see for myself... he say "that woman, she is good for *two* men" and I say, "no, impossible" but, now I see, yes, he is telling truth... Dora is impressive girl. I go back to shore now and tell Heino to get back on board...'

Dora scrutinised him like a stud bull sniffing a heifer. 'You start at nine,' she said.

Owen attempted a jaunty stride as he returned up the corridor but, in reality, he was almost physically sick.

He risked a quick look behind. The hatch was closed. This was the lowest deck, and the corridor ran down the middle of the hull all the way to the tender pens which were situated about a third of the way back from the front of the yacht. The corridor gave access to cabins on either side, which were the low-ranking crew quarters. They had no windows of any description because they backed onto service rooms and other cabins. This part of the so-called mega-yacht was like a prison. In all, Owen thought there were roughly twenty cells. One of these cells was reserved for Linh.

He entered his cabin and pulled out a pair of underpants from his bag. The label around the elastic band featured decorative coloured dots. With his fingernail, Owen carefully pried a grey dot away from the band. He licked the inside of his right thumb and stuck the dot to it. He then dribbled some spit over the dot. He went out into the corridor and pretended to stretch as he made up his mind. Then he bent down and pulled his sock up in his shoe, all the while leaning against the closed door. His thumb pressed the dot onto the door—Linh's shoulder height, and one eighth the distance from the hinge. The hinge side corresponded to twelve midnight—thus, his dot suggested three in the morning—the end of his first shift. He wriggled his foot and leaned against the wall to adjust the other shoe—this time to have a good look at the grey dot against the grey wall. Not obvious but easy enough to spot for someone scanning doors at that height. The saliva activated glue would set in about ten minutes.

So, Linh would know his room and his shift times. It was a start.

He walked further up the passageway to the stairs that accessed the canteen. The metal rungs had a depressing resonance. There was no one at the tables, but there was a woman behind the counter. He went over and gave a little wave and a smile. The woman stood in front of him, bowed slightly and kept her eyes down.

… okay, we don't fraternise… we don't have fun…

Owen ordered a cup of tea and some biscuits and sat at one of the tables. Again, there were no windows. The casual staff were pretty much confined to the inner parts of the ship. Only the waitresses had occasion to go beyond the restricted areas. From his table, Owen could see as far as it was possible along the service corridor that connected the kitchen with the main dining room and further aft to the lido deck. This would be the preferred table if he was to maximise visual contact with Linh. That way she would know to use it as a post box. The tables were aluminium, so magnetic holders wouldn't have worked anyhow.

He slugged back the last of his tea and rose.

… may as well make my way to the engine room…

He was just wondering whether or not to return his cup to the counter when he noticed a woman walking swiftly down the corridor towards the kitchen. She was speaking into a two-way and was out of sight before he could get a good look. But there was no mistaking her voice—it was Gina Wu.

Owen turned away from the servery just in case she should appear there. She would recognise him in an instant. She'd spent a fair while studying his face through that gadget of hers.

He wanted to leave the canteen as soon as possible but wondered whether it would be more prudent to stay seated until she had gone. He heard her conversing in English with someone in the kitchen— something about having the full quota of meals ready.

... so, the other staff, including Linh, will be coming on board soon...

Owen's knees went weak. He sat down. How was Linh going to avoid Gina? They had spent so much time together in Cambodia. It looked as though Gina was in some sort of catering or staffing role. Linh would be exposed in a matter of minutes.

... who the hell is she working for?...

Purposeful steps resounded in the corridor. Gina Wu was making her way back to the main dining.

A vibration transmitted through the ship—the engines were being started.

Owen rose quickly and headed for the stairs. He would have plenty of time to think about Linh's predicament while he was looking after the engines.

Owen depressed the lever on the hatch door and pushed. The onslaught of sound was terrifying. Despite being the most efficient engines for their size on the planet, and despite the sound deadening room-lining, the four engines together produced a physical pulsation that vibrated his organs—and they were just warming up.

Dora had her eyes on the read-outs on the central LCD screen. She was wearing heavy duty ear muffs. Owen went to a corner of the bay to a cabinet and pulled out the top drawer. Inside were his earmuffs and ear plugs. He adjusted his gear and turned around just in time to see Dora whip off her hearing protection and pull out the second bottom drawer. She flung her gear in and without so much as a glance at Owen, strode to the hatch and let herself out.

This was it—he was now the supervisor in the engine room. For a moment he stood in anxious indecision until he remembered that he literally did not have to do anything. He was there in case a fire broke out, a hydraulic line split, a circuit breaker tripped, a drive belt shredded... he was first aid. Major repair work was done by Knowles and his team, who spent most of their time on the bridge monitoring engine data and actuating the controls.

Owen took in the size of the engine room. It was vast. Each of the four, 8000 series twenty-cylinder MTU diesels, stood taller than Owen could reach. Silver grey and intimidating, they looked pumped full of steroids. There was a thin gangway between the engines that continued along the individual propeller shafts. The shafts exited through the bulkhead about two metres below water level. At high speed, the five bladed props, rotating at a thousand rpm would push *Zeus* along at upwards of forty knots.

At the head end of each engine was an electronics panel, and below that was the final fuel filter. It was easy enough to get at. Owen inspected the retaining handle for the filter cap. Everything was oversize but it was essentially no different from normal truck equipment. He checked for the fuel cock on the inlet line. It would be very messy if he attempted to take out the filter without cutting off the fuel first. The other three engines were identical. There were plenty of ways of stopping the motors, but spiking the injectors was probably the method that would attract the least attention. On the front bulkhead, along with the LCD monitor, was the black dome of a security camera that gave coverage to pretty much the entire engine room.

The engine revs suddenly increased. The clamour was like a vibrational matrix. Owen strode quickly past the engines to a recess on the side that led forwards to the fuel tanks. According to Heino, this refuge was the least noisy place in the engine room. Here were the air-conditioning compressors. In a similar nook on the other side of the boat were the electrical generators and the battery bank.

The engine revs stepped up even more. The *Zeus* was obviously on its high-speed run to a rendezvous.

Chapter Twenty-Six

At the other end of the engine room passageway, the door into Knowles' room swung open. Gina Wu casually sauntered in and confronted Knowles with folded arms.

'How is everything with the casuals?' she asked with a hint of disdain.

Knowles looked up and eyeballed her for a moment before answering. 'Yeah... good. We got the other mechanic and the Italian waitress. Why?'

'Just checking... doing my job. We'll pick up the rest in Tunis. If there are any inconsistencies, I want to know about it. Okay?'

Knowles lent back in his chair and exaggerated the act of deliberation. 'Sure, Gina... I will do that... just for you.'

Wu turned on her heels.

'Oh,' Knowles added facetiously, '... Virtanen is clean shaven now. You can add that to your data base.'

The woman stopped in the doorway and without turning, called back, 'And how did he come up on the scan?'

'How do you think? He failed. So, I had to see him in person.'

Wu faced Knowles from the doorway. 'Are you sure about him?'

'Nah, but I figured we needed a second mechanic, so I thought, what the hell... yes, of course I'm sure about him!'

Wu stepped forward. 'Okay, well, bring him up. I don't want to make a fool of myself by challenging the newly shaven mechanic.'

Knowles stabbed at the keyboard on his desk and scrolled through some images. 'Here!' He swung the monitor around to face her. He waited with a resigned look while she perused the screen.

Wu remained still, her face unreadable. 'And he is presently on board?'

'On board and in the engine room. Dora said they're splitting the shift three and nine.'

'Thank you, Mr Knowles,' Wu said softly. She turned and headed out of the room.

Four levels above, directly underneath the bridge, Gina Wu pressed a button beside an oaken door and positioned her face in front of the hidden camera. The door opened smoothly and silently. She went in and stood on a timber floored space above the sunken lounge which, in turn, had expansive views forward of the sea rushing towards them.

A man's voice, tremulous but authoritative, called out. 'Gina... come in.'

Wu turned and marched to a door to the side and let herself in. The room was panelled in a honey blonde timber that had such a translucent quality to it that it was difficult to grasp the size of the space. Near the front windows, that looked forwards over the moonlit sea, a large, silver egg hovered above the floor. It undulated gently relative to the ship's movement. It was the back of a chair. A thin, human arm rested on the cut-away contour of the armrest.

Gina Wu coughed lightly. 'Good evening, Eamon.'

'Good evening, Gina. Do we have a problem?'

'I think so.'

'Tell me.'

'The second mechanic that we have on board to monitor the engine room is not who he says he is.'

'Go on.'

'We employed a Finnish engineer called Heino Virtanen. The man who is currently assuming his role is a twenty-eight-year-old Australian cowboy called Owen Lucas.'

'An Australian cowboy,' the man mused. 'I think you will find that over there they are called stockmen, Gina my love.'

'Yes, they are. Sorry. He has a degree in mechanical engineering.'

'Well, well... now *he* would have to be a handy young man. Are you sure we can't convince him to apply for the job through the usual channels?'

'Eamon, I have encountered this man on previous occasions.'

'Is he dangerous?'

'... ah, well... on the face of it, no. In fact, he is probably the least dangerous man that one would ever be likely to encounter.'

'Then what is he doing posing as a mechanic on the *Zeus*?'

'I have yet to find that out. However, I have strong reason to believe that he is working with the Meridionali faction.'

'Really... Alasdair. And why do you believe this?'

'About two years ago he came across the Gulfstream crash and found the Viridian data. He hid it when he realised that it was probably important. As you know, we failed on our first attempt to retrieve it when we encountered the Meridionali drone but, with Lucas' help, we got it back. In the meantime, one of our agents got friendly with his girlfriend, an Australian Vietnamese girl called Linh Vuong, and we used her to expose some of the Meridianoli network. I'm pretty sure though that Lucas and Vuong have been recruited. I didn't pursue it because it was no longer relevant to me.'

'But, now it seems it is relevant.'

'Something just occurred to me... if I may pull up the file on the casuals, I would like to make a check.'

A claw-like hand protruded from the egg and made an indistinct wave.

Gina went to the far wall and pressed a button. A keyboard emerged from a hidden slot. A section of the blonde panelling configured into a screen. She tapped out commands and scrolled through the images on the monitor. Then she straightened and moved back to her original position. 'I'm afraid it's a more concerted plan than I first thought. His girlfriend has been enlisted as well.'

The egg hovered silently for a long while.

Wu rocked with the motion of the ship. In this room it was completely quiet. At forty knots, the *Zeus* was surprisingly stable, but every now and again it would respond to the swell with a languid heave and fall. With nothing to hold on to, Wu couldn't help occasionally repositioning her balance point.

At last the chair rotated. It moved closer to her. She raised her lowered sight to the occupant of the chair and looked directly into the pallid blue eyes of a skeletal head with skin as pale as parchment.

With not much more than a whisper, she asked, 'Do you mind if I kneel, Eamon?'

The gaunt frame, slumped in the oval cocoon, began a rapid wheezing. He was laughing. 'No, Gina... not at all. I love it when women kneel before me.'

'It's just that with the motion of the ship... I might be pitched forwards...'

'Of course, darling—kneel away.'

The ovum moved closer. The old man held out his hands. Gina delicately grasped his cold fingers. She ran her thumbs over the plain gold rings—one on the fourth finger of each hand. She rested her hold on his bony knees and smiled warmly.

Gina Wu had no regrets—the reason being that she never looked back. She existed on the event horizon—all information was dealt with or discarded the instant it came to her. With a prodigious memory, she was able to synthesise solutions to the most complex problems—but she never allowed herself to dwell on what she was running from.

Gina was ruthless and relentless and had come to the attention of powerful people very early in her life. She performed beyond expectations—and grasped beyond any limitations. She changed sides with uncompromising conviction.

Now, as they sped across the warm waters of the Mediterranean, Gina allowed herself a moment to reflect on her journey —from a high-rise in Hong Kong, trapped in a middle-class aspirational grind of excessive schooling and parental oversight, to her chance encounter with the city's underworld and her passage through the ranks and across borders.

This wasn't the first time that she had knelt before an overlord of some sort or another—but it was the first time that she had felt any affection. And, as she thumbed the curvature of the rings, she knew that she would not be destined to wear them—she knew that, for all her skills and abilities, she was never likely to be chosen—that mantle would befall someone else.

This realisation had come to her one night as she and Eamon lay against each other on the magnetic levitation bed. The warmed, humid air in the room enabled him to wear just his under shorts whilst she was completely undressed. He clasped her with surprising vigour and nestled to her breast. Intimate contact, he had told her, was something that he couldn't live without, and they would doze in a gentle embrace for hours as the bed warped and pulsed beneath them. It was his belief in love that bared her inadequacies; she knew that for her it was too late; her intellectual dominance would never reconcile such a human need; a need so undeniable to Eamon that it replenished his will to live. 'Not that I'm about to snuggle up to the bosun,' he said one night, '... a woman's body is a corporeal endowment that I don't question... some things are not meant to be questioned...' which is when Gina realised that she had a lot to learn.

She had admired him from their first meeting. 'Mrs Eales wants to retire, Gina,' he told her as they leant on the rail, watching the subject of their conversation waving from the passenger seat of the tender as it headed for the shore. 'She has struck up a very hearty relationship with the engineer, and I know she wants to engage in a life with him before she gets much older. She doesn't look it, I know, but she's in her seventies. I will miss her terribly. She has been with me for thirty years. But, I'm aware more than anyone, that life goes on and change keeps it real.'

Gina felt emboldened. 'Well, now you can retell all of your stories to me.'

Eamon wheezed his characteristic laugh. 'I'm two hundred and seventeen years old, Gina, and I've recounted my stories too many times. I would prefer it if you told me about yourself.'

They turned and walked back along the deck to the suite.

It was many weeks before she realised what Eamon was doing—catching her off-guard with subtle probes about her past. She would find herself elaborating on an experience, and then catching the intense interest in the old man's eye.

'I have never seen a person so attuned to their destiny as you, Gina my love,' he told her one day, '... I'm frightened for you. I want you to know that I care for you, not in any sensual sense, but simply because you are human, and that the longer you deny your hurt, the greater will be your pain. I can't offer you the comfort you need, but I can offer you the love that you deserve; because it's fearless people like you who test our human frontiers and for that we should all be grateful.

'I thought I was just a soulless over-achiever,' was her glib reply.

Eamon raised her hand to his lips. 'You are anything but soulless, Gina.'

She thought about that; nothing that she had ever done had a soulful origin. And yet, here she was, on the verge of loving someone purely for their mind. She moved closer to the frail being. Their bodies touched. She and Eamon were much the same height, despite his stoop. Their hands remained by their side; they communed silently, closed their eyes and touched foreheads.

At last he said, 'I want you to share an experience with me... come to bed with me. You will be revitalised.'

Gina smiled. She knew what he meant. She put her arms around him and drew him in. 'I've been longing to go to bed with you, Eamon.'

The magnetic field in the suite supported two objects—the ovum and the bed. They floated above the floor with Zen-like austerity, supported by the invisible matrix. The main purpose of this arrangement was not to show off the latest gadgetry but rather to prolong the life of its owner. Extended exposure to the powerful field had rejuvenating properties on human cells.

Gina felt the effects almost as soon as she had wriggled next to Eamon. 'Oh, my god... it feels wonderful,' she said with breathless awe.

'That's what every woman I bed says,' Eamon murmured.

Gina gave him a light dig with her elbow.

The slanted side windows were in transparent mode which had the effect of turning the suite into a solarium. The warmth of the sunlight sank into her nakedness. Even her mind seemed to clear of everything but a reverence for living.

They lay there holding hands, she, at his quiet prompting, harking back to episodes in her life that she had never had the need to revisit. They watched the sun set over the water. Eamon told her that she was a child of the universe, no less than the trees and the stars, and that she had a right to be here, and, whether or not it was clear to her, no doubt the universe was unfolding as it should.

Gina looked over and saw the tiniest smirk on Eamon's lips. 'So, that's what you've achieved in two centuries—memorising the Desiderata for a pick-up line.'

'Still true though, Gina,' he said off-hand, '... still true.'

For days after the experience on the magnetic bed, Gina felt pulses of vitality rippling through her. However, there were jobs to be done to which she had been especially assigned, so, with renewed energy, she addressed every detail of security management on the *Zeus*. That included cleaning her Beretta PX-4 which she did before she went to bed.

She slipped the gun from its special holster in the small of her back. Men could never understand that for a woman, used to doing up bras, a concealed pistol in the small of the back was more accessible than one competing for space next to a breast. Being concealed under her clothing meant that there was always the possibility of some lint or fibre getting into the trigger mechanism. She checked it thoroughly and placed it on her desk. Her cabin was small and sparsely furnished. That's how she liked it. Fewer places to hide and fewer places to scan. Not that an ambush was likely on this vessel, but it was second nature to her. And she only came here to sleep. She unbuttoned her top and unclipped the studs at her belly that held the fabric of the built-in holster in place at her back. The top, elegantly styled with pleats both back and front, was of her signature design—the pleats at the back disguising the fact that there was a convenient slit through which she could reach her weapon. She practised often enough so that she could drill the centre out of a target at ten metres in less than one second from the draw. Throwing her top onto the bed, she unclipped her bra and held the garment in front of her. She carefully checked the underwire where it came together at a little rosette. The connections were all good. Her brow darkened at the memory of an airport security guard who'd scrutinised her lecherously after she'd been through the metal scanner. She imagined herself shamelessly sauntering up to him and then pulling at the rosette and slitting his throat with six inches of twined surgical steel. Airport security—what a joke! A well-endowed woman could carry enough metal under her breasts to wreak unimaginable carnage.

Gina stripped and stepped into the shower.

Chapter Twenty-Seven

Owen staggered along the passageway and tried to find his door. Now he knew why they employed casual labour in the engine room. After being confined with thirty-six thousand horsepower for the best part of six hours he was ready to die. His cheery workmate, on the other hand, if not chatty, seemed well rested. Dora had waltzed in dead on time and had donned her hearing protection before Owen could yell a futile 'hello'.

He fell onto his bunk and moaned to himself out of sheer self-pity. He wondered if he would even be able to fall asleep, his head reverberated so much. In six hours, he would have to be revived, dressed, fed and ready to do it all again. He did not think it would be possible.

The engine sounds abated. They must have reached their destination. Where could that be? Short of tattooing a map of the Mediterranean on his thigh, he had done everything he could to memorise that part of the world. He knew that it was pointless trying to guess where they were going. He couldn't even tell which *direction* they were going. And now the ship was idling.

... trust Dora to get that shift. She must know something...

Well, if he couldn't fall asleep straight away, he might as well get something to eat. He let himself out and trod up the stairs to the canteen. He was going to have to risk it as far as Gina was concerned—he had to eat. The same girl was behind the counter. He ordered toast and butter. That's all he felt like. The girl gave a tiny shake of her head and pointed at the bain-marie. There was lobster, crab, joints of lamb, ribs, veal... anything a healthy appetite could desire. But toast, apparently, was out of the question.

He took a plate and selected a thin piece of veal. Nibbling on that could be enough exercise to settle his brain. With elbows on the table and hands holding his head, he chewed listlessly and tried not to think about his responsibilities.

...just get over this... just get to the next level of energy... don't burden yourself with the impossible...

Noises in the corridor drew his attention. A line of women began to enter the canteen. They quickly found empty chairs and seated themselves as though by instruction.

Owen hid behind his hand.

... the new recruits...

As they entered, he searched their faces from under his palm. The last girl to enter was Linh. Owen almost leapt up at the sight of her. His involuntary movement made the chair squeak loudly. Linh turned to him. She perused the room over his head and, seeing that it was filling up, sat down in the most convenient chair, which happened to be at his table.

Owen's emotions were out of control. In his agitated state, he wanted to reach out and hold her... to reclaim the security and peace that was always there whenever she was with him.

Just for a second, Linh locked eyes with him. The intensity of her expression revealed the alarm she was experiencing at seeing Owen so distraught. Her immediate response was to reach out with her foot to stroke his leg.

Owen gave a shuddering sigh and trapped Linh's foot between his calves. He didn't know how to look at her without being unnatural, so he dropped his head and stared at his plate.

Linh slowly moved her foot within Owen's hold.

A booklet landed on the table in front of him. Linh's slender hand reached for it. Her fingers spread over the cover and lingered within Owen's sight. He couldn't help it; he placed his hand on top of hers, savouring the familiar contours, feeling the warmth of her skin. He pressed down and pushed her away from him in what he hoped would look like a perfectly natural gesture of proffering.

Linh slid the book towards her and flipped it open.

The female crewmember distributed the last of the books and then began to hand out headphones.

The women donned the phones and turned to the first page.

Linh pretended to read the cover of the booklet and mouthed, 'I love you'. She darted Owen a quick look, kicked him under the table then smiled at his astonishment.

Owen almost fainted with happiness. It was real!... she was here!... he had her lovely smile to take with him.

She was about to don her ear phones when he remembered who was on board. He covered his mouth and pretended to sneeze. 'Gina Wu is here!' he blurted in a harsh whisper. He looked meaningfully in the direction of the passageway.

Linh's eyes widened. She stared at the table. Her foot stilled.

The assistant glared at Owen with a peevish mien.

He rose from the table and cleared his throat with a guttural 'Be careful'.

He headed for the stairwell.

Ten minutes later, Gina Wu sat cross-legged on the magnetic floor of the suite while Eamon hovered in his cocoon at her side. The screen materialised on the timber wall panelling.

'What have you discovered, Gina?' There was a noticeable eagerness in Eamon's voice.

'Well, sir...' Gina began.

'Gina...' the old man interrupted in a plaintive tone.

'Sorry, Eamon... it's just a habit...'

'I know... I know,' he reached out and stroked her ear.

At the time when Eamon had offered Gina the position of girl Friday, he'd stipulated that he desired an informal and relaxed relationship. She'd proven herself in the field and now was the time to operate beyond the typical hierarchies of command. He needed her to feel free—that way he could access the most of her potential. He wanted her to use his name.

An image of the canteen came up on the screen. 'As you can see, Eamon, he looks completely exhausted.' The image zoomed up to

Owen's tired eyes.

'Yes, he does, poor boy. Are you sure he's cut out for this sort of thing?'

Gina threw her hands in the air. 'Obviously not. Wait till you see the rest.'

The resolution on the screen was incredible—it was like looking directly through an opening. Owen nibbled at his veal and looked up at the arrival of the casual staff. Then he covered his brow with his hand. His body jerked, and the chair squealed as it slid on the floor. A woman stood before him searching for a seat, deciding with laboured uncertainty to sit at Owen's table. The two of them studiously avoided eye contact except for a moment when she searched his face, lifting her leg towards his and remaining connected in this odd embrace.

'I assumed he'd chosen the table next to the corridor exit to get a better view of the comings and goings to the main dining room. I asked the girl at the counter and hoped that he would sit in the same place again. That's Linh Vuong.'

The old man squeezed Gina's shoulder. 'She looks like a nice person. You can certainly see the emotion on Owen's face.'

On the screen, the assistant began to distribute the booklets, and when one landed on Owen's side of the table, Linh curiously laid claim to it without drawing it towards her. Then, even more intriguingly, he tenderly covered her hand with his. Eventually, she slid the booklet her way with his hand still covering hers. The love and relief were clearly visible on the young man's face, especially when she mouthed, 'I love you'. That's when Owen sneezed.

'He just told her that I was on board.'

The old man clasped his hands to his chest. 'It's beautiful,' he whispered.

The assistant came into view and Owen withdrew his hand. He stood and walked away from the table.

The image disappeared.

Eamon placed his hands in his lap. 'So, these two are our spies, and I would have to assume, our potential saboteurs.'

Gina rested her arm on Eamon's knee. The magnetic matrix was composed of cross-fields that enabled the ovum to be pretty much locked into position—a necessity on an ocean-going vessel. 'I know... it's hard to imagine. I've met them both and I know that, while they are both intelligent and highly socialized people, I find it impossible to believe that they could be turned into spies, let alone saboteurs.'

'And yet, here they are... obviously both very uneasy. Why?

Gina took the old man's hands in hers. 'Maybe we have to find out *who.*'

He looked down knowingly. 'Go on then, Gina... what have you uncovered?'

'Well, I checked Virtanen's bank details. He has definitely been paid off, and the deposits seem to originate from a Meridionali source. Can't be certain... pretty well covered. My only deduction is that Lucas is here because he is a close match for the mechanic, and the clean-shaven bit just helps to throw our biometrics into disarray. No one has said that the casuals can't shave off their facial hair. That leaves the girl—ideal actually—she speaks fluent Vietnamese and just had to be substituted for one of the domestics in the casual pool... though how they knew about that I can't answer.'

Eamon looked into the distance. 'Alasdair is no fool... though what he hopes to gain by putting these two neophytes on my boat is anybody's guess.' He made eye contact with Gina. 'They are very much in love, aren't they?'

She searched the crystal-clear eyes and gave a little nod.

'I don't want to hurt them, Gina, and I don't want to lock them up. But, just to be on the safe side, I don't want the girl to be anywhere near food preparation or even serving.'

'I'll have her scraping out the chain locker.'

'No... no... she has to believe that she is part of the usual team.'

'I'll put her in the laundry... that's an easy place to isolate... she won't be able to roam.' She noticed Eamon's far-away look. 'What are you thinking about? I know it's not work.'

A wan smile preceded his answer. 'I can't help thinking that a love forged in adversity and in an alien place will be a strong love... don't you think, Gina?'

His girl Friday heaved an exasperated sigh. 'I suppose so... I wouldn't know—I haven't been in love like that.'

'I have.' He absently caressed her cheek with the back of his hand.

Gina glanced at her watch. 'Well, the induction will be finished shortly. I'd better organise Linh Vuong's work detail. It's annoying that I don't have free access to the casual staff quarters any more, but they would recognise me instantly.' She separated from Eamon and squeezed his hand.

'Gina,' he called after her.

She turned.

'It's so difficult for someone like you to fall in love.' There was a sonorous quality to the old man's voice, as though he was expressing something that he'd long prepared. 'Even the expression—falling—goes against your instincts. Finding love is random, unplanned and mysterious... not something you'd be comfortable with.' The ovum floated closer to her. 'May I suggest though, that the first step to finding your own love is to be able to recognise it in others.'

Gina's gaze drifted away. Okay, so now she had two agendas—nail the security on board ship and keep a lookout for burgeoning love. 'Yes, sir,' she said and turned on her heels.

Linh closed the door to her cabin and joined the other girls in the passageway. It turned out that she was quartered just two doors away from Owen's room. As the women moved along the corridor to the stairs, she passed the camouflaged sticker on the wall. Its innocuous presence filled her with hope. Just metres away, Owen was sleeping. She wasn't alone.

No, indeed... Owen's warning about Gina Wu was a matter of grave concern. How on earth was she going to avoid her?

At the bottom of the stairs, the woman in charge gripped her arm and held her back as the rest climbed up towards the canteen. She then pointed further along the corridor and gave Linh a little shove in that direction. This took her forward towards the tender pen where she had arrived earlier. About halfway along there was an intersection. She was guided left by a rough hand and then left again at the next intersection. They continued down a corridor and passed the open door of a cabin on the right. With a quick glance, Linh could see that this was a nicely appointed room with two portholes. A little further on they came to a door on the left marked Laundry through which she was ushered.

The woman remained at the door and carefully articulated, "You stay here... boss will come... stay."

Linh nodded and bowed and made it look as though she was comprehending something difficult.

The door closed. Linh looked around the facility. It was quite big with industrial size front loading washers and large tumble dryers. Along the wall opposite the door there were narrow trolley bins that were obviously designed to handle the confines of the ship's passages.

The thought came to her as she looked at the steel wall—was there a chance that Owen's cabin might be on the other side? She tried to imagine the distances she had travelled to get to the laundry—up the corridor from Owen's cabin, turn left, turn left again and down the corridor... how far?... was it far enough?... too far? Linh felt a surge of elation. Something told her that there was a very good chance that he was sleeping on the other side of somewhere along the laundry wall. She would be able to communicate with him! Tapping out messages in Morse code!... they didn't know Morse code... well, they'd have to invent their own code... how?... how would she even get his attention?... and when?... now!... it had to be now... while the other casuals were getting their induction... the cabins were presently unoccupied... but where to start tapping?... she had to have a better idea of where his cabin was... pace it out... but she'd been told to stay... what the hell, no one can fight a tummy bug... she needed to go to the toilet, an excellent excuse.

Linh went to the door and opened it. There was no one in the passage. Leaving the door open, she strode away, counting each measured step. She turned at the intersections and began counting again, continuing past Owen's cabin, past her cabin and into the toilets. She assumed that there would be cameras monitoring the passageways, so her whereabouts would have to be able to be explained.

After a while, she entered the passageway again and did the whole exercise in reverse. She could barely contain her excitement when she entered the laundry; the measurements indicated that Owen's cabin was in fact exactly opposite the laundry door. She moved a trolley out of the way and struck the wall with a balled fist. There was barely a sound. She tried with her knuckles—nothing, and it hurt. What was needed was something metal.

She searched the cabinets for tools, but the place was surgically clean. At last she found a key that had fallen between two basins.

With the key clutched in her hand, she commenced tapping—periodic intervals that she hoped would sound as though it was being made by a human intelligence.

Owen was rigid with terror. He knew that it was just a matter of time before Dora found him. She was wielding that big spanner—he knew it. Every now and again she would tap the wall, and she was getting closer. Tap... tap... tap... it was the ominous passage of a maniac, and now she was right at his head.

He cried out and leapt from the bed. It was pitch black. He felt around and found the bed. It took him a moment to realise that everything was okay—he was confined to a stuffy cabin, tasked with sabotaging a ship. Phew! It had just been a bad dream.

Tap... tap... tap...

Sweat trickled down his back. Very slowly he turned to the doorway and felt for the light switch. The sudden brilliance disorientated him. He breathed heavily and waited. The tapping continued... there, just at the head end of his bunk. He listened and tried to work out what was causing it. It was a definite sharp tap... not a scrape, not a bang. And so regular.

The sudden realisation that it was Linh made his skin crawl. This was her only means of communication! Something was happening to her!... where was she?... next door! Yes, obviously—she must have jagged the cabin next door... what a relief—what luck! But wait... the noise was definitely coming from the back wall... was she in a cabin on the other side?... but how would she know where *he* was?... was it something else making that noise?...

The tapping stopped. Owen stared at the wall from where he was kneeling on the ground. Was he imagining things? Maybe his stretch in the engine room had scrambled his brain.

The tapping recommenced. Tap—tap-scrape-tap-tap—tap-scrape-tap-tap—tap… The pattern repeated itself.

On the third time through, Owen almost wept with relief. It *was* Linh, and she was tapping out the intro to *I Can't Get No Satisfaction*. This was a little joke that they shared whenever they witnessed an outrageous disparity about someone's complaint and their actual position of privilege; like if someone complained about getting a skinny latte when they'd ordered almond milk. They would innocently hum that tune.

But with what could he answer the tap? His belt buckle! He dived for the small bag that held his own clothes and reefed out his jeans. There was no longer a belt in the loops—Knowles had taken it out. He had no coins, nothing. Then his eyes rested on the steel capped boots that he'd been issued. Perfect. He hefted one of the boots and sat on the bed. Then, at the start of the next pattern, he joined in. The heavy boot made a surprising amount of noise. He tapped as lightly as he could without losing the sound because of the leather covering. After the second time through, the tapping on the other side broke out into a rapid crescendo. Owen knew that it was applause. She was congratulating him. After a pause, he returned the applause as best he could with the heavy boot.

Then it was quiet. What now? Who was going to make the first move? What move? He tried to establish some logic in his mind. The bed rose and fell. It was only then that he realised they were under way again and that the subliminal sound to which he had awoken was in fact the constant background drone of the engines.

One sharp tap emanated through the wall. An A perhaps—first letter of the alphabet.

After a pause, three taps followed. C?

A pause. Owen was suddenly aware that he might have to count a whole cluster of taps next. Count? No, what would be the point of that? Say the alphabet!

The taps began before Owen was ready. *A B C D… M N O P…* the taps ceased.

… oh, hell. What was it? An N, an O or a P?

After a pause the taps resumed. Four. *D*

Pause. Five taps. *E*

The silence on the other side of the wall continued.

... okay... A, C something D, E... Must be an O. So, ACODE... A CODE! Oh, you little beauty!

Owen rapped his applause on the wall.

He waited for Linh to take the initiative.

One tap. *A*

Long pause. One tap, continued scraping, seven taps. *G*

... A... A something G?... Okay, not sure where we're going with this.

Two taps. *B*

Long pause.

Eight taps. *H* scraping, fourteen taps. *N*

Long pause. Owen looked wildly around for something to write with but he knew there was nothing in his room. He licked his finger and tried to write H and N but it didn't really stand out on the wall.

Three taps. *C*

Long pause.

Owen went through the alphabet along with the fifteen taps that followed. *O* scraping, twenty-one taps. *U*

The silence on the other side prolonged.

... okay, now it's up to me. A—A and G: B—H and N: C—O and U...

Owen recited the results to get it into his brain.

... A—A and G: B—H and N: C—O and U...

His emotions were running so high that, despite the troubled awakening, he felt totally focused.

He repeated his mantra and tried to think at the same time. Maybe the initial A, B and C were in fact one, two and three. So, it became;

... one is A and G: two is H and N: three is O and U...

Then all at once he realised;

... One tap is A through to G: two taps is H through to N: three taps is O through to U...

He could see what Linh was trying to do. Instead of rattling off bulk taps for each letter, now the letters could be grouped so that the prefix—a one, two or three taps—would indicate which group the next letter was in, then the following taps would give the position of the letter in that group.

He drummed his applause on the wall. The sweat poured off his body and dripped to the sheets. The emotion, the challenge, the success—he was almost quivering with exhilaration.

He took the initiative.

Two taps—H to N. Two taps—I

A scrape. This was his idea—it would help to separate the letters.

Two taps—H to N. Five taps—L

A scrape.

Three taps—O to U. One tap—O

... Oh, what now... just tap it out...

Twenty-two taps—V

Scrape.

Three taps—O to U. Seven taps—U

The applause started straight away. Owen sure hoped that it was Linh he was communicating with and not the cook. He'd never experienced such a degree of euphoria—to accomplish this level of communication under such difficult circumstances was beyond bliss. He held the boot above his head and bent his forehead to the wall, letting the sweat drip from his nose, hoping that he might hear a sound from the one he loved.

The door to the cabin burst open. Owen turned his head in a flurry of spray.

Kendrick Knowles stood in the doorway with his hands on his hips. Behind him, Dora was trying to get a look inside.

'WHAT THE BLEEDING, BLOODY HELL ARE YOU DOING, YOU SORRY SACK OF SHITE! Knowles screamed from three paces away. YOU'RE SUPPOSED TO BE ON DUTY. GET YOUR GEAR ON AND GET YOUR FAT BUM TO THE ENGINE ROOM BEFORE I KICK YOU RED RAW!

He'd forgotten to set his alarm. His exhaustion—seeing Linh in the canteen—the tumult of emotions as he crashed into his pillow. He'd forgotten all about the next shift.

HURRY UP YOU PATHETIC, SNIVELLING LITTLE CREEP OR, SO HELP ME, I'LL SUFFOCATE YOU IN MY ARMPIT!

Owen had the presence of mind to give one long scrape of the boot down the wall as some sort of alert to Linh, but all that did was to raise Knowles' ire another notch.

He stepped right up to the bed. ARE YOU DERANGED? he shrieked with spittle spraying from his mouth. I SAID MOVE! I'LL BELT THE LIVING BEJESUS OUT OF YOUR STUPID HEAD—DON'T THINK I WON'T!

With the boot in his hand, Owen scurried to the end of the bed, trying his best to avoid contact with the bosun. He jumped to the floor and stepped into his overalls. When he had his boots on, he stood for an indecisive moment at the end of the bed. But a glimpse of Knowles' fuming jowls impelled him to scuttle through the doorway, push Dora's bosom out of the way and run down the corridor.

Linh heard the vague slamming of the door. She drew her ear from the wall. Poor Owen. She'd heard it all... the yelling... the abuse. Through sore knees, she raised herself and walked to the lone chair in the room. Next session, she would put the chair against the wall and communicate in comfort. Her spirits had soared with Owen's message. She so badly wanted to tell him that she loved him. He needed it, now that he was going back to his lonely post in the engine room. She put the key in the top pocket of her blouse.

Now, here was something odd. She was dressed for waitressing. What was she doing in the laundry? Overalls would be more appropriate, surely.

The door was open, as she had purposefully left it. Was she supposed to use her initiative here and start doing some washing? She could end up flooding the place. No, she'd been told to wait.

Footfalls sounded in the passageway. She turned to the door in time to see a thin man with long wispy hair enter the room. He leant against the door and closed it slowly with his back, all the while eyeing Linh with brazen lewdness.

'Ohh, honey,' he uttered, smoothing back his hair, '... aren't you just too lovely for words.' He loosed himself from the door and came towards her. 'And here I was thinking I'd drawn the short straw... I won't mind giving you instructions at all... no I won't... not at all.'

Linh stayed seated—there was nowhere to run. She might be able to defend herself better from this unusual position. He circled behind her... that wasn't good.

'Now, let me guess,' his voice was so close, '... you would have to be... um, now, don't tell me, don't tell me... Filipina! Am I right? See, I'm an educated man... I know what you are called.' He put his hands on Linh's shoulders.

Now was the time for her to create some scope. She pointed to herself. 'Vietnam,' she announced.

'Oh!... you're from Vietnam. Well that changes everything, baby. I thought you were some slum dweller looking for an easy way out, but hey, now that we're having a conversation, I'll have to treat you with respect... all the respect you deserve, sweetheart.' His hands slid down her arms. 'Isn't it great that there's no work on just at the moment... it's just you and me.'

Linh could feel his breath on her head.

Knowles had made his way back to the bridge. His face was still swollen with anger. A slug of whiskey was what he needed before he killed someone. Tefay had some in the communications room. He changed direction.

Gina Wu stepped out of the com room just as Knowles arrived.

She looked him up and down. 'What's wrong with you?'

Knowles barged past her. 'Nothing!' He went to close the door. 'Actually, there is something—ever since that Finn shaved his face, he's been acting weird. He missed his shift—I had to boot him out of bed... though, whatever it was that he was doing on his bed... I don't want to know!'

Wu squared up to the bosun. '*What* was he doing on his bed?'

'How the hell would I know?... dripping sweat and holding on to his boot... the guy's got to be losing it. I'd take him off the shift if it wasn't for the fact that I enjoy seeing him cooped up in the engine room.'

The floor took a plunge. Wu automatically put her hand out to the wall. She seemed to be staring straight through it.

Knowles grunted and closed the door.

Wu strode swiftly to the stairs. The spiral treads took her directly to the oak door. It opened straightaway and the lithe, head of security made her way straight to the magnetic suite.

The ovum rotated. 'My goodness, Gina... you look flustered,' the old man raised his eye-brows.

'I'm sorry to trouble you, Eamon, but I have every reason to believe that our two spies have been communicating with each other.'

Eamon's brow fell. 'But how is that possible? You've separated them, and no electronic devices will work on board.'

'You wouldn't believe it, but the laundry, where she is consigned, happens to share an internal wall with Lucas' cabin. Something Knowles said made me realise what was going on.'

'But she's only been there less than two hours—that's awfully quick work for amateurs.'

'I don't understand it either. With your permission, Eamon, I'd like to sort this out once and for all.'

'Yes, of course, my love. But, Gina... don't be too harsh... I'd like to meet this couple at some time in the future. I don't know why—a premonition perhaps.'

Gina looked hard at the frail, huddled creature in the egg. 'We have no idea what's in their minds,' she said with a dispassionate shake of her head.

Eamon nodded his assent. 'I know... I know. I'm sure you'll find that out soon enough.'

With a contemptuous smirk, she turned on her heels and strode away.

Chapter Twenty-Eight

Linh bowed her head.

The man's breath followed her.

She closed her eyes.

He mouthed her hair.

Linh took her mind to a time when she was fifteen.

She and her father were facing each other, both wearing the sky-blue garments of an exponent of Vovinam—the martial art form that evolved in response to the occupation of Vietnam by the French.

She had been doing the drills and exercises with her father since she was eight years old. It was always fun. Her father was a highly skilled fighter. He subtly trained Linh's young body to be fast, evasive and powerful. And up until the age of fifteen, the rigour and the movements were not dissimilar to ballet.

But one day, he faced her from one pace away and informed her that the strength and agility that she had developed would now be directed to a specific purpose—disabling an opponent. At first, she was repulsed by the notion. The family had always chosen to avoid the overt expressions of violence that are so prevalent in films and books. There was plenty of thought provoking material out there that didn't devolve into graphic displays of aggression and brutality. The family steered around those aspects of the culture and focused instead on upbeat themes.

Linh's father was all too aware of how sheltered her upbringing had been. He began with break-holds and passive defence. He created plausible scenarios where she would have to defend herself. A strong feature of Vovinam is to assess the whole situation and not just the immediate conflict, so that a defensive strategy works towards achieving an exit from danger.

Their sessions together were as much about bonding socially as training for combat.

Gradually she learnt about aggressive defence, using her environment to her advantage, and finally, lethal termination of combat if there was no other way to survive a conflict.

Linh weighed up the pros and cons of remaining in the chair. Her assailant would feel empowered by his position behind her. Good—he would not expect an attack. The disadvantage was that she could not direct any of her explosive power. If she was going to have any chance of disabling him, it would be easier, face to face.

His hands travelled further down her arms, to her hands, finally clasping the seat edge. Linh was trapped. The man's upper arms pinned her shoulders against the chair back. His head was next to hers. She suddenly realised that she was in the presence of a man who was used to subduing women. A head-butt would be ineffectual, and he could turn his face into her neck if she tried to rake him with her nails. The subsequent retaliation on his part would be devastating.

'What's the matter, darlin'… you've gone all quiet on me. Don't you like me embracing you?'

Yes, it was a very convenient embrace. He could roam about her with one hand, and still keep her under control with the other arm.

… use the environment…

What environment? She was wedged in a chair with no way of reaching anything nearby—not that there was anything remotely weapon-like in the room.

… use the environment…

The man's mouth was at her ear. 'Baby, do you mind very much if I help myself to your scrumptious little body? I'll be very gentle, but you have to promise to be still, now.'

Okay, so he has a bit of a grope. Eventually, she would find the moment to serve him one.

… use the environment…

One hand left the seat. He reached for her blouse and fiddled with the top button. 'Oh, dear... women's clothing. I never get used to the buttons—you undo them for me, sweetheart.' He tapped at the button.

... use the environment... language! That's part of the environment...

Linh's hands came up inside his arms to her blouse. 'You should try it face to face,' she said clearly, slightly turning so that she could see him.

The man's head jerked to the side in astonishment.

As the last sibilant hiss escaped Linh's mouth, she drove her rigid thumb straight into the man's eye. In a continuation of movement, she writhed around in the chair and propelled her fist from her shoulder to his nose. His head arced. His arms came up in defence. Linh gripped some of the strands of hair, and levered downwards, helping to lift herself out of the chair. The hair tore out in her hands. The man groaned loudly and attempted to rise on buckling knees. With a dull crack, Linh's second punch skewed his nose across to one side. He covered his head and managed to stand. Linh laid out a side kick that reflexed, with her full, balanced weight behind it, straight into the inside her assailant's knee. He screamed and sprawled to the floor.

Linh stood near him and massaged her hand. Punches were desperate measures—likely to hurt the thrower as much as the receiver, even if you targeted soft parts like the nose.

Her father had warned her to be wary of injured combatants. Pain usually made them doubly dangerous—though looking at this guy, it was doubtful he would be troubling anyone for a while.

A noise made her turn around.

Gina Wu walked slowly into the room. 'My, my, my... Linh Vuong—that was pretty to watch.'

Linh's mouth unconsciously sagged. 'Gina...' was all she could manage.

The head of security looked down at the squirming, groaning crewmember. She shook her head and put her hands on her hips. 'Tut, tut you bad boy... taking liberties with the casual staff.' She turned to Linh. 'Do you want me to kill him?'

Linh sucked in some deep breaths. 'No... no, not really. I think he's learned his lesson.'

Gina threw back a scornful laugh. 'Oh, Linh... you really are priceless.' She was suddenly serious, 'No!... he hasn't learned his lesson... he'll just become nastier, won't you, Holroyd?'

Holroyd became quiet. He stared at his superior with undisguised malevolence, his nose running blood and his eye tearing uncontrollably.

Gina glanced at Linh with exaggerated sympathy. 'I will kill him,' she uttered. With barely a movement, a gun appeared in her hand and discharged loudly. Holroyd convulsed. Linh leapt backwards against a basin, her hands to her mouth. The crewman twitched and shuddered on the floor. Linh sank to her knees.

Gina stood over the body for a moment then turned to Linh. She came over and held out both her hands. The gun had mysteriously vanished. 'Come on. You don't want to be left in here with a dead body.'

Linh accepted the lift and got to her feet.

Gina strode to the door. 'Follow me,' she said without looking back.

Linh skirted around Holroyd's body. A red patch was growing in the centre of his chest.

'Where are we going?' She asked the stupid question more as a means of affirming that she still had a voice and that she had come out of this whole episode in one piece.

Gina's voice echoed in the passageway. 'We're going to my cabin.'

'Why?'

'To have a drink—I've just killed a man.'

As the two women made their way higher in the ship, Gina spoke into her bracelet.

Someone was going to have to clean up in the laundry.

Owen paced underneath the security camera for the umpteenth time. The wall of noise didn't register in his mind. His thoughts were of Linh. To see her in the canteen, and then to communicate so profoundly with her on the other side of his cabin wall, had disturbed his already agitated equilibrium into a state of uncontrollable restlessness.

He turned at the end of the gangway and headed back. Was everything alright? Was she *supposed* to be in a room adjacent to his? How did she know his location? Was she in a storeroom... a cell? Had Gina identified her already? That would mean that they'd be coming

303

for *him*—but they hadn't—yet. Would she resist revealing his presence on board? It'd be pointless—he couldn't accomplish anything without her. And anyway, they'd been told to confess everything if they were caught.

'You are very much like the proverbial "spanner in the works",' Alasdair had said to them, 'If they find you, they will pull you out from amongst the gears and set you aside. They will not vent their anger on you—it would be as pointless as scolding a spanner. You are a tool of their opposition—you will be restrained and then jettisoned at the first opportunity—or, they may try to find a place for you in their tool box.'

He and Linh had subsequently discussed this analogy at some length and had come to the conclusion that they themselves represented the best opportunity for sabotaging the gamma-ray scheme, and that it was their duty to accept the mission despite its dangers.

But now, the uncertainty about Linh's circumstances was driving him crazy. Suddenly the oppressive clamour of the engines was all too real—he needed to get out.

He turned to the door and pushed on the handle. He would do a quick recce—try to find the room that Linh was in—that would begin to answer some questions. They surely wouldn't miss his presence on the monitor for a few minutes. If he was caught, he'd just say that he was on his way to Knowles' office and that he got lost—anything!

Owen strode past his room and started counting. At the intersection of the corridors he turned left and started counting again at the second left turn. He paused outside the door marked Laundry. It was open, and inside, on the floor, he could see a person lying sprawled in an odd way. With a glance up the passageway, he entered the room.

A bright pool of blood had formed underneath the man's body.

Owen scanned the room. There was no one else inside. The room continued to gyrate around him. A distant roaring filled his ears.

... oh no, not now... not now... Linh is in trouble... a body... a code... Gina Wu...

Voices came to him. It wasn't his imagination—someone was coming.

Owen moved towards the laundry bins on the far wall. They loomed in his vision. He looked inside one of the bins. It was empty. The voices were very close. He allowed himself to topple, head first, into the bin. He pulled up his legs. Footfalls resounded.

'Jaysus!' came a voice just metres away.

'Who did it?' a second voice questioned.

'Wu did,' came the reply.

Being head down in the bin restored Owen's awareness—not that the conversation he was hearing made any sense.

... so... who did it?... answer the question, man...

'Why?'

'Wu knows.' The men chuckled heartily, then grunted with exertion as they hefted the body.

'Here,' said one, '... let's put him in one of the trolleys.'

A disembodied voice echoed in the room. It was Knowles. 'Briers—location please...'

'Hang on.' The sounds of labour diminished. '... yeah, we're in the laundry... dealing with um, Holroyd...'

'Leave him for the moment. Go and check in Virtanen's cabin... his transponder seems to suggest he's in bed. Drag him out and bring him to me.'

'Yeah... okay...' There was a moment of quiet. 'C'mon... may as well chuck him in the trolley. We'll collect him later.'

The men heaved once more.

Owen took the opportunity to turn himself upright in the trolley. This was bound to become complicated. He couldn't allow himself to be captured.

He suddenly understood. *Oh... Wu did it!*

Danger had never felt so close. This was worse than he could have imagined—and totally mystifying. He was going to have to chance it—there was no other option.

Gina sat in the only chair in the room. She passed a small bottle of Cognac to Linh, who was sitting on the bed.

Linh sipped carefully. It was reassuring for her to see the drawn appearance of the woman opposite. She'd noticed the almost imperceptible tremor as she scrabbled about in the desk for the bottle.

'Do you drink much?' she asked out of genuine curiosity.

'Very, very rarely,' came the reply.

'Only after you've killed someone?'

Gina smiled. It seemed as though certain muscles in her face had finally released their tension, revealing that there was a vulnerable human being behind the mask of severity. 'I'd be an alcoholic if I drank each time I killed someone,' she replied languidly.

That was disturbing news. Linh took another swig and handed back the bottle.

Gina tilted the cognac to her lips and quivered as she swallowed her mouthful. She placed the bottle on the table and looked squarely at her guest. 'You are very much in love with Owen aren't you, Linh?'

The mention of his name and the coolness with which she framed the question revealed to Linh that their mission had been well and truly exposed. She suddenly, silently burst into tears. She held her hand to her mouth and, through brimming eyes, looked at the cold-blooded assassin opposite her.

Gina stood up, went into the ensuite, and came back with a handful of tissues.

Linh reluctantly accepted them.

The host sat down and crossed her legs. The cabin had no window, no decorations—there was nowhere to look except at each other. 'Tell me what it's like to be in love with a stockman,' she smirked.

Linh wiped her eyes and blew her nose. This development was a lot less upsetting than a bullet in the heart. She scrunched the tissues into a ball and took a big breath. 'He's one of a kind... he's naïve—because he chooses to ignore the bad things about people. He's generous, because he gives everyone the space to be themselves. And he's lucky, because he's happy with what he's got. Oh, I know he's got much, much, more than most people, but you know how it is—people with a lot often feel overly entitled and end up wanting still more. Owen doesn't. I know that if all his material things vanished, he would find a way of connecting with the simplest things until it became his fortune.'

Gina scrutinized her guest as though she was a specimen. She suddenly laughed. 'You two really are from another planet, aren't you.'

Linh took in the perfect teeth, the breasts that bounced with her laugh, her shapely legs. 'You must have had untold numbers of men,' she proclaimed boldly.

Gina slanted a coy grin. 'Yes... yes, indeed I have... untold numbers... all without the slightest encumbrance of love. Until now.' She reached for the cognac, 'Now it's love without the encumbrance of sex,' she chuckled and put the bottle to her lips.

'Who is the man that you love?' Linh took the bottle from Gina's proffered hand.

'The man you want to kill.' Gina kept her eyes closed as she savoured the lingering heat in her throat.

'I don't want to kill anybody!' Linh protested.

'Then why are the two of you on this yacht?'

Their instructions had been clear—if they were discovered, they were to tell their interrogators the complete truth. Linh looked down at her hands holding the bottle. 'Is Owen safe?' she said with an even detachment.

'No,' Gina quickly replied, '... he's being tortured as we speak.'

Linh drew back her hand to throw the bottle. With cat-like fleetness, Gina lunged forward off the wall and intercepted Linh's hand. They fell onto the bed with Gina's elbow at Linh's throat, their faces just centimetres apart.

'I'm joking... I'm joking,' Gina breathed, '... he's in the engine room, slowly being driven mad by the noise. It's okay... yes, he's safe.' She looked at the hurt in Linh's eyes. 'I'm sorry—bad joke.' Her grip slackened and she sat up. 'Oh, great... now there's cognac in my bed.'

Linh quickly turned the bottle upright. 'Sorry,' she said weakly. She sat up.

Gina adjusted her place on the bed and put her arm around Linh. 'Hey, that was a bad joke, under the circumstances. I'm sorry.'

Linh looked askance and asked the rhetorical question, 'So, you love someone.'

Gina levered herself off the bed and sat back in the chair. 'Yeah...' she replied wistfully. 'At least, I'm feeling something for this person that I have never felt for anyone else.'

Linh reached forward and put the bottle on the desk. 'Well, without starting another fight, who is he?'

Gina activated her bracelet. 'You'll see.' The bangle glowed. She spoke at it. 'Can you get the mechanic out of the engine room... yes, now... take him up to the green lounge.'

Linh could hear no reply.... *the auditory signal must be very precisely aimed*...

Her host resumed eye contact. 'Where did you learn to fight like that?'

Linh told her about the instruction with her father.

'I saw every bit of that fight, Linh. You were lethal.'

'I was fighting for my life. I'm not proud of what I did, but I'm glad I managed it.'

The back of a man's head swayed above the rim of the trolley.

Owen stood up. His arm was already drawn back—his feet braced inside the bin. He unleashed a vicious chop straight at the neck of the man nearest to the trolley. The force of his attack translated through his body to the bin—it rolled a few centimetres in the opposite direction. His strike landed harmlessly on the man's shoulders. His victim goggled in surprise and let go of the body in his hands. Owen had the presence of mind to maintain his hold on the man's shirt. He lunged with his other arm and gripped the man's collar. Thrusting his leg forward, he pulled his opponent towards him. The trolley corner slammed into the man's knee. As he bent forward in pain, Owen yanked at his hair and drove his head onto the edge of the bin. He vaulted over the rim.

The second man turned to sprint for the door. One stride landed in the patch of blood. His leg slipped out in front of him—the other knee landed heavily on the floor. He twisted out of an awkward splits and turned around just as Owen's boot caught him under the chin.

The room was deathly silent again. Owen took some deep breaths. The action hadn't been long, but it had certainly been violent. Now there were three bodies littering the floor.

The radio squawked into life. 'Briers! Change of plan—it looks like he's in the laundry. Get back there...'

Owen looked at the unit on the floor, still attached to Briers with its coiled lead. He reached down and picked it up, unclipping the power pack from Briers' belt. He moved back against the far wall and lifted the radio to his mouth.

'Ah, he's asleep in his bed,' he whispered, '... do you want me to wake him up?'

The radio crackled with distortion. *'Of course, I want you to wake him up, you idiot.* Bring him here!'

'Okay,' Owen whispered in reply.

'And stop whispering into the radio, damn it!'

Owen couldn't resist a little smile. He threw the radio into the bin then felt around his overalls. Along the rim of his collar he found a peculiarly hard strip.

... okay, so I'm bugged...

He tried to rip the collar away but it was not possible. Even if he took off his overalls it would probably be impossible to tear the heavy material. He unzipped the front.

... here we go—time to bare my soul...

He placed his overalls against the wall and positioned the trolley on top. Standing in his underwear, he looked at the unconscious bodies.

... hmmm... two with blood stains on them and one that's miles too small for me. What to do...

The radio blared into life. 'God almighty, Briers... why haven't you left his room yet? I don't care if he's starkers, just get him here, pronto.'

On an impulse, Owen bent into the trolley and retrieved the radio. He was going to have to leave the laundry and having access to their means of communication might be a definite advantage.

He looked down at the bodies and decided that stripping them for their clothes would not only take too long but was something that he just couldn't do. He'd have to find something on the run. As well, he felt some relief at discovering that the men were not armed—taking a weapon would have presented another moral hurdle.

With the radio in his grasp, he moved to the door. Going right was the only option. Astern was the engine room bulkhead. He loped up the passageway, feeling distinctly exposed in just his briefs. At the intersection he peeked around the corner—all clear.

... no point in going down the centre of the boat... that's where all the trouble will be...

He jogged across the intersection into the continuation of the passageway forward. On his left were more doors to cabins. He gently tried the first door he came to. It was locked. He tried every door until he came to the end of the corridor—all locked. The passageway now turned to his right. With a quick glance around the corner, he realised he was at the tender pen bulkhead. However, there was a stairway that led up. He glided to the base of the stairs and, after a furtive check, ascended.

... at least bare feet are nice and quiet...

Cresting the next floor level, he found himself in a carpeted foyer, complete with ornamental lighting and plush furniture.

... beauty... guest accommodation. Bound to find some clothes here...

In his hand, the radio came noisily to life. 'Briers! So, help me god... if you're not out of that room in seconds, I'm coming after you...'

Owen hastily adjusted the volume knob so that Knowles' disembodied bellow became a distant murmur. He turned aft into the wide hallway and tried the first door he came to. Locked.

... of course... they're all locked... I'm on a boat with conspirators and secret agents...

The radio vibrated in his hand. A different voice, crisp and urgent emanated into the hush of the hallway. 'Kendrick... we've got him... he's on level two, for'ard... he's got a radio... change to the maintenance channel.'

Knowles' answer was immediate. 'Seal the exits... I'm coming up.'

Owen looked back towards the foyer. Somewhere hidden amongst the sumptuous decor there was a camera.

... can't win a trick here...

Linh rubbed the knuckles of her right hand which was beginning to swell. She'd put everything she had into the punch at Holroyd's nose.

Gina smiled under an intense stare. 'Why did you aim for his nose and not his throat?'

Linh looked at the hands in her lap. Her father had rarely repeated instructions to her—he would reinforce the correct moves through demonstration, and it had only taken one demonstration where his fist blurred to a stop centimetres from her nose for her to understand how devastating such a blow would be. 'If I'd missed his throat and clipped his chin, I could have broken my knuckles. My father told me that, whilst a strike to the throat may be lethal, it doesn't incapacitate an adversary as quickly as a punch to the nose—it blinds the victim for a vital second longer. Then, if I needed to, I could...' but she didn't want to think about it anymore.

'That was well executed, girl.' The bangle on Gina's wrist glowed. 'What?... well find him!... get Knowles onto it... *what*?... shut down every entrance to the third floor... the fourth floor will be completely sealed—anyone caught there will be shot dead. Meet me at the com room.' She leapt to the door and turned to Linh. Stay here. You could be killed if you leave this room. It looks like your boyfriend has sprung into action. Tell me—was this part of the plan?'

Linh looked bewildered. 'No... he was supposed to put rice in the filters...'

Gina looked hard at her then gave a curt nod. 'Right—it looks as though Knowles has got to him. Stay here.' She slipped through the door and pulled it shut.

Linh put her hands to her face. She'd had to tell Gina about the rice. It was the only way of convincing her of Owen's innocence in this present situation.

There was no point in trying to find the location of the camera— they'd be filing up from the lower deck in no time. Owen raced down the hallway towards an ornate timber staircase that wound upwards. He propped on the ornamental baluster. There was nowhere to run to. Every part of the boat was under surveillance. He was trapped. And yet, the thought of Knowles at his back induced him to climb the stairs. What could he expect to find when he reached the next floor? A formal gathering of wine sipping research scientists? A cleaner, vacuuming the carpet? He was in his underwear—it didn't matter. It was going to be painfully embarrassing no matter who he met.

It was, however, reassuringly quiet up there. From halfway up the stairs, he bent low and tried to take a last look down the hallway. The lighting was very subdued and it was difficult to define any shapes— Knowles or otherwise. Would he be better off just surrendering to the inevitable, or was there still a chance—to do what?—save Linh? It remained to be seen whether or not he could save himself! A movement deep in the shadows of the distant foyer caught his eye. A broad shape moved into the hallway. It was Knowles—with a gun at the ready.

There was no time to lose.

... anything but that psychopath...

Owen straightened and propelled himself upwards—and halted instantly.

With her hand on the rail, Gina Wu was poised just three steps away. She regarded him with superior amusement. 'Owen... that's no way to present yourself,' she drawled lazily.

Along with the rush of blood that the last few minutes had triggered in his body, Owen felt a peculiar ascendancy; he was living in the present as never before. The options cascaded into his brain—she was very close by—she was unarmed—she represented a bargaining chip—a hostage. He reacted instinctively.

So did Wu. He was three steps below—she had assessed the situation while he was bending over the rail—he was in his underwear—and she had spent an intensive year in the Israeli military learning combative Krav Maga. She nimbly leapt over his lunge at her feet and, so as not to waste the energy of her descent, she flicked one foot into his forehead and drove the other close to his neck. Then, taking her landing on her hands two steps above her, she thrust him away from her. Owen slid on his back, headfirst down the stairs. He came to rest on the lower floor with his arm skewed in the pins of the baluster.

He knew he'd fainted, but this time felt different. There was the pain for a start. His neck was on fire. And most times he wanted to resurface. But not now—his arm was seriously uncomfortable and his back hurt in numerous places. He didn't feel ready to regain consciousness. He wanted to die.

He opened his eyes.

... wish granted...

Kendrick Knowles glowered at him. 'Get up, you smarmy, perverted creep... and pull up your underpants, for god's sake.'

A fine spray of spittle arced down in the light of the stair void.

Owen wasn't sure about which part of him he should attempt to move first.

'Leave him alone, Kendrick—I'll take care of this.' Gina Wu's calm voice filtered through to Owen's semi-consciousness.

'Of course, you will, Gina. Although, I hope you won't mind if I give him a little something to remember me by—he's taken out two of my men.'

'Touch him at your peril.'

There was a moment of quiet. Owen tried to look up. He caught a glimpse of his assailant, half-way up the stairs, standing with indomitable bearing with her hands on her hips. Above his head, Knowles' swung his gun in her direction.

'Really,' he uttered, '... I don't see any peril. I'll tell you what I see, Miss Wu—I see you with a bullet in your pretty head... I see our boy here similarly dead... I see a trail of death and destruction created between the two of you, and I see me putting an end to it all. How does that look to you?'

Owen would have loved to come to Gina's assistance, because at least she hadn't mentioned killing him. The only trouble was, he was having difficulty staying conscious.

'You wouldn't want to do that on camera, Mr Knowles.'

Knowles scoffed. 'You should know better. There's no camera in the void.' He glanced up as he said it.

Owen saw Knowles' gun go off. It was just above him. A light-yellow flame leapt from the barrel. Knowles dropped his head and looked straight into Owen's eyes. The arm fell. The gun swung centimetres short of his face. A red dot just above Knowles' left eye began to spurt blood. His body filled Owen's field of vision. His heaviness crashed onto him.

Owen waited for his senses to contract. It was inevitable—Knowles' blood had squirted all over him. That would be enough—and the fact that he was being suffocated in Knowles' armpit. What a terrible irony. So... what about the shot he got off? Must have been a nerve thing... what a trained killer Gina Wu was though... never seen anyone like her... where did the gun come from? He could have surprised her on the steps though, if he hadn't been such a gentleman... he'd just wanted to sweep her off her feet—in a manner of speaking—and hold her in a bear-hug. She would have struggled, sure, but he was considerably stronger... he'd hold her close—she wouldn't be able to escape... have to be careful not to squeeze her breasts too hard... oh, well, maybe a little squeeze... she was certainly a handsome creature... wild... her lips snarling next to his face... pleading with him to release her... Owen... Owen...

'Owen... Owen,' Gina's mouth was at his ear, '... c'mon, get up. We haven't got much time...'

Owen took a huge gasp of air. Gina helped him to sit up. His arm was free. His whole body hurt.

Knowles' body lay at the foot of the stairs.

Gina put Owen's arm around her neck and hefted him to his feet. 'C'mon... up the stairs.'

Owen's faculties, physical and mental, began to revive. 'You shot him?'

'Uh huh,' Gina grunted.

'Lucky he didn't get you.'

'I fell to the left... he's right handed... his reflex would pull to his left... my right... can't you do any better than that?'

'Well, excuse me for limping—but you did nearly break my neck.'

'Yeah... sorry 'bout that. I just managed to rein in my responses in time—otherwise you would have been dead.'

They were staggering through a huge lounge area. Quite a few people were staring at them from behind couches and bars. There was obvious terror on their faces.

'So, you rearranged my attire for me, I notice.' Owen was suddenly conscious of his state of undress and the fact that he was spattered with blood.

They stopped in front of a lift. Gina pressed the button and it opened right away. 'You worked out that you were bugged, huh?'

'Yeah... not a lot of trust on board this vessel.' Owen managed to stand unassisted as the lift went up.

'The only place where there is any trust is on this floor, Owen.' The lift doors parted.

'And who would that be between?'

'You'll see. In here.' Gina rapped on a cabin door. 'It's me,' she called out.

The door opened inwards. Linh put her hands to her mouth when she saw Owen. She walked out with unbound concern on her face, then held out her arms.

Owen could barely believe his eyes. He moved forward to embrace her but held her at arm's length. 'I'm covered in blood, Tot. It's not mine.'

Linh clutched his hands.

This was not the sort of reunion that Owen had imagined. He felt suddenly guilty at having failed so spectacularly. Nothing was turning out the way it was supposed to.

'Go in and get showered, Owen,' Gina called behind her as she strode away. 'I'll get some clothes.'

Owen and Linh entered the tiny cabin. They looked into each other's eyes and squeezed hands.

'What's going on, Owie?' asked Linh, shaking her head.

'I was hoping that you might be able to tell me that,' he responded softly. 'What's with Gina helping us now?'

'Let's get you in the shower first. I'm no better informed than you. All I know is that our mission is well and truly blown... what are you doing?'

'I'm taking you into the shower with me...'

'In Gina's shower!'

'I don't care. I want to have a shower—I want to be with you—I want to ease this pain in my neck where she kicked me...'

'She kicked you?'

'Did she ever. By the way, it's great that she's being nice to us, because if she didn't like us we'd be instant history.'

'Tell me about it—I was only in her presence for one minute and she shot someone.'

'Hey, that was my experience too—except that she laid me out cold first.'

Linh reached up to Owen's face as the warm water splashed onto them. 'Oh, you poor boy.'

Owen held his girl close. 'Is this really her cabin?'

Linh nodded.

'Wow... it's not what I would have expected... although she has splurged with the shower head—it's the size of a pizza.'

Linh laid her head on Owen's chest. 'Lucky for us.'

Chapter Twenty-Nine

Gina entered Eamon's suite. The panels were in transparent mode and the sunlight produced natural, radiant warmth. She was surprised to see him lying on the bed. She kicked off her shoes and went over on bare feet.

'How are you feeling, Eamon?' She climbed in next to him. 'You're very cold, my love... what's wrong?'

The old man produced a wan smile and covered Gina's hand on his chest with his own veined hand. 'Gina, my darling... I think that I am, at last, dying.'

It was a glorious day outside. The forward-facing vent was open and, despite the forty knots of boat speed, a gentle zephyr blew across the bed. Its occupants remained balanced with an immutable inertia—riding across the earth's surface on a magic carpet.

Gina raised herself and looked into the sunken pale eyes. 'Do you want me to summon the doctor?'

'No... no,' Eamon shook his head, '... I'm not about to depart in the immediate future, and the last thing we need is more helicopter traffic. What's more important is you—there's worry on your face. Tell me about it.'

Gina unbuttoned her blouse, lifted her bra over her breasts and settled Eamon's hand on her. 'I will... in a minute. I want to relax with you.' She stroked the hand on her breast. 'Tell me something wise.'

This was a routine that Gina had initiated when she became aware of just how much life experience Eamon could draw on. "Tell me something wise", she would say whenever they needed a moment to

317

distil the events of the day. The fact that he invariably obliged her is what she loved about him—a man who possessed so much wisdom.

'Well, Gina,' he answered just above a whisper, '... as I feel your breast, I am reminded that we live in a material world. There are so many things to love about the material world—we can't escape it—we are not meant to escape it—we are meant to embrace it... as I am you, with my dry, gnarled hands. The thing is, we have to attribute the correct emotions to everything material—when objects become bargaining chips they lose their inherent value. That is what is meant by divesting oneself of possessions—not so much actually giving everything away, but rather that one shouldn't become beholden to objects as symbols—they will only make you happy if you appreciate them for what they are.' He rolled against her and nestled his mouth against her shoulder. 'Sorry, it's not very wise—it's the best I could do.'

'And what do you appreciate about my breasts?'

'That it's as close to your heart as I will ever get... and that you have lovely breasts.'

'Just like a man!'

'At my age, that is unbelievably complimentary.'

They laughed.

Gina pursed her lips in thought. 'Why did you choose to remind me about the material world?'

'Well, you eschew material things—which is very evolved of you. But maybe there's something material out there that you need... and who needs you...'

Gina leant her head against Eamon's. 'Maybe. Not while there is still breath in your body, old man.'

Eamon sighed deeply. 'Ah, yes... to breathe in anticipation of the future...'

Gina lifted away Eamon's hand. She sat up and readjusted her bra. 'It's the past that is causing a few headaches for us now. As you know, I had Linh assigned to the laundry. Sometime after the two of them communicated through the wall, Dillon Holroyd went to the laundry to instruct her on the machines. It was a bad choice. He's one of the remaining ne'er-do-wells from Knowles' original crew. He tried it on with her and she very effectively neutralised him.'

'Really! How?'

'Well, she was trained by her father in the style of Vovinam. Absolutely fluid... borne of desperation, she freely admits. Admirably lethal!'

'And Owen? Is he an exponent of martial arts?'

'Ah... no. He's good with horses, apparently.'

'Oh...'

'However, young Owen took it in his mind to go in search of his girlfriend and found his way to the laundry after Linh and I had already left. He was there when two of the crew came to collect Holroyd's body. Amazingly, he managed to disable them. He ran into Knowles at the staircase on level three. I was there. Knowles was going to kill him...'

'So, you killed Knowles...'

Gina gave a nod of affirmation.

Eamon reached for her hand. 'I'm sorry you had to do that.'

'I'm not.'

'I know—he was evil. I'm just sorry you had to soil your hands. So where does that leave us now?'

'The two love birds are in my room. He's getting cleaned up— covered in Knowles' blood. I was wondering whether he could borrow some clothes... slacks and a shirt.'

'Yes... of course,' Eamon drawled distractedly, '... but I would like you to fit him for a dinner suit.'

'A dinner suit! Why?'

Eamon's eyes gleamed with mischief. 'Will Linh fit into one of your gowns?'

Gina sat up straight in the bed and appraised him with a look of disbelief. 'Okay, I get it—we're going to give them a sea burial and they've got to look nice.'

'Oh, Gina... you have such a macabre sense of humour. Well... will she fit into something of yours?'

'I'm a little taller, but yeah, we're about the same size.'

'Good, good. Make her stunning—memorable. And I want you to scan him for a suit—neck-tie, kerchief, shoes... Caraceni in Milan... to be ready in a week...'

'What are you scheming, Eamon—are you sure you're feeling

alright?'

'For a dying man I feel fantastic. I did some research of my own, and I found out why those two came onto the yacht.'

Gina slid to the end of the bed and began gently manipulating the old man's feet. 'Why?'

'Their mission is to sabotage the gamma-ray program.'

'How? None of the technology is on board.'

'No, but the brains trust is. Each time we step up to the next level of the program, we concentrate all the living knowledge on the *Zeus*.'

'It's the only way to prevent leaks.'

'I know—and it works really well—and so far, apart from these two arriving, it seems to have remained concealed.'

'And you should keep it that way, Eamon. It is *the* most powerful weapon ever—not so much in its destructive capability, but in its disruptive capability. You have the means to both wage war and ensure peace—that is why you have fostered this research—gone out of your way to support these crazy, soulless scientists... because, like your worst enemy, you wanted to keep it close.' Gina dropped her head. She ran her thumbs lightly over his insteps. 'I'm sorry—I'm speaking out of turn.'

'No, Gina, no... you have said exactly what I want to hear. I'm tired of being alone. It's unavoidable, I know, but since you have been with me, I've felt that you have the fierce resoluteness of purpose that I can rely on.'

'Then why am I detecting a change of heart?'

Eamon held out his hands. Gina took them and assisted him in sitting up. He took her hands and kissed them.

'Gina... I was born in Prague in 1800. My parents were both doctors. We lived in the countryside. I had an idyllic childhood. I grew up to be very healthy, well-educated and I chose to travel. By the time I was sixty, I had had many different careers, explored many countries, had a few brushes with death, had four children with my gorgeous wife, Sabine and decided that I should retire. We bought a farm in northern Italy, close to the French border. It wasn't anything so magnificent, but it was ours and we enjoyed living there. One day an enormous entourage came up the valley and came to rest at the manor house that bordered our farm. In due course we were introduced to the owner, a widower of, it seemed to me then, fairly advanced years. He was an immensely charming and cultivated man, and Sabine and I became very attached to him. He was quite independent and not at all needy in any way, but it became an established routine that we would eat together most days, either at his place or at ours. He had a wonderful sagacity—I thought that *I* was a bit of a man of the world, but I felt like a callow farm boy in his presence. As well, he had enormous vigour, not just physically but also in his imagination. Between us, we reinvented the village—revitalised the farming, began new industries, improved schooling and training—we were very busy people, and it wasn't until Sabine and I were approaching our nineties that we began to suspect that something was amiss…'

'You weren't getting any older…'

'That's right! I mean, people in that part of the world are notoriously long-lived, but we were exceeding all expectations. We had the advantage of having moved into the area at an age where the locals may have remembered us as being in our fifties or even our forties. You have to remember that age was a badge of honour in those days—people were quick to pull rank based on their seniority. So, we managed to wave off any meddlesome questions, but when we were well into our hundreds, we had to leave.'

'What about your neighbour?'

'During our last week in our house, he confided to us that the special wine that he had always insisted on serving at our meals was indeed an elixir that kept us from aging.

'Did you ask him why he had chosen the two of you to benefit from this elixir?'

'Gina, we asked him hundreds of questions—who was he? what was his purpose? why us?… endless questions. He told us that we were chosen to oversee the development of humanity—at least in our neck of the woods—and that, if we were lucky, we might live to be one hundred and fifty years of age.'

'You've done especially well, then.'

'Ha! He hadn't counted on the medical advances of the twentieth century.'

Gina looked away. 'Where is Sabine?'

Eamon reached up and stroked Gina's hair. 'Oh, Gina… it's too sad… I will never forgive myself. We were living in England in 1940. She was a hundred and thirty-eight years old and we had a nice little farm in the countryside. We were well aware of the dangers because we were very well connected, but one night, a stray bomber dropped its load. One bomb landed right on our cottage. I was away that night. We should have moved right away.'

'And then you could have ended up on a ship that was torpedoed.'

'Exactly, Gina… we both came to the decision not to allow our prolonged lives to breed paranoia. Death is everywhere—so is life. We took chances and laughed about it. It was a terrible shock to me that she died in our little farm house—all because of a war.'

'Is that why you have spent so much time developing this anti-weapon?'

Eamon wheezed with laughter. 'That's very astute of you, Gina. Yes, the war changed me. I was a hundred and forty-five years old when it ended, yet I felt that I had enough energy to devote to finding, as you said, an anti-weapon. I didn't know what shape this weapon would take—all I knew was that, after Hiroshima, it was going to be in the realms of nuclear research. I was well connected, but the problem was that technology was exploding in all directions. Where was the answer? In nuclear warfare? bio warfare? information technology? Space?'

Gina held up her hand in apology and addressed her bracelet. 'Yes?... Okay.' She turned to Eamon. 'The disturbance has been cleaned up—everything is back on track.'

Eamon nodded. 'Well, the paradox was that the answer was in front of us the whole time—every day, Buck Rogers dealt with the forces of evil using ray guns. They were a popular symbol of the modern era, but strangely they were never developed. We went to space, we flew beyond the sound barrier, and we blew up entire atolls with atomic bombs… but we never developed the ray gun. When I investigated what was required, I realised why—they required an enormous amount of power. At the time, various institutions were experimenting with nuclear fusion, and my team realised that therein lay the source of energy for an all-powerful ray gun. In time, we realised that fusion technology was never going to work—it is impossible to replicate the conditions inside a star that is well over a million times bigger than the earth. This is when we changed the narrative to one of sub-atomic research.

'It was an era of fascination with particle physics—the constituents of matter itself held so much promise. What exactly we would achieve was anyone's guess—flying cars? sub-cellular surgery? teleportation? It didn't matter. Numerous exalted magazines produced mind-boggling graphics that attempted to explain the inner workings of the most elemental components of our realm, and all that achieved was to make people feel inferior and beholden to the alter of science. It played into our hands.

'We did the same with space exploration. Obviously, our ray gun would have to be positioned in an orbit around the earth, and so we promoted the allure of the cosmos. To be fair, the technology available just after the war was undoubtedly exciting—jets, rockets, atomic power—higher, faster, further—the populace was searching for something to replace the memories of the recent past. However, realistically, we should have been spending what money there was on repairing our nations—but, inevitably, our technological advances were steered towards military purposes.

'That spurred me on—the need to find a neutralising weapon became more vital with every decade. Even though we were at the cutting edge of so much research, my team was constrained by the technology available at the time. Paradoxically, just when we wondered how we would ever find the obscene amount of money to build the collider, public sentiment turned very much in favour of exploring the unknowable whilst ignoring the obvious—we found funds to pour into, literally, a black hole, whilst Europe staggered with social unrest. I mean, we contributed to the promotional campaigns, obviously, but it always surprised me how well our brain-washing worked.

Gina raised an eyebrow. 'Many dictators have discovered that fact.'

Eamon wheezed alarmingly. He allowed himself to fall backwards onto the bed.

'Did you direct some of your research into finding ways of making you live longer?'

The old man massaged his eyes. 'Yes... oh, yes. That is the beauty of sponsoring research. Do you think that all students have an equal chance when they apply for doctorate funding? They don't. There is much examination by vested interests with prescribed agendas and insidious influence. The only justification for my longevity is that I was trying to save the world.'

Gina swung her feet off the bed. 'Well, I'm relieved to hear that you still intend on saving the earth. But I'd better head to my cabin. One of the crew has reported steam coming out from under the door—god knows what those two have gotten up to.'

'Of course, Gina. Grab some things of mine for the present—it's not as though they are two hundred years out of date.'

Chapter Thirty

The warm rain dissipated the pain in Owen's shoulders. The water brimmed at the raised sides of the shower recess and flooded onto the floor. An edge at the entrance of the ensuite contained the flow as it emptied through the drain.

Owen was seated with Linh's legs wrapped around him. They dozed with their head on each other's shoulder. Steam swirled thickly around them.

It was surreal—buoyed in the water—enveloped in a cloud—hugging Linh. Maybe he *had* been shot. He didn't want to think—he just wanted to be—like this—it was beautiful. It was even better than the sand-hollowed bath at the waterhole—with the scent of ti-tree—and Linh, naked, taking her turn to add hot water...

Gina's voice echoed in the confines. 'For god's sake, you two—the whole cabin is damp with steam.' She reached in and turned off the shower. 'I'm going to get some dry towels and you'd better both be out of there when I come back.'

'Or what?' Owen mumbled against Linh's shoulder.

'Or,' Gina responded instantly, '... I'll grab the fire extinguisher from across the hall and spray you both with freezing cold carbon dioxide.'

'We're getting out,' Linh said hurriedly.

'Do you want us to save the water for you, Gina?'

The slam of the cabin door was Owen's answer.

'God, Owen... don't get her upset. She's got a gun, you know.'

'Yeah,' Owen cranked his head in question, '... where, exactly?'

'In the small of her back—I felt it when we were on the bed.'

Owen's eyebrows rose as his face fell. 'Come again?'

'Owen!' She slapped him playfully. 'We had a fight—a scuffle—I spilled cognac on her bed.'

'She had a go at you because you spilt cognac on her bed?'

'No... we were drinking, then she said something that made me really angry, and I tried to hit her with the bottle.'

Owen held out his hand. Linh helped him out of the recess.

He stood with his arms out and dripped. 'I have a great idea—seeing as how there is cognac in her bed anyhow, we could just slip in between the sheets and wait for her to come back with the towels, and you can tell me the whole story of you and Gina and your little drinking session.'

'No! I'm not getting into her *bed*!'

'And I don't want to be standing here stark bollock naked in this tiny cabin when she comes in. C'mon, it'll be fun.' Owen threw open the covers. 'Hey, that smells really nice.' He wrapped Linh in his arms and the two of them collapsed onto the bed. Then he threw the covers back over.

'Owen, seriously, did you receive a knock on the head or something? The woman is an assassin.'

'You're telling me—and I'm alive because of it. So... your intimate soirée with the assassin—especially the bit where you felt her up.'

Linh couldn't help laughing. She kissed him on the mouth. 'Did she really beat you up?'

'Ah... well, now, let's get this into perspective—I was at an extreme disadvantage...'

'Being in your underpants an' all.'

'Ha, ha... look, if you're not going to take my side of the story seriously...'

'No, I am, I am... I'm taking your side of the story very seriously... very seriously...'

The two lovers held each other close in the narrow bunk and kissed tenderly.

Gina swung open the door and stood speechless for a moment. '... really!... in my bed!'

Owen squirmed around and held up his hands. 'Now, Gina!—don't shoot me... don't shoot me... it was her idea,' he pointed at Linh, '... she asked me whether I'd ever tried lovemaking in a bed splashed with cognac, and I said no, no I hadn't, and that it sounded a bit kinky, but...'

Gina dropped a bundle to the floor. 'Oh, shut up, Owen. Here are the towels—not that you need them any more after drying yourselves in my bed—and some clothes to see you through. I'll be back shortly. We're having dinner with the most important person you're ever likely to meet.' She turned and slammed the door.

Owen pulled a face. 'Okay, that went well.'

'Thank you very much for your gallantry, Owen Lucas... blaming it all on me.'

Owen stepped out of the bed. 'Is there any more of that cognac about, or did it all end up in the bed?'

Linh lunged forward and grasped him around the waist. 'No! Owen, No... it's in the drawer. We can't look in there.'

'No, here it is... on her desk.'

'Oh, that's right. I'd forgotten she'd left it there... with all the steam and everything.'

'I vote we have one tiny sip each—just to celebrate that we no longer have a mission on this boat, and that we're not likely to be killed for having tried.'

'Likely?'

Owen came and sat next to Linh. He held the bottle between them. 'Linh, my darling, Linh... here is to you for doing everything right in your first time as a spy.' He put the bottle to his lips and sipped.

Linh took the bottle. 'Here is to you, Owie—the dead-set luckiest bloke to walk this planet.' She put the bottle to her lips and gulped a healthy swallow.

Owen still hadn't taken a breath after his taste. His eyes watered and his face reddened. At last he coughed. 'Holy hell! Talk about fire water.'

'Oh, Owen... you're hopeless. C'mon, let's get dressed.'

Linh gathered up the bundle on the floor and laid it on the bed. 'She was right—we don't need the towels any more. Oh, wow! Look what she's brought for me... all wrapped in a plastic coverlet.'

Linh carefully undid the string on the wrap and pulled out a narrow-waisted, fifties-style swing dress in storm blue with a fine cream and teal geometric pattern and full-length pleats in teal. She held it against her.

Owen towelled himself and admired her from the end of the bed. 'Wow, the colour really suits you.'

With a peek inside the collar, Linh let out an exclamation of disbelief. 'Huh!... this is the real thing, Owen.'

'What do you mean?'

'This is a vintage Dior.'

'It's not going to fall apart, is it?'

'Owen, this dress is from the mid-fifties... and it's original. Oh, my god, it's gorgeous! And look, there is the belt.' She pointed near Owen's knee.

'How come you know so much about fashion?'

Linh looked contrite. 'In between my usual history studies, I also delved into fashion history—like modern fashion. It was just an indulgence—wasn't anything serious.'

'Well, that dress is going to look seriously fantastic on you. Put it on.'

Linh opened up the bodice buttons and flung the dress over her head. With little shivers, she settled it around her. Then she did up the buttons and twirled on the spot. The full circle dress spun almost to horizontal, the teal inserts flashing like a strobe.

Owen observed her with an attentive eye. 'How come I am suddenly massively attracted to you, knowing that you are naked under that dress.'

'You keep away from me, Owen Lucas. I am not going to allow you to besmirch this garment with your... your, whatever it is that you're thinking...'

'Just a little bit of besmirching?' he pleaded.

Linh rolled her eyes and moved to him. 'Alright then... just a little bit of besmirching.' She stroked his forehead.

Owen wrapped his hands around Linh's calves and slid up underneath the folds of material. She was still warm from the bath.

The door swung open and Gina let herself in.

Linh gasped and turned in a spray of skirt.

Owen pulled Linh to him. 'Don't you ever knock?'

'Hello… mister cowboy, this is my room, remember. Oh, wow, Linh… much as I hate to admit it, you do look ravishing,' she slanted Owen a woebegone look, '… whilst not actually *being* ravished, I hope.'

Owen dropped his hands from underneath Linh's dress.

Gina walked over to her desk and sat down. She repositioned the cognac to the corner of the desk. 'You two really have made yourselves at home, haven't you?'

Owen held his thumb and forefinger fractionally apart. 'Just a little toast to having made new friends.'

Linh rolled her eyes. 'In his case, a *very* little toast.'

'Not much of a drinker are we, Owen?' Gina crossed her legs. 'That will stand you in good stead with your new friend.'

'My god! It's unbelievable—no sooner are there two women in a room, and I'm the enemy. I'm getting changed.' Owen scooped up the rest of the bundle on the bed and went into the ensuite. Out of Gina's view, he winked at Linh.

She didn't try to supress her smile.

Gina called out around the corner. 'Don't go any further than your underpants—I have to scan you for a suit.'

Owen poked out his head. 'What?'

She waved her phone at him. 'The boss wants you in a suit—about ten thousand dollars' worth. Come out when you're decent. I put some briefs in there.' Then she turned to Linh. 'We have like a shop here if you need anything—just let me know.'

Linh ran her hands down the dress and said in a harsh whisper, 'Where did you *get* this?'

Gina reached for the belt. 'I know, isn't it divine. I have someone scouting for me. He picked it up in New York. I've only worn it once myself. Here, wrap this around you.

Linh clasped the belt in place. 'What am I going to do for shoes?'

'We'll go around to my wardrobe in a minute, as soon as Roy Rogers here gets measured.'

Owen stepped into the room and stood obediently with his arms slightly away from his sides. Gina referenced the phone on the carpet then walked slowly around him, all the while raising the scanner.

When she got to his neck she switched it off. 'Okay, you get dressed—Linh and I are going in search of some shoes.'

'And some underwear,' Linh added.

Minutes later, the two women entered a stateroom. Expansive views of the sea let in a vivid light. Linh glided in and gazed at the restrained opulence—ivory tones with silver birch trims and turquoise fabrics underscored by a charcoal floor of Portuguese cork.

'It's a beautiful room, Gina—is it yours?'

'Yes... but I don't use it, other than to store my clothes when I'm on assignment. I like the simplicity of my cabin—for various reasons.' She moved to the aft wall and placed her hand on the panelling. A seamless join parted to reveal a glowing walk-in wardrobe. It was like an elite boutique with dresses and gowns, not on racks, but displayed throughout the space on silhouette mannequins.

Linh entered and moved through the apparel, letting her hands stroke the fabrics. It was like she'd been conveyed to a glittering function held in suspended animation. 'You are corrupting me, Ms Wu,' she murmured. In front of her, at hand height, were rows of backlit slanted shelves, displaying a collection of shoes.

Gina observed the young woman with a self-satisfied curl to her lip. 'If this is corruption, then so is the aspiration to achieve it. I'd rather be enjoying it.' She went over to Linh and handed her a packet of new panties. Underneath the shoe shelf was a drawer that she slid open. 'Now, let me see... you're a little bigger in the bosom than I am.' She withdrew a box. 'This would probably be the most comfortable fit for you.' She handed the packaged bra to Linh. 'Do you see any shoes that you like?'

Linh stepped back and caught Gina's eye. 'I think I will defer to your good taste, Gina. You've selected a dress that really suits me, and I have no doubt that you have the perfect shoe to complement it.'

'Very well. Do you want to make yourself a little taller?'

Linh shook her head.

'Okay, no platforms then,' Gina reached for a pair of cream stilettos with an open, beaded lacing, '... these will pick up the cream in your dress... Jimmy Choos, not too formal and surprisingly comfortable.'

Then, she lifted a pair of red soled, mesh stilettos, also in cream, '... Christian Louboutin pump in a classic fifties style—absolutely lovely to wear... next, a curvy heeled, teal Walter Steiger sandal, which suits the era but is possibly a bit too aggressive for you... Lanvin stiletto criss-cross strap sandals in black... DSquared2 bejewelled open toe in pebble... nah... Dolce and Gabbana medium heel in ivory... not if your intention is to end up flat on your back with your toes pointing at opposite corners of the room...'

Linh burst out laughing.

'Ah, Miu in opal... but that would detract from Mr Dior's creation.' Gina moved to the next row and gave a little squeal of delight. 'Here we are... an understated, exquisitely comfortable, silk-finish, classic Manolo Blahnik pump in cream with tiny grey/blue bow... does it match the dress?... yes, I think so. Try it on.' She stooped and pulled out an upholstered drawer/seat.

Linh seated herself and lowered her parcels to the floor. She took the proffered shoe and carefully worked her foot into the soft leather. When she had them both on, she cautiously moved her weight forward and stood. The cool, pliant grip on her feet seemed to hint at intentions that were not her own. She rotated her pelvis to compensate for the provocative stance.

Gina uttered, 'These will have you nice and moist by the end of the evening.'

Linh almost overbalanced with laughter. 'Gina Wu! You really *are* corrupting me.'

'Well, excuse me, girl, but there is only one reason why we dress like this, and that is to prepare us for love—and don't blame me for corrupting you—you're not even wearing any pants.'

With a huge gasp, Linh flung her hands to her thighs.

'Go for a walk and tell me what you think.'

In the golden glow of the wardrobe, Linh hesitantly strode between the two-dimensional mannequins. In no time, she had perfected a confident step. She came back from the entrance swaying with self-assurance. 'Gina... these are absolutely amazing... there's something about them... I feel as though I'm walking on a cloud.'

'What you're feeling is thirty thousand dollars' worth of technology,'

Linh gaped. 'Thirty thousand!'

'If you rock back on your heel, you'll feel it.'

Linh experimented with a small adjustment of weight then gradually increased the movement until she could depress her heels a few centimetres. 'They've got suspension!'

'Titanium gas struts... takes the shock out of the heel landing and allows you to lengthen your stride. It gives you incredible poise.'

Linh beheld her new friend with softness. 'You are truly amazing.'

'It's not all about gadgets that kill, you know.'

Linh approached and hugged her gently. 'Thank you.'

Gina placed her hands around Linh's waist. 'Come on, we'd better see what your man is up to. For all I know, he's converted my cabin into a stable.'

They moved towards the bedroom.

'Better take off the shoes—you'll get stuck in the cork. By the way, you and Owen will be occupying this room for the next few days.'

In the cabin, Owen was blissfully asleep. He'd dressed, then lain down to await the return of the girls and was asleep within a minute.

Gina and Linh crept inside and appraised him from beside the bed.

'Whose clothes are these he's wearing?' Linh queried.

'They belong to a man who has supported and fostered haute-couture for a very long time. Owen's ensemble is from his collection.'

'He looks like the Great Gatsby,' Linh murmured into Gina's ear.

'I was hoping more for the Tom Buchanan,' Gina softly returned.

Linh looked taken aback. 'Yes!... I could imagine that. He had that, oh... what's the look?'

'... dissolute...'

'... yes, a dissolute look—much more your type?'

'Well, such a man would less likely be surprised by my immorality.'

'True. I can't imagine Leonardo DiCaprio offering to top up your glass after you told him you'd just shot someone.'

The two women tittered quietly and resumed their scrutiny of Owen.

'I wasn't certain about his shoe size, that's why I opted for high-waisted, oxfords with a polo shirt—he'll fit right in with bare feet.'

'It makes him look really athletic.'

'He *is* athletic—not too lumpy with muscle. I like willowy men—they have a natural confidence. I can't be in competition with my lover—he has to be his own man.'

Linh's gaze unfocused. 'Owen is his own man,' she said dreamily, and then, abruptly, 'and you can't have him—he's mine.'

Gina slapped Linh's shoulder. 'Oh, c'mon... I lent you my shoes!'

Owen awoke to the sound of laughter. 'Ah, good morrow, ladies. Nice to be the object of your amusement...'

'Wrong era, Owen,' Gina muttered as she went to the desk, '... you're not dressed as Oscar Wilde.'

Remaining on the bed, Owen pointed to his waist. 'I take it that the belt is *supposed* to come up as high as this? Seriously, these pockets are deep enough to stash a bottle of bourbon *and* the still.'

Linh kneeled on the bed and wrapped her arms around him. 'I've got a surprise for you.'

Owen kissed her mouth then whispered in her ear.

Linh giggled and pulled back. 'No!... well, yes, but I've got some here that I'll put on as soon as I show you these...'

'Don't do it,' Gina warned, her eyes on something inside the drawer.

Linh held up her shoes.

Owen smiled approvingly. 'They're shoes.'

'Oh—too late, damage done,' Gina retorted.

'Owen, these are Manolo Blahniks!'

With shrewd eyes, Owen nodded deeply. 'Uh huh, a weapon of mass destruction disguised as a shoe...'

'No... it's just a shoe!'

'That's what I said in the first place!'

Gina guffawed. 'Hello... your first fight. Shoes tend to do that.'

Linh winked secretively at Owen.

The wall adjacent to the desk flickered with light. A diagram appeared. It was a floor plan. Tiny red dots, distributed throughout the diagram, began to converge towards one spot. Gina touched on one of the dots. A data bubble appeared below.

Gina read aloud. 'Eiji Hasegawa. Speciality—high energy quantum field theory, making his way to the conference room.' She touched on a menu bar. The numeral 23 came up. 'Twenty-three delegates. All present and accounted for.'

Gina turned sharply. 'Were you two told what form the cavalry would take when it arrived to save you.'

Two heads shook in unison.

'Submarine, perhaps?'

Owen cleared his throat. 'We have no idea—we weren't told about that. But, if you were to ask me, I'd say, yes... most probably a submarine. Because your satellites would know exactly where any surface ships would be.'

'Got that in one.' Gina perused the image for a moment longer. 'Hmmm... all good, it seems.' She reached into the drawer. The image died. 'Well, children... it's almost time to go to dinner, but before we do, I will escort you to your quarters.' She glanced at her bangle. 'In fact, you will have time for a little snooze. I will come to get you, and this time I will make sure to knock. Come on—follow me.'

Chapter Thirty-One

Owen and Linh luxuriated in the warm glow of the setting sun. They'd draped their new clothes over convenient furniture and were lying on the massive bed in their underwear. They sank into the softness and stared at the sculpted ceiling, both of them at the point of exhaustion. The view through the broad stretch of windows revealed a limpid sea. The yacht had come to rest.

Linh groaned with the effort to speak. 'Owie... this is where I'm supposed to fall overboard.'

Owen made the effort to hold her hand. 'I know, my love. I think the window at the far end can be opened. It's a bit higher than what you trained for, though.'

Linh flung her arm over his stomach. 'Boy, that seems like a lifetime ago.'

'Doesn't it just.'

'Owie... I'm exhausted from... everything. Today, I saw a man get shot... she just shot him. She didn't need to...'

Owen turned to her. 'Yeah... why do you suppose she shot him?'

Their noses were almost touching.

'I don't know,' Linh whispered, '... she didn't need to... in view of what is happening now.'

Owen turned to look at the ceiling. 'What *is* happening now? I mean, you and I are doing a great job of keeping things light and sassy, but hell... this is about world domination... conspirators at war with each other. Jeez... I'm totally confused. The only good thing to come out of this is being with you... just suddenly seeing what an incredible person you are.' Owen kept his eyes on the ceiling. 'When you winked at me, earlier on, my heart nearly burst with love for you, Linh... I realised how much you were doing to try and make this work.'

Linh licked Owen's ear. 'There's something else you should know.'

'... hmmm... what?'

'Those shoes that Gina leant me have got gas strut stilettos...'

Owen nodded slowly. 'That's it! We have to stop this mad conspiracy whatever the cost.'

Linh laughed and climbed on top. 'Don't you want to evaluate the technology first?'

'No way... I've been humiliated plenty enough already on this boat, and the last thing I need, even if I did fit into them, is for Gina to walk in while I'm road-testing her stilettos in my underwear.'

They rolled together into another sunny spot.

Linh looked up at Owen. 'Do you think we're being bugged?'

'Who knows... who cares anymore. I mean, it's bizarre—they kill two of their crew, and put *us* up in the lap of luxury. Go figure!'

There was a moment of silence before Linh asked, 'Why do you suppose the boat has to come to a stop while they're having their meeting?'

'Yeah, I thought about that. The only thing that I can think of is that they must be exchanging data during the meeting, and because they're using a very concentrated satellite beam in order to eliminate eavesdropping, they have to keep the boat still. That's all I can think of.'

Linh reached her hand down along his belly. 'We make a good team, don't we, Owie?'

He groaned. 'Hey, Tot, I thought you were feeling exhausted?'

Eamon pointed at the wall and flicked the virtual speaker graphic to off. 'Alright... we might leave them to restore each other. What do you think, Gina?'

She lent her elbow on the old man's knee. 'I'd put my money on she being on top.'

The room was filled with a faltering, wheezing sound. Eamon grabbed at his chest and slowly sighed to quiet. 'Gina, you are wicked in so many ways—some of them adorable.'

She stood up and stretched. 'Well, I think they are the most naïve couple I could ever imagine.'

With a prolonged lurch, Eamon pitched out of the Ovum and walked barefoot to the forward windows. 'No, no, Gina... you don't mean naïve—you mean virtuous. Often, it's hard to tell the difference in these times of cynicism. They are two truly virtuous young people. They are a tremendous resource.'

'And to think that I nearly shot one of them during that fight with the drone.'

'Yes... yes, but then, he wasn't realised the way he is now. This whole episode, from him finding the briefcase, to being recruited for those other jobs, to finding his way here—it has all come to a serendipitous moment where, if we put things to him, and her, in the proper way, we will gain valuable allies.'

'Just remember, Eamon, that the two of them signed up to an impossible mission on board the *Zeus*—I think they have already proven that they have the requisite fortitude to commit to a dangerous mission if it squares with their ideals.'

'Eamon bowed. 'Well spoken, Gina. Alright then, set the table for two extra places.'

Owen was starving. He hadn't eaten a decent meal for days. He was actually at the first stage of starvation. His body had very little in the way of fat reserves, and the absence of nutrition was beginning to affect his thinking. Along with the sharpness in his stomach, he felt a sharpness of mind. It was as though his intuition had come to the foreground—the environment had much greater depth.

He'd woken from a disturbing dream. Linh was asleep beside him and the room was bathed in the deep orange glow of the sunset. In his dream, he'd been standing on a barren planet that was revolving closely around a sister planet. He wondered whether the gravitational pull of each body would cancel out and make him weightless. The planet responded to his thought by allowing him to rise from the terrain to a space equidistant between the two surfaces. As the planets revolved around him, he was told that it would only be a short while before they merged and ground into each other. The thought of the two planets colliding upset Owen, but a superior voice told him that it was the nature of things to become one. He'd felt a surge of humanity at the thought of so many individual lives, struggling with such overwhelming burdens, meeting their demise as one entity.

Owen stared at the glowing ceiling and pondered on the meaning of his dream. He could suddenly see that being an individual enabled him to experience empathy... being separate, gave him context... being distinct heightened his alikeness. It all *seemed* to make sense.

Linh stirred and draped her arm over him.

... colliding and melding...

'Owie... you're all hot and sweaty.'

'I'm starving.'

'You *and* me, baby.'

The room was becoming grey.

Linh nuzzled into Owen's armpit. 'Did Gina mention a time?... for dinner?'

'I don't remember.'

'Owie,' Linh lifted her face close by Owen's, '... are you okay? What are you thinking?'

Owen stared distantly. 'About my dream... about people... they're so heroic... and the obstacles are so big.'

'Not all people are heroic.'

'Maybe... but babies aren't born just to give up... they start their search early, and all too often there just isn't enough love to make them heroes.'

Linh sat up and massaged her lover's chest. 'Owie, you're thinking too hard on an empty stomach. Why don't we get dressed and make ourselves ready for dinner?'

Owen scooped his girl around her bottom and dragged her over the top of him. He kissed her on the mouth and stroked her back.

A chime sounded somewhere in the room. Gina's dulcet voice filled the room. 'Hello, young lovers... it is time to prepare for dinner. I'll pick you up at your door in twenty minutes.'

There was a bold glint in Owen's eyes.

Linh tried to push him away. 'No! Owie, we haven't got time... we'd have to have a shower!'

Owen shook his head. 'That's not what I was thinking of, Tot. No, what I'm thinking is that we are going for the biggest job interview of our lives. Have you got your CV in order?'

'*Us?*'

'You bet.' He nuzzled her some more.

'You know what, Owie... since our moment of soul searching in the coffee shop, way back in another lifetime, we seem to have become deeper and deeper involved with these... secret... whoever they are. And now you're saying that the group that possesses the supremo weapon of mass destruction is going to attempt to recruit us?'

'... ah, yeah. Got it in one.'

'What are you thinking we should do?'

Owen pursed his lips.

'No, Owen, I'm not kissing you—I asked you a question.'

'This is my thinking face.'

'Thank goodness. For a moment I thought it was your kissing face.'

'Well,' Owen mused, '... it's not very often you get invited to join the winning side...'

'Oh, so we've abandoned our scruples, have we?'

Well, scruples can be very over-rated, Linh. Just think for a moment—you work in a coffee shop, and you buy your shoes from the discount shop in the plaza, *or* you loose off a few random gamma rays here and there and you get to wear Mandela Blimps with comfy cushion heels...'

'Manolo Blahnik... Oh, Owie... that's not fair! How do you expect me to make a choice if you're going to reduce the issue to footwear?'

The two of them suddenly burst out laughing and rolled in each other's arms across the bed.

The door opened and a very determined Gina Wu strode in. 'Change of plan, children. I will sit here,' she pulled out a chair tucked against a bureau, '... and brief you while you dress. That way I know we'll be on time for dinner.' She looked gorgeous in a heavily pleated, halter-neck evening gown.

Owen flipped himself off the bed and strode casually to his clothes hanging over the back of a couch. 'That's not very fair to the other applicants, Gina.'

Gina scowled at him. 'What?'

'... giving us a special briefing.' He slipped into his shirt.

'What are you talking about, Owen?'

'The job interview... for deputy despot of the world.' He wriggled into his pants and hefted them to his waist. 'I mean, don't get me wrong... I'm definitely the man for the job... make a good despot...'

Linh, who had been discretely dressing herself, moved closer to Gina. 'He hasn't had anything to eat...'

Gina lounged back in the chair. 'You really are a pair, aren't you. And yes, Owen... you are going for a job interview. My master has taken a shine to you two, god knows why, and he really wants to meet you. Let me just say, that to my knowledge, he has not had guests at his table for at least fifty years. He's had meetings aplenty... dignitaries, corporate shakers and movers, film stars, you name it... but never for dinner.'

Linh approached. 'We'll behave ourselves... won't we, Owen.'

Owen walked up to her and gently held her. Then he looked into the eyes of the woman who, earlier in the day, had laid him out cold. 'We'll behave ourselves,' he said with soft assurance.

Gina nodded. 'I'm glad to hear it. Now, a little bit of a heads-up... what might you be expecting to be served by the world's most influential conspirator?'

Linh dipped her head to Owen.

He massaged his face with one hand. 'Well, the person I would admire would eat a simple meal. And I imagine that someone who is dedicated to preserving themselves would eat a simple meal. But then, someone who goes charging around the Med, burning enough fuel to supply the energy grid in Tasmania for a month, would probably have a very exotic meal. I don't know, Gina... I'll take a punt on braised endangered species garnished with powdered rhino horn.'

Linh closed her eyes and sat heavily on the bed.

Gina draped an arm over the back of the chair and regarded Owen with a droll look. 'You know, young man, I'm finding your unwarranted confidence exhilarating and exasperating in equal measures.

Owen settled next to Linh and straightened the cuffs of his trousers.

'What can I say, Gina—I'm an enigma.'

With stricken eyes, Linh looked at Gina and made a face as though to dispute that fact.

Gina raised an eyebrow. 'You're an open book, Owen, but your training is coming along nicely. Now, are we all done?'

'Just my hair,' Owen stood and walked to the bathroom, '... it's not messy enough.'

The trio exited the stateroom and entered the nearby elevator. They stood in silence as they were lifted to the floor above.

'Let me guess,' Owen ventured as they walked out, '... there is no other access to this floor.'

Gina led them to the oaken door. 'Correct, Owen. There are no exterior access points either. The man you are about to meet prefers controlled environments, so there is no need for decks and balconies.'

Linh ran her eye over the magnificent door. 'Does he have many visitors?'

'No... not on board the *Zeus*. He only comes aboard during the weapons summit.'

'Oh. It's such an amazing door.'

Gina stepped back to allow the guests to enter. 'It is very old. It was retrieved from the citadel of Acre during the First World War, and it was built to secure the bedchamber of King Richard the First during his crusade in the Holy land.'

Owen gripped the door edge. 'Say what?'

Gina casually slapped his bottom. 'Don't be vulgar, Owen. There are trinkets in the space you are about to enter whose provenance would astound you. Follow me.' She moved into the dark room towards the sunken lounge and indicated the step lights. 'Please excuse the dimness of the room. My master wants to avoid confronting you at first introductions. The lights will intensify as the evening progresses. Make yourself comfortable. Would you like something to drink? Cognac perhaps...'

Owen had the distinct impression that she was smirking, even though he couldn't clearly see her face.

Linh responded. 'I'd love a small cognac, please, Gina.'

There was a moment of quiet while Owen made up his mind.

'I'll have a sip of Linh's.'

Gina remained where she stood. It suddenly became uncomfortably quiet, and there was the overwhelming impression that there was someone else in their presence.

Owen scanned the other settees in the subdued light. Silhouetted against the forward-facing windows, he could make out the form of a man. The shadow made some distinctly human sounds as it slowly came forward.

In a thin, breathy voice, their host spoke. 'May I suggest that we partake in a lovely red wine and, in consideration of our Australian guests, can I offer you a glass of Penfolds Grange Hermitage from nineteen fifty-one?'

'Oh, yes please,' Linh replied within a heartbeat, '... I would love to try a glass of Penfolds Grange Hermitage from nineteen fifty-one.'

'Good for you, Linh!' returned the feeble voice, '... and you, Owen?'

Owen sat forward in his seat. 'Thank you. I would very much like to drink a wine as rare as that.'

'Ah, so you know a little bit about this vintage?'

'My family runs a small restaurant, and in the course of working there I've become acquainted with the Grange label, though I have never had the pleasure of tasting one myself.'

The shadow moved towards them. 'Well then, this evening, I would like to honour you with the most exceptional example of this unique wine. It arrived by helicopter just a few hours ago—belonged to a collector in Venice. The flight alone raised its cost some three and a half thousand dollars—about ten percent of its value—not that I mean to be brash—but at some point, the two of you must become familiar with an altogether unrivalled tier of affluence, if you are to understand the work of the conspirators.'

Owen tried to determine the features of the speaker. Obviously, the plan had always been to commence with a toast. Gina walked into the lounge carrying a tray. She offered a glass to her master, and then to Owen and Linh.

The reedy voice continued. 'I'm aware that you are participating in this tribute on an empty stomach, but I feel strongly about commencing our relationship with something suitably mature and refined. Please approach me.'

The two guests, each with their glass in hand, stood and moved towards their host, close enough to be able to toast with their drink.

Owen wasn't sure whether his vision was becoming accustomed to the dark, or whether the lighting had improved, but the man just one metre away from him, stooped and swaying slightly, seemed to have a face made of straw; most of the lines were vertical apart from where they coalesced in blackness at the eyes. He could sense the steadfast gaze on him. Something glinted dully in Owen's vision. The old man had raised his glass.

His words came in little more than a laboured whisper. 'To you, Owen Lucas… and to you, Linh Vuong… I welcome you to nothing less than our Earthly realm. Too many people live their entire life without acknowledging the way of the World; whether they are rich and privileged or poor and disadvantaged, there is only one credo that suffices, and that is to live compassionately.'

Owen and Linh lifted their glass and simultaneously uttered, '… to compassion…' and Owen thought about Knowles' last moments on the step, and Linh remembered the plop and thud as the bullet travelled from Gina's gun to Holroyd's heart.

In the gloom, they put the wine to their lips and sipped its sumptuousness. It was a taste that defied description; Owen could only think of an antonym to depict the contrast—engine coolant, and Linh abashed herself for imagining what it would be like to mix this wine with sex.

'Come,' said the voice in the darkness, '… let us adjourn to the dinner table. Gina—would you mind activating the light trail, please.'

At their feet, pinpricks of light appeared that led diagonally away towards the forward windows on the starboard side. Owen's excellent night vision enabled him to detect the surrounding furniture, as well as Gina's dark profile as she approached her master. There was an exchange between them and the sound of metal on glass. Owen realised that the old man had given his glass to Gina and that he was wearing a ring. He knew that Gina's hands were unadorned.

… oh, great—he's poisoned the wine…

Owen put his arm around Linh's waist. She reciprocated with a tight hold of her own.

Gina's gown swished across the floor lights. 'Follow me.'

The old man stood aside as Owen and Linh were led to a circular dinner table. The windows were much larger than they first appeared and sloped rearwards so acutely that they acted almost as a skylight. There was enough starlight to illuminate the table and its setting for four.

Owen scanned the sea for reflections of moonlight, but saw none.

... moon not up yet... late summer—moon low... maybe it's as bright as it's going to get...

Gina indicated that the two guests be seated diagonally facing the windows.

... okay—so it's harder for us to read their faces against the background light...

'... or, if you prefer,' Gina continued, '... you can sit here,' she indicated the two seats on the window side, '... but I thought you might like to look at the stars.'

The two of them stood dutifully behind their allocated chair and waited for their host to make his way to the table. He clung to the back of his chair and turned his head to look out across the sea.

'I've arranged for there to be a small show whilst we're having dinner. Look, it's beginning now.' He pointed heavenwards.

A jagged bolt of lightning slashed through the night, but instead of being visible for mere fractions of a second, this flash persisted, and instead of being a white streak, it was made up of roiling coils of red and green. The colourful convolutions swelled and diminished and transformed in shape and colour. It was as though there was a mad dragon in the sky.

Linh sidled up to Owen. Together they moved closer to the window and craned their necks as the phenomenon materialized above them.

'It's beautiful,' Linh uttered with a glance at the stranger a mere arm's length away. She stiffened in horror. Their host's ancient face was canted to the light show, and the colours painted his withered features in ghastly hues. He directed his sight at Linh. His lips parted in a black smile, emitting a palpitating high-pitched wheeze. Linh clutched at Owen, but she couldn't take her eyes off the dreadful apparition next to her.

The old man's arm reached towards her. 'I'm sorry to frighten you, Linh.' The shrunken visage changed from purple through to indigo. 'I was hoping to introduce myself rather more considerately, and now I've frightened you.' The arm remained outstretched.

It felt to Linh as though her heart had stopped beating. Owen's hand at her elbow, encouraged her to extend her arm. She delicately grasped the old man's dry fingers in hers.

'My name is Eamon,' he pronounced with renewed vigour. The black eyes peered from under crinkled folds of skin.

Linh managed to find her voice. '... hello, Eamon. My name is Linh... this is a very strange meeting...'

Once more, a disembodied wheezing arose. The room flashed to green. The old man bowed and touched his mouth to the back of Linh's hand. She could feel Owen's grip around her waist tighten as he held her steady.

'This is almost as strange for me as it is for you, Linh. I haven't engaged with young people like yourselves for over a hundred years. I can't tell you what a privilege it is to be in your presence.'

Linh's heart melted at that moment. The lurid flashes reflecting off the wizened face, revealed a soul that was too old to harbour malice, and she realised suddenly that one could only endure for as long as he had if there was a love for life. She carefully separated from Owen and slowly embraced the creature in front of her. Her arms clasped bones through the thin tunic. She pressed the softness of her cheek to the raspy slabs of his face and held herself against him. She felt the points of his fingertips travel from her waist to the small of her back.

A tiny groan escaped his lips as he in turn hugged her close.

For a suspended moment, Linh felt as though she had an infant in her arms—a being unselfconsciously dependent on tactile nourishment. Tears sprang to her eyes.

... he hasn't met young people for a hundred years!... how old is he?...

They remained connected for quite a while; what did it matter? She wasn't going anywhere. Through misty eyes she watched as the subdued colours in the room shifted from pink to gold then, in a particularly bright instant, she saw Gina, sipping Eamon's wine, looking directly at her through narrowed eyes, and she knew then that she would never be able to completely trust her no matter how cosy their circumstances might be.

Eamon separated from her and lifted his arms to her shoulders. 'Thank you, my dear, for your faith in me,' he said in a voice rough with emotion.

Linh smiled and searched his sunken eyes.

... a window to the soul, right to the end...

He stepped to the side and held out his hand to Owen. 'It's nice to finally meet you, Owen.'

The two men shook hands.

'Yeah, mate... it's nice to meet you, Eamon,' Owen replied in slightly exaggerated Ocker.

Linh turned to him and wiped her eyes with the back of her hand. 'Oh, Owen... you're such a show-off.'

He grinned.

Eamon wheezed. 'Come,' he indicated the table, '... let us make ourselves comfortable.'

As they seated themselves, Eamon continued speaking. 'You'd be interested to know that the last time that I was in Australia, nobody spoke like that. That unique accent is something that has developed from the blends of many languages over many years.'

Owen raised his eyebrow in query. 'So... when exactly *was* the last time you were in Australia?'

The old man sat with his hands folded on the edge of the table. Outside, the lights continued to pulse and morph. 'Well, it was a long time ago. I was asked to captain a ship sailing to Australia—and when I say sailing, I mean, literally, a sailing ship. It was 1852, and the developing nation was in urgent need of manufactured goods. I was chosen for this trip because the owners knew that I would return; you see, it was just at the time of the gold strikes and many ships' crews decided to abandon their vessels to try their luck on the gold fields. I assembled a trusted crew and, over the years, we made five trips to the antipodes with cargoes of highly sought-after equipment. We came back each time with far more gold than we would ever have dug with our bare hands.'

Gina arrived at the table with two plates in her hands which she placed in front of the two guests. They murmured their thanks.

Eamon nodded vigorously. 'Are you hungry?'

Linh gave a wan smile. 'Eamon, we are almost beyond hungry.'

'Oh, I know... it's been a trying time for the both of you, as I understand. I hope this meal will satisfy you. It is unhusked rice cooked in ginger, with crushed walnuts and Nori seaweed, shitake mushrooms simmered in marrowbone and fresh Japanese Black Trifele tomatoes.'

The aroma wafting from the plate made Owen feel faint.

... not now, buddy... you need this, otherwise you might never regain consciousness...

There was concern in Eamon's voice. 'Are you alright, Owen? Is it not to your liking?'

Linh answered for him. 'It's very much to his liking, Eamon. He tends to feel light-headed at certain times... extreme hunger being one of them, it seems.'

Gina returned with two more plates and set them on the table.

'Thank you, Gina. Perhaps we'll put on the table lights—but not too bright.'

The table glowed miraculously from an unseen light source but its members remained largely shaded.

'Let's not tarry, then!' Eamon placed a napkin on his lap.

They ate in silence, taking small portions to chew. The ginger and marrow flavours lingered long enough to make the chewiness of the rice enjoyable, and the fruitiness of the tomatoes was the perfect complement to refresh the palette.

Owen barely moved, except to bring food to his mouth. He had never before absorbed himself in the act of eating as he did now. Each nuance of flavour, every textural encounter, he appreciated. He could feel his energy being restored.

... let's not tarry?... he really is old... and marrow bone... so, we're not completely vegetarian, then...

The lights outside subsided and soon it was dark again.

Owen's mind was less cluttered and more at peace than it had been for a long time. He felt as though he was able to select a train of thought without immediate events interrupting. He made a choice— to compliment his host.

'Eamon,' he began, when his mouth was clear of food, '... thank you very much for the brilliant light show. I feel very privileged that you arranged it just for Linh and me.'

The gnarl of wrinkles around the old man's mouth shaped into what could have been interpreted as a smirk. He exchanged a brief look with Gina.

That was all the confirmation that Owen needed. '... but, am I correct in saying that the weapons team will have been pretty thrilled to see their baby in action... even if it was only to create a spectacle?'

Eamon wheezed alarmingly. Gina put down her utensils, ready to come to his aid. Finally, the old man settled.

He addressed Gina. 'It must be the ginkgo in the rice.'

She, in turn looked unimpressed. 'I somehow doubt that a few grated leaves could be responsible for that deduction.'

Eamon nodded in agreement. 'It's all about the ability to synthesise what is already there.' He turned to Owen. 'You are absolutely right, my boy—we have been awaiting this trial for some time, and it is marvellously serendipitous that the two of you are here to share it with us.'

Owen gave a loaded look across the table. 'May I?'

Eamon dipped his eyes in assent.

Owen smiled smugly. 'Well, I would say that, whatever high energy ray is being used up there, it's aimed or tuned to excite the charged particles in the upper atmosphere, and that it produces the same effect as the aurora borealis... except that it is much more localised. By altering the intensity, it is possible to change the colours as the ions drop down into lower states of energy and release light.'

'You know more about this than I do, Owen. Well done.' He turned to Gina. 'You see what a contribution this young man could make!'

Gina acquired a superior mien. 'He'll make the wrong impact if he tries to be smug with tomato seeds on his chin.'

Owen hastily applied his napkin.

Gina put her bracelet to her ear. Her expression became vacant.

Eamon also became subdued and toyed with the remains of his meal. Linh and Owen felt obliged to withdraw from any interaction at the table and quietly resumed eating.

Gina murmured to her master. 'She's sent another message... this time from Cologne.'

Eamon took a deep breath. '... and the cypher?'

She shook her head.

The silence was heavy. Owen was conscious of every scrape on his plate.

Linh reached her hand across to Eamon. 'What's the matter?'

Owen held his breath.

... whoa, cheeky...

Eamon smiled at Linh's gesture and covered her hand with his. 'We have been monitoring phone messages from an agent who has become separated from her team. We don't know the circumstances exactly, but somehow, she has become embedded with the target group, and her only recourse is to send coded messages by phone. It's ridiculously complicated, but it would be catastrophic for us, and her, if she was discovered. She can't last much longer, but so far, we've had no success in deciphering her impromptu code.'

Eamon suddenly leaned forward over the table so that he could reach Gina's hand as well. 'Gina...' he implored, but she had already anticipated his request. With her other hand she pointed to the back wall. The textured pattern dissolved into a screen. She prodded the air with her fingers as various icons flashed on the screen. Then, with a final stab, a line of text appeared.

I got have to nobly for tow says left-wing Bedford then equipment nectar stops bet.

The four of them scrutinized the screen.

Linh turned to look at Owen. There was a hint of expectation in her face.

He returned her stare and gave the tiniest shrug of his shoulders.

Without being conspicuous, she replied with the subtlest big eyes that she could.

Owen's eyes in turn widened with surprise.

She nodded minutely in return.

Owen mouthed, 'You know?'

Linh gave an ambivalent shrug to indicate her level of confidence.

Owen's mouth opened in amazement.

Gina sighed heavily. 'Go on then, you two... what have you got?'

Owen readily blurted, 'I haven't got a clue.' He leant out of the way to give Linh her moment.

Eamon searched Linh's face. '... Linh?'

Putting a hand to her mouth as though to swallow a mistaken word, Linh ventured in a small voice, 'I think it's a predictive text code.'

There was a moment of silence before Gina shot up from the table. Her chair toppled to the floor. 'She's right!' she exploded. She glared at Linh. 'What else?'

Linh remained surprisingly calm. She looked away in thought. 'You would have to know the brand of phone as well as the regional installation—not all phones are alike.'

'And there would be a protocol—a convention,' Gina almost yelled, '... first word on the left or last word on the right... total or partial substitution...'

'... depending on how the predictions are implemented...'

'Oh, clever girl!' Gina leapt around the table to high five Linh. 'Is this just a notion that you had, or do you have a developed method?'

Linh vehemently shook her head. 'No, just a notion!'

'You're a genius, Linh.' Gina turned in a swirl of pleats and strode across the sunken lounge to the door. Her voice could be heard issuing instructions until the door shut.

Calm descended once more. Eamon smiled generously and once more laid his hand upon Linh's. 'We have a very nice stewed plum and yogurt dessert, but I'm afraid our waitress has abandoned us.'

Linh patted their host's hand. 'It's alright, Eamon. We have eaten most delightfully, and we thank you for your kind hospitality... though, I wouldn't mind a top-up of the old 1951.'

Eamon reached across for the bottle. 'Linh, my darling, if your code is correct, I will happily buy the remaining nineteen or so bottles that are left in the world, for you... no matter what the price.'

Linh looked aghast. 'Nineteen?'

'Something like that.' With a shaking hand, he topped up the glasses.

Owen noisily cleared his throat.

Linh burst out laughing and tossed her head onto Owen's shoulder. 'It was just a hunch, Owie... I don't know where it came from. It just came to me—a desperate situation—had to disguise a message on her mobile—like Eamon said—synthesis.'

'... hmmm... he also said ginkgo, which makes about as much sense.' The two of them laughed. Eamon wheezed.

Linh looked at the two men. 'Well, when you send a phone message on a modern phone,' she was considerate of Eamon's possible unfamiliarity with mobile phones, '... they often try to predict which word you might want to use next, and the program puts up a small list of options. If you were to begin a message say with "I", the predictive text might put up "have", "will" and "am" for your possible next word. The code might require you to choose the word on the right, "am". Then you would put in your next word which might be "have" and the predictive text will then put up "you", "got", "the". Then you chose "the". Anyhoo, depending on what sort of protocol you have agreed on, the system effectively allows for a message to be hidden in an incomprehensible sentence, and it would be, I imagine, completely random.'

'But,' Owen contributed, '... everyone has to be on the same type of phone.'

'Uh huh. And you could insert actual words of the message, or you could choose substitute words from the list, as Gina pointed out.'

'Whoa... that sounds like it could compound into something very difficult to decipher within a short time.'

'Probably.'

Eamon had been nodding enthusiastically the whole time. 'It's very similar to the Enigma cypher machines that Germany used in the Second World War, in that each operative has a compatible device, and that the protocols, as you suggested, Linh, are rotated on a daily basis—ingenious.' He anxiously looked about the room. 'Honestly, I was really looking forward to dessert.'

'I could get it!' Linh volunteered.

This offer was met with a resolute raised hand. 'No... you could get into a lot of trouble if you were to wander about on this floor. We will

351

adjourn to the lounge and finish this bottle.'

As they made their way to the settees, Owen quietly enquired, 'I thought you didn't drink... apart from the occasional toast.'

Eamon settled himself heavily. 'Ah, that's very observant of you, Owen. Yes, I gave my glass to Gina. But now, I feel carefree enough to join you both in this excellent libation. Ah, Gina is back.' He felt around for something in his pocket.

The door opened and Gina swished into the lounge. 'We've got it,' she announced curtly. She turned to Linh and held out her hand. They shook. 'Well done, Linh. You have made a massive contribution tonight.'

'It was my pleasure,' she answered softly.

Chapter Thirty-Two

Gina left the room to get the desserts. Eamon sat poised and upright in the settee with his hands on his knees as though in anticipation.

Linh and Owen settled into a settee. He felt an almost irresistible urge to lie down with his knees over the armrest. Instead, he slid in very close to Linh and held her hand, allowing himself to sink back into the cushions. The oppressive stillness made him suddenly sleepy—it was as though he had fallen into a void.

... okay, make polite conversation with an... how old is this guy, exactly?...

Owen decided that *polite* was too much trouble. He took a short cut. 'We're here to sabotage the gamma ray project,' he offered tonelessly.

Eamon remained sitting there like a weathered statue. 'I know,' he croaked, '... and I'm going to make sure that you succeed.'

This response just didn't compute for Owen.

Linh came to the rescue. 'Do you think that supplying the power for the gamma ray is too risky?'

The old man waved a dismissive hand. 'No!... not at all. All that nonsense that you've probably heard about time dilation and destroying the fabric of space is just that—nonsense. No, the reason why we want to quit the project is because of what we've termed *exponential redundancy*, where new technology is overtaking older technology at ever increasing rates.'

This stirred Owen's interest. 'Is that like, when a space mission to a distant planet finally arrives after decades of travel, to find that other Earthlings have already set up a base even though they departed earth at a much later time?'

'Exactly, Owen,' Eamon slapped his knees, '... well done! Yes, that is the sort of paradox that we are faced with at the cutting edge of technology. We constantly need to investigate how emerging scientific know-how will change our ability to engage in the future. For instance, we can look back at the decade of moon exploration and ask ourselves, would that money have been better spent on creating social benefits while we waited for just a few more decades until the technology arrived so that we could explore the moon much more cheaply and safely using remote technology, much as we're doing on Mars now.'

Linh interjected. 'But doesn't the very pursuit of something like a space mission drive the development of technology?'

'Very astute, Linh. Yes, that has certainly been the case in mankind's advances in most fields, and sixty years ago, when we realised that we had the mechanical might to reach the moon, it seemed the most natural thing to do. However, no one at the time could have predicted the advent of the data processing age in which we are presently immersed. We are at the forefront of a new age; we've continually developed the mechanical phase of our evolution; we are perfecting communications technology, and now we find ourselves at the threshold of the information age even though we are still thinking linearly instead of holistically. Our technological ability to create futures, far outstrips our human ability to pursue a future. We have arrived at a point in time where we can theoretically reconcile humanity's needs by merging the powers of mind and modelling. We just need to commit.

A cunning smile spread on Owen's face. 'I suppose the risk is that we spend ages and ages perfecting the ideal while, in the real world, society is falling apart.'

Eamon rocked backwards and forwards and wheezed alarmingly.

Linh tensed and looked around for Gina's presence.

She entered the room with a tray of desserts. 'Honestly, you two... I'm not altogether convinced that you *haven't* been sent here to assassinate Eamon.' She deposited the tray on a side table and settled next to her master. With evident affection, she placed her arm around his shoulder and held him securely.

Eamon calmed down and lent his head against Gina's shoulder. 'She's right... you probably will be the death of me. It's been too long; I have dedicated so much time to overseeing various projects over the years that I lost touch with the vitality of youth. It wasn't until I had occasion to converse with Gina while she covered me with a gun, that I realised what I was missing out on.'

'Is that how you met?' Linh stroked her wineglass.

'Yes... oh, Gina hasn't told you? She was sent to kill me—and would have done so, if it hadn't been for my persuasive charm,' he wheezed with laughter.

Gina touched her head to his. A soft look transformed her face.

The two guests each felt that it would be improper to enquire about the details of this confrontation and maintained their silence.

'She is the only person ever to break through my security. She doesn't want to talk about it, I know. I simply put it to her that she could continue to work for the hidden conspirators behind her organization, or she could work with me. It's a well understood phenomenon in the circles of power—changing sides creates hybrid vigour. Suddenly, the resources of two combatants merge to form a united force. It's observable throughout history. And it worked for me. I'm not dead, and I got to meet Gina.' He turned his head towards her and they lingered with their foreheads touching.

Owen thought he would add to the spontaneity of youth. 'Would you like us to help ourselves to dessert?'

Linh put her head in her hands.

From underneath her brow, Gina threw Owen a look of suffering, and motioned for him to go ahead.

Eamon raised his head just as Owen lifted two bowls from the tray. 'That's what I like about Australians—you are uncultured in the most refreshing way.'

Owen harked back his head and laughed.

The old man made a deferential gesture with his hands. 'No—I mean that in the best way possible. You have no idea what it is like to live in a town where you are connected by generations of history. It becomes impossible to step outside your station in life, to reinvent yourself. You are bound by cultural conventions. Often people become neurotically obliged to conform. It's only in pioneering countries with open spaces, that one has the freedom to think and behave outside the norms. Well, that's my theory.'

Owen offered the bowls to his hosts. 'Maybe... but old Europe has plenty of examples of brilliant individualism.'

Eamon accepted his dessert. 'Thank you, Owen. Yes, you are absolutely correct...'

'... and the problem with new frontiers is that they usually attract all the ratbags that aren't fitting in in the old country.'

Eamon almost choked on his plum. His shoulders shook with silent laughter.

Gina pointed to the settee and spoke like a school teacher. 'Sit down, Owen, and eat your dessert quietly.'

Owen did as he was told. He gave Linh a reassuring grin on his way back.

Once more, a heavy silence settled. The windows were utterly black, but the ambient lighting had increased enough to dimly illuminate the interior of the sunken lounge room.

Gina rose carefully and took Eamon's bowl from his hands. She placed them on the tray and returned to her master. His head was lowered and he had tilted to one side.

'Help me, Owen,' Gina ordered quietly.

In three big strides, Owen was at the old man's side. Linh, holding his bowl, looked on with concern.

'Eamon needs to go back to his room.'

By interlocking their arms, the two of them made a cradle by which they lifted the slumped body.

Owen was surprised at the tenacity of Gina's grip on his wrist.

They carried their burden to the higher level, towards the opening of the magnetic room with its cobalt blue floor. The ovum hovered nearby and it was a simple procedure to settle Eamon into its magnetically tethered springiness. Gina gently lifted his feet onto the rest.

Eamon smiled wanly and looked lazily at his two helpers. 'I seem to have become over-excited, and it's all your fault, Owen.' One wrinkled eye winked at him. He looked around with concern. 'Where is Linh?'

Owen stood aside and pointed, 'She stayed in the lounge.'

'Well, bring her in here, man... I haven't finished talking to the two of you yet.'

Owen went out and quickly returned with Linh on his arm. Gina's shoes were now at the perimeter of the floor. Linh removed her shoes and the two of them came and stood next to the chief conspirator's girl Friday.

Eamon seemed to have revived a lot. He adjusted his position in the hovering pod. 'Welcome, young lovers, to the room that sustains me,' he swept his arm to encompass the expanse that included the bed and the sunroom. 'Owen, I defy even you, with your gift for engineering, to work out how this floor achieves its magic,' he gazed into the stockman's eyes. '... but, I will give you every chance to do so. I would like you to rest on the bed and see what you can come up with.'

Owen's mind was already engaged in that analytical task as Eamon was speaking to him. But this invitation interrupted his train of thought.

... oh, yeah, right... go and have a little nap on your bed... how weird is that...

He looked around for Linh.

She had already moved to the suspended platform and had seated herself on the edge. By the time Owen walked over, she had pivoted herself towards its middle and lain down with her arms by her side. The windows above her, in transparent mode, gave an extensive view of the stars which, because of the dimness in this area of the room, made them appear particularly luminous.

Linh let herself relax... totally relax... the way her father had instructed her to... allowing her mind to grow with latent capacity, yet not focusing on anything in particular. But now, she was rushing to a state of centeredness quicker than she ever had before. A strange effervescence commenced within her. Her head felt as though it was expanding, and she brought up her hands to check if that indeed was happening. Along with the perception of swelling, her thoughts seemed to separate, giving her the impression that she could observe various compartments of consciousness from a remote and omniscient state. Then, she became aware of an ability to direct tremendous focus onto any part of her body. She looked at the stars and understood the utter amazingness of sight—that ability to process information that came on nothing more substantial than reflected photons. She felt her heartbeat—those bunched muscles that never tired and that filled her body with pressure and power. Her hands ran over her abdomen. The flow of energy into her body from the food she had ingested became a visual transfer. Owen stirred beside her and she was immediately aware of an overpowering magnetism to him. In her mind she morphed into a single multi-faceted soma that corresponded inversely with every peak and trough of his body. They became an organic whole that quivered with fecundity. A lush, vibrant sound filled her senses, and she exerted all of her concentration to turn to the man beside her so that she could experience it with him.

Owen was lustily snoring. On his back, with his mouth part open, the tumultuous events of the day had finally caught up with him. Pleasantly sated and at ease, sleep had stolen upon him before he had a chance to consider the implications.

For Linh, the spell was broken. It felt as though her body had retracted from the endlessness of space in an instant of intense gravity. She punched Owen in the ribs. 'Wake up!' she whispered harshly.

Owen's bleary eyes opened. He breathed heavily. 'Did I fall asleep?'

'Yes!'

'Oh, that's surprising.'

'Why?'

'Because the bed is a bit hard… do you find it a bit hard?'

'Didn't you *feel* anything?'

'Ah, no. I must have nodded off.'

'God, Owen… I wouldn't be surprised if I was pregnant to you after what *I* just experienced.'

'Erotic dream, huh?' He rolled towards her.

'No!' She lifted her head and looked behind her. The ovum hovered in the same place, but Gina was nowhere to be seen. She writhed into a sitting position and ran her fingers through her hair.

Owen slid off the bed and massaged his face.

The ovum began to turn towards them. Simultaneously, it translated across the floor and came to rest by the side of the bed. Eamon had regained his previous animation. He held out his hands. 'Well?'

Owen was desperately thinking up a diplomatic reply when he realised that the question wasn't directed at him. Linh's fearless appraisal of the old man, however, informed him that something significant had happened to her.

'Do you experience that every night?' she ventured.

Eamon shook his head. 'I have things set much milder. And I tend to focus on one part of the body at a time... to initiate healing, to focus the forces of life... much milder.'

'It was both out-of-body and into-body, if you know what I mean...'

'I know exactly what you mean, Linh.'

Owen raised his eyebrows and looked from one to the other. 'Well, I have no idea what you mean.'

Eamon nodded deeply. 'Unfortunately, the settings can accommodate only one gender at a time—this time, it was tuned to accommodate the fairer sex.' He glanced at the doorway. 'Gina has had to take care of a matter.' He folded his hands in his lap. 'She must be experiencing considerable jealousy, with me paying so much attention to you. She has become very devoted to me, and I to her. I hope you can find some way to reassure her at some time in the future.'

Owen said uncertainly, '... or she might kill us both?'

Eamon threw back his head and wheezed. '... no... no... at least not while I'm alive.'

'Oh... great...' Owen looked about self-consciously, aware that the three of them created an odd tableau.

Eamon gestured with a thrust chin. 'Lie back down, you two. I will modify the setting so that Linh doesn't inadvertently orgasm.'

Owen darted a look in her direction, expecting to see mortification in her face. But, no—his lover smiled contentedly and wriggled prone onto the bed. He hesitantly placed himself beside her and felt an overwhelming reassurance when her hand slipped into his.

'I must place your mind at ease.' The ovum gave Eamon's voice an echoic quality. 'Your mission here is based on the belief that the Hadron collider interferes with the fabric of time, and that meddling with the constructs of our realm could destroy the universe. This is not actually the case...'

'Then how do you explain the time discrepancies around the village?' Owen was not going to allow himself to be side-lined by some old codger with a mysterious power over his girlfriend's orgasms.

'Good observation, Owen. May I begin by saying that time and space is an illusion, and that this realm is a wonderful construct to which we are unescapably bound. The concept of infinity is an impossibility, and it is this very deduction that establishes that we are part of an illusion. The answer has always been in plain view—unambiguous and accessible even to those without the contrivances of schooling. Animals recognise this order and live their lives with sublimely, fatalistic composure—they live in the present, and they live for the present—there is nothing more compelling. Even the animals that horde for the winter are occupying the present.

'We, on the other hand, have applied our considerable intellect to conjuring the most bizarre fabrications, in religion and science, removing ourselves further and further from nature and the truth. However, our observations and deductions have accrued over time to form a collective cleverness that has great potential to validate this realm—to achieve, from nothing, something transcendent. But we are still early in our journey—and, despite my age, I have no more idea of where we are headed than you young things.'

Owen decided to put forward the rhetorical question, his speech slightly slurred with drowsiness. 'But releasing a few rogue strangelets into the universe is not a matter for concern.'

Eamon grunted softly. 'There is no such thing. Do you seriously think that in the realm of suns that are thousands of times bigger than ours with gravitational forces that defy belief, we puny humans can manufacture a device that will gobble up the universe? It is the height of hubris and an unconscious remnant of our search for God—we become terrified when we discover nothing but more stars, and so we direct our search inward to see if God exists there.'

'Then what is affecting the watches in the villages?'

'Owen, when you place thousands of high-energy magnets in a circle around a village, you create a level of artificiality in the environment that has never been experienced before. We have discovered that time anomalies do exist in the village—or, more correctly, *timepiece* anomalies have been observed. Our researchers discovered that the degree of time lag is influenced by the orientation of the individual watch to the collider. Certain orientations make watches operate more slowly. Basically, their mechanisms, even the crystals, are affected by aspects of the magnetic radiation. We readily admit that we don't know exactly what's going on, but it definitely won't create the Apocalypse. It's more like running a wind-up clock in an atmosphere of argon or some other heavy gas—the additional air resistance on the moving parts will make the clock lose time.'

Linh's voice suddenly brought new life to the room. 'And I suppose that the factions that want to close down the collider have been jumping on those rumours about strangethings, or whatever...'

'Quite so, Linh. As you are probably very aware, the community's opinions are in the hands of those who control the media—whatever the mindset required, it will be achieved.'

'As you admitted to doing with the "reach for the stars" campaign over the last fifty years,' Owen slurred.

Eamon looked over at Linh. 'Does he always become so tetchy just before he falls asleep?'

With his eyes closed, Owen grinned and squeezed Linh's hand.

Eamon sighed. 'Look, amongst the conspirators, propaganda has always been the dominant force. Actual combat is a last resort.' The ovum lowered itself and the old man swung his legs to the floor. 'Well, be that as it may... it is time for you two lovely things to go to bed, and whilst I would love for you to remain where you are, I'm afraid it would become a little crowded if I was to join you. So, I bid you goodnight. We will speak in the morning about your assignment.'

Owen levered off the bed and held out his hand for Eamon to take. 'Thanks for the chat. I didn't mean to be rude—just need to get to the truth.' He led his host to the edge of the bed so that he could sit down.

'My boy, I am delighted by your perspicacity—both of you. You fill me with hope.'

Linh slid off the bed next to where Eamon was seated. On an impulse, she reached out with both arms to hug him—and dropped to the floor.

Eamon cried out. 'No, Cato!'

Owen's mind roiled. His first priority was to Linh. He knelt beside her and slipped his hand under her neck. He lifted her head off the hard floor. Then he looked up at the old man.

'She will be alright, Owen,' Eamon was breathing heavily. 'Just lift her onto the bed.'

Working his arm under Linh's knees, Owen hefted her limp body and laid her gently onto the bed. 'What just happened, Eamon?' He turned around angrily.

Eamon reached out and put his hand to Owen's shoulder. 'I'm sorry, Owen. She'll be alright in a minute. Just let her lie there. She'll come around soon.' He dropped his head to his chest and groaned.

'Are you okay, Eamon?' Owen gripped the old man's shoulder. 'Was that a defensive weapon that just came into play?'

Eamon nodded weakly.

'Do you want me to get Gina?'

'She's already on her way.'

Owen scanned the ceiling. The skylight had transformed into a smooth, opalescent surface, without any obvious apertures for weapons.

Eamon's voice came weakly. 'You won't find anything. The pulse comes from various corners of the room. It's at a special frequency that renders humans unconscious virtually instantly. Her sudden movement to give me a hug was interpreted as a hostile act. The system reacted as it was designed to.'

'So, we've been targeted the whole time?'

Eamon's slitted eyes slowly turned to Owen. 'One doesn't get to be two hundred years old without taking precautions.'

... two hundred!... and now is probably a good time to ask him what he meant by assignment...

Quick footsteps approaching alerted Owen to Gina's arrival.

She moved like a leaf in the wind and knelt in front of her master. With her hands cradling his head, she searched his eyes.

'I'm alright, Gina,' his voice was feeble. 'It was an accident... unintentional...'

Gina cast a measured glance at Linh's prostrate form then flicked her head at Owen to indicate that he should move her out of the way so that Eamon could lie down.

Owen scooped Linh to his chest and walked around to the other side of the bed.

She groaned sensually and ran her hand around Owen's neck. 'Don't put me down, Owie,' she said quite clearly, '... take me back to bed... I want to have sex with you...'

Owen stood there with his girl in his arms and silently mouthed, 'What have you done?' in Gina's direction.

Her answer was a curt nod towards the entrance and, '... wait at the front door.'

He turned and padded heavily across the cobalt floor, deciding to leave Linh's shoes behind, because in this sterile place they were completely unnecessary. He sat in one of the settees in the sunken lounge and cradled his girl in his arms as he waited for Gina.

Linh's colour had returned and she clutched lightly at his shirtfront, smiling and burying her face to his shoulder. 'Owie,' she murmured without opening her eyes, '... this is so lovely. Do you mind carrying me? I can walk if you want me to.' Linh intuitively understood that, for Owen, this moment was a much-needed affirmation of his masculinity. After the confrontations he'd endured, she knew that he badly needed to restore his self-esteem and letting him care of her was the best and most pleasurable way that she could think of.

'It's alright, baby. It's not far. You've had a bad knock. I'll look after you.'

Gina strolled into the lounge and silently signalled for Owen to follow her.

A few minutes later, he was lowering Linh to the broad expanse of bed in Gina's cabin.

Gina paused at the door. 'Breakfast is at eight. Eamon will outline his proposal. Should you accept, we will leave the ship at ten. Linh will be okay. Goodnight.' She closed the door.

Chapter Thirty-Three

It was 10:05 am. Owen couldn't help but feel a trace of terror as he, Linh and Gina made their way to the tender pen. All three were dressed in baggy jump-suits, deep grey and water resistant. Their neoprene boots squeaked lightly whenever they crossed glossy surfaces.

It was the sight of the staircase that had precipitated Owen's anxiety—the memory of lying on the bottom step looking up into Kendrick Knowles' vicious face just before Gina shot him through the head. His step had faltered and he'd grabbed hold of the handrail. Linh had tweaked him a grin and asked if he was okay—she, lightly compliant with everything that had transpired at the breakfast meeting.

Eamon, fresh and buoyant and had outlined his astonishing plan to them as they spooned date and coconut yogurt.

Owen's mind reeled with the bizarreness of it all. He felt as though it was him that had been zapped by the automatic defence system. He stepped resolutely onwards and entered the tender pen.

Linh guessed his thoughts. 'He needs us to set things right, Owie. We'll be okay, everything will work out fine... I'm very happy to be doing this.'

Owen felt an urgent need to restore some levity to their situation. He turned to Gina. 'So, whose idea was it to name the room defence, Cato... after the character in the *Pink Panther*?'

Gina turned her head. 'We needed a quick, clear command... it was his idea. He has a surprising sense of humour for a man who read the original Dumas and Dickens.

She led the way into the pen and marched towards the Zodiac nearest the hatch opening. This was a place of undisguised technology, with gleaming pipes neatly bundled, and polished instrument panels with glowing diodes. The speedboat in which he had arrived was in a cradle out of the water. Owen realised then that he and Linh would never have stood a chance of escaping the *Zeus* if things had turned ugly.

Gina motioned for them to get into the inflatable while she extracted a remote from a compartment under the steering console and activated the hull hatch. A sunlit diorama slowly revealed itself as the panels slid apart. The azure blues and russet browns of a picture-perfect Venice shone into the hold. Wavelets from the Canali di Venezia gently rocked the Zodiac.

Linh gasped in amazement.

The knot in Owen's stomach tightened.

... why us?... why do we have to do this?... this is not what I'm good at... I'm a stockman, for god's sake... Linh's a waitress...

The outboards came to life with a muted roar. Gina deftly loosed the lines off the cleats and began to turn the craft around on the spot. In front of them the basilica of San Pietro di Castello rose above barges tied to the wharf, and as they slowly exited, they were confronted by the huge and elaborately crenelated walls protecting the harbour of the Torre dell' Arsenale.

When they were out of the shadow of the *Zeus*, the morning sun enveloped them. With a shunt of the throttles, Gina steered towards the narrow aperture that led into the harbour. The Zodiac carved a frothy wake.

Owen turned his head towards the diminishing bulk of the *Zeus*. Following the sheer from its pugnacious bow, he looked up at the black windows that slanted from underneath the bridge deck of the super-yacht. He raised his arm in a small salute. He imagined Eamon, in the ovum, hovering right by the solarium windows, no doubt wondering whether or not he had made the right decision in entrusting this mission to a young couple from Australia.

They passed the towers on either side of the gateway and entered the shipyard. Warehouses stood neatly against the square perimeter, their brick facades emblazoned with the names of the various businesses.

Gina corrected her course towards the far diagonal corner. Soon it became apparent that there was a connecting waterway that led into a canal. Owen glimpsed the smile on Linh's face as they entered what would be best described as a quintessential Venetian canal. He shifted closer to her.

She looked into his eyes and moaned, 'Oh, Owie... we are on the adventure of a lifetime. Isn't this wonderful?'

It was at this moment that Owen was filled with courage. His girl was showing him the way—meeting their future head-on—not encumbering herself with what-ifs—relying on her reflexes to deal with any surprises. Eamon had obviously recognized this quality in her. He'd said to him, with a pointed look, 'You can't do this by yourself... this is not a mission that you alone are capable of, Owen. Both you and Linh have been nurtured by your families and your experiences, and you possess the very attributes that give you the best possible chance of success. So, don't allow yourself to be alone—your woman punches well above her weight—literally, so Gina informs me.'

The four of them had taken their time over breakfast. There'd been much to discuss. They dunked fresh figs and dates into a most delicious yogurt and nibbled on crisp walnuts and blueberries.

This time, Linh was on the front foot. 'I suppose the obvious question is, why us? Surely you can dismantle the gamma laser project without our assistance.'

Eamon, though hunched and frail, emanated a vitality that surprised both his guests. 'Oh, dismantling the project is a simple procedure. The tricky part is to get the most publicity from the act. I want to leave the world a message, and I want that message to be delivered by two ordinary people whose histories can be traced back to their very ordinary, urban environment. I want there to be an indisputable authenticity, so that the subsequent media frenzy will only add to the significance of what occurred. Unfortunately, you will, for a time, become the most prominent individuals on the planet, but I have no doubt that it will not take long for you to return to the degree of anonymity that any sane person cherishes.'

Linh sipped on her ginger tea. 'Well then, you'd better brief us on our mission. Owen and I have been on a few and, in every case, we were pretty ignorant of the bigger picture. This time I'd like to know exactly how we fit in.'

Eamon wheezed heartily and slapped his knee. 'Bravo, Linh.' He turned to Gina. 'Shall we commence the slide show?'

Gina rose and pointed at the back wall. Again, the blank wall resolved into icons, barely visible in the streaming daylight. She activated one icon. The room began to darken. When it was almost pitch black, she initiated another icon and a broad image appeared across the wall. Underneath the tiled rooftops of an antiquated metropolis was the title—*Venice Film Festival*.

Now, as the Zodiac plied the confines of the Rio de l'Arsenal and went under a curved footbridge, Owen was filled with a sense of purpose. Eamon was right— he and Linh were ideally suited to carrying out this task.

Just as the opening to the end of the canal appeared in the distance, where it led into the main lagoon, Gina cut the motors and expertly swung the inflatable side-on against the stone wall of the plaza. Before Owen could take the initiative, she took a mooring line to the nearest bollard and secured the craft. She leapt off the front of the inflatable and beckoned the two to follow.

The flat facades of the houses were disappointingly derelict. Thin wire mesh covered the grills of the lower windows and there was no obvious sign of the buildings being occupied. Gina led them to a very narrow laneway. They ventured into its constricted shadows, passing doorways on either side. Gina stopped at one neglected door, flush to the front of the building, and knocked.

Owen looked up and down the alley. He felt rather conspicuous, the three of them standing there in identical jumpsuits.

... not a soul about... weird...

The door was opened by an old woman who didn't question their arrival but stood aside to let them enter. Without a word, Gina continued to the end of a dim hallway where there was a flight of stairs with wrought iron balustrading. Their steps were muffled by the booties as they climbed to the fourth floor. They entered what appeared to be a self-contained flat with four beds and a selection of antique wardrobes.

Gina went to one of the wardrobes and pulled open the door. She riffled through the hanging clothes and gave a grunt of satisfaction. 'Our clothes are here. The trip to the Lido is not so far but it is impossible to predict the weather conditions, and if a wind blows up, we will be thankful that we're wearing this,' she tugged at her grey suit. 'Wouldn't want to arrive looking wet and bedraggled.'

Linh walked to the nearest window. 'Is it okay if I look out?'

Gina sat on the edge of a bed, unzipped herself, wriggled out of the top half of her suit and focused on her phone. 'Sure, but there's nothing to see.'

It was true—the window looked out over the alley at another barred window facing them not three metres away. If she cranked her neck, she could see the pigeons alighting on the television antennas on the roof.

... not so romantic at all, really... in fact, quite squalid... and the water smells...

She turned to Owen who was looking a little lost. She didn't want him to assume all the responsibility. She knew she had to fulfil her role in this. 'So, at last we get an insight into the way Gina Wu operates— the stealth, the planning,' she wrapped her arms around him, '... the exhilaration of executing the perfect plan.'

Gina smiled without taking her eyes from her phone.

'... it'll be a shame though if someone steals the boat. I noticed you left the keys in it.'

Gina pocketed the phone and allowed herself to flop backwards onto the bed. 'No one will steal it. There are more high-level crime figures that make Venice their home than you could ever imagine. No one would be stupid enough to steal a piece of high-tech kit because, apart from the fact that it has at least three transponders in it, they could come to a grisly end in some abandoned warehouse.'

Linh sighed. 'Oh.'

'We leave in about four hours.' Gina nestled into a pillow and closed her eyes. 'I suggest you two try out your costumes just in case we have to make some last-minute alterations. And, I'm not snoozing—I'm planning.'

Apart from the occasional flapping of a pigeon's wings, it was very quiet in the room.

Linh led Owen to the wardrobe. 'Okay, my darling... let's see how you scrub up in a Milanese suit.'

They took out the hangers with their clothes and laid them on the bed. Gina had already primed them about their outfits and Owen couldn't help feeling some curiosity for a suit with a price tag that approached ten thousand dollars.

He held the protected suit at arms-length and unwound the cord from the buttons of the brown paper covering. Then he handed Linh the hanger and stripped down to his underwear. It was a relief to feel the air on his skin, even though it was quite warm and humid. His first touch of the cool, lightweight silk-cashmere blend reminded him of a dark grey skirt that his mother wore for many years when he was a child. He always felt particularly comforted when she wore it, not being aware at the time that it was an expensive gift to her from his father, and that she wore it whenever there was a special, joyous occasion.

'Shirt first, Owen!' Gina called from the bed. 'You are not going dressed like some rapper with nothing more than a gold chain on his chest. In the drawer,' she pointed to a squat cabinet.

He went over and pulled out the top drawer. Inside lay a number of packaged shirts. He felt Linh at his side. Together they held up the possible choices.

'I like this one, Owie,' she held up a thin striped canvas cotton shirt in ecru and stygian blue.

Owen smiled. It wouldn't be too hard to wear this—it was practically a uniform with cattlemen all over Australia. 'Can I take this home with me when we finish this gig, Gina?'

She shook her head despairingly.

He ripped open the packet and put on the shirt. It fitted perfectly.

They turned and together looked at Linh's ensemble lying on the bed. In the bland décor of the room, the redness of the Lanvin, knot waist gown was as provocative as a bullfighter's cape.

Owen stood behind his girl. 'Here, let me help you undress.'

Linh held out her arms as Owen undid the back zip. 'You are so obliging when there's any disrobing to be done, aren't you, my love.' She looked down at the velvety slimness of the gown. 'Ah, Gina... this isn't something that I need to be sewn into, is it? It looks awfully small, even for me.'

Gina opened one eye. 'Well, there's a special feature to that gown that Mademoiselle Lanvin would probably have disapproved of, and that is that it is actually a slitted skirt with a top. We had to make it like that so that you could still wear your jumpsuit. When you get there, you will take the skirt part out of a case and slip it on.'

By this time, Linh was standing in her underwear trying to work out how to disengage the two parts of the gown.

'The fabric knot around the waist disguises the join. Owen's an engineer—see if he can work it out.'

The two of them sat on the bed and eventually discovered that the top had a fabric bow and so did the bottom. When the two lengths of fabric were twined in a special way, they combined to make one knot which held everything in place and made the ensemble look like a contiguous gown.

'Wow, Gina, that is so cool,' Linh gushed. Then she frowned. 'So, does that mean I'm going over in my underwear—underneath the jumpsuit.'

Gina raised a careless brow. 'If you want to. Bear in mind that most red-carpet celebs would die of embarrassment if there was a panty line visible under their skin-tight get-up.'

With a sharp intake of breath, Linh thrust her hands to her mouth. 'I am *not* wearing nothing!'

Owen tut-tutted. 'But think of how embarrassing it will be if the cameras pick up the outline of your full-brief, comfy grannies...'

Linh flung him a doleful look. 'These are not granny pants, Owen,' she snapped the elastic at her bottom.

Owen stood back with a finger to his lip. '... hmmm... I don't know. What're your thoughts about this, Gina?'

The svelte assassin flicked herself from the bed into a standing position in one reflexed motion. 'Me, personally?... bare... without a doubt.' She sidled over and appraised Linh's semi-nakedness.

'Stop it, you two.' Linh put her hands on her hips. 'I wouldn't do it even if the mission depended on it.'

'Yes, you would,' Gina added. 'Anyway, there's nothing to worry about. The drape goes underneath your tush and upwards to your navel. You can wear witches-britches for all I care and it will still look sensuous and sensational... so much more alluring than seeing slashes of flesh. She moved to the staircase and turned. 'Anybody hungry?'

'Ooh, yeah,' Owen went to Linh and held her softly. 'What's on offer?'

'Home cooked Italian, Owen,' Gina stood back as the old woman rose up the stairs carrying a tray with plates of food. Gina relieved her of the tray and watched for a moment as the woman descended. She took a luxurious sniff, 'Fegato Alla Veneziana,' she pronounced with relish... liver and onions. This will fortify you for the mission.'

Linh's face contorted.

Owen blanched.

Gina gave them an urgent look. 'Really?... a girl with Asian heritage, and a man from the land?... and you turn up your noses at liver?' She deposited the tray on a small side table. 'Well, all the more for me! But I would urge you to give it a try.'

The two lovers sauntered over in their underwear and looked on as Gina delicately forked a thin slice of liver and nibbled its edges. The aroma was quite pungent, but the caramelized onion transformed the fusion into a wholesome bouquet. Two forks tentatively ventured to the plate.

'Hey, wow... this is really delicious,' Owen nodded to Gina.

Linh went for a second helping. 'I don't think I've ever eaten liver.'

The three of them sat on the beds and slowly devoured their meal. Beside them, each had a small bottle of Pellegrino.

In the quietness, Owen occasionally darted a look at Gina as she performed that most essential of acts—eating. He noticed that she had an unhurried manner and that she chewed her food well. He recalled his promise to Eamon—to dispel any notions of ambition on his and Linh's part. This looked a timely moment. He swallowed and took a swig of water. 'Gina...' he began.

'I know what you want to tell me, Owen.' Gina put down her plate and unscrewed her bottle. After a long sip she placed her hands between her thighs. 'You two are destined for... well, what exactly, I don't know—no one knows. We operate in a very dynamic realm that requires a very replete skill set, but for the job that he has in mind for you, there's one attribute that Eamon values more highly than any other, and that is a conscience. You can imagine why—it's one thing to have all the powers in the world devolve to an individual—it's another thing entirely as to whether that person has the morality to utilise them in the interests of humanity. Such integrity has to grow within the individual from the time they are born. Then it is resolute, immutable—only then does the organization stand the best chance of enduring.

'Recruits are selected at an early age—there is no formal method. The conspirators, as you call them, have all the time in the world and have plenty of encounters with likely candidates. Many of the chosen ones are retained to work in various capacities but might never end up in principal positions. After all, the leaders tend to be around for a while, and who knows where our technology will take us in years to come. By the way, we have done exhaustive DNA testing on both of you, and the good news is that you both have the requisite genetic strength to bear the rigours of an artificially prolonged life.

'But, I'm projecting too far into the future—other people will prepare you for that in the years to come. It's just that the two of you have been thrown into this cauldron of subterfuge and have made a big impression with Eamon. And I know he's concerned about me—I have a strong component of jealousy that I can't do anything about. I'm sure that Eamon has asked you to address that in some way.'

'He did,' Owen murmured.

With a rustle of wings, a flock of pigeons took off from the roof opposite.

Owen caught Gina's eye and smiled openly. Her candidness stirred an unexpected affection. 'But, I suppose you wouldn't hesitate to shoot either of us in the back if there was ever a compelling reason to.'

Gina's return smile was unguarded and with a distinctive wrinkle at her eye.

Owen rose. He sat close beside her and enveloped her in a gentle hug.

She didn't resist and leant her head against him.

'Thank you, Gina… for being there for us… for saving my life.'

Opposite them, Linh put her hands to her mouth. A look of anguish suddenly transformed her face. She propelled herself from the bed and sat on Gina's other side. 'Yes, thank you,' she choked with emotion, '… for being there for me too.'

Owen looked at the floor and smiled. 'That would have been a waste of rigorous genes, hey… if Knowles had gotten his way!'

Gina shoved him away. Then she turned and kissed Linh on the forehead. 'You two finished with your outfits, then?'

Chapter Thirty-Four

The spray thrust forward by the speeding Zodiac was blown back by the rising wind into the faces of the occupants. Not that this was in any way an inconvenience. The trio on board wore helmets fitted with full-face visors. Each was also wearing black body armour, a bulging utility belt, a holster with a fully loaded 9mm Beretta and a shoulder slung communications module. The deception was obvious—without any emblems of identification, they looked exactly like an elite counter-terrorism unit engaged in securing the waterways around the island of Lido. They had passed a similarly crewed inflatable going the other way as they came out of the lee of San Servolo Island. There had been no challenge. Owen's derisive snort articulated his scorn on the intercom.

'What is it, Owen?' Gina raised her chin in his direction.

'Nothing... just another example of security being too complicated for its own good.'

Linh gleefully chimed in. 'They don't know who we are, but they don't want to question us in case they look foolish.'

'That's what we're counting on,' Gina replied as she scanned the water ahead through the bursts of spray. 'It's crazy—you'd think that with our resources we could place ourselves in the midst of the Palazzo del Cinema without the need for this,' she drew her hand along the accoutrements strapped to her body, '... but, sometimes it's easier not to use our established resources. We don't want to run the risk of compromising them... and we can never be totally certain of their allegiance. It's a case of balancing the human element against evolving technology.'

Owen wasn't quite sure what to make of that, but another thought came to his mind as a particularly dense wave of spray engulfed the Zodiac and washed in a foamy cascade to the back of the craft. 'Now, Gina... I just happen to know that this time of year is fairly benign as far as breezes go. My parents holidayed here two years ago... so what's with the blow? Did you guys predict this?'

Gina laughed. 'You have no idea, Owen, how accurate our weather mapping is. When one has sufficient data, the outcomes are surprisingly predictable. Okay, keep a lookout for the entrance to a canal... it's not very big...'

The three kilometres that they had travelled from the waterfront on the Rio de l'Arsenel to a point just off the island of Lido had taken less than ten minutes, but to Owen it seemed much longer. He thought back to Gina's briefing in the room above the shadowed alleyway.

'We're going by boat because we need to avoid the facial recognition locations. It's not that this event requires such high security, it's just that, nowadays, as a matter of course, everyone is secretly scanned. At an exclusive occasion like this, filtering is easy—everyone in the vicinity is bona-fide—they are either rich or connected or both. There is no reason for strange faces to pop up. The digital security will pick us out in an instant. So, we go in the back way... through the canal that loops behind the Cinema. Not that there aren't security cameras there—many of the guests will arrive by launch at the casino wharf— it's just that the trajectory is short and we can negotiate that before security is mobilised. By that time, we'll have changed and admitted ourselves into the main party.'

Owen's thoughts were interrupted by Linh's sharp command.

'A bit to the left, Gina... that's it.' Her sharp eyes had located the canal's northern entrance.

The Zodiac sagged in the water as Gina pulled back on the throttles. 'Scan the place for security, guys. We want to do this with as little fuss as possible.'

All three of them raised binoculars to their eyes. It became immediately obvious that there were a number of different craft on patrol in the vicinity, some off the foreshore and one police launch at the entrance to the canal. A flash of light from one of the boats confirmed that someone had glasses trained on the Zodiac.

'We'll do a run parallel to the shore... let them get used to us.' Gina nudged the throttles and the inflatable hopped onto a laboured plane. They travelled south for some distance until they were hidden behind the island of Lazzaretto Vecchio. Rounding it, they could see the southern end of the canal loop. After scanning the water as well as nearby buildings, Gina guided the Zodiac into the narrowness of the waterway and under the Riva di Corinto footbridge.

The inflatable burbled steadily past the luxurious mansions on either side of the canal. 'Come on, you two,' Gina's voice came too loudly through the intercom, '... be assertive. You're seeking out trouble not slinking from it. Raise your visors and look alert.'

The two new recruits were about to assume a more aggressive stance, when the police launch that they'd seen previously, cruised slowly into view from around the bend ahead. Owen and Linh reflexively straightened and began methodically sweeping the canal sides with their binoculars.

Owen glanced casually at the oncoming launch. There were only two occupants, but their attention seemed riveted in the direction of the Zodiac. 'Should we be worried about this, Gina?' he murmured.

'No,' was her emphatic reply.

The two craft closed to within twenty metres. One of the policemen raised himself above the windscreen and looked ready to communicate.

Gina spoke in a low, urgent voice. 'Put your head down, you two... low...' She reached down into the control console and pulled out a loudhailer.

Owen looked across at Linh as she ducked below the level of the gunwale.

... *a loudhailer?... you'll be popular with the neighbours, Gina...*

'Head down, Owen!' Gina spat.

He hunkered down against the front of the console so that he could still see over the bow.

Gina raised the loudhailer to her mouth but stayed mute.

The police launch swung towards them in a lazy arc. The inflatable continued on its course with Gina maintaining her silent aim on the launch.

The policeman with his hands cupped to his mouth, suddenly sat down. The driver's head dipped until it touched the steering wheel.

Gina kept the loudhailer trained on the cockpit of the launch as the Zodiac moved past. The launch drifted slowly towards the bank and nudged nose on into the stone embankment. Only when the inflatable had rounded the bend, did Gina stow the loudhailer back in the console.

'Can we resume our positions again, Gina?'

She didn't reply but focused instead on negotiating the very narrow confines under a bridge which then led onwards in a sweeping bend to another bridge.

'Neat weapon, Gina. Do they make a pocket-sized model?'

She tapped her breast pocket without taking her eyes off her course. 'We're getting out just up ahead. Drop your visors. You know what to do.'

Just after passing under the second bridge, Gina nosed the Zodiac to a private mooring on the right-hand side. There was a boat already tied there, and as the inflated side of their craft came into contact, Owen leapt off and clambered across with a line, struggling somewhat with the encumbrance of his kit. He quickly tied off, caught the case that Linh hefted at him, then watched as the two women scrambled over the boat and across to the walkway that ran alongside the embankment. The three of them paused for a moment, then headed down a tree lined path... straight into the arms of a clutch of four immaculately dressed, white belted Carabinieri. Such is the climate of terror-preparedness that none of them so much as flinched at being confronted by three helmeted special-forces types.

Without a word, Gina strode quickly to the midst of the group and produced a map that she proffered to one of the officers. He took it without hesitation and held it out as the others huddled around. Gina pointed to a spot, holding her finger on the paper for an extended period. The men seemed transfixed. They stared resolutely at the map, but Owen could see they were not processing anything.

... she must be zapping their brains with that thing in her pocket... it's like they're hypnotised...

After half a minute, without any of them making a coherent move, Gina pulled away the map. The four police officers seemed to distantly acknowledge her presence but made no move at all when the trio continued on their way.

Whilst it was deserted in the park area next to the Palazzo del Cinema, out on the Lungomare Marconi it was wall to wall glittering humanity as the invitees to the Lion Awards milled about on the concourse.

The trio emerged from underneath the trees facing a block of units. Gina flicked her head towards the portico of the nearest entrance. They jogged up the steps and through the open doorway. A stairway to one side led upwards. Further along was the door to an apartment.

With a key at the ready, Gina strode forward, unlocked the door and swung it open. In the middle of the room, an elderly man in formal dress turned around with a gape of surprise.

Gina flicked off the lights at the door. In the subdued light she confronted him at arm's length. 'Do you understand English?' she barked.

The man nodded. 'Si... I mean, yes...'

A woman swished into the room, inspecting the contents of her purse. 'Penso che sono pronto ora, Tesoro...' she muttered without looking up. Upon bumping into Owen, she emitted a squeal.

Owen hastily reached out to steady her and mumbled his apology.

At the sight of the visored helmet her face began a rapid transformation into hysteria.

In an instant, Linh was behind her with a hand clasped firmly over the woman's mouth. 'Bite me, and I'll break your neck,' she hissed into her ear. The staring eyes rotated upwards. Linh held her as she sagged and, together with Owen, they dragged her to a divan.

Meanwhile, Gina had steadied the protesting husband with a sharp palm to his forehead... just enough to forewarn him that resistance would not be tolerated. The old man swayed and collected himself.

Owen could see that, in his time, the old feller had probably been in enough brawls to know the effects of violence—unlike some people who wade into a physical match and are totally surprised by the brutality.

'Do you have a spare room?' Gina motioned with her head towards the hallway.

'Yes, down there...' the man nodded.

With a gentle hand, Gina guided him. 'Take her in as well,' she indicated the unconscious woman.

Owen and Linh took a side each and hefted their burden through the hallway to the spare bedroom. They laid the woman on the bed.

'Stay here with your wife,' Gina demanded, '... I'll be back in ten minutes.' She held out her hand palm up.

With a visible sigh, the man reached into his pocket and pulled out his phone. He placed it in Gina's hand.

'Take her handbag, Linh.' Gina motioned at the prostrate form on the bed. She moved to the doorway and waited for the other two to exit. 'Just sit here quietly for ten minutes until I return,' she warned the husband again.

As they walked back to the lounge, Gina shoved Owen in the back. '... ooh, I am sorry!' she mimicked.

Owen spun to face her. 'Oh, my apologies for having been raised with manners.'

She ignored him. 'Well done, Linh... nicely executed.'

They entered the main bedroom and commenced stripping off their gear.

Owen was beginning to overheat with all the layers of protective gear he had on. It was a huge relief to cast off the armoured vest and the utility belt. Underneath he was wearing his striped shirt and dress pants. He sat on the bed to pull off his neoprene boots and leaned into Linh who was doing the same.

She turned her face to his and kissed him on the cheek. 'You do have lovely manners, Owie,' she cooed in his ear.

'And I suppose you did deportment classes for delinquents,' he grunted petulantly as he wrenched his sweaty foot from a boot.

Linh gave him one more peck then, stood up and wriggled a foot into her high heels.

With her panty clad bottom so close, Owen couldn't resist gently embracing her and kissing the thin material.

Linh brought her arm around and fondled his neck. 'You'll have to help me twine on my skirt, Owie.'

Gina threw her boots into a corner of the room. 'Hurry up, you two!' In just her underwear, she came around to their side of the bed. 'Here, I'll do the twining—you get yourself dressed, Owen. You're the one that's going to be in the spotlight.'

She inserted herself unceremoniously between them and commenced gathering Linh's dress.

Owen's face was inches away from the fine mesh girdle that supported the holster in the small of Gina's back. The pistol was positioned hand-grip upwards, and a special cut-away in the holster gave the freedom to thumb-off the safety. He imagined her hand—a finely built and flexible woman's hand—twisting into position and grasping the weapon with ease and speed.

Rising from the bed, Owen went to the case and extracted his shoes and socks. In his mind he went over the plans for the mission.

Gina's briefing at the apartment had been very thorough and, so far, the ad hoc approach to dealing with the unexpected had worked out well—the mission leader had technology to cope with every contingency. They were not expected to be in the main auditorium for another hour, but Gina liked to keep time in reserve. 'We can always stay in the apartment until we're good and ready,' she'd said, '... the owners will just have to deal with it.' She'd glanced at her phone and turned it to the others. 'See... security video footage of the concourse in front of the main entrance. We can monitor the crowd and slip right in. I've got all the camera angles right up to the auditorium.'

'Come on, Owen!' Gina's voice brought him back into the moment. 'Get happening!'

Owen reached into the case and lifted out his anthracite grey coat. The folds in the expensive silk/wool blend fell out without leaving a single wrinkle. He moved in front of the full-length mirror and checked out his form.

... hey, wow... I really am tall, dark and handsome...

Linh stood beside him. She held his hand and smiled at him in the mirror. Her short-sleeved gown, as red as Poinsettia flowers, hung from her shoulders in a cascade of diminutive pleats that gathered at her waist and entwined into a Celtic knot sitting bunched at her navel.

The newly attached skirt fell in vertical ripples as though it had grown organically from the ground up.

Owen could just see her toes enclosed in glossy red stiletto sandals. He turned, and with his hand in the small of her back, drew her to him. He lowered his head to her upturned mouth and kissed her lightly.

Linh slipped her fingers under his coat and ran her hands over Owen's shoulders. They lingered and swayed against each other.

A man's voice at the door said, 'Please, do not do anything that might give me cause to shoot you.'

The two lovers went rigid with surprise.

'... and you, young lady... take your hands from under his jacket very, very slowly.'

Owen raised his hands so that Linh could more easily extract her arms.

Inside the door frame stood the owner of the unit. With a pitiless expression, he levelled a gun at Gina as she gathered herself into her gown.

Her eyes never left the mirror. 'Put the gun away and go back to your wife, Mr Orsatti,' she intoned, '... we are not going to hurt you—we just need to use your premises.' She turned to face him. 'I know who you are... and so do the people I work for. Go back to your room... we won't be much longer.' She looked at the discarded equipment on the carpet. 'I apologise for the mess. You have my permission to sell all of it online.' Her face remained composed with utter authority. 'The guns I would throw away. We don't have any bullets for them anyhow. See for yourself...' With a neat little flick-kick, Gina lobbed one of the belted holsters towards the doorway where it landed in a twisted coil at the man's feet.

He looked down and bent as though he was intending to pick it up. Instead, he carefully placed his gun on the ground and stood back up. He raised his hands above his shoulders. A voice behind him issued an order. Mr Orsatti stepped over the weaponry into the bedroom and stopped at the foot of the bed.

Into the doorway stepped a squat, blond man. Held loosely at his side was a pistol with a long-barrelled silencer. With his foot he carefully moved the clutter out of the way.

The calmness by which he surveyed the occupants of the room, and the fact that he wasn't exerting his dominance with a more threatening show of his weapon, gave Owen more reason to be fearful. Here was an operator who was very used to dictating the play.

The newcomer addressed Mr Orsatti who still had his back to him and was staring at the floor. 'Are you calculating your chances, old man?' His speech was surprisingly refined.

Owen's holster lay in a tangled coil at the foot of the bed where he had stripped it off. The butt of the Beretta pointed invitingly upwards near Mr Orsatti's foot.

'*Tell me!*' The command left no room for ambiguity—the man really did expect an answer.

Mr Osatti lowered his arms but remained with his back to the door. 'The thought had crossed my mind.'

'Really!' The gunman's face revealed the first hint of emotion—derision.

Owen observed the curl of his lip and immediately felt the first wrench of nausea. The line of questioning—the old man—an opportunistic means of asserting dominance—the chase to catch them—limited time to get an answer. He was going to use Mr Orsatti... the old man was going to die.

The whirring began in his head. He spread his stance a fraction. The gunman's voice came from a great distance.

'Do you think you could reach down, unclip the strap, flick off the safety and turn around and shoot me?'

Mr Orsatti shook his head.

'Tell me why not!'

Owen's vision began to tunnel. He took some deep breaths, leant his head forward and scrutinised the man's face... the hint of perfect teeth... the full lips.

'*Tell me!*' the gunman insisted.

'I would be too slow,' Mr Orsatti's voice was remote. 'Even if I was young and fast, you would have ample time to shoot me dead.'

'Indeed. Now, if you wouldn't mind turning around, I will do just that.' The blond man raised the pistol.

Owen began to pant. It was the only thing that kept the looming void of darkness at bay.

Linh looked into his eyes. 'Oh, no... Owie... not now,' she murmured.

The gunman changed his focus. 'What the hell's wrong with him?'

The colour had drained from Owen's face. His pupils had dilated so much that his eyes were almost black. Linh put her hand to his chest.

'Don't get any ideas there, young feller.' The gun thrust forward.

On the other side of the bed, Gina mounted the mattress on her knees. 'He's having a fit... he does that.' Keeping herself facing the gunman and with her hands raised, she carefully shuffled her way to the other side. 'If we don't deal with it, he could die...'

'*You* could die, if you move again without my say-so.' The heavy silencer covered her as she stepped off the bed next to Owen.

Gina slowly raised her hand to Owen's neck. 'He needs to be gripped here to stem the flow of blood to his head.'

'Uh, uh... girls... now, just keep your hands where I can see them... and frankly, I don't care if he does drop dead.'

'Don't you? He's the one you want to talk to, isn't he?' Gina pressed herself against Owen, giving the impression of supporting him and administering some sort of recuperative massage.

A disembodied voice spoke from the gunman's top pocket. He answered. 'We're in the units next to the cinema... ground floor... extreme right building... I think... not sure... which is the one we want?... all of them?... okay... yes, I've got them covered... not a problem.'

Owen couldn't resist smirking. The man's voice was so, so slow... and his movements seemed to take forever. He'd never managed to hold off from fainting for so long, and now, he was experiencing a heightened state of awareness as the synapses fired with increased intensity. He was able to process his world with supreme concentration. Already, the plan was coming together...

Gina... nice move... you are so wonderful... pressing your sharp nails into my neck... pressing against me... rubbing your breasts over my arm... here, let me hug you... let me slip my hand through your dress...

The gunman's voice boomed in Owen's mind. 'Now, ladies, keep your hands where I can see them!' His gun panned back and forth ever-so-slowly, covering Linh, then covering Gina.

... but not covering me. Ah, girls, let me hold you both... that's the

way... squeeze up close... it won't be long... Mrs Orsatti will open her door... let me embrace you, Gina... that's the girl... turn your body into me... uh, huh... nice... let me get a good hold... oops, sorry, didn't mean to stroke your bum...

'What the hell's wrong with him... why is he smirking like that?' The man's voice echoed from far away.

... mmm... focusing too much on me, mate... when Mrs Orsatti opens her door, it will be just so much more of a surprise for you... arch your back, Gina... oh, yes... yes... oh, god, you're wonderful... let me get my fingers around it... little bit more... there, how's that... smooth as, huh... now, where's that little safety catch... I know you're there... let me feel... oh!... there you are... just gently, with my thumb...

Once again, the gunman addressed his two-way radio but his gun stayed resolutely trained on the trio in the bedroom. 'No, it's okay... I can hold them here... yeah, whenever...'

... now, change gun to right hand... mmm, you're so with me on this, aren't you girls... we make a great threesome... really, we do... okay, exchange successfully executed... hold weapon around girlfriend... that's the way, darling... oh, god, am I stroking your bum?... was that deliberate?... mmm, I think it was... yes, I'm deliberately stroking your bum... ooh, that feels so good... is it good for you?... what?... what's with the glare?... don't worry, we've got all the time in the world...

'Right! Sit down against the wall with your hands on your knees. Slowly!'

... not a problem... it doesn't change anything—except that now I've decided to shoot you in your fat, ugly gob, feller... Oh! What's this I hear?... the turning of a doorknob... won't sit down just yet...

'Did you hear me? I said sit down... before I shoot you in the leg...'

... way too much focus on us, mate... to the exclusion of everything else... whoops, here she comes... hear the squeak?... oh, you heard it!... great, because this is the distraction that I've been waiting for... one to the body... two to the body... that was unexpected, wasn't it? Yes... now, before you think about rearranging your priorities, I might just pre-empt that outcome with one to the head... two to the head... let me see... what the hell, one more to the head...

The gunman slumped against the doorframe then toppled out onto the floor.

Far in the distance, Owen heard Mrs Orsatti's scream of terror. Gina's nails were no longer in his neck. There wasn't the need for him to hold on—the gunman's face was covered in blood. The last thing Owen saw was Linh as she mouthed something to him that he could no longer hear. The last thing he registered before he lost consciousness was the acrid smell of gun smoke in the room.

Chapter Thirty-Five

Owen regained consciousness in the back seat of Mr Orsatti's Alfa.

Linh stroked his forehead. 'Hey, Owie. We carried you in here... Mr Orsatti helped. The garage was at the back of the unit. We are parked just a hundred metres or so from the cinema... just to keep away from whoever is after us... but we really have to get a move on. Do you feel up to it?'

The plush leather of the seat felt so very, very comfortable—and Owen felt so very, very tired. He groaned just to rouse his voice. 'Might have to get Gina to dig her nails into my neck... that seemed to do the trick.'

From the driver's seat, Gina turned around. 'You were wonderful, Owen. I didn't know what we were going to do... I just knew that so much more was possible if we were together. There was no way that I could have nailed him... he was a dead-set killer.'

Owen took stock of this revelation. 'Ah... so, what?... *I* killed him?'

Gina closed her eyes. 'Oh, Jesus...'

Linh looked aghast. 'You can't remember?'

'... um, not at the moment.' Owen didn't want to be the cause of any added anxiety at this crucial hour. 'I just remember looking at him. Did I *kill* him?'

Gina peered through the rear window. 'Yeah, but only after you fondled my bum.'

'... and mine,' Linh added.

Owen made an apologetic grimace. 'Whoa... seems I've got more in common with James Bond than I thought.'

Gina flicked her head to the front. 'Right, are we ready to go? C'mon then.' She flung open the door and stepped out into the night.

The walk up the Lungomare Marconi towards the cinema was just what Owen needed to restore his senses. The crowd had dissipated and it was only as they approached the expanse of doors at the foyer that they had the opportunity to mingle.

Gold embossed cards were retrieved from glittering purses and handed over with ostentation to the concierge who divulged just enough obsequiousness to flatter the patrons. Owen thought it was amusing that it was the women who carried the invitations.

... better than pulling a dog-eared ticket out of your back pocket, I suppose...

When their turn came at the entrance door, the usher spent an unusually long time perusing the cards but didn't object when Gina pulled them from his hand and strode into the hall.

Their strategy was simple—they would linger at the bar until the formalities began. Every guest was expected to be seated. The trio had no designated seats. They would try to be unobtrusive, but if someone did become officious, they would feign concern over Owen's well-being—*he suddenly felt a bit light headed... we'll go to our seats shortly... hope he doesn't have to accept any awards.* That, or the mind ray. They stood behind a large pillar.

The assembled guests began moving towards their seats.

Gina came to Owen's side. 'Okay, time for me to go into the control room. Our man there should be in charge by now, but just in case. Security will be notified to remain in position—no one will interfere. Don't forget, the teleprompter is in front of the camera. The script will appear on all four cameras—you can choose which one is the most comfortable for you. Your cue is when the lights dim. The two MCs are supposed to walk out, but they'll be getting a message to stay put. Don't be too long getting out there, though. Linh, you're back-up—you know what to do if Owen fluffs it.'

Owen rolled his eyes. 'Hey, apparently, I've just killed a man—I'm sure I can manage to read a speech.'

Gina faced the couple with a surprising amount of ardour in her eyes. 'Do well, you two—it's very important.' In a swirl of skirt, she departed.

Linh held Owen's hand in hers. 'Are you nervous, Owie?'

He shook his head. 'Nuh… this is so far beyond the usual for me that I wouldn't even know what to get nervous about. You?' He kissed Linh's hand.

'No. No, not at all. I just really want to go home, Owie. I want to see my family, just to let them know I'm okay—and I want to lie with you in your day bed… and maybe get Jenna to bring up some food…'

Owen hugged her close. He closed his eyes and kissed her brow.

… I know what you're doing, you clever thing… taking away any undue focus from this mission and reminding me of the important things in our lives…

'They'll know you're okay, sweetie—you're going to be on telly in a few minutes time.' When he opened his eyes, the auditorium lighting had dimmed noticeably. He gave Linh a quick squeeze. 'C'mon, we've got to hustle.'

The couple stepped from behind the pillar… straight into the arms of an usher.

'Stop, stop… dove stai andando…' The usher held out his hands.

Linh pressed herself close to him and commenced opening her handbag against his chest. She looked up into the man's face with a silly smile, turning him around so that Owen could escape to the side aisle.

The hum of conversation covered Owen's footfalls as he made his way to the stage. He tripped lightly up the steps and emerged into the glow of the podium.

… and suddenly, I'm here…

The dais was a minimalist, glass affair that he wasn't certain how to approach.

… where the hell is the microphone?… and where do you rest your notes? Okay, no notes—no need to nowadays… the exultant recipient probably follows an impromptu speech on their phone… can't see a thing!… oh, here we go… super thin microphone stand…

Before Owen could grip at the stark structure in front of him, he recalled Eamon's exhortation about looking comfortable and non-threatening. He casually clasped his hands in front. He found a camera positioned just above the rim of the stage and looked at it. On the pane of glass appeared his first words to the world.

'Hello, my name is Owen Lucas. I'm a stockman from Australia. I've got nothing to do with the Venice Film Festival, and I apologise for intruding. The thing is, I have been asked to give a very important message to the world, and we are using this occasion to deliver it. I am appearing on every television station around the world—you can't escape me.

'In a short while, we will leave the cinema and walk across the road to the beach where you will witness the most spectacular light display ever created by human hands. You will be able to see it across most of Europe. This stunning illumination of the atmosphere is the parting gift of a man who has been observing our society for over two-hundred years, and who has decided to redirect the forces of aggression into a vision of peace. The energy required for tonight's phenomenon could just as easily be directed to destroy our communications network in a matter of hours. In a matter of days, we would be fighting each other tooth and nail. Tonight, when you see the roiling energy above you, be thankful that you are outside looking up at the sky and not crowded in a bunker wondering what the world will look like if you ever get the chance to leave.

'We, as a global population of humans, are on the cusp of disaster. Everywhere, we are threatened by more forces of destruction and doom than we are of healing and cooperation. In fact, we have no plans at all to save ourselves—not one plan by any nation, big or small, technologically advanced or not—even though we are living so far beyond our means that we would strip the earth bare within two generations if we continued to consume like locusts. But we will be reduced to warfare long before then. This is the disaster we are facing— attaining our wants through aggression.

'The answer to our dilemma is so achievable, that it will seem like magic—and in a way, it is like a spell. Because, all we have to do to save ourselves is to change our mind. Some of us, in wealthy circumstances, have to think about how much we really need—and those of us in poorer circumstances, have to think about how much we really want. Our survival depends on how well *all of us* live within our means. That is what is meant by the meek inheriting the earth—meek being able to know what is rightfully yours. Just *how much* is rightful to you? Just how much is rightful to your neighbour?

... no one has come to crash tackle me yet... oh, good, here comes Linh...

'We desperately need to reconsider our community. The better you understand community, the better is your chance of fulfilling a place here on earth. Do what you can to help shape your community—you don't have to create it—it's already there, but it needs you to help in whatever way you can. It won't happen overnight—for some it may not happen for years and years, but your *view* of tomorrow *can* change overnight. Your commitment to a better future doesn't have to be a burden—it requires no physical expenditure at all—just a change of perspective.

... let me hold you, Linh. We'll look good together on television...

'Be at peace with yourself—you don't have to grasp for what you need—you are part of a community. Don't clutch at your wants—other people have the same wants and I'm certain that we can find a way of sharing.

'If you, personally, find it difficult to come to terms with the way things are going to change, then at least do one thing, and that is to allow your children to believe in a new world. Don't burden them with your past. There are things being put into place at this moment that will make it easy for your children to embrace a sustainable community, but you have to allow it to happen.

'The future is rushing to meet us—that is inevitable. On this finite earth, it is beholden of us to refine our conscience. When you look up at the sky tonight, remember that, as individuals we are insignificant, but as an expression of humanity, we can be awesome—we simply need to allow ourselves to change.

... wow, seriously compliant audience... no one brave enough to yell "get him off"...

'Now, it is time to look at the night sky. The future that is possible is up to you. Please follow me and my friend Linh to the beach. I'll see you out there.'

Owen and Linh, hand in hand, walked slowly away from the podium and off the stage. A spotlight illuminated their progress. At first there wasn't a sound. By the time they were halfway up the aisle, they could hear a hush of whispers.

Linh turned to Owen. 'The ladies are probably wondering how they're going to cope with high heels on the beach.'

'Oh, right.' Owen paused. He put one foot on an armrest next to a surprised patron. 'I'll tell you what,' he said loudly, 'everyone—take off your shoes. We are.' He untied his laces. 'It's a beach, after all...' He commenced taking of his shoe.

Behind him, Linh bent and unbuckled her sandals. She giggled. 'Reminds me of *The Life of Brian*.'

There was the rustle and roar as hundreds of people began to move and talk. A few of the ushers and some other, more serious security types, tracked Owen and Linh as they walked to the back of the auditorium.

Linh clutched at Owen. 'Do you think that the other killers will still be out there?'

They paused at the entrance to the foyer and waited for the first people to emerge from the auditorium.

Owen drew his girl to him. 'Probably. Bit late now... the message has been delivered and the show is about to start. Too crowded for an assassination.'

'... or maybe just nicely crowded,' Linh offered in a far-away voice.

The first of the audience tumbled out into the foyer, shoes in hand, laughing and giggling. Owen and Linh led the way outside and stood in the carpark of the Palazzo del Cinema. Bodies began to pour into the open night.

It was time to initiate movement towards the beach. The couple strode across the road towards a line of canvas beach shelters above the high-tide line. There was only a short distance to the water but, in front of the never-ending row of shelters, there was sufficient space to spread out on the sand. Many decided that getting wet would increase the novelty of the occasion and entered the water. The sea surface was utterly black, because all the light sources were behind them. In the warmth of the evening, couples waded out, some up to their waist in the still sea.

On the beach, suits and gowns pressed from all directions, and Owen and Linh soon found themselves surrounded.

'Owie, I'm not totally comfortable with this.' In the darkness, Linh searched the pale, surging faces. Being fairly short, she was quickly losing her bearings. 'Have you seen Gina?'

'Well, I could put you on my shoulders, but I don't think we should attract attention to ourselves. I'm sure she's factored this into the mission—there's probably a bug in your shoe.'

'Okay, just as well I didn't abandon them, then.'

A sudden, collective sigh issued from the throng of people.

The couple looked skyward. What seemed like a fat, green meteorite had appeared in the starlit sky and was travelling slowly out to the seaward horizon. Its tail dripped luminous globs as it progressed, but instead of fading, the globs grew, and some began to change colour to red. Then, amazingly, white points appeared that grew like slow-motion starbursts. Applause erupted from the enraptured crowd.

Owen bent his head to Linh's ear. 'I don't know whether it is intentional or not, but Eamon has created the colours of the Italian flag.'

The green and red flushes lit Linh's upturned face with a hideous tinge.

Soon the sky became black again. Then, amongst the stars, there appeared countless tiny pinpricks of yellow. The effect stretched across the horizon. The balls of light gained intensity and soon the beach scene was bathed in a golden light. All colours seemed to be washed out. Everything appeared to be made of gold. People looked at their hands and marvelled at how solidly gold they seemed. The water's surface looked like liquid gold. Figures became golden statues. It was as though the nightmare of King Midas had come true. Then, the sky turned to Platinum and everything gained a silvery white sheen. It was both wonderfully beautiful and eerily frightening. The light seemed so dense and very unnatural.

Just when the effect might have begun to create claustrophobia, the sky went dark. Then slowly, a new phenomenon revealed itself. The sky was emitting an ultra-violet type of light that imbued living tissue with a blush of deep blue. The men threw off their coats and shirts and bared their chests. Forms in ultra-blue morphed and clotted into bizarre shapes as the revellers danced about. Soon, almost the entire spectrum at eye-level was a pulsing, indigo dimension—the women had divested themselves of a fair bit of their clothing as well.

Owen and Linh laughed. Even the inside of their mouths emitted tints of blue. But their teeth and their eyes were black. They took stock of each other and stopped laughing. Around them, the gyrating bodies looked eerily like the abandoned sinners from Dante's Inferno.

Linh buried her face in Owen's jacket.

Owen cupped her head. It was then that he saw the still, black shapes intermittently revealed by the twirling crowd. Only five metres away, three men were not in party mode. They stood in a tight huddle and surveyed the crowd with ominous deliberation.

Owen wasted no time. He grasped either side of the neck of Linh's gown and wrenched it apart. Before Linh could react, he'd reefed the material down below her hands so that her arms were free.

With a stricken gape, Linh allowed Owen to pull the rest of the gown all the way to her feet. Hiding behind her, he flung off his jacket and clawed at his tie.

Too shocked to resist, Linh merely watched as Owen, bent low, struggled with his trousers, finally casting them to one side.

'They're on to us, baby. They'll spot us if we keep our clothes on.' All around them were shrill screams and laughter. 'Come on!' he yelled in her ear.

Overcoming the inertia of shock, Linh unclipped her bra and let Owen, now totally in a blue sheen, lead her towards the water. When their feet became wet, Owen, still searching the crowd behind them, followed the water's edge towards the walkway access to the road. All around them, naked blue bodies moved wildly in and out, recklessly bumping and colliding.

Their progress was very slow, but eventually, as they neared the boardwalk, the crowd suddenly thinned. They were on the periphery of the event.

Owen held Linh to his chest. The human din had noticeably receded.

Her black eyes looked up at him. 'You realise that you stripped off my pants in the process?'

'I'm sorry, Tot... I had only seconds to decide.'

'Nothing's changed then.' Her smirk was a thin, cobalt line.

Owen looked towards the road. The beach was littered with clothing. 'We should be able to at least preserve our modesty,' he mused.

'But they'll have someone up there,' Linh pointed to the access between the rows of tent shelters. 'And the other thing is, if we did have a bug on us, we don't anymore.'

Owen bit at his lip. 'I suppose we should at least secure some more clothes. Don't know what the next light show is going to be, but I don't want to be like this if the night turns into stark white fluorescent lighting.'

Maintaining a hold of Owen's hand, Linh retrieved a glittering red gown off the sand. 'At least we won't be alone.' The sequins of the gown glowed like red-hot metal. Linh held the garment out in front of her. 'Hey, I remember this dress... but it wasn't red at the time. It had silver sequins.'

Owen ran his fingers over the material. 'I think I know what it is. When I was taking off my pants, I noticed that the belt buckle was exactly that colour.'

'The light makes metal go red!'

'Who knows? Looks like it.'

While they had been standing there, the crowd perimeter had moved inwards. The two of them were now standing a little apart from the thronging revellers.

Owen took Linh's hand. 'C'mon, let's find some togs.'

There were no shining blue heads or bodies up at the shelters. It looked as though everyone had moved onto the beach. The amount of discarded clothing, men's and women's, was overwhelming. Neither of them had any trouble finding something that fitted.

Owen was just buttoning up a shirt when he looked towards Linh who was holding out a dress. Beyond her, the throbbing mass of blue bodies were still happily making a spectacle of themselves—except for one blue person, who was heading up the beach towards them. Something in his right hand glowed dull red.

Owen raced forward. Linh was less than ten metres away but by the time he reached her, he knew it was too late. The gunman was striding well within the range of accuracy. He didn't even bother to raise his weapon when he saw that Owen wasn't going to make a run for it. Wearing just his briefs, he pulled up some distance from them and put a fist on his hips.

'Phew... I was hoping you weren't going to run... because then I would have *had* to shoot, and you know how badly that can go.' He waved them towards the exit to the road. 'Don't do anything rash... I can see that neither of you would like to live without the other.'

Owen put his arm out to Linh. She hesitated with her eye towards the melee of blue dancers for just long enough to alter the gunman's mind.

He half turned. 'Oh, so your other little buddy is still in the mosh-pit, is she? Thanks for the intel.' He impatiently indicated for them to move on. 'She'll be joining you shortly.'

They got onto the short boardwalk and followed it up to the shelters. All of the nail-heads and bolts had a deep, red radiance.

Owen rubbed shoulders with Linh. 'Good job, baby. Now he thinks Gina is back there.'

The voice continued very closely behind them. 'That blue light, or whatever it is, has put me in a rather bad mood—leaving me in just my underpants when there's a thousand-dollar leather jacket lying somewhere out on the sand. Are you going to tell me who's doing this? No? Your call. Don't say I didn't give you a chance. Stop here.'

The two of them came to a tentative halt. Behind them, the gunman called softly.

'McCleary... you there?'

They were beside the canvas shelters. A gun fired. Owen and Linh instinctively ducked. A heavy thud behind them made them turn. The gunman was lying face-down on the boards.

A grotesque, black figure with a huge head emerged from under one of the shelters. In the dim lamplight, it looked like a partly unravelled mummy. It came towards them, regarding the stunned couple with a curious tilt to its bandaged visage.

Linh took a step forward. 'Gina?'

The mummy gave a muffled reply. It raised its arms and began to unwind the cloth around its head.

Linh leapt forward to give assistance.

Gina took a gasp of air as the last of the cloth unwound from her neck. 'Oh, dear god... I thought I was going to asphyxiate. I just managed to swipe a bunch of these bar-runners to hide my blueness. *That* was a surprise, I have to tell you. I'd taken care of one of them,' she harked back her head, 'and I was waiting for you two to rock up. Knew you'd probably have an escort.'

The trio looked at the dead gunman.

Linh put her hands to her mouth. 'He's gone green!'

Gina disentangled the remaining bar-runners from her legs. 'Yeah... let's not hang around. The other one has gone a putrid, yellow colour—it's awful.' She looked Linh up and down. 'So, you happy with what you're not wearing?... or do you want to wrap yourself in these?' She held out a runner.

Linh hastily clutched the gown she was still holding to her chest. 'God, I've completely forgotten...' She flicked out the material and stepped into it. She presented her back to Owen.

As he pulled up the long zip, Owen peered into the darkness beyond the boardwalk. 'What's the plan now, Gina? Have we still got Mr Orsatti's car?'

'No. It's been bugged. Fortunately, we have a better option. C'mon.' She waved them onto the road. 'Eamon has sent a chopper out to meet us. Hope it still flies with this crazy light.'

Just then, there was a change in the air. The severe contrasts that were so apparent before, softened into natural night. In the streetlight, the trio's faces and hands went back to normal shades. The red glow of metals around them disappeared. Above them, the sky began to pale. The stars vanished.

As they walked south along the Lungomare Marconi, the vault of heaven became a luminous ivory—it was as though the earth was inside an egg shell. There were no shadows. Objects appeared to float in isolation.

Owen marvelled at the image of Linh and Gina walking in front of him. They appeared like animations disconnected from their environment. He called out, 'Good luck with the mob back there trying to find their clothes.'

Linh turned and laughed. She reached for Owen's hand. 'Is this what Eamon wanted?... for there to be a debauched beach party? It seems so out of context after your speech and everything...'

Gina looked back. 'Do you think they'll remember this night? You bet they will. Now, it's all about shaping their minds from this pivotal point in time. And don't forget, not everywhere are people letting go quite like this—this crowd was ready to party from the outset... they just skipped all the formalities of the presentations.' She veered off the road and followed a path that took them back onto the beach. 'Here we are.' She turned to face them. Her eyes crinkled in that very rare manner when she was truly happy.

Linh understood immediately and rushed into her arms. She sobbed on Gina's shoulder.

Owen looked out at the sea. It had a dull metal tone that reflected no light. He had a sudden longing to be near a waterhole—to feel the sweet, tannin-stained water through which he could see the rippled sand. A strong emotion clutched at his chest and he sighed audibly. It was time to go home. Tears sprang to his eyes. The horizon blurred. He looked up at the lucent sky and cursed the fact that humans had the power to tamper so much with nature. Now it would become beholden upon them to manage that power, and it was anyone's guess as to how well that was going to go.

A pair of arms slipped through his and gently hugged him. He closed his eyes and put his lips to the head beneath him. She was taller. It was Gina.

She rested her head on his shoulder. 'Farewell, Owen. I just want to let you know that if it doesn't work out with Linh, for whatever reason ... well, I'll get you two to make up at gunpoint.'

Owen held her tight and nodded. In the distance he could hear the steady beat of a helicopter. He took a shuddering breath. 'Next time I hear about you, I expect you to be mothering a brood of little assassins.'

Gina's laugh came freely—it was the first time that Owen had seen her abandon her reserve. He opened his eyes. The night was black once more.

'We *have* to see each other again, Gina—we've got enough material to last a lifetime of afternoon teas. And only *you* know that it's all true.'

'You don't know the half of it. When you fly back to Australia, go via Melbourne—it's important.'

'Melbourne... okay.'

Linh added her embrace and held them all tightly together. A harsh light pierced the night.

Owen moaned. 'Oh, no... what have we got this time? Oh... a searchlight. Our ride has arrived.'

Gina thrust forward her head and kissed Owen on the mouth. Just as suddenly, she swung Linh towards her and did the same. Then she turned and walked out of the glaring light.

Chapter Thirty-Six

The passenger compartment of the Augusta-Westland 169 was like being inside a kaleidoscope. The light from hundreds of huge, static, coloured balls high up in the atmosphere shone through the windows and lit up the beige interior with solid tints and hues.

'How can the pilots fly through this, Owie?' Linh was looking up at the heavenly display.

'My guess is they've got their visors down and they'd be following a virtual map.' He placed his mouth against Linh's hair and peered through the porthole. 'This would be enough to give anyone a fit.'

'Eamon was right about creating an unforgettable spectacle. And it's all coming from the lasers in space, right?'

'I have no idea, Tot. I presume so. There's so much we don't know.' Owen smelled Linh's hair. He closed his eyes. 'I imagine there must be heaps of people videoing this... mmm... do you think so?... I think so... I hope so...'

Linh straightened. She pushed Owen's chin so that his head came back on the rest. Then she pressed the recline button.

Within seconds, Owen's mouth sagged partly open. He was asleep.

The helicopter dropped them off in a field outside Ancona. There was a Fiat Bambino waiting for them which had in the glove compartment, a credit card and a phone. They drove through the remaining night along the east coast, coming into Naples via Foggia. Much of the time, the sky was filled with bizarre illuminations. In every little hamlet they drove through, people were out, in camp chairs, on mats, looking up at the night long exhibition.

The weirdest trick was the false sunrise. About an hour before it was due, the sky paled with the first light of dawn. The sky became orange and proceeded to become progressively brighter. The whole countryside was suffused in a deep amber. Somehow, it created a sensation of optimism—as though the world was being bequeathed a special energy. Then, in seconds, everything became black. The effect was devastating—the darkness seemed especially malign—even though it was just ordinary night. Even from inside the little Bambino, the panning headlights revealed that the sky watchers out in the open were becoming fearful. They were clutching children, arms full of gear, and making straight for the safety of houses.

The two of them looked at each other. This last effect was deliberate. It was a reminder of what *could* be—endless darkness after a terminal war. Humans had the capacity for it.

After about ten minutes, the sky became pale with the real sunrise.

'A lot of *very* relieved people will be looking out of the windows now, I expect,' said Linh. 'Now, tell me, why is it so important for us to leave for home from Naples? ... hmmm?... you've been very evasive. You haven't lined up another job with the conspirators, have you?'

'Absolutely not!'

'... um, you have long lost relatives here?'

'No.'

'You were conceived here on your parents' honeymoon?'

'No... hmmm... well, they did go to Italy, so, maybe... but, no...'

'You have a past—or maybe even, current—girlfriend living here?'

Owen paused long enough for Linh's eyes to grow.

'You have a *girlfriend* here?'

'Well, she *is* a girl, and she *is* sort of a friend—a very recent friend...'

'Owen Lucas, are you telling me that while I was slaving away in a noodle bar, you were out squiring young Italian girls?'

Owen's nod was almost imperceptible. '... yeah, I was...'

Linh crossed her arms and produced her most theatrical pout. 'What was her name?'

Owen's eyes were on the road, but there was a definite dreaminess to his look. 'Her name... her name...' He frowned. 'Oh, her name is

Marlene.'

'That doesn't sound very Italian. Are you sure you're not just making this up to make me jealous?'

'No.'

'How old is she?'

'Oh, I don't know... early twenties...'

'Is she pretty?'

'Of course, she is! I only go out with pretty girls.'

'Don't even *think* that I'm flattered. Does she have any *other* redeeming features?'

'Well, she is *fantastic*—watch out! You fool! God, what is it with Italians and round-abouts?'

'... hmmm?... *fantastic*?...'

'Oh, yeah, well, she wanted to show me a good time so I let her take the lead and... are they beeping at me, or is it just part of the road culture?'

'... she showed you a good time, did she? How, exactly?'

Owen pointed in front of them. 'On the back of one of those.'

'You did it on the back of a *scooter*?'

They both burst out laughing.

'Yeah, she steered and I hugged her.'

Linh reached out and held Owen's hand. 'Oh, Owie... that's sweet. That is so quintessentially Italian.'

Owen's eyes lit up. 'That's what *I* said to her! I wanted to do something quintessentially Italian. So, I bought her a scooter and away we went.'

Linh rested her head on Owen's shoulder. 'This, I want to hear.'

Half an hour later, as they pulled up at the Grand Hotel Vesuvio on the via Partenope, Owen was just ending his story.

'... and I kind of promised Marlene and Adelina that I would come back to let them know how I went.'

'*Two* girls, *and* you blurted out the details of your secret mission.'

Owen laughed. 'Yeah, I wish I'd *been* in possession of a few more details at that stage. I would probably have turned my back on the mission and married Marlene... or Adelina.'

'... and leave me at the mercy of Gina Wu!'

They looked at each other. Owen kissed Linh's hand. He loved the way that she so willingly moved her hand to his lips.

Linh dipped her eyes at Owen. 'So, Romeo, how do you know she's on a shift today?'

Owen shrugged his shoulders and made an indistinct noise. 'We're staying here anyway, so I'm sure we'll encounter her at some stage.'

'Or we could go to her house,' they said simultaneously. They laughed.

Owen had especially asked for the same room that he'd occupied just a fortnight before.

'Is it just me, Tot, or do you also feel like we've been on this mission for months and months?'

'Months and months, Owie. And that doesn't even include my time in Ho Chi Minh City. That seems like another lifetime.' Linh came out of the shower and towelled herself. 'Were you thinking of me when you were in this room?'

Owen put his arms around Linh's warm body. 'Oh, was I ever. Every time I saw something interesting, ate something new, spoke to someone, I wished that you were with me. You would have made everything better. I would have gone crazy if Marlene hadn't come along... you know what I mean?'

Linh kissed Owen's chest. 'I do, Owie. You're such a caring person— it wouldn't have been good for you to be alone. I'm glad Marlene was there for you. As soon as I'm dressed, you can introduce me to her.'

They knew she was on shift because they'd seen the lime-green Vespa in the carpark on the way to their room.

Owen chose the same spot on the rooftop for lunch.

'Are you going to order the same food as well?' Linh teased.

'I don't know what it was—she ordered it for me... it was nice.'

Linh rolled her eyes. 'And to think that I had to follow you through a pitch-black park, get abducted in a helicopter and get hoisted into a tree in virtually my underwear... and she only has to press her skirt against the table...'

'... against my shoulder, actually...'

Linh gave Owen a kick under the table. 'And I don't want to *know* what you had for desert.'

'He have Armagnac Fig with Salty Caramel,' said a soft voice.

Linh spun around. She looked up at Marlene with horror on her face. 'We weren't really arguing.'

'I know that, because Owen smiling whole time. Hello, Linh... I am Marlene.' She came around to the side of the table and held out her hand.

The three of them had a wonderful afternoon. They drove to Mount Vesuvio, the girls in front and Owen scrunched crossways in the back seat, up the winding Contrada Osservatorio into the caldera. From there they walked to the rim of the volcano.

'It's your classic volcano shape, isn't it, Owie?' Linh's head was wrapped in a white and black polka-dotted scarf and, with her retro sun-glasses, she very much evoked the fifties era look.

Owen was wearing a fedora and large, dark glasses. 'It's not likely to go off today, is it, Marlene?' Both girls had an arm around him as they peered into the crater.

'It would be a shame, yes... the day after you are so famous.'

Owen turned to her. 'Did you watch us on television?'

'Most of it. I am cooking... perfecting a dish for exam. I hear loud banging on door. It is Assunta, the widow next door. She say, *Turn on TV* so I turn it on and you are on it. I can't believe it. Assunta say, *that boy you take back home with you—if you want to get out of Napoli, you marry someone famous...*'

Owen and Linh laughed. Despite their exposure on television, not a single person had so far come up to them. Everyone was too hung-over from the previous night.

The trio drove on to Pompeii. It was too late to visit the museum, so they had a gelato at a café on the via Lepanto. Then, with a golden sun hanging low over the sea, they did the winding coastal circuit from Salerno to Sorrento. At dusk, they were back at Adelina's flat after having walked from the hotel. Owen was conscious of limiting any obvious connection to the two women. He waited inside the doorway for ten minutes and scanned the street while Marlene took

Linh inside to be introduced to her auntie. Adelina had returned early from a rehearsal so that the four of them could have Marlene's special examination dish for dinner.

They talked endlessly about the meaning of the light show. Everyone had seen it. The rooftops had been jammed with humanity. Linh enquired about how other groups had dealt with the mysterious blue light—had anyone seen anything quite as debauched as what she and Owen had?

The two hosts were shocked.

'The film festival attendees?' Adelina burst out laughing, '... who'd have thought? They all look so formal and serious.' She stroked Owen's shoulder. 'But, you two have all the integrity in the world... no skinny-dipping for you.'

The little, private look between Owen and Linh was all it took.

'*You didn't!*' Adelina put her hands to her mouth.

'We had to, Adelina!' Owen spread his hands in protest, '... otherwise we would have been killed!'

Linh hid her face in her hands and shook with laughter.

Adelina guffawed. 'You had to get it all off, or you would have been killed? By whom?'

Owen rolled his eyes. 'I don't know... about half a dozen gunmen. They were everywhere.'

Marlene's eyes were as big as pizzas. 'Gunmen! Why?'

With a smile of capitulation, Owen waved away the question. 'Ah... look, we can barely believe it ourselves. In the short time since I left you to go on that boat, I have been shot at, beaten up...'

'By a woman!'

'... yes, thank you, Linh... fought for my life... been terrorized...'

'By another woman!'

'... indeed, but in each case, I was severely disadvantaged...'

'... because he's such a gentleman.' Linh reached forward and hugged him.

'Be that as it may, there were times when I acquitted myself quite admirably...'

Linh looked suddenly serious. 'He did.' Then she squealed with laughter, '... but he can't remember it!'

Owen's face took on a woebegone look. He stared at the ceiling. The other two women clasped at their faces with anticipation.

'What happened?'

There was a moment of silence. Linh quickly composed herself and held tightly to Owen's hand.

She looked at his face. 'Owen had to shoot one of the gunmen,' she replied softly.

Their two hosts, in unison, inhaled sharply.

It was very quiet. Somewhere in the distance, church bells chimed. Most people had gone to bed early.

Linh shifted right up against her man and hugged him around the shoulders. She looked at the women opposite. 'We would be dead if Owie hadn't saved the day.'

Both women reached across and held Owen's hand.

Owen smiled broadly. 'I love this.' He squeezed their hands.

Marlene looked very concerned. 'Why can't you not remember, Owen?'

Linh saw the beginnings of a smile on his face. She recalled that odd smirk that had overtaken him when the gunman had them up against the wall—and how his arm had moved stealthily behind her—the gun pressing against her spine as he slid it around her waist to her side. She'd angled her elbow out just far enough for him the snuggle the weapon into position—and all the while, his head had been pitched slightly forward and his eyes had held a terrible focus.

Having been trained in the martial arts herself, Linh was scrutinizing the gunman for the tiniest lapse in concentration. When the distraction occurred, and he looked down the hallway, Owen had fired before she had properly registered the moment. Somehow, he had tuned into the scene with such amazing intensity that he had been able to capitalize on that fraction of a second when the gunman was vulnerable. Five rounds—in lightning succession. Two to the body and three to the head. What extraordinary abilities had he tapped into— that made him leer like a killer.

Linh abruptly put her fingers to Owen's mouth and cried out, 'Don't Owie!... don't. Don't try to remember... please, don't try to remember... oh, my darling... darling...' She cradled his head and kissed his face, her tears streaming onto his cheeks.

Owen's head turned to one side. His arms came up, as though to fend off something. He slid sideways. Linh wasn't well positioned to stop him from toppling off his chair and the two of them crashed to the floor.

They made Owen comfortable on Marlene's bed. Linh could barely keep it together. She needed sleep so badly herself. She was shivering uncontrollably. Adelina wrapped a soft rug around her and hugged her as they sat on the couch. Marlene made a honey chai that restored some of the balance to Linh's body.

The next morning, Owen felt marvellous. He was surprised not to see Linh beside him and wondered whose bed he had commandeered. He let himself out of the room and found Adelina asleep on the couch and Marlene curled up in an armchair. Sunlight was just starting to light the walls of nearby buildings. He peeked into the other bedroom. Linh was asleep on her tummy as was customary. That was good—because it meant she would be well rested.

Their flight was leaving around mid-day. The four of them would be able to have a lovely breakfast—maybe order something in. He didn't want to venture out from the house.

He found a sunny spot on the balcony, pulled up a chair and put his feet up on the railing. Life for the two of them was going to go back to a sensible pace. That was a good thing... wasn't it? He and Linh had barely had a moment to digest the incredible journey they had just undertaken—a few moments on Gina's bed in the stateroom before sleep overtook them...

... oh, no, that's right, Linh had wanted to... that girl is amazing... such strength of mind. How would she ever have known what she was capable of if she was still a waitress?...

There'd been a few private moments to reflect on things as they took the Zodiac into the heart of Venice.

... mostly I was almost sick with worry and nerves...

They hadn't had the opportunity yet to debrief. Everything was still up in the air.

... who were those killers, anyway?...

Had they successfully completed their mission? Neither of them had any issues with the content of the speech.

... what things have been put in place to create sustainable communities?...

Were the last two years all that he and his future wife would ever talk about? Just like war veterans, always harking back to those vital few years where life hung in the balance.

... got a suspicion that we haven't seen the end of these mysterious missions...

Would they be living in suspense the whole time? Never knowing when they might be summoned... never knowing if they were a target.

... trouble is, there's nowhere on earth where they can't find you... even Yappar River...

Owen stared unfocused at the intensifying morning light on a nearby building. Soft lips kissed the back of his neck.

'Did you come in to check on me?'

'Yeah... I did.' Owen massaged Linh's calf with his trailing hand.

Linh came around and sat astride Owen's lap. She nuzzled her nose against his brow. 'Do you think we've been followed? Are the girls in any danger?'

'The girls will be fine. But I'm certain we've been followed.'

'By who?... whom?'

'Eamon's crowd.'

'How do you know?'

'Literally, a flying bug... about the size of a cicada. I first saw it when we climbed Vesuvio. I was looking out for something like that, and sure enough, it was hovering around in the distance. I figured it must have its home in the car and, when we fuelled up, I pretended I couldn't find the filler cap. It has a little home in the rear bumper panel—looks like a sensor insert, but it's a tiny door. That's where it gets charged. It followed us here and it's probably doing guard duty out the front of the building.'

Linh stroked Owen's chest. 'Aww, how cute...'

'Yeah, real cute. But, at least we know the girls will be safe.'

The sound of distant voices signalled the waking community.

'Owie... I'm really glad that you met Marlene and Adelina. They're lovely people and they must have restored your composure just at that time when you were about to embark on a dangerous mission so far from home.'

Owen closed his eyes and recalled Marlene's wild laughter at the end of their scooter trip. He raised his chin. 'You have no idea...' He kissed Linh's mouth.

Chapter Thirty-Seven

The arrival at Tullamarine was early. It was a typical windy and overcast winter's morning in Melbourne and, at that hour, people hurried to get inside anything—taxis, trains, foyers.

After twenty-plus hours of first-class travel, the two lovers were *still* jet-lagged and felt so utterly dissipated that they resorted to claiming the advantages to which they had access—they summoned for a chauffeur.

Brenden was befittingly servile and made no attempt at familiarity. He was even prepared to retrieve baggage from the carousel except that there was none. Linh and Owen possessed nothing more than the clothes they were wearing. Brenden wholly understood Owen's wish to be taken to David Jones so that they could outfit themselves with new clothes. Their hotel was a few blocks away, but they wanted to get the shopping and a restorative cup of coffee out of the way before they collapsed onto a bed. The car would be at their disposal for as long as they needed.

At about mid-day, they both roused from their slumber and reached out to each other.

Something had changed. They were back in their home country, but both of them were aware of the shift in the order of things. They had taken advantage of the means that would always be available to them if they wanted it.

Linh spoke first. 'It won't be long, Owie, before your motor design becomes commercialized. And even if it takes ages, we'll still manage.

I'm sure I can get better paid work than waitressing—not that I mind waitressing for however long I need to. And you'll be able to get work. We don't need this...' she cast her gaze about the luxurious apartment.

Owen squeezed her hand and gave a reassuring nod. 'I know.'

It was too easy to remain dependent on the limitless reserves of the conspirators... and to be at their beck and call. Just this once though, they deserved a bit of pampering.

'We'll let Brenden go,' Owen began, '... as soon as we work out why we're here.'

Linh nodded. She took some big breaths and sat up.

'What's wrong, Tot?' Owen stroked her back.

With a sudden gasp, Linh shot off the bed and into the bathroom.

Owen's face remained impassive. He propped himself against some pillows and listened as Linh vomited noisily into the basin.

After a few more spasms, Linh's worried face appeared at the doorway. 'Owie... have they poisoned us?' she said with a towel to her lips.

Owen nestled deeper into the pillows and said with a doubtful pout, 'You, maybe... but I'm okay.'

With a stricken face, Linh moved towards the bed. 'Owie...?'

Owen moved across a little and patted the sheet beside him.

Linh's eyes were full of fear and confusion.

'Sit down here, baby.'

Linh hesitantly went to the bed and sat down.

Owen placed her head on his chest and hugged her near. 'Hey... hey...' He kissed her hair. 'When was the last time you had a period?'

'Oh, Owie...' She flung her arms around his neck and sobbed against his shoulder.

They stayed in their room until late afternoon. Owen tried to make Linh as comfortable as possible, but there wasn't much that he could do. She didn't want to drink anything and preferred sitting upright in a chair.

Then, as suddenly as it had appeared, the nausea went away.

'I feel fine now, Owie... hungry.' She cast him a sidelong glance. 'How come you knew what it was?'

Owen grinned. 'I'd thought about it on and off throughout our adventures. We've had some wonderful opportunities...'

Linh rose from her chair and went to him. 'Nothing like the element of danger to get a girl pregnant, hey.' She sat on his knee. 'But, why am I sick now? It's not morning.'

'It is in Italy, sweetie.'

They laughed.

Linh searched the ceiling. 'When do you suppose...'

Owen's eyes twinkled. '... on Gina's bed?'

'Not enough time to get this far... must be back...'

'... at Alasdair's canyon hide-away!'

'Or in the camper.'

Owen hugged his girl. 'I hope so, Linh—it is so Australian to get your woman knocked up in the back of a van.'

She slapped his shoulder. 'C'mon then, let's get something to eat.'

'Eating for two, suddenly, are we?'

Owen received another hearty slap.

'Where shall we go then?' Owen rubbed Linh's belly. 'What shall we do?'

Linh reached for the phone and began a search. 'Oh, this looks interesting,' she said, and leant across for Owen to see.

'Dinner and a movie... okay, I'm in.'

Linh stared out of the window. Her smile altered and became strangely serene. She turned to Owen. 'I know why we're here...'

'Great! Because I have no idea whatsoever.'

'This theatre café is in Brunswick... does that ring a bell?'

Owen's eyes roved the room. 'Noo... but then, I don't know Melbourne at all.'

Linh's gaze bored into her lover's eyes. 'You met someone, quite recently, who came from that part of town.'

'Oh, yeah... Francesca. Her parents had the playhouse or something.'

Linh put her hand to her mouth. Her brow worked with emotion. 'We owe it to her... we should check to see that her parents are okay.'

Owen nodded. 'Yeah, let's do that.'

Brenden picked them up from outside the hotel. The two of them

411

settled into the back seat as the Audi moved off. Owen was about to announce their destination when Brenden interrupted.

'If I may make a suggestion, Mr Lucas. If you're going out for a nice meal, and you're looking for some entertainment, may I suggest a little theatre place in Brunswick that shows short films.'

Owen glanced at Linh.

She showed genuine delight. 'Oh, yes, darling... let's do that. It'll be fun.'

'Yes, okay, suits me.'

Brenden allowed the tiniest smile to grace his lips.

'By the way, Brenden, we won't be needing the car after this. Thank you very much for your service though.'

They were let out on Albion Street and watched the Audi drive away.

'So,' Linh nodded thoughtfully, '... we were destined to be here even if we hadn't accidentally discovered this place ourselves.'

'So it seems... but why?'

Linh took Owen's hand. 'I think I know why, Owie. Come on.'

They walked the short distance to the theatre entrance with its façade of glass doors. Once inside, the foyer led into the main auditorium which had a level floor and a very high ceiling made to look like the night sky with shadowy, moonlit clouds and hints of stars. The walls had large openings that led outside which produced the effect of creating a vast space. Interspersed were tables, each with a plasma screen, but positioned in such a way that the occupants lounging in easy chairs at one table would not be irritated by any screen nearby.

They were shown to a double settee in front of a low table.

The waitress pulled up a menu on the screen. 'The control is on the armrest. I'll be back shortly.'

Once they'd ordered and paid for their meal online, they looked through the selection of films. These were all short or shortish films made by amateurs using the vast array of technology that has become so easily available. There were the various genres of fiction as well as documentaries and animations, all made on limited budgets and relying heavily on good storytelling.

'Nothing mainstream here,' Owen mused. 'What do you feel like watching?' He looked up.

Linh surreptitiously scanned the darkened venue.

'Tot? What's wrong?'

Reaching across with her foot, Linh rubbed Owen's leg. 'I feel fairly certain that we're going to have a visitor to our table.'

With a resigned groan, Owen sat up straight. 'Not another mission... I want to go home.'

'No, not another mission.'

The waitress arrived with their meals. 'Here you are... two Thai Laksa. Is this your first time here?' She had that bouncy, familiar tone that has become universal in the service industry and, even in the subdued lighting, it was obvious that she had adopted the dissolute Gothic modishness that invariably goes with it.

'Huh? Oh, yeah... sorry. Never been to Melbourne before.'

'Well, you're off to a good start. This place is becoming the cultural centre of the country... y'know, where people can digest, not just good food, but the latest in thinking... docos an' stuff—so we cover art, writing, politics, science... the whole shebang. And then there are short films, if you just want something lighter—and that can be insightful too, y'know—allegorical...'

Owen nodded politely as he sipped from his spoon. 'Tell me, is this establishment owned by an elderly couple who have owned the place since way back?'

The waitress threw up her arms in a shrug. 'Don't know. There's the eccentric couple that are always out and about and come here a lot, but I don't know if they own it.' She turned on her heels and called back. 'I'll get your film started.'

Owen nodded in reply.

Linh delved into her noodles with chopsticks. 'See!'

'What?'

'About the visitor...'

'She's the waitress...'

'I know that... and she's also organising our film for us... that we hadn't yet decided on...'

'Oh, right.'

The screen glowed into life. The image was of the inside of a room looking towards a dormer window.

Linh shifted closer to Owen. She gripped his arm.

The screen blurred as someone came and sat in front of the camera. It was obviously a laptop.

The face resolved into focus. It was Francesca. 'Hello, you two,' she said with a mischievous smirk, '... I've been wanting to talk to you for such a long time. I'm so glad to be able to now... and I'm so sorry to have caused you such grief. I had no choice—I needed to die in order to protect you. It's complicated. How are you both?'

Owen didn't know what to think. He felt slightly displaced. 'Is that the room with the dormer that you had when you were a child, Francesca?'

'Yes, Owen. You're an attentive listener.'

'Hello, Francesca,' Linh said softly, '... you look well.'

'Particularly for a dead person,' she laughed. 'Well, haven't you both totally made a career out of the conspiracy industry. I couldn't believe what I was seeing on my screen. You have completely eclipsed anything I ever achieved.'

Owen replied with an edge of bitterness. 'I don't think so, Francesca... we're still in the dark except that now we're public figures. You, on the other hand, are doing what you love in complete anonymity.'

Francesca gave an exaggerated pout. 'Ooh, Owen... I know how you must be feeling. Both of you must be utterly exhausted. Look, why don't you have your laksa, and then you can come up to my room. How does that sound?'

Linh drew Owen closer. 'We'd love to, Francesca.'

'Oh, good. I'll see you soon, then.'

The screen went dark.

Owen nuzzled Linh's hair. 'You knew?'

She nodded. 'I remembered what you had told me about her life and how she supported her parents... even though they weren't aware of it... and, when I saw the advertisement for this place, I suddenly realised what a perfect hide this would be for her. Then, when the driver recommended it, I just knew she was here. She and Gina must have some contact still.'

The laksa was heavenly, and Linh ate with obvious pleasure and hunger.

Owen couldn't help but smile. He kissed her neck. He was going to enjoy every moment of the making of their baby.

The waitress approached them as they dabbed their mouths with a napkin. 'Follow me,' she said, '... but you will have to leave your phones on the table. It's okay, it's safe.'

'Only have one phone.' Owen put it down.

They followed her through the simulated moonlight, past other table settings where people were lounging comfortably as they viewed their film. At the back of the auditorium was a screened opening that led to a narrow staircase. The waitress indicated that they should ascend.

There was barely enough light to see the treads and, at one instant, Owen felt enough suspicion to turn around.

The waitress had gone.

Linh knocked on the door. Francesca opened it and immediately took Linh in a heartfelt embrace.

Then it was Owen's turn. He smelled Francesca's spicy perfume and held her body close. He wondered whether she had a lover.

... she's so undeniably sensuous...she shouldn't be stuck in an attic ...

'What are you thinking, Owen? Are you worried about me?'

They separated. Francesca led Owen by the hand to the dormer window. It looked out onto the brick façade of a warehouse. 'Is this how you pictured my bedroom when I told you my story?'

On the dimly lit roadway below, a truck backed up to a delivery dock. The clinking of chain could be faintly heard as the industrial roller door was raised.

'Yep, this is exactly as I imagined your home to be.'

Owen hugged Francesca around the waist and looked down at the single bed, neatly made, against the wall. Above it was a faded poster promoting the Australian tour of the Bolshoi Ballet in 1989. The floor had the finest film of dust that reflected the light from the single hanging bulb. Owen turned to look at the door. He could just make out the faint track that the three of them had made whilst in the room. He dipped his head and kissed her hair. 'Go on then, Francesca... surprise me. Where have you invested all your money?'

She laughed and turned to Linh. 'He's become a regular spy, he has!' She moved to a wall unit and opened the doors. Inside were clothes on hangers. She turned to her guests with a knowing look and reached inside. The whole wardrobe began to move forward, towards them. At about a metre space between it and the wall, the wardrobe stopped. Francesca beckoned them and disappeared behind the unit. Linh and Owen followed.

Francesca faced them in a lift. She smiled broadly. 'Exciting, huh? I put this in place quite some time ago just in case I ever needed to bunker down.'

The three of them were a close fit. Francesca operated the doors.

Owen squeezed up and held the two women close. 'I love my job as a spy.'

Linh kept her arms by her side. 'Well, just remember that you've knocked up one of the Bond girls and that it won't be just your martinis that'll be shaken and not stirred from here on.'

Francesca let go a piercing squeal and, in the constrictions of the tiny lift, the two women bounced and hugged each other while Owen kept a staunch face above them.

... how long was that?... less than three minutes?... and I'm on the outer in a space where I can't help but feel every part of their bodies...

The lift jerked to a stop. Francesca hugged Owen and reached up and kissed his chin. 'Congratulations, Owen. That is such wonderful news. I'm going to be an auntie at last!'

Owen couldn't help smiling as the three of them disgorged from the lift.

They were in a very narrow tunnel. There was room only to walk single file.

Francesca led the way. 'Do you know where we're headed, Owen?'

'Yep, across to the warehouse.'

'Well done. You do have an excellent sense of spatial orientation.'

... yeah, pity about my sense of social orientation...

The tunnel was dimly lit by movement sensitive LEDs.

'How far below the surface are we here, Francesca?'

'Far enough to avoid the sewer, water, electricals. Naturally, I had to kill all the workmen involved—they're entombed nearby.'

'Naturally...'

They came to another lift.

'I had thought about a ladder and even a fireman's pole but, the actual height is about twenty metres and if I fell or needed to use this if I was injured... y'know... awkward.'

Again, they had to squeeze into the lift.

'Any more news you'd like to tell me, Owen?'

'Only that I have a flatulence condition when I become claustrophobic.'

Two sets of arms reached their way around him.

... curiouser and curiouser...

The lift exited into an enormous space—a home. The industrial heritage of the building was obvious—massive exposed wooden rafters and metre thick brick walls with floor to ceiling double-hung windows imparted a sense of permanence. The view was to the south, where the jagged horizon of the city could be made out in the ambient glow.

There were no interior walls at all—even the plant shrouded bathroom was a vast expanse of stonework and limestone tiles completely in the open.

'The plants get watered when I shower—it actually rains. There's a warm section just by the boulder. I want the two of you to experience it before you go... no point in having an indulgence if no one knows about it.'

Artworks, sculptures, multi-media hangings and geometric constructions interlaced to create pathways and living spaces that flowed into each other.

Francesca gave some hushed verbal commands. Indirect lighting in the high ceiling changed from white to non-ultra-violet. The greenery became almost iridescent and every hue deepened. The effect reproduced the moments before a sunset.

Owen and Linh stood mesmerized.

'Go on, go for a walk... look around.'

Owen moved towards what he thought might be the kitchen. 'Got any beers in your fridge?'

Francesca laughed. 'I haven't actually. I don't drink beer. The fact is,

I don't need to cook and eat here—I just walk across the road. I only sleep here.'

Linh perused the surrounds of the little rainforest. 'Oh, so, it's not a secret then... that you live here?'

'No... not a secret. But it's not me that lives here—it's Penelope Fairchild... mysterious heiress to a fortune who comes and goes with no one to account to, and who is such a regular face in this locality that everyone assumes someone else must know her life story.'

Linh turned to her. 'Ohh, Francesca...'

'Hey, it's better than dead.' She walked to a place in the diagonal corner. 'Come on, I want you to see something.'

The trio exited the space through a door that led out onto a steel mesh walkway above the old warehouse floor below. They descended the steel steps and came to rest on a smooth concrete floor.

In front of them, lit from above, was a city. They walked out onto the roadway and made their way to a corner shop. In the display window was kitchenware for sale—fry pans, tea pots, cutlery sets, tea towels and more.

Linh put out her hand and felt the roughness of the paint. It was all a façade—the items, the shop window, the shop—the entire streetscape was a veneer. The buildings on either side of the narrow roadway were painted onto thin ply and, in some cases, just cardboard. As they strolled through the miniature town, they came to a sidewalk café with just two small, round tables on the footpath. The door into the shop was ajar. Linh pushed the door open and peered through. She beckoned Owen. Inside was a commercial kitchen whose normal proportions looked suddenly out of place.

Francesca indicated that they should enter.

There were blenders and baskets of fruit, hotplates and an oven with pots and pans hanging overhead, drinks fridges and cakes inside cooled display shelves. Crockery and utensils lay in the drying racks.

Francesca opened another door.

They exited the front of another café on a different street with different footpath furniture. On the other side of the street were tall buildings that tapered at the top so as to emphasise the illusion of height. Parked in front of one of the buildings was a small car. Owen examined it closely. It was a pedal car built to fit a small child. He lifted it up and spun the pedals. Both rear wheels turned.

'Hey, wow... it's got a diff!'

Linh came up and had a turn of the pedals. 'Owie, this whole place is made for kids.'

'Are you creating a theme park, Francesca?'

'Sort of—it's actually more than just a commercial recreational site. What we're doing here is creating an interactive world for modern kids. It mirrors the adult world, just at the child level. It's going to be a new place of learning.'

Owen noticed that there was a building site nearby with miniature frontend loaders and forklifts parked against a wall. He went over for a closer look. The mechanicals worked either off the pedal crank or by progressive ratcheting of a handle. He toyed with the mechanisms and marvelled at both the simplicity of the design and the efficiency of their operation. 'So, these components are all relatively simple to make, by the looks of it.'

Francesca stood nearby. The contentment in her eyes surprised Owen.

'The whole idea is that teenagers can build the equipment—cut out the panels and frames using jigs and templates—assemble all the componentry using cordless technology. The city,' she waved her arm to encompass their surroundings, 'is made from simple panels that younger children can have a hand in making, and just about every kid that comes here after school wants to have a go at painting a building. So, what we're doing is bringing in all the age groups and building an instructive world for little kids... and at the same time providing opportunities for older children to gain construction and design skills.'

Owen rose from the backhoe that he was inspecting. What he was hearing was not at all what he expected from Francesca.

Linh walked over and stood next to him. 'Francesca... what's going on?'

Francesca made big-eyes at them. 'Nothing!... can't a girl have a hobby?'

Owen frowned. 'The totally radical apartment,' he pointed upwards, 'I can understand. It's excessive, indulgent... it's you. But this...

building glorified cubby houses for kids... I'm... completely surprised. Since when did you care this much for the community?'

Francesca folded her hands in front of her. 'Since I fell in love.'

Now it was Linh's turn to squeal. She rushed over and madly hugged the soon-to-be auntie.

Owen rolled his eyes. 'Jesus...'

When the girls settled down, Owen gave Francesca a warm hug. 'Nice one, girl. It *is* a man you're in love with, hey? It's only that I do recall you saying that you appreciate a little bit of animal... or beast... or something.'

'You don't forget much do you, Owen. No, he's a gentle man... quite a bit older than me... separated with a grown family. He lives just up the road... runs a mechanical workshop... not my type at all... and yet, I love him so much.'

'How did you meet?' Linh gave an involuntary jump.

'Out on the footpath. I was going for a walk early one morning. He was putting out his bin. Two young louts bailed him up and threatened to come back and trash his house if he didn't give them some cash. Roy—that's his name—didn't seem to be in need of help, but I just knew these kids were up to no good. So, I moved in. I always carry a piece,' she put her hand behind her back and when it reappeared there was a small pistol in it, 'and I threatened to riddle their bums if they didn't shove off.'

'Blowing your cover a bit?' Owen interjected.

'Maybe. Anyhow, Roy stood up for them. Waved me aside and invited the two of them to come back with their crap cars so that he could show them how to fix them. They said that they didn't own even a crap car, so Roy said he did, and that they should come back and sort something out. I hung around because I was curious. When we were alone, he asked me in for a cup of tea.'

Linh smiled and took hold of Francesca's hand.

'That's when I started to see what could be done to change things. I just joined the dots—Roy's vision of a place of relevance for kids and my money.

'Not many dots.' Owen smirked.

'That's just the thing, it's really very obvious except that our society is too conceited to accept any change.'

'So, Roy is the brains behind all of this?' Linh pointed with her chin at a ply façade.

Francesca nodded at the tractor beside Owen. 'Roy is the mechanical genius. I came up with the idea of a replicate world housed in an abandoned warehouse where many of the physical challenges of everyday life can be duplicated and shaped to fit the abilities of children.'

Linh put her fingers to her chin. 'That is so awesome, Francesca. So, little kids are given tasks that they can manage?'

'Not straight away. Kids are kids. They just want to play. They come here and all they want to do is pedal their car around the city. We have "the countryside" just over yonder,' Francesca indicated with a wave, '... in the old carpark outside, where there are sheep grazing on chaff and fields of corn growing in brick beds... all made by the older ones. But, eventually, little kids see what the bigger kids are doing and they want to do the same. That's when you can motivate them. They get their truck licence so they can carry real loads—like compost or building materials. Then they graduate to tractor licences—forklifts and such—initially very simple jobs, supervised by suitably trained older children. It's a work in progress, but the best thing is that we have a fabulous resource to help us achieve things... big people! You wouldn't believe how many adults want to be part of this in some way. They can see how this is helping their children.'

'But, aren't volunteers a bit problematic?' Owen asked cautiously, '... you know... well-intentioned, but can get in the way...'

'Oh, my god, yes,' Francesca waved both hands in a dismissive gesture, '... it can become problematical—but we invite them to try out to be trainers, and if the kids, big and little, like the courses that they're offering, well, then they've got regular work. If the kids choose not to elect their courses, well... too bad. Interestingly, we find that children are choosing courses held by just ordinary people with an obvious passion for their subject—be it in metal work or botany or whatever—over trained teachers. I mean, that's one of the fundamental conceits of our system—that we believe we can train teachers to be inspirational. It rarely happens. *Inspired* people are inspirational, and then only to the receptive student. What we focus on is the interests of the children—they make the choices. They know it's their future—they don't want to waste time. They choose trainers and courses that will prepare them. That usually takes care of a lot of weeding. We do use trained teachers as facilitators, y'know... helping with getting courses into the best instructional shape.'

'But,' Owen mused with a finger to his lips, '... you can only do so many jobs driving a vehicle of some sort. When do they graduate to the not-so-fun challenges of life?'

'Natural growth, Owen... a combination of peer aspirations, inspiring opportunities and an inherent desire to develop what's inside. We don't know what we're wasting in the one-size-fits-all system that we have at present. If we were really smart... *really* smart, we would tap into the unknown instead of imposing the ordinary.'

Linh sat down on a nearby café stool. 'So, there's a lot more going on here than just kids racing around in pedal cars.'

'Very much so. It's early days still, but behind these façades, there are real projects going on. For instance, in the building behind you, a young woman has set up a facility researching the fabrication of everything from bricks to bowls and artificial leather using mycelium biology, or fungus technology, as it's popularly known. The kids love it. They're watching the growth of spores and fibres through stereo microscopes. They're learning so much incidental stuff, like data logging, chemistry, fabrication... and it's all totally relevant to them. And, the best thing is that all the kids here find somewhere, something, somebody that makes them feel good about themselves. We're fostering direction and fulfilment. Once a child has that, creating a well-adjusted adult is easy.'

Owen and Linh had so much to think about, they were speechless.

Francesca came and sat next to Linh. 'Roy's been thinking about something like this for years and years... but he had no way of realising his dream. When I listened to him, somehow it all fell into place for me... how to structure the whole thing...'

'... and how to finance it,' Owen interrupted.

'Well, that was easy... with my own money. But the funny thing was that, as we were going about the applications for this project, I sensed that there were greater forces at work making it easy for us. I should know. I mean, getting permits to use an old warehouse for a school—that could take years. But no... no objections, all hurdles conveniently pulled out of the way... go ahead... make it happen...'

'The work of conspirators?'

'Without a doubt.'

Linh leant forward. 'We were told that things had been put in place to make the changes necessary to improve society.'

'Yeah?... well, that's interesting, because I've just been dealing with an "entity" that wants to do just what we're doing here and is prepared to pay us big money to ensure that our model can be replicated elsewhere around the globe.'

'Which it would be,' Owen offered, '... because the designs and management and what have you are all easily copied and will work just as well here as in any other city.'

'Very true, Owen. It stands to reason that change should begin with the young... and in such a way that the parents' generation will be supportive. Maybe I've finally made a positive contribution to the world.'

Linh reached out and took Francesca's hand. 'You and Roy are in the process of making a monumental change to the way we live. You will be able to instil notions of sustainability and community that are impossible for older generations to adopt. It all begins here... in microcosm.'

Owen nodded his support. 'Yeah, it's the most obvious way of going about it really... creating a child-size world. I noticed the theodolite over there... or a rudimentary version. So, the older kids are doing surveying and using trigonometry? Brilliant.'

'That's correct. And the kids are running the cafes, making things for the gift shops, repairing appliances, growing crops, putting on musicals... we have a stage just around the corner... it all depends upon who comes to us and what skills they have to offer. The default work for the older kids is making the vehicles and building the set. It's very structured, and they like that.'

Linh shook her head in wonderment. 'You've achieved a massive amount in a short time, Francesca.'

'Well, now that you've alerted me, I do think I'm getting a lot of support. Still, it shows you what can be done if we want to make it happen and the bureaucracy is on your side.'

Chapter Thirty-Eight

Three days later, a cream coloured campervan made its way through the streets of Orbost and headed north along the Bonang road towards the Snowy Mountains. The few cars and trucks that occasionally crept up from behind found it easy enough to pass because the van was motoring at a very leisurely pace.

At the wheel, Owen looked across.

Linh had the seat back as far as it would go and was resting with a pillow against the door frame. The morning sickness, whilst never prolonged, did take its toll on her.

He recalled the night after their incredible meeting with Francesca when they staggered into bed.

'Let's not fly back.' Linh had her head cradled in the crook of his arm. 'I don't want our adventure to end... maybe we can stretch it out if we get a camper.'

He'd stroked his girl's forehead. 'You won't feel uncomfortable with the morning sickness?'

'No... just open the sliding door and blah!...'

'Lovely. Not staying anywhere for more than one night, then.'

'I want to see Mum and Dad, but I want to wind down too... talk about everything... somewhere peaceful and quiet... around a campfire.'

'I'm with you there, Tot.'

They decided to hide themselves.

'This credit card is obviously a dead give-away.' Owen flicked it onto the bed the next morning. 'But, I'm inclined to take advantage of it one more time.'

'How?'

'Auction.'

'... auction?'

'Yep. We buy a camper—a really expensive one—at the auction, which is on today,' Owen showed Linh the website on the phone, '... and we resell it straight away to one of the other bidders for five grand less. With the cash, we can buy a private van, which I have also sourced while you were in the bathroom calling for Ralph in the toilet,' he showed her the ad on Gumtree, '... and, we'll have enough money left over not to have to use the card.'

Linh was convulsing with laughter. 'Where on earth did that come from, Owie. I've never heard that expression before.'

'No, well, that's because you live in a cultured environment and you've been denied the richness of the full, Australian... whatever...'

'Oh, Owie... you're so full of surprises.' She hugged him close. 'I forget that our school experiences were so different.'

'I'd say that expression has been around for centuries, but it was made popular in an Australian film from the late sixties, I think it was. Anyhoo, *we* will be flying below the radar, and the other camper will probably be tracked from outer space until somebody questions why it's been parked on a suburban kerb for the past two weeks.'

'Very clever, Owen. I can't wait to be on the road in our new camper.'

The few farms outside Orbost soon gave way to endless tracts of forest. The road became more and more winding as the campervan gained altitude.

Even though it was still early, Owen was on the lookout for any interesting side roads that might lead to a creek and a pleasant spot to camp. They'd made further calls to reassure their parents that the return trip was going to take a while. Happily, everyone was good with that. As Linh had suggested, a few days on the road would be just the time they needed to debrief—and to fully embrace the prospect of impending parenthood.

Owen felt a sudden surge of emotion at the thought that his beautiful girl was going to bring a new life into their world. His perception of

Linh had been under constant change ever since she had been thrust into his arms by the track-suited thug at New Farm Park. She had shown so much character and resourcefulness—and now she was going to be a mother.

A car drew up to pass. Owen collected himself and moved over a fraction to give the other driver a better view of the road ahead. He recognized the old XC Ford from when they refuelled in Orbost. It pulled out and overtook.

Owen thought about his room in the loft. Would they be able to stay there with a baby? Well, of course they could! The thing was, *should* they stay there with a baby. It would be wonderful for his parents, but it could become hurtful for Linh's parents. No, they'd have to find a place of their own. That would be exciting... house hunting. He suddenly remembered a ramshackle old house in Dutton Park that had been up for sale for a while before they'd left on their mission. It was circa 1930's and completely original, down to the bathroom and kitchen fittings, but just woefully neglected. What a project! And not too close to the relatives.

A road sign ahead indicated a logging track that seemed to go down to a nearby valley.

... excellent... bound to come across a nice little creek...

He slowed and turned into the dirt track. Immediately, it became enclosed by shrubs and trees on either side. The twin ruts obviously didn't see a lot of traffic, and the going was smooth and winding. The trail descended steadily. Owen could see that the bottom of the gentle valley was not far away. Not being in a four-wheel-drive, he was mindful of being able to turn around should the track deteriorate.

'Hey, Owie... have you found another candidate for your *Best Bush Tracks of Australia* book?'

'I hope so, sweetie... it's looking good so far.'

After about a kilometre, there was a shallow creek crossing, and a clearing to one side.

'Perfect.' Owen steered onto the clearing. 'It doesn't get any better than this.'

'It's beautiful.' Linh sighed.

The two of them sat motionless. They looked out over the expanse of rapids and listened to the collective gurgles of hundreds of eddies. The reflected sunlight dazzled in all directions and lit up the overhanging casuarinas. A kingfisher swooped from bough to bough.

Eventually, Owen spoke. 'So, what have we got to eat?'

Linh gave him a sorrowful look. 'Cucumbers… remember?'

'Oh, yeah… and some whole grain crackers and soft cheese and berries!'

'But, that is for me… because I'm special. You, on the other hand, have been eating too much pasta and you need an appetite suppressant—cucumbers. We spoke about this…'

They looked at each other and burst out laughing. Without his usual exercise regime, Owen had actually managed to put a bit of weight over his lanky frame, despite the privations of the first part of their mission.

'Come on then, starving boy. Let me make you something nice.'

The van came with a huge fridge which had inspired the couple to shop for supplies in a completely different way than Owen was used to. It also had permanent solar panels on the roof which looked a bit industrial and reduced the cruising speed by twenty kilometres per hour but kept the food nice and chilled. The retired couple who sold it to them were so elated at getting their advertised price without any haggling that they threw in chairs, table, annex and everything else necessary for a trek.

Now the chairs were opened up on the river bank.

Owen nibbled on a cracker. 'It's surreal, isn't it, Linh… our adventure. I hardly know what to make of it…'

Linh reached out for Owen's hand on the armrest. 'I know. The more I think about it, the more I realise what a deluded world we live in. But what is right?… is it this?—being here in this blessed place… that we'd have to leave as soon as we'd eaten all the food in the esky—or is it dodging detection by murderous agents while we do our bit to shore up the defences of some world dominating conspirator?'

Owen was silent for a while. 'At least we have a choice.'

'Yeah, but I don't know if that's a good thing. And, to be honest, I don't know that we have a choice anymore.'

Owen caressed Linh's hand. 'Hey… there is no doubt that we have an unusual destiny... and I would get all overwrought about it if it wasn't for one thing—you.'

The riffle of water over stones was a background noise most of the time but had the ability to come to the fore during breaks in the conversation.

Owen closed his eyes. The winter sun was already on its way down and there was enough chill in the breeze for him to feel snug in his chair.

The sound that made him stiffen with dread was almost subsonic. It was the sound of a car's suspension bottoming out in a pot hole. That, and an engine just above idle. There was a car approaching. He opened his eyes.

Linh was staring out across the creek. 'Hey, you... I thought...'

Owen held up his hand.

Linh stopped speaking. She followed his stare up the track.

It was too late to do anything. The old Ford swayed into view from behind a clump of casuarinas. It stopped and slowly rocked still. There were three occupants—men who continued to observe them after the engine had been switched off.

Owen gave a cheery wave.

There was no response from the car. It was the same one that had passed them earlier out on the main road.

... here's trouble. They must have pulled over and waited for us to pass. When we didn't, they doubled back and found this track... wonder what their game is...

'Be on guard here, Linh... these guys are up to no good.'

Three doors opened. The driver looked like the one in charge—goatee, wiry with piercing eyes. The front passenger, thickset, shaved head and pink, pulled a baseball bat from behind the backrest. The rear passenger was very pale and, despite his vacant look, conveyed a sense of malice.

Owen gestured again and raised his voice above the noise of the stream. 'Afternoon, men... looking for a good fishing spot?'

The thickset guy thought this was pretty funny. 'Yeah... yeah, you could say that.' He backhanded the bat lightly against the front tyre.

Goatee came forward a few paces. 'Saw you down at the servo...

fillin' up.'

Owen didn't leave his chair. He nodded and crossed his legs. 'Yeah, I remember... got my licence in an XC,' he lied.

'Did'ja... bet you don't drive one now...'

'No... no... moved on since then...'

'Yeah?... good for you. I noticed you paid with cash back there.'

'Well, I figured that seeing as how I was travelling in the backwoods, I'd better take something the locals would recognize.'

Goatee looked around. 'You got any other friends here, smartarse?'

'No. Just me and the girl. We're a touring circus act. She's a knife thrower.' Owen looked down at the vinyl picnic-set case. 'Show the boys what you do, love.'

Linh flexed her fingers and reached down.

The three visitors took steps back to the car.

Owen laughed. 'Just kidding, boys. We're completely defenceless.'

The pale, vacant one thrust out his chin. 'You think that's funny, mate... threatening us with a knife?'

'Sorry... bad joke. So, why are you blokes here? Not on your land, are we?'

'Nuh.'

'Oh, good. Wouldn't want to be doing anything illegal.' Owen took off a boot and emptied some imaginary grit.

The big guy with the bat sauntered over to the back of the van and swung at the tail-lights. Plastic crunched and scattered to the ground.

'You *are* doing something illegal... got a tail-light missing.'

Owen spread his hands. 'I can get another tail-light... but you're stuck with your brains.'

The bat came to the shoulder and he moved forward.

The driver called in a low tone. 'Watch it, Dooley... he might have a gun.'

Dooley stopped.

Owen held up his hands. 'I told you... we're completely defenceless. Come on up. Sorry we don't have more chairs.'

Dooley moved forward again. 'Just throw me your wallet, and I won't bash the livin' shit outa you.'

From five metres away, Owen could detect the manic flicker in his eyes.

... wired to the max...

Owen looked perplexed. 'Don't have a wallet... truly, I don't have a wallet. Sweetheart, that's what we forgot to buy at David Jones—a wallet. How stupid of us.'

Linh leant forward in her chair and fiddled with her shoe laces. 'We talked about that... you don't need a wallet, because I'm in control of all the money—I told you!' One foot was under her chair. She was shaped like a sprinter under starter's orders.

Owen shrugged helplessly. 'Yeah... she is...' He bent to put on his boot.

Dooley commenced another step.

Owen's boot flew through the air straight at Dooley's face. Owen lunged forward.

So did Linh.

Five metres is a lot of ground to cover in the heat of battle.

Dooley easily dodged the boot and had sufficient time to anticipate Owen's trajectory. But Linh's charge was a surprise. Should he swat her first? No. Hit the guy first, then take care of the chick.

Owen pulled up and straightened just out of swing range.

Smart bastard. The girl was still coming at him. Okay, the girl it is then. He unleashed at where her head would have been if she hadn't also suddenly pulled up. The blow went unconnected and spun his shoulders out of shape.

Owen lunged again.

Dooley was used to brawling—*okay, cop the butt end then, buddy*. He reefed his arms across with the handle aimed at Owen's face.

Owen knew he wasn't going to be able to land an incapacitating hit. First things first—he had to protect himself. Linh was going to have to hassle Dooley until he could get into a better position. He put his hands up to take the big guy's return swing. Their faces came centimetres apart. Dooley's scream was an unexpected and off-putting development. He was probably descended from some feral band of Celts who lived to fight. The return swing didn't eventuate and the screaming didn't abate. Owen had time to deliver a punch to the neck and was surprised at how quickly Dooley dropped. The bat fell from

431

his hands and he clutched, not at his neck, but at his knee. Through the tangle of limbs, Owen saw Linh's foot retract as she rolled out of the way.

Owen and Dooley collapsed in a pile just as the scream of pain faded in the big guy's throat.

With a sharp elbow to Dooley's nose, Owen scrambled up.

Linh was already standing with the bat in her hand.

'Watch out!' Owen caught a glimpse of the pale guy running at Linh. She didn't seem aware of what was happening. Then, she unexpectedly lofted the bat into the air when her assailant was about five metres away. It remained perfectly horizontal as it made an arc that would intersect perfectly in pale guy's path.

He saw his chance. His arms came up for an easy catch.

Linh exploded into a round-house kick.

The guy's focus was on the imminent catch—he didn't see the heel that rammed into his solar plexus. He probably didn't feel it either— the bat landed on his head, and he was out cold when he hit the ground.

Owen had never seen such a fluid whip-lash of human movement.

Linh stood poised above the guy, completely relaxed and looking into the mid-distance.

At the car, the driver was just in the act of pulling the keys out of the ignition.

Owen knew it was too late. 'Linh! Run, baby... go... go!'

But Linh didn't run. She walked back to Owen who met her halfway.

The driver had opened the boot.

The clearing wasn't that big—they could easily run into cover. The trouble was that the cover was so thick and, depending on what was coming out of the boot, being trapped in difficult terrain could prove fatal.

What came out of the boot was a double barrel shotgun. The driver pointed it towards them and took a few steps in their direction.

Owen held Linh by the shoulders. 'We can't run now, Tot... but it's okay... we're going to be okay.' He scanned the glistening water, then panned to the driver who was advancing with a methodical step, the shotgun firmly pointed in their direction.

Linh put her hand up to Owen's. 'This isn't looking good, Owie.'

He was just about to reply when the driver yelled at the still prostrate big guy.

'Get up, Dooley!'

But, all he could do was whimper, '… can't, Tex… my leg feels broken…'

The newly identified Tex knelt down beside their other comrade who still hadn't moved. 'Casper… get up.'

Casper remained inert with his eyes half open.

Dooley moaned. '… Tex, I seen these two… they were on telly…'

'What?'

'… they were on telly… that night… on Foxtel… when the fight just went off… and they came on… remember?'

Tex looked hard at them. 'You've copped a hit in the head, Dools… that was in Monaco, or some place.'

Owen slowly steered Linh towards the river.

'Where the hell are you going?' Tex looked up and readjusted the aim of the barrels.

'Just giving you some room, Tex… you'd better splash some water on him… bring him around… see if he's okay.'

Linh looked at Owen with alarm in her eyes. 'Oh, my god,' she pointed at Casper, '… he's got the death stare, darlin'… look, he's gonna die… do something, for god's sake… he's gonna die…'

Owen held his hands wide. 'I don't know the procedure, sweetheart… you're the nurse. Are you sure he's going to die?'

'He's got the death stare, I know it… oh, I can't look.' She buried her head in Owen's chest.

Tex leant over to look at Casper's face. 'What's she on about? What's wrong with him?'

'Don't ask me, mate. He just looks unconscious to me. He'll be alright… just give him a few minutes.'

Linh's head shook violently against Owen's chest. 'He'll be dead in a few minutes… he's got the death stare, darlin'… I seen it… I seen it heaps of times…'

'Well, I don't know sweetheart… you're the nurse… then help him, for god's sake.' He gently pulled her away from him and turned her around. 'Go on… we don't want anyone to die.' He gave her a little push.

Linh held her hands over her face as she shambled towards Tex and Casper. 'I can't do it by myself... I never saved anyone from the death stare by myself...'

She came so close to Tex—so close to those awkward, heavy barrels—before caution overrode Tex's concern for his offsider.

'Whoa there, lady... you're the one who put him there—don't want you doing the same to me. Go on then... fix him up... I'll cover you.'

Linh knelt down behind Casper's head. She gently cradled his neck—except that she dug her fingernails into his flesh.

Casper groaned.

Keeping separated from Owen was the preferred strategy. She could see him edging towards the stream. She knew he had something in mind and that he'd been about to tell her. She didn't know where to go from here.

Owen spoke softly.

Tex turned to him. 'What?'

'I said, listen to me very, very carefully, Tex.'

'Now why would I do that, feller?'

'I want you to point the gun down, and once it's down, please, please don't raise it again.'

'What if I don't want to?'

'Then you *will* die. Please, just point the gun away... it'll make a lot of difference to you, believe me.' Owen nodded earnestly.

To Linh, it was almost as though Owen was pleading with Tex from a position of command.

Confused about what was happening, and worried about having Linh behind him, Tex half turned. For a moment, the shotgun covered neither of them.

Tex's head dipped. The barrels dropped, and both discharged. The blast was deafening. The shot gouged a furrow in the dirt, and the recoil wrenched the weapon from Tex's limp hands. His knees buckled and he stretched his length face down on the ground.

Casper's eye's flashed open. Linh held his head down. He began to struggle. She brought her elbow down on his temple.

The only sound was the rush of the rapids.

Owen moved towards Linh. She got up. They gently embraced each

434

other.

Dooley groaned in pain.

Linh looked out into the stream. 'What's happening, Owie?'

Owen pointed to a spot upstream where there was a large black boulder. 'Watch.'

After some seconds, the boulder raised itself on spindly legs. Two vortices of spay appeared on either side and the black shape rose from the water. It hovered and moved towards the clearing, eventually settling in a spray of dust and leaf litter, ten metres from Owen and Linh.

Once again, Owen was surprised at just how big the drone was.

When the ducted rotors had wound down, Owen went to it and opened up the two hatches that had popped. He pulled out the tripods and set them up where the laser directed. When he turned, Linh was putting the camping chairs into position. He walked over to Tex's body and picked up the shotgun. Then he joined Linh.

She put her hand on Owen's. 'How come all this exciting stuff happens, and we hardly get time to draw breath, then something else pops up—literally.'

Owen eased himself out of the chair and knelt in front of Linh. He took both her hands and kissed them as they rested on her knee. 'Linh, I don't know what to say... except that you saved our lives... you saved my life.' He looked deeply into her eyes. 'You are wonderful... truly wonderful. Thank you...'

Linh's mouth crumpled. 'Thank you, Owie... you saved my life.' She looked to the sky as the tears welled in her eyes. 'I don't know what to say, either.' She leant forward and hugged his head to her belly.

They stayed like this for some time—feeling the heat of each other's exertions and smelling the sweat.

A polite cough emanated from the drone.

Owen took a deep breath and lifted his head. Casper was on his feet looking very wobbly. Dooley was still on the ground.

He turned around.

Alasdair was seated in what looked like a hovering chair. He waved. 'Hello, Owen... hello Linh.'

They returned their greeting.

'You could have done with me a bit sooner... but then I would have missed a textbook example of self-defence. Well done, you two.'

'Thanks. We had to play it by ear. I didn't think they were going to back off.'

'You're absolutely right there, Owen. That is in fact the reason why we are here.'

'Really?'

'You did a nice job of trying to elude us, but we had you back on the radar before you got back to the hostel with your new camper.'

'*Really?*'

'And then, when you got fuel in Orbost, our processors recognised that you were in very close proximity to some very bad company—that lot,' Alasdair pointed with his chin in the direction of Casper, who was now bending down to Tex. 'Based on intel we have on them, that not even the police have, we determined that you would be a likely target for their typical modus operandi. When their car followed yours, we scrambled the closest drone.'

Linh was obviously ready to say something. 'Do we have *any* privacy? How can you trace us so easily... and out here?'

Alasdair gave an emphatic nod. 'Yes, you do have total privacy—it's only that you two are extremely high on the list of priorities. We have a very densely networked data gathering ability—everything from stoplight cameras to dash cams on ordinary cars. That's how we figured you came down this track—you suddenly disappeared off the dash cams. And that's without even touching on transponders and stuff. Look, we don't observe you at all, okay? But we keep an eye on you—and just as well, because, Ricky—he's the drone operator—could not see how you were going to get past the shotgun level. Ricky's a gaming champion,' Alasdair rolled his eyes. 'He took a shot when he could... pretty safe bet with the pulse gun.'

Owen turned around. Tex was sitting up with his head on his knees. 'Oh, so he's *not* dead then.'

'No, no... the pulse is far more reliable. *Then*, if we really don't like him, we'll use a bullet.'

Linh's face wrinkled in disgust.

'Oh, come on, Linh... you're the one that disabled two of the three amigos.'

'I know... shooting just seems so... premeditated...'

'Linh... Owen... are you both okay? No injuries?'

They shook their head.

'Okay, great. Look, now that I'm in front of you, I may as well tell you a few things that you need to know... the shape of things to come... so that you can see how the big picture is unfolding. So, get comfy, and I'll begin.'

Owen harked back his head. 'What about those three?'

'Ricky will take care of them if they get naughty.'

Chapter Thirty-Nine

Owen ran his hand over the roundness of Linh's belly. 'No more round-house, Kung Fu kicks for you, young lady... although, the little one in there seems to have potential.'

They were lying on the day bed in Owen's old room. It was a Sunday morning visit, and they'd gone up to the loft to get a few more of his things to take back to the house.

Linh stroked his forehead. 'Does it matter either way, even just the teensiest bit, whether we're having a boy or a girl?'

'No... not in any way at all. We're having a baby, and... well, I'm looking forward to being a father.'

'In today's world, it really doesn't matter, does it? It's almost as though it's some sort of infringement of rights if you dwell too much on your baby's sex.'

'Yeah. But if we have a boy, I want him to be able to stand up for himself... learn how to fight—you'll teach him, won't you?'

Linh took Owen's face in her hands and kissed him liberally.

It had taken a few months for Linh to come to terms with the events at the clearing by the river. She seemed relaxed at first, and the road trip continued with light hearts and no particular plan. But gradually she became distracted and impatient, which wasn't like her at all.

One day, in Nightcap National Park, as they sat on a log watching the mist float away from the face of a waterfall, she began to cry.

Owen had been anticipating this moment. He knew she was experiencing a post traumatic condition. And, he thought he knew what the problem was.

He sat beside her with his elbows on his knees. 'Linh, you engaged at a supreme level of combat. Your intention was to badly hurt some people so that you, and me, would survive... and you had the skills to be able to do it... skills and techniques that your father taught you, at first, patiently and gently—because you were young and couldn't really see the relevance of what you were doing. Then, when you became fluent, and old enough to understand, he directed your powers towards lethal intent. He showed you how to become a killer... should you ever need to defend yourself in an extreme situation. That training you reinforced with repetition and routines... even though you didn't *believe* in the scenarios... you did it for your dad... you did it because the physicality felt good. It's not *who* you are... it's what you can do if someone is fool enough to threaten you. You didn't do anything wrong, Linh. You made the conscious decision to unleash what you have committed to memory, because not to have done so could have been terminal for both of us. You would have done the same if it meant pulling a trigger... you wouldn't beat yourself up about how destructive a gun is—you would confine your self-examination to working out just how much right you had. Well, you had every right—there by the creek—in the laundry on board the *Zeus*... you were fighting for your life. How much more right do you need?'

Owen put his arm around his girl. 'You are beautiful... because you are so much, and okay, some of what you are is downright dangerous, but that's no reason to feel bad about yourself. You conduct yourself with such poise and aplomb... you should be proud of who you are— who you have become. You are Linh Vuong—very, very capable young woman.'

Linh leant her head on Owen's shoulder. 'I hope I can be a capable mother.'

Their return to Brisbane was manic. Naturally, everyone wanted to see them and, the underlying question, the irresistible, tantalising question, after their appearance on all television channels, was... *what on earth have you been up to?* as well as, ... *where did you get that fantastic suit/gorgeous dress?*

It was with heartfelt relief that they moved into the dilapidated house in Dutton Park just two months later, because its shabbiness seemed to restore some balance to their image. Now, when friends and acquaintances, and even curious passers-by, dropped in, Owen and Linh, dressed in their work clothes, could hold a conversation as they continued with sanding and painting. The old house didn't really need much more than that. It was well built from timber that would long outlive the softwood frames of newer houses, and the original coloured glass window panes just needed a touch of putty here and there before a major restoration at some time in the future.

The work would have gone much faster with some hired labour, but the young couple found that the project allowed them to slowly distil the events of the past, so they chose to work alone, with just a few good friends chipping in.

Alasdair's words on the river bank came up frequently in conversation.

He'd told them that he had been in touch with Eamon, and that there was an unprecedented amount of cooperation between sides that had always been implacable enemies.

'At last we're seeing the obvious—the world will be a wasteland unless the human species changes its behaviour,' he'd said at one point. 'It's not that people are suddenly so much more altruistic or environmentally minded—it's just that within a very short time we won't be in a position any more to put in place what is required to save ourselves. We need functioning governments, productive industry, educated and proactive societies for the changes to be implemented with any guarantee of success.'

He spoke briefly about how the change to alternative energies was becoming widely accepted, not so much because of environmental concerns, but because they presented a more desirable sociological choice.

'Why would we foster a mining industry, which will be run by robots soon anyway, when we can create the technology that engages people directly with harnessing energy from renewable sources? We'll look back in years to come and wonder how we ever thought that burning a rail carriage full of coal every single second of the day was not going to have an impact on the atmosphere. We're creating so much gas, mainly carbon-dioxide, that we are actually increasing the size of the atmosphere—the layer of air around us is getting fatter. Which sounds comforting in one way but has two rather uncomfortable consequences. One is that, adding mainly the heavier molecules of carbon-dioxide, means the air around us can store more heat, which is energy… so we have more energy to influence the weather, and the other consequence is that, a thicker atmosphere allows for much more energetic weather events to develop… bigger storms, bigger floods. And just to make matters worse, the heavier carbon-dioxide tends to sink to the surface of the earth. Then, it absorbs sunlight energy, gets very hot, and rises high in the stratosphere. Then, it cools down, becomes extra heavy, and sinks in a rush to the surface…'

'… causing abnormally high winds as it fans out,' Linh interrupted.

'Precisely! It's like having some sort of agitator in the air mass.

'But, the percentages of change are only very small, aren't they, Alasdair?' Owen probed.

'Indeed, but the effects increase exponentially… so think about that, Mr Sceptic. You seem to be parked on a reasonably flat bit of sandy soil… why don't you describe a circle with a stick, six point four metres in radius, to represent the earth, and then add another three centimetres to your radius to represent the thirty kilometres of our atmosphere that constitutes about eighty percent of the actual air, and in which all the weather phenomenon take place. That'll give you a good idea of the fragility of the film of air around our planet.'

One day, a courier delivered two large parcels to the house at Dutton Park. Owen and Linh sat on the bare floorboards of the loungeroom and unwrapped a parcel each. Inside were a total of eighteen bottles of Penfolds Grand Hermitage vintage 1951. The occasion was too significant not to celebrate. They strolled to the junk shop around the corner and bought a set of ornate crystal wine glasses. Each made a phone call. Back at the house, they sat cross-legged opposite each other and opened one of the bottles. They sipped the superb flavours as the setting sun shone through the doorway. A short while later, both sets of parents arrived. Don carried in camping chairs for everyone.

Owen explained that he could only appreciate one small glass and that Linh was restricting herself to half a glass. They needed help to finish the bottle. Inside their new house, everything felt good.

Later that evening, Owen received a message on his phone. As instructed, he and Linh sat up till very late and looked up into the clear, moonless sky. From the east, a ball of light, about the size of the moon, traversed the sky. It travelled quite slowly and was visible for a few minutes before it faded to the western horizon.

He and Linh held each other and wept quietly.

Eamon had passed on.

Linh sniffed in Owen's ear, 'He was ready to die. All he needed to think about was the love of the people he'd known and his heart would just stop.

The astronomical event didn't even make it onto the front pages of the paper.

'Is there any hope for us, Owie? When will we recognise that it's not for us to presume understanding of the unknowable, but just to marvel at creation.

Owen looked up from his phone. 'Sorry, Tot... you were saying?... I was just checking my Facebook posts...'

Linh punched his arm. 'Anything about him on Google?'

'No... nothing.'

'I feel so much for Gina. I hope she finds a way of coping.'

'Yeah, as long as it doesn't involve visiting us.'

'Speaking of visiting... when do you think we should go north?'

'Late Autumn... the baby will be able to cope and the weather will be nice. But we'll fly to Darwin. Too long to drive. Alasdair will arrange a military chopper for us. Hope it's not too noisy.'

Linh came up and hugged him. 'I know he wants to see us, but I was thinking more of when are we going to Yappar?'

A distant look came into Owen's eyes. He absently kissed Linh's forehead. 'It'll always be there... might be a bit difficult with a small baby...'

As well as renovating the house, Owen had resumed some of the responsibilities at the engine facility. Bearing in mind Alasdair's predictions about renewable energies, the team decided to look more closely at utilising hydrogen as a fuel for the motor and came to the conclusion that the engine was ideally suited to hydrogen and water injection. The short duration power phases allowed the water to turn to steam before the cooling explosion created a negative pressure which would occur on the exhaust side of the turbine blades. Luckily, the engine had a high degree of configurability which allowed the team to quickly explore the optimal parameters for hydrogen fuel.

The team was not discouraged at the prospect of delaying commercialisation of the motor; the new direction had mysteriously attracted generous research grants and everyone involved benefited.

Owen stayed mum.

In the time leading up to the birth of their baby, there was one announcement by the government that surprised and delighted Linh and Owen. It was announced that the proposed space research academy had been axed, and that the money was now going to be directed into truly innovative training and educational projects directed at establishing sustainable industries and promoting opportunities for youth employment.

Owen gave Linh a wry smile. They were grouting the new tiling in the bathroom, with Linh taking care of those sections that didn't require bending down. 'That'll be Francesca's model in play—creating a viable alternative society in miniature and gradually integrating it into the mainstream.'

'I know... the time is so right for something like this to happen.' Linh sat down on the rim of the cast-iron bath. 'Twenty years ago, something like that would have seemed irrelevant and perhaps even patronising. But now, with so many young people at a total loss as to how to venture into the next phase of their life, it's a relief for them to know that they can be part of a parallel society—an idealised analogy of what's out there, I suppose— and that they can gain employment and even secure accommodation, all within a protected setting that, okay... it's artificial, but it's productive in helping to train workers and to nurture a healthy social outlook.'

Owen sat next to her and massaged her knee. 'It absolutely beats going on the dole, which is an admission of failure on everybody's part.'

The soon-to-be parents would regularly visit the *Roadways* website to see how things were progressing. Each day, live links revealed crowds of tiny commuters, bustling through townscapes, or travelling along country roads, each child energetically pedalling from one location to another, sometimes for no particular purpose, and sometimes carrying useful loads destined for a worksite somewhere on the premises. And, behind the scenes, older children and youths helped with organising construction projects and coordinating the growth of the complex. Beyond the painted facades, corn and beans grew in long brick troughs and children tasked with a picking assignment, parked their vehicles and opened up paper bags ready to fulfil their quota.

The *Roadways* movement had arrived at a time when there were any number of vacant warehouses available within easy reach of the suburbs. Dedicated bus routes made it possible for all age groups to travel safely and efficiently to the complexes, which, in effect, became satellite communities that even offered accommodation for older children as a means for them to make autonomous choices about their future and the degree to which they wanted to engage in their new, virtual environment. It was not just about training; the structures in place also encouraged participants to seek independence, and to allow them to separate from influences in their lives that kept them bound and beholden.

'We must get more involved, Owie.' Linh looked up, already knowing his reply.

He hugged her close. 'We will.'

They both knew that, for the moment, they needed to keep things really simple.

'Do you want me to do around the shower rose, Tot?'

They studied the un-grouted back wall where the shower spout exited. They began to laugh, each knowing what the other was thinking. As far as showering went, there was one moment in their lives that neither of them would ever forget, and that was showering with Francesca.

'We will be taking care of so many social issues with this one movement,' she'd said, as the water ran over her naked body, '... that I truly believe we can transform our communities to be much more cost-effective and sustainable.'

They were in Francesca's astonishing apartment, standing in the rain. It was really more of a swirling mist, except near the boulder, where Francesca had returned to the heavier, warm shower.

Owen hugged Linh to him as she gave an involuntary shiver. It felt wonderfully free to feel the eddies of spray on his skin.

He'd surprised himself with how readily he'd followed Francesca's cue as she stripped off on their way back through her amazing apartment. He and Linh threw their clothes on the back of the couch facing a window with a view to the city and followed Francesca's curvy body along the winding stepping stones to the 'rainforest'. It began to rain with fat, cool drops that gave him instant goose bumps. Francesca beckoned them to join her in a little alcove of boulders. The rain there was hot and heavy. Occasionally they would wander out into the cool mist and stand amongst the dripping plants. It was surreal.

Later, after they'd dried with warmed cotton towels, and had each fallen into one of the many plush lounges, the two lovers stayed awake just long enough to finish their glass of port before Francesca's enthusiastic words melded into sleep.

When the sunrise poured in through the massive windows, Linh crept over to Owen's lounge and snuggled into his nakedness. It seemed an unlikely place to feel transformed, but that is how both of them felt in that new day, with fruit and coffee at their side and covered only in a towel, realising that they had been reincarnated as much as the old industrial warehouse that sheltered them. It seemed obvious now; creating the future should begin with children; they were the only ones who could accept the changes that needed to be made without feeling they were making sacrifices. That was the means by which an overly entitled society could restore the balance of consumption towards a more sustainable level; by allowing the emerging generations to realise the benefits of social connectivity above that of materialism.

'This is something we should be proud to own,' Francesca said, as they waited for a taxi out on the footpath near the huge roller door. 'We are fortunate that the answer is so simple, but we must never allow ourselves to be complacent; without inspiration, humans quickly revert to indulgent behaviour.'

Owen and Linh nodded, and resisted the urge to look upward towards the luxury apartment.

Francesca hugged them both. 'I was waiting to have one last shower with someone who would appreciate the sacrifice that I was making before I turn it,' she flung her gaze aloft, '... into a playground.'

The trio wriggled and laughed in each other's arms.

The two young homebuilders paused for a moment in contemplation. Some of their recent adventures defied belief.

'You grout, Owie... I'll put on the billy.'

Just then, a voice called from the open front door.

Linh replied, 'We're in the bathroom, Jenna. Come on in.'

Owen whispered, '... she must have passed her driving test—awesome!'

Jenna arrived at the bathroom door with a guitar in her hand. 'I passed!'

'Well done, Jenna!' There were hugs all 'round.

'Hey, great idea. I'll sing you my new song in here because the acoustics will be really good.'

Jenna and her friend, Aurora had a little duo going—two guitars and nice harmonies—and played regularly at the gallery. They were writing a lot of material and gaining quite a following.

'They've got just the right amount of confidence for their ability,' Owen had said one day, '... or, the right amount of ability for their confidence.' Stony faced stares was all the reply he got from the group. The era of jousting with his sister had come to an end. It was still her right to nettle her big brother at every opportunity, but those occasions had mellowed a lot now that she was becoming an aunt. And, in her own way, she was aligning herself with Owen's destiny, choosing to do volunteer work and living among the dispossessed. 'It's really the only way that you can get a true picture of our society,' she told him. 'I know I'm not making any money, but I still get to live...

even if I don't know where I'll be sleeping from one night to the next.'

Jenna settled herself on the edge of the bath. 'I wrote this while you guys were away.' She cradled her guitar. 'I suddenly had this feeling that there was going to be a lot of change, y'know... in the world, or in my life... dunno. Anyway, all this stuff came out of my head, but I think it's pretty good.' She strummed the strings and began to sing.

Come with me to my secret place
Change your heart and change your pace
Close your eyes and feel love's soft embrace
Livin' for the songs we sing
Our throats vibrate like butterfly wings
Naturally and clear you tell
All that makes you feel so well
Shangrila and Eden are places that don't seem so far
When I hold your hand in mine and lean against your shoulder

Breakin' hearts and movin' fast
Building castles that won't last
It isn't you and it isn't me
Such desperate hopes die endlessly
Friends we are, we won't betray
So give your secrets all away
The only laughter you will hear
Is from your heart because it's free
Shangrila and Eden are places that don't seem so far
When I hold your hand in mine and lean against your shoulder

The Earth can sigh and while away
A million years in rain and tears
And every tree that ever grew
knew just what it had to do
We are just like specks of dust
Looking at the stars too much
Grating each and everyone
To smallness and oblivion

447

But in the rivers we unite
Grain to grain we're held in tight
And in time the wounds will heal
And we can build a mountain
Shangrila and Eden are places that don't seem so far
When I hold your hand in mine and lean against your shoulder.

The room became utterly quiet after the last notes of Jenna's song had faded. Linh, seated in the only chair, had streaks of tears running through the fine dust on her cheeks. Beside her, seated on the floor, Owen clasped her hand in his.

Jenna raised an eyebrow. 'Wha'd'ya think?'

Neither of her listeners could speak.

A few days later, Linh and Owen were at a health bar in the grounds of the University of Queensland. It was a nice walk for them across the bus bridge, and they usually did it once a week, stopping at the bar for a vege-juice.

'I definitely think this will be the last time, Owie. The baby is getting awfully heavy.'

'Sure, Tot... do you want to get the bus back?'

'We'll see...'

Some distance away, in the shade of a large Morton Bay Fig, a lone woman sat at a table, and when Owen happened to catch her eye, she beckoned them over.

'It's Cassandra,' Owen indicated with his head. 'We must be getting our de-brief at last. C'mon.' He grabbed their drinks.

The agent looked lovely in a floral-patterned frock, swinging a delicate sandal from her toes.

'It's hard to believe, Cassandra, that you possess intimate knowledge of the most highly protected secrets in the world today.' Owen held out a chair for Linh.

Cassandra slipped off her sun-glasses. 'I know... but it's a bit like trying to pay for your shopping with a gold brick. It's impossible, no matter how much it's worth. What I know is unusable to most governments. So, I just keep it to myself... except when I'm told to share it.'

'And, what are you sharing with us on this lovely morning?'

'Alasdair wants you to know how well you did in Vietnam...'

'Amanoi resort?'

'Yes. Your deductions were beyond profound, Owen. It took us a long time to fully appreciate just what a quantum leap you had made with the concrete submarine theory... and the relationship with the undersea vents. We couldn't believe what was coming together... but there it was—the construction materials, the building processes and, eventually, a compelling reason why. Do you know why, Owen?'

'I think so.'

Cassandra leant forward with her arms on the table edge. 'Please tell me.'

Owen sighed deeply. He took Linh's hand in his. 'How do I know that I'm speaking to Alasdair?'

Cassandra dipped her eyes to him. She leant back in her chair and flicked at a strand of her hair.

Owen gave one nod and waited patiently. A water dragon scuttled down a buttressed root into a pool of sunlight.

Leaves crunched behind him as someone approached. They grasped the back of Linh's chair.

Linh reached behind her and put her hand on the person's hand. 'Hello, Alasdair.'

Alasdair bent and gently kissed Linh on her cheek. 'Hello, lovely Linh. Congratulations... you will have you hands full within a couple of days, if I'm any judge.'

Owen pulled out the chair on his other side.

Alasdair sat down. 'Thank you, my boy.' He clasped a hand on Owen's knee. 'So, you think you know what's going on?'

'And, if I do, you're here to tell me personally just how crucial this knowledge is.' Owen remained staring at the table.

'And, how dangerous. If it turned out you were ignorant of the circumstances, we would leave you thus. But, if you think you know... you'd better tell me... and, I believe you do know.'

Owen smiled to himself. 'I won't lie... I think I know.'

Linh put her hand up to Owen's shoulder.

'Naturally, it's about competition for space on this earth... and self-defence,' Owen's voice was low and even. 'Up until recently, ownership of the low, sandy islands of the Spratly's remained uncontested, not because there wasn't a will to claim them, but mainly because the energy and resources to do so would be irreconcilable with any likely benefits... defensive or economic.'

'You're sounding like a conspirator, Owen,' Cassandra interjected.

Owen chuckled. 'I've had a good think about this. Anyway, that was the situation until the Red Dragon awoke. It stretched and yawned, and its paws easily reached out into the South China Sea. This was its territory... and it was going to mark it with permanent structures and bases. The move was subtle, pre-emptive and ever so unambiguous... and no one could do anything about it. There was only one other nation that had the ability to do what the dragon had done—Japan, but they were constrained from any expansionist engagements because of the nearness still of the Second World War. So, they waited for the inevitable occupation of that lonely segment of sea and planned their own defence.

'This is the undertaking that engages them off the coast of Vietnam—the construction of giant submarines, strong enough to dwell in the deepest troughs and channels of the undersea topography—and so massive, that they will become permanent habitats directly underneath the sweep of Chinese radar. Only the dedicated inventiveness of the Japanese could solve the problems associated with living in an environment more hostile than the surface of Mars, and only they could have imagined themselves suckling from the teat of a dragon far more powerful than the Red Dragon—one that has terrorized their island nation since time immemorial—the long-tailed dragon of volcanoes that lives in the bowels of the earth.

'I imagine that they plan to construct matrices of ceramic pipes around the tectonic vents that criss-cross the South China Sea and beyond, and that they will be able to dock with these ambient-pressure grids to supply super-heated liquid water to heat exchangers to provide energy for their vessels. Japan is the only country wealthy enough and clever enough to undertake such a mind-bogglingly adventurous project, but once they have their fleet of ultra-deep submersibles in place, they will be untouchable, because they will be able to control the ocean above them with impunity, and anyone with hostile intentions that ventures above, will be shot out of the water. But this whole quest is not just about a reaction to regional power-plays... it is also a pragmatic attempt to meet the changing environment on earth—it's a journey that needs to be taken, simply because it's possible... just like the first steps out of Africa and our awkward forays into space.'

No one spoke at the little round table under the shading fig. The enormity of such a frontier, fully occupied everyone's mind. It seemed incredible that something so akin to the realms of science-fiction could actually exist.

Alasdair was the first to speak. 'Welcome, Owen... you have truly gained your place. Our best analysts haven't even come close to what you've described. I came here with the intention of allowing you to free yourself from our domain—you and Linh have more than enough potential to fulfil a life with your own pursuits... but now, I realise that we can't let you go... we just can't. We will work together. Your gifts will add vigour to whatever we undertake... but I do promise you both this... no more risky missions.'

'You're right about that, Alasdair. May I enquire, though, how you managed to get hold of our information?'

Alasdair waved a careless hand. 'Oh, that... we had monitoring gear in position at the place where the crew first gathered after they'd photographed your notebook. They were a bit excited and unprofessional, and while they waited for a lift from the harbour to their ship, they blurted out all sorts of scenarios based on your data and sketches.'

'And who were the people that Francesca and I encountered in the building in Edward Street?'

'That we don't know. They came out of nowhere. I actually suspect they were a contingent from Gina Wu's previous employers—before she went over to Eamon. They were probably exploiting all of the loose ends available to them to see where it would lead... but between the two of you, you took care of them. Well done. We always intended to get back to you, but then the gamma project took precedence.'

'Oh... speaking of which—it's not really a gamma ray, is it?'

'Hard to imagine that it could be. Probably still at the X-ray stage, but nonetheless, a very powerful weapon.'

'Thought so. Not that it matters—the technology has been superseded, according to Eamon. There is something else out there, more powerful and less hostile, more persuasive and less confrontational... that's what he told us.'

Nearby, a child squealed as she ran down the grass slope to scare a magpie. People's conversations drifted hypnotically towards them. Water splashed delicately somewhere close by.

Linh took Owen's hand and lifted it to her mouth. 'Owie,' she said, '... my waters have broken.'

THE END

Did you enjoy this book?

I'd love you to leave a review at
www.amazon.com.au/dp/B07DRBT6G9/

Snap a pic of yourself and this book and post it on
Instagram using #petelansbooks

Please consider this book, or one of my other
books, as a gift for someone.

Find more of my books online at
www.amazon.com/pete-lans/e/B07D6FKB4Y/

If you would like to communicate with me
personally, please email
author@petelans.com

Free Short Story!

Email me at author@petelans.com for a FREE copy of
my short story, *Good Morning Sunshine*.

Thrum
- A Conspiracy to Create Euphoria -

Thrum is a light-hearted, humorous, respectfully erotic and delicately romantic novel about how little it takes to make people happy.

In a time-worn country town, one woman's accidental, erotic discovery sets in motion a comedy of errors as she and a naïve group of residents conspire to transform their community.

Iris, the angry baker, rediscovers her love of French cuisine and feels bold enough to dress as she pleases. The derisive Ellen, no longer hides her scars and sets about painting the town.

Octogenarian, Moira Gatton, divests herself of all her treasured possessions and gives up smoking. Miranda the dragon, discovers who she really loves. Max, the bikie tattooist, becomes a man as he could never have imagined.

Tiffany fills her life with the things from a shared love. Phoebe's unfettered laugh rings out in her salon ...

... and Ian, for once, knows more about everything than anybody else.

The Difference
~ Twelve Journeys of Humor and Fulfilment ~

The twelve short stories in this anthology illustrate how pathos shapes our experiences and that we are mostly unaware of the direction of our journey through life.

A harmless foray into the theatre leads to love... A man, mysteriously cursed, finds salvation in abject humiliation... Another, continually thwarted, discovers the legacy of all his ardour... A reckless young woman tests the boundaries of her privileged life... Can a man, a sportscar and a nymph exist in the same story?... Two cousins, worlds apart, discover that family comes first... ASIO and the Department of Education misplace their files and save the nation... An android reviews her journey amongst humans... A scurrilous landlord creates his own doom when he tries to save the world... Eternity is not something to look forward to... and, can a man redeem himself by not saying a thing?